Dead Kids Don't Speak

A Novel by Ron Costello

Dead Kids Don't Speak

Gold Sun Publishing
A Novel
Published in the United States of America

ISBN Numbers: Paperback: 978-0-578-53091-8
EBook: 978-0-578-55939-1

Dead Kids Don't Speak is a work of fiction. Any resemblance to actual events or persons, living or dead, is entirely coincidental. Names, characters, businesses, places, events and incidents are either the products of the author's imagination or used in a fictitious manner. The opinions expressed are those of the characters and should not be confused with the authors.

Dedication and Introduction

Denise E. Costello

For ten years, Denise has been asking me to write a book about how and where I grew up. So, the first book I wrote was *Charter School General*.

"Ron, that's not it," Denise said, "Write a book about how you grew up."

Then I wrote *Darkness They Could Not See*, about Christopher Columbus's first voyage.

"Uh-uh, Ron," she said, "that's not it, either. You have to write about how you grew up. You know, on that wacky place you called the Hill. Write about the lunatic things you did there, and of course, the friendships. Isn't that what you said made the Hill so unique, the bonds?

"How about pulling raccoon tails across Centennial Road at midnight with cars slamming on the brakes and spinning around to avoid hitting them? With 20 nutty kids hiding in the woods alongside the road laughing their posteriors off. I bet that was fun.

"What about this one: Skyrocketing down Fairview Avenue in a refrigerator door with no way to stop? That was imaginative; I have to give you that. And ringing doorbells and running. Now that's not unusual; all kids probably did that. Okay, right, but not at age five.

"Ron, when will we see that book?"

Well, Denise, here it is.

Contents

PART ONE

CHAPTER 1

The Crime Scene

June 18, 1964
Belmont Hills

It was a night meant for the dead.

Dark. Dark as a funeral scarf. Dark as death's eye.

Some link darkness to evil as if evil things surface on nights when shadows don't tell.

It's not good Lower Merion Township police officer Jack Bek thought. *Don't like these nights. Even the streetlights are useless; dim of light swallowed by blackness. These nights give me the creeps.*

The officer's precognition proved worthy. His radio crackled.

"16 what's your 20?"

Officer Bek reached for the handheld mounted on this his cruiser's dashboard. "Sixteen in Penn Valley checking on a prowler," he responded.

"16 we have a possible 10-31 (a crime in progress) at 618 Mary Waters Ford Road in Belmont Hills."

"Proceed with caution 16, reported shots in or outside the house; suspicious persons on the property, copy?"

Office Bek U-turned on Woodbine Avenue and gunned the engine, moving swiftly toward Conshohocken State Road. His head filled with thoughts: *Damn kids, that's what this is, the Otts and the*

*cherries. They probably set off a couple of firecrackers. Every year it's
something different. One generation has to outdo the other.*

Bek knew about the cherry trees in front of the Otts' house. The
majority of Lower Merion cops grew up on the Hill, so Bek was a
card-carrying cherry stealer. But the Hill kids never considered it
stealing — they just picked and ate them. It was a right you were en-
titled to growing up on the Hill.

Same as stealing Tastykakes at old lady Myers' store on Jefferson Street. Piled high on an easily reachable shelf, lemon and cherry,
chocolate cupcakes, butterscotch Krimpets, and of course, every kid's
favorite, peanut butter Kandy Kakes. They had to be eaten fast in the
summer. Sugar laced treats that taunted and teased broke kids. She
always ordered extra; she knew a portion would be ripped off. It was
the cost of doing business on the Hill. Kid psychology: As long as you
don't get caught, it's not stealing.

Bek kept his emergency lights off so not to chase away the intruders, *kid intruders no doubt.* He smiled at the memories of growing up
in what he called "seventh heaven." But Bek also knew that the Hill
kids had a sixth sense about cops. He knew they'd be long gone when
he got there. Notably, on a night when the darkness and gloom shifted to their side, helping them disappear. Fast as the sleight of hand.

Bek spoke softly into the handheld, *"16-10-23"* (arrived at the
scene). He turned off the headlights and pulled into the Otts' driveway. He cut his engine. The house was dark and lifeless. It was eerily
quiet. From behind the wheel, Bek looked around. Nothing.

He looked into his rearview and scanned the ballfield behind
him, nothing. *Yea, the damn kids are home watching the Late Show;
eating cherries.* He cracked his door and as slowly and quietly as he
could, stepped out onto the gravel driveway, his hand on his holstered
revolver. He left his door partially open, the dashboard lights consumed by night too dark for its own good. Bek — still convinced it
was kids stealing cherries — ambled up to the front porch. The door
was slightly open. It was the night of June 18, 1964, 11:20 p.m., when

4

Officer Bek pushed the door open with his foot. It creaked like a hurt chicken.

"Hello, is anyone home? This is the Lower Merion police. Is anyone there?"

He waited briefly then reached for the flashlight on his belt, clicked it on, and scanned the downstairs of the home. What he saw stunned him and shattered his cherry stealing theory. He focused the light on two bodies lying together face up in the dining room. Blood on the floor encircled their heads. He shined the light on their bloody faces. Officer Bek had seen the look of death before. Their chests lay still, no movement of breathing; mouths and eyes open, staring at the ceiling. *They probably didn't know what hit them*, Bek thought. Death can be swift and hideous, clean and painless, or cruel and slow. Were they dead before they hit the floor? Or did they die violently, twitching and jerking, their brains were disconnected from their bodies? He was sure the faces he saw, even from the distance of the front door to the dining room, were the faces of death

He pulled out his revolver, switched off his flashlight and, holding the gun in front of him, slowly backpedaled toward his cruiser without removing his eyes from the front door. He pushed the cruiser's door open wider with his knee, knelt behind it, and reached inside for the handheld. His voice was shaking.

"16 at 618 Mary Waters Ford Road, Belmont Hills, requesting back-up.

Two bodies on the floor inside the home appear to be shot. Officer 16 moved back to car in driveway and covering the front door. Do you copy?"

"Roger that 16. Assistance on the way. Use caution and stay with your vehicle. Back-up on the way."

It was only a few minutes — but it seemed longer to Bek — when he heard the first police sirens in the distance. They were coming from two different directions — getting louder by the second — the closest coming from Conshohocken State Road. The flashing lights danced in the corners of his eyes; even so, he kept his gaze focused on the front door. The first arrivals split up — one slid on the gravel and stopped at the curb, the other bounced over the curb and stopped on the lawn. The policemen emerged, guns drawn, and crouched behind their opened doors.

"Jack, you good?"

"Good," Bek responded.

"What do we have?"

"Two bodies in the dining room. Appear dead."

"Anybody else inside?"

"I called out from the front door," Bek said, "no one answered."

The officer on the lawn switched on his spotlight, lighting up the front porch, as more police cars arrived. Two spun around and sealed off Mary Waters Ford Road, blocking traffic. More sirens blared in the distance.

Bek wiped sweat from his forehead and waited. He knew they had to secure the house before the detectives arrived.

"Okay," Bek said, "let's move to the front porch."

CHAPTER 2

The Clues

At 11:45 p.m., Lower Merion detective Tommy Lochran's wife Delores told her husband she was off to bed. Tommy nodded and said he wanted to see the sports. "Are the kids in bed?" he asked.

"Yes," she replied, "Shane is reading, and the girls are waiting to be tucked in. I think tonight's their story night, too." And she smiled.

"I'll clean up down here, Dee. Goodnight, hon."

"Goodnight, Loch." She placed her hands on his shoulders, leaned down, and kissed him on the cheek.

But a call on Lochran's Motorola police radio changed their evening.

Lower Merion dispatch called detective Lochran and summoned him to a double homicide at 618 Mary Waters Ford Road. He put on his socks and shoes, grabbed his service revolver, and opened the front door. "I'll be out for a while, Dee, police business," he called out.

When he heard her answer, he slipped out the front door and walked to his car. Lower Merion Detective Michael "Butch" Frost received a similar call. Both detectives grew up on the Hill and lived there as police officers and detectives — Lochran on Maple Avenue in the "Heights" section, and Frost on Springfield Avenue. They were only minutes from 618 Mary Waters Ford Road and arrived simultaneously. Lochran went inside. Frost remained out front getting information from the first arrivals.

Inside three officers, including Jack Bek, were standing over two bodies on the dining room floor. When Lochran entered, officer Bek nodded. "Loch," he said, acknowledging Lochran, whom he'd known since kindergarten. Lochran nodded and knelt beside the male victim. "Anybody check to make sure they're dead?" he asked. "Didn't think so." He gently picked up the male's hand and placed his fingers on his pulse.

"They look dead to me," said officer Nobbs, half in jest, smiling and looking at the other two cops. "You don't see too many people walkin' round with their heads blown apart like that." He laughed until he saw Lochran lookup.

"We'll put that in the police report," Lochran responded, holding his fingers on the female's wrist, "they're dead because they look dead to officer Nobbs."

"The coroner is on his way," Bek said. "And an ambulance."

Lochran nodded. "Yea, they're both dead, all right. Nobbs, you're in the wrong profession." Lochran had a dry sense of humor and with quirks and short remarks could go right for the jugular. His parents had both emigrated from Charlestown, County Mayo, Ireland, and sometimes his partner Frost could detect a slight brogue. Lochran boxed in a Manayunk club called Ike's, and he had the facial scars to show it. With the look of a fighter, broad shoulders and a 'don't–take-shit' attitude, Lochran parlayed the toughness of his ring experience into his job. His hands were curled slightly from throwing too many punches that hit their mark. His receding hairline gave him an older look, and he'd developed somewhat of a gut — barely detectable when he sucked it in — from overeating Dee's soda bread and banana cream pie. And of course, the beer and wine he consumed.

"You should've been a doctor instead of pissing your life away as a cop," he told Nobbs and gently lay the female victim's hand down. Nobbs grinned but didn't know how to take it.

Lochran got up and approached Bek and took him by the arm. The two lawmen walked several steps away from the other officers. Lochran and Bek were in the same class at Lower Merion High School and played football for legendary coach Fritz Brennan. Lochran, a "tough son of a bitch" linebacker, and the lanky Bek, a wide receiver.

"Beckie. Hey, you get the new Mossberg yet?" Lochran asked his friend.

Bek smiled and shook his head. "Hell no, Loch, Margie thinks we can't afford it. She's giving me all kinds of shit about it."

Lochran chuckled and patted his friend and colleague on the back. "Well hang in there, buddy, maybe you can cut a deal with her when she wants those high heels at Wanamaker's."

Detective Butch Frost came through the front door behind them.

"Loch," he said, "some things you should see out here."

"All right, don't touch anything here until the coroner comes," Lochran told the officers. "Jack, call off that ambulance." Bek nodded as Lochran turned and followed Frost out the door.

Frost focused his flashlight on the ground around two cherry trees in the front yard. "Look at this," he said. "Pits and cherries all over. Over there under the two corner trees, too."

"Keep your light down here, Butch," Lochran told his partner. The detective got down on one knee. He picked up several pits and half-eaten cherries. Holding them in his palm, he moved his hand into the light; he smelled them, ran the tip of his finger against one that was half-eaten, and tasted it. "They're fresh, Butch. Still juicy."

"Kids?" Frost asked.

Lochran looked up at the tree branches. "Yep," he said.

"Think they were here and saw the murders?" Frost asked his partner, motioning his head upward.

Lochran stood up. Still holding the pits and cherries, he said, "I hope for their sake they weren't. Let me have your flashlight, Mike," Lochran asked a nearby officer, as he flung the cherry bits to the ground. "Butch," he said and motioned with his head.

The two detectives walked to the street. Lochran shined his flashlight out across the ballfield. "If there were kids here," he told Frost, "that's where they went."

"I sent a patrolman to the field to check," Frost said. "He didn't find anything."

"Yea, hell," Lochran replied, "they're long gone. Might have gone to that patch of woods, what do the kids call it, 'Smithy's woods?'"

"Yeah," Frost said. "Or maybe somebody chased them there."

"Wait a sec, Butch, is that a sock in the middle of the street?"

They stepped out onto Mary Waters Ford Road, and Lochran reached down and picked up the sock. "Jesus Christ smells like he just lost it," Frost complained.

"Yea, it hasn't been here long, Butch," Lochran replied, smiling.

"Loch, if that's the sock, where the hell is the shoe?"

The men stared at one another and turned toward the Otts' front yard. "Come on," Lochran said.

They walked back to the cherry trees and Lochran shined his flashlight around on the ground, looking for a shoe. "Loch, up there," Frost said, as he focused his light into the tree, "is that a goddamn shoe?

The shoe appeared caught between two branches not far up the tree. Frost only had to climb up a couple of limbs to pull it off. He jumped back down,

"Holy hell," Frost said, "this is like a fairy tale. What is it?"

Smiling, Lochran said, "Cinderella. Think we have a match here, Butchey?"

"So, your conclusion? Frost asked.

Lochran looked up at the tree branches. "Only a kid in a panic climbing down a tree would leave a shoe up there," he said.

"And a sock in the middle of the street," Frost added.

"Those kids got out of here in a hurry, Butch."

"Because they witnessed two murders?"

"Right, and ran for the field," Lochran said, nodding toward the ballfield. "There must have been four or five of them; all four trees have pits and cherries under them."

"The most the Otts would have done was put on the outside lights and threaten to call the police," Frost said, "that wouldn't have sent those kids off in a panic. "

"No, they would've laughed and taken their time getting down, yelled for the Otts to go ahead and call them, and ran for the field, knowing that if the Otts did call the police, which they usually didn't do, they had plenty of time to get to the woods."

"Hell, yea, plenty of time," Frost said.

Lochran nodded. He half-turned and looked at the house. "No, something panicked those kids, and we know what that might have been, Butch."

"We have a double homicide in there," Frost said, as he jerked his thumb toward the house, "with possible eyewitnesses, kids in the trees picking cherries."

Frost looked at Lochran's face, silhouetted in the light from the two flashlights. They'd been partners for 12 years and had worked on over 180 cases together, more than a few murders. "The homicides," Frost asked, "any thoughts?"

Lochran half turned again and looked at the house. "Husband and wife in their 80's, both shot in the head. No signs of forced entry or anything stolen. Old man Otts lengthened a lot of hand-me-down pants for free on the Hill. He was damn good at it, too. I'm not sure Butch. Everybody knew the Otts; they were nice people. Did they see something they shouldn't have? Could it be a mob hit?"

"Or maybe the killer had the wrong house?" Frost offered.

Lochran looked at his partner. "Butch, we need to find the kid who wore these before the murderer does."

Frost stared at Lochran and rubbed his chin. "Yea, shouldn't be too hard to find, should it?"

CHAPTER 3

'From the Hill'

The Hill, short for Belmont Hills, was a working-class village on the edge of Philadelphia, nestled on steep hills between a moat, the Schuylkill River, and castles, the Main Line. It was a community where kids roamed by day and night and settled disputes in the old-fashioned way. A neighborhood where people rarely locked their doors and knew everyone else's business. Where kids were as plentiful as ants at a barbecue.

In 1964 the people on the Hill were a hard-working, blue-collar mix of Italian, Polish, Irish, and German, and more than a few were immigrants themselves. They didn't employ lawn services or expensive security systems, and they cleaned their own homes. They fixed their cars and trucks in their driveways and frequently helped each other with a leaking roof or pipe.

Their children got bussed to the posh suburb of Rosemont where they attended the scholarly Harriton High School. Harriton was built in 1958 to ease the overcrowded conditions at Lower Merion High School. At Harriton, the kids from the Hill mixed with the la-di-da kids from the most exclusive Main Line neighborhoods — well-heeled boys and girls with expensive cars and nice clothes. Many of those kids came from big homes that sat on sprawling landscapes, with caretakers, and automatic sprinkling systems. Snowplows cleared their driveways in winter — and sometimes, at least in the neighborhoods that bordered the Hill, small packs of roaming kids did it faster and cheaper.

At Harriton, the majority of the kids' fathers were doctors or attorneys, commuted to Wall Street; headed law firms and banks, or owned businesses they could pass on to their sons and daughters. Unlike the Hill kids, they never worried about lunch money or buying school clothes and were on track to attend the best private universities. The majority of the Harriton kids were as different as night and day from their Belmont Hills' counterparts.

I lived on Ashland Avenue, the main street through the Hill, across from the Curry's. George and Meta Curry had five children, as my folks did. Billy, their oldest, was a tough kid who had an unsurpassed work ethic — it seemed he was always fixing or building something. He had a heart of gold, too — when you needed help, Billy Curry never hesitated to help. Billy's grandmother lived next door to us, so I often saw him there, just as I did on the pleasant afternoon of June 18, 1964. He drove his motor scooter from across the street and into his grandmother's driveway. We called Billy and his boys the Ground Crew because Billy's motor scooter, with a sizeable wagon-bed attached, looked like the one the ground crew used to smooth out the infield at Phillies' games.

"Got it runnin' good, huh Bill?" I yelled, the bat on my shoulder, doing my Richie Allen impersonation in my backyard. Billy wasn't easy to talk with, and he was entirely mechanical. Me? I was lucky to know the difference between a screwdriver and a pair of pliers. But Billy could take an engine apart and put it back together before you finished supper.

"Gettin' ready to load it with cherries, Ronny," Bill hollered, glancing over his shoulder. "It's time, and we're gettin' them tomorrow night when they're peakin'. You and your fart-bird friends can have the leftovers." He laughed and disappeared into his grandmother's house.

I nodded and smiled in appreciation. I stood still a few minutes, leaning on the bat, letting what Billy said sink in. Impulsively, I tossed the bat and rushed up the back-porch steps and went inside. I made three phone calls.

"It's Ronny; we got to meet after supper. It's cherry pickin' time, and it's got to be tonight."

Later that evening, around dusk, we met at the old church and school building on Jefferson Street. It was a massive stone building with plenty of crannies, doorways, steps, and walls. It was the first Ashland School, built in 1883 and rebuilt in 1892. In 1918 the school was moved to Madison and School Streets, but the old building on Jefferson Street remained, sometimes used as a church, a boy's club, and finally demolished in the early seventies. For us, however, the boarded-up building that sat on a knob served as our hangout starting that summer. As usual, we arrived individually.

"Jesus H. Christ if it's not the Brun." Gary hollered.

"Fuckin'—a, you got that right," Pete replied. Pete Bruno was not short on self-confidence or bravado. Even the way he walked showed confidence, and he could take and give insults as good as any kid on the Hill. The bantering back and forth between Gary and Pete continued all summer. That night was no different. It was a night perfect for stealing cherries, so dark, as Gary said, you could play with your pecker and not get caught. We — Micky, Pete, Gary, and me — had not yet discovered the allure of the Harriton girls. That would begin in the fall when we entered the 10th grade. For now, the Manayunk babes — girls Gary said were sweeter than smart — had our attention that summer.

"Them El girls got one leg shorter than the other," Gary joked.

"Yea? How's that?" Mickey asked.

"From walking up those hills to Roxborough," Gary laughed, then froze momentarily to gauge our reactions.

"I don't get it," Mickey deadpanned.

Gary, slightly irritated, countered, "Jesus fuckin' Christ, do I have to explain everything? You assholes are the dumbest assholes I know." That opened up a clear shot for Pete.

"That's because your entire family are idiots," Pete said. "Fuck, everybody knows that." Pete often guffawed at his jokes and insults so vigorously that his glasses slipped down his nose, and he had to push them back into place. He loved to hammer Gary or anyone for that matter, but indeed Gary was his favorite target.

Gary returned fire. "Hey, blow me dago, who's dumber than you?"

"He would, but he probably couldn't find anything down there," Mickey said. Mickey was the intellectual insulter among us. He made us think before we laughed — and many times, we still didn't get it. But we laughed anyway. Mickey was the only one of us who didn't play baseball; he watched our games, however, and served as our sharpest critic. He was tall and somewhat lanky, a bit uncoordinated, and he sometimes mumbled under his breath. Pete, on occasion, called him Jughead because he resembled the character in the Archie comic books.

"All right I'm wasting my time on you guys," Gary said, "who's gettin' the cherries tonight?" We knew Gary would bide his time to hammer Pete again when he was least expecting it.

"Jesus Christ," Pete said. "What's so big about cherries?" Pete had just moved to the Hill from Conshohocken. His family had emigrated from Italy when he was seven. They came over on the Santa Dora, which sunk not on Pete's voyage, but the next one. Pete told Gary the Polacks tried to sink his ship but, as usual, they sunk the wrong one. Pete started elementary school in Conshohocken without knowing how to speak English — and Gary claimed all summer that he still didn't.

He'd only been hanging with us for a week or two and discovered we did some strange things like stealing cherries. Pete never picked cherries in Conshy. It didn't take Gary long to zero in on that, either.

"Bet they didn't have no cherries back in dago city," Gary laughed. 'Dago city' is what he called Italy.

"That's cause we shipped them to the Polacks, who stuck them up their asses," Pete said.

"Shit," Gary shot back, "Italy was on Germany's side. They let Mussolini lead them around."

"Yeah, that's better than fighting the Germans with spears, which is what the Polacks did," Pete laughed. "It took the Germans, what, three days to take over Poland?"

Gary and Pete argued all summer over who had a better army, Italy or Poland. Neither one knew jack shit about Italy or Poland's armies; they just made stuff up.

"Look," I said, "are we gettin' the cherries or not?"

"Let's go," Mickey said, "I'm ready to pick and eat."

"Petey," Gary said, "you can sell them cherries to all the dagos on Jefferson Street."

"No, I'll sell them to your mother after she blows me," Pete responded.

An outside observer might have thought Gary and Pete were bitter enemies from the way they bantered back and forth. But nothing was further from the truth. They were good friends and became the best of friends as they went through Harriton and played together on two different baseball teams. The four of us didn't realize it, but in that summer in 1964 we were forming bonds that would last a lifetime.

Oddly, we enjoyed trading insults about each other's sexuality, intelligence, athletic ability, relationships with girls, and surprisingly, mothers. Whenever a kid was on the losing end of an insult bombardment, he'd go to the mother salvo. This was used frequently: Did you bring your lunch today, or did your mother walk? We all knew it was the worst of a kind, lowball slap, but no one knew what it meant. It didn't even make sense. I've often heard kids from the Hill, strolling down the hall at Harriton, say to a kid, "Yo, Jimmy, you bring your lunch today, or did your mother walk?"

"Look," Gary said, flicking his butt away as we watched the sparks dance on the concrete, "We gonna shit or get off the pot?" a saying our baseball coach used.

"Gary's right," I said. "Let's go."

The four of us headed to Price Street and up to Ashland toward the ballfield.

CHAPTER 4

Stealing Cherries

"**S**hit it's dark," Gary said. We each lit cigarettes, cupped them so not to advertise our whereabouts. We were on the pitcher's mound of the softball field directly across from the Otts' house, where four beautiful cherry trees sat in their radiant splendor.

"Dark's good," Mickey said, "darker the better."

"The Otts are home," I observed, as I drew on my Winston, "lights are on."

"That shit's good," Gary said. "They can't see ten feet anyway, and it'll light up the cherries so we're not eatin' the shitty ones."

"I can't believe I'm doing this," Pete complained, "if you want cherries just buy them in the store."

"It's more than that," I explained, "we're beatin' the Ground Crew. They'll come here tomorrow night and see the pits on the ground. They'll find the low hangers gone. And besides, it's the danger of the thing."

"Come on, ass-wipe," Gary said, "them cherries will make your pecker grow, but you got to eat a lot of them."

"Speak for yourself," Pete said. "Trust me, Italians don't need to eat cherries."

"Everybody ready?" I asked. "Don't throw your butts, stamp 'em out. Let's go."

Like mice moving across the kitchen floor watching for the cat, we snuck through an opening in a chain-link fence and crossed Mary Waters Ford Road. Gary led the way as we crept into the Otts' front yard. A dog barked in the distance, temporarily freezing us. *Mickey was right,* I thought, *dark is good.*

Since this was new to Pete, Mickey took him to a tree that was easy to climb and helped him up. Gary and I, veteran cherry stealers, were already picking. We spit the pits and bad cherries on the ground. Sometimes we'd spit the pits at each other. Once, Gary spat a pit at Mr. Otts, who came out on the front porch for a smoke, and the pit stuck to his cheek. He went back inside, and we heard Mrs. Otts yell, "How'd you get that on your face?"

"Get what?" Mr. Otts replied.

"You've got a cherry pit stuck on your face. You been eatin' the cherries outside?"

"No, I haven't been eating any cherries," he said, as he wiped his face. From the trees, we could see the entire downstairs through the windows. And we could hear everything.

"You're lying," Mrs. Otts yelled. "You've been eating those cherries.

You know they give you the runs." On the Hill, a story like that would spread faster than measles. Of course, lots of kids changed or added their version of it. By the time the story made its final rounds, it had gone like this: Gary had spat a cherry pit on Mr. Otts' face, and right there on the porch Otts shit his pants.

It was quiet inside the Otts' place that night and so dark nobody could see us in the trees; and as Gary predicted, the lights from the house danced softly on the cherries. However, the peace didn't last long. We were well into picking and filling our bellies when we heard yelling inside the house. Still munching and spitting, we focused our attention on the windows. The Otts were arguing with someone inside.

"Hey," Mickey whispered, loud enough to hear. "Something's going on inside. Be quiet."

"All right," Gary hushed, "dinner and a show."

Gary had the best view; he was in the tree closest to the windows. As we ate and spat, the yelling got louder.

"Anybody seen him before?" Mickey whispered.

"No," I said, "I don't think he's from the Hill."

"Must be some relative," Gary said. "Let's watch and see what happens."

Without warning a gunshot went off inside the house. It sounded like an atom bomb. It reverberated through us as if we felt the gun's recoil. Mrs. Otts' screamed and called out her husband's name. The visitor told her to shut up, but she didn't. He told her to shut up and lie down. A second shot went off, and the screaming stopped. It got quiet, creepily quiet. We stood in the trees frozen as we watched the visitor drag the Otts' bodies into the dining room.

"Jesus H. Christ," Gary stammered, "he blew their brains out."

"We got to get out of here," Mickey called out.

"The ballfield and into woods," I said, barely audible.

"Holy Shirt," Gary said again, "he blew their brains out."

It was as if we were paralyzed, trying to move but couldn't.

"Let's go," I said, "we can't stay here; he'll kill us, too."

We started down. Slow like turtles, if turtles could climb. We were scared shitless. Mickey jumped first and hit the ground hard, and he grunted. Then Gary. We were jumping from high up; fear pushed us on. I jumped and rolled. The grass was soft and cool; I looked up. Pete was still in the tree, unable to move.

"Pete," I muttered, hopefully, loud enough for him to hear. "Come on, you can jump from there."

And he did, he hit a few branches on the way down — it was an awkward jump. He landed hard next to me and he grunted, too. But there was a problem. He was missing a shoe; his shoe got caught between two branches. Light from the windows illuminated it.

"Oh, shit," Pete said, "where are my glasses? I can't see anything."

"Here, I got them," Mickey hushed. "Hey, where's your other shoe?"

"Damn," I whispered, "look up there; it's still in the tree."

"Oh shit," Mickey cried, "we better get it."

"The hell with that," Gary whispered. "We got to get out of here. That pecker-head is coming out here, and we'll be target practice. I don't see him inside anymore, where is he?"

Nobody answered. We bolted for the street. Halfway across the street, Pete cursed out in pain. "Aww shit."

"Come on, Pete, come on."

"I lost my goddamn sock. Where is it? It's too dark. I can't see shit."

I went back to help him. We couldn't see anything on the street; it was too dark. A noise on the front porch startled me. "Come on," I said, "we've got to go."

Just as we started for the opening in the chain-link fence, I heard the front door squeak open, and light from the house reflected on the fence. Pete went for the opening, and I followed, I looked back. A man watched us from the porch. It was scary: a dark figure outlined in light from the open door. It looked ghostly. The man said nothing, and I turned and dashed through the fence opening and followed Pete across the softball field. We ran like our lives depended on it.

Gary and Mickey were just ahead of us as we crossed left-field of the baseball diamond running toward the woods. I looked back again and saw a pair of headlights sitting in front of the Otts' house. Pete, running on a sock and shoeless foot, and not a fast runner, was flying. I couldn't catch him.

Adrenalin made us Olympic sprinters. We raced along the side of the tennis courts and passed two picnic tables on our way down an embankment. Gary and Mickey were already in the woods. We entered the woods running full speed — didn't know or care where we were going. We tumbled through razor-sharp stickers, tree limbs, rocks, dirt, and tall weeds; low hanging branches ripped at our faces. We kept bulldozing our way deeper into the woods; stumbling, rolling, getting back up, swearing, moving forward until we hit a creek. That stopped us.

We sloshed into the creek — two inches deep, maybe five feet wide — and tumbled into the mud and rocks on the other side. We were drained and couldn't get up. We sucked in the cool night air, filling our lungs as fast as we could. Coughing, spitting, our chests heaved as we gasped for breath.

"We…we have to…we have to be…we have to be quiet," I managed to get out as I sucked in more air. We lay there in the dark, in the muddy water, knowing that we were somewhere in Smithy's woods. Burrs and stickers covered our clothes; our pants were torn and ripped apart, and we were wet. It was so dark; I couldn't see Pete, less than ten feet away. Only heard him gasping for air.

"My goddamn foot hurts," he said.

"I don't see any lights," I groaned, "I don't think they followed us. But they know we're here."

"Who's they," Pete asked, "I thought it was one guy."

"No, a car pulled up in front of the house."

"Oh, shit, can they drive down there?"

"No, I don't think they will. The ground's too soft. But they saw us, that's for sure."

"What are we going to do," he asked.

"Skippy and I hunted down here. I helped him lay traps along this creek. I know if we follow it, we'll come out to some tall grass. The quarry will be to the right, the elementary school to the left."

"You sure?"

"Yea, pretty sure."

"How did I get myself into this?" Pete moaned. "I have to be an ass-wipe. Stickers and shit all over my arms, goddamnit. My foot's killing me."

"Can you walk?"

"Fuckin'-a," he said. "I want to get home."

I was right. We followed the creek for maybe fifty yards — it eventually banked to the left — and we came to the tall grass I'd envisioned.

"What's in there," Pete asked, "anything that can bite us?"

"I don't think so. Let's go."

As we moved out of the creek and into the tall grass, I heard Pete whisper, "He doesn't think so, that's some shit."

We didn't get bitten, but I missed the opening to the elementary school by twenty yards. Finally, we found it. We crossed the school field and came out onto School Street. We hobbled down Elmwood, and I saw the car sitting on Springfield Avenue.

"Pete, come on, in these hedges."

"Now what," he said, "I want to go home."

As we burrowed into the hedges, I pointed out the headlights from a car sitting on Springfield Avenue. "I don't think they saw us," I said. "It's still sitting there; it's not moving."

"So what? So, what if a car's sitting there? Some kid getting some feels, or don't they do that here. No, they just steal Goddamn, asshole cherries."

"Wouldn't be sitting there with the headlights on," I explained. "When we were running to the woods, I saw a car pull up in front of the Otts' house. If it's the same car, they could be looking for us. It doesn't seem right a car just sitting there."

"Oh shit, this is getting worse. Come on, man," Pete said, "I've got to get home. Can't we go another way?"

"All right, I know, let's watch this car for a few minutes. Maybe it will leave, and we can go on."

The car pulled away, and we continued down Elmwood. Pete went straight, and I turned right onto Springfield Avenue. I could see the taillights of the car ahead of me, moving at a snail's pace.

I decided to get close to it. I stayed to the left, careful not to get picked up in the rearview. I went through yards and over porches. I served newspapers on the street, so I knew short cuts from one yard to another. I got close enough to see that it was a big white Cadillac with huge tail fins. It's a car you'd never forget. It inched down Springfield. I turned up Maple and broke for home.

CHAPTER 5

On the Payroll

It wasn't like any of us could hide in the cellar until it all blew over. We had stuff to do, like making good in our first year on the big team, what we called the Hill's American Legion baseball team. I also had my paper route — 100-plus *Bulletin* customers, who I supplied with the news every afternoon. On our ball team, a new kid, our new friend Pete Brescil, who left his shoe and sock at the murder scene, was an impressive hitter. He had a short, powerful swing and drove the ball to right field like no kid we'd ever seen.

I'll never forget the first time I met him at the intersection of Highland and Ashland on the way to our first practice. He was a bit stocky, not fat; he just ate well. And talk about self-confidence. Upon self-introduction, he called himself 'the Brun.' He was extremely likable and quite handsome, too. His hair was thick and black, and he wore black wide-frame glasses.

The ballfield was a Hill kid's Shangri-La, from school closing to Labor Day. Hundreds of kids a day would meet there to make up baseball teams. Completely unsupervised by adults, kids would go to the ballfield and play ball all day, other kids waited to make up the next team. Those who didn't — kids chose up the sides using the fist over fist method at the handle of a bat — would sign out a basketball and go to the blacktop court. Tennis courts sat between the baseball field and basketball court, and kids signed out tennis rackets and balls, too.

The ballfield was famous for something else, too: rumors. Kids could take bits of information, true or false, and add outrageous stuff of their own. A week after the double homicide on Mary Waters Ford Road, the rumors were flowing like smoke from a house fire.

"It was JoJo-Apeshits," one kid said, "I swear on my mother's grave."

JoJo-Apeman, alias JoJo-Apeshits, was a mentally challenged middle age man who spent his days roaming the streets of the Hill talking to himself. Kids unmercifully tormented him. His demeanor and walk resembled that of a gorilla. The rumor made perfect sense: since JoJo was half-ape, he roamed the streets in the day and lived in the trees at night.

"It was Apeshits," the kid said, "he was up in the tree, and old lady Otts tried to chase him. Apeshits blew a hole in her head. Then did the same to old man Otts so there'd be no witnesses. Swear to God; it's the truth."

Kids always swore to God; it made the tale more believable. Or they swore on their mother's grave, even if she wasn't dead. The other popular rumor was that Mumbles did it. Mumbles was a broad-shouldered giant of a man who also roamed streets of the Hill. When you said stuff to him, he'd answer, but nobody ever understood a word he said. Because of his size, most kids tormented him from afar. The story around the Hill about Mumbles was that he fell off a Manayunk beer truck making deliveries. They had to put a metal plate in his head, so whenever there was lightning, Mumbles went nuts. It didn't matter that there was no lightning the night of the murders. Nobody cared about that; the story made sense.

The truth was, we were happy the rumors circled JoJo Apeshits and Mumbles. Although we, of course, knew those rumors were bullshit. Even so, we hoped the cops would believe the stories and investigate them, not us.

The Otts' shooting made *The Philadelphia Bulletin*'s front page, a boxed-in feature at the bottom. And, in the *Main Line Times*, a hoity-toity paper which most people on the Hill didn't read, anyway. Except for us paperboys, kids never read newspapers, either.

The 201 Bar on Jefferson Street was on my paper route, and frequently when I took the paper inside, the bartender gave me a Coke. I sat at the bar and thought I was hot stuff; not there waiting for my father. Coming out of the 201 is when I saw it, the white Cadillac coming down Highland Avenue. I was sure it was the same one I saw on the night of the murders. It had those big-ass-fins. I got my wagon and began working the homes on Jefferson hoping the Cadillac would either turn up Jefferson the other way or pass by me. I kept my eye on it and nearly dropped dead when it pulled up to the curb on the opposite side of the street from me. The driver put down the window. "Hey, kid, come here, we want a word with you."

I stood on the sidewalk; afraid I was about to get shot. "Yeah, what?" I said.

"Come here, kid. We're not gonna bite you. Get over here."

I let a car pass and approached the car, stopping in the middle of the street. This time the passenger spoke up. "Kid, what the hell, get over here we want to talk to you, you deaf or something?"

I took a couple of more steps toward the car. "Look, kid, how much you make delivering these papers?" the driver asked.

"I don't know," I responded, "four bucks a week, I guess."

"Four dollars?" the passenger said. "Kid that's slave labor, for Christ's sake. What you sweatin' on a hot day like today for, for four dollars?"

I didn't answer, just shrugged my shoulders.

"Look, kid, we want to put you on our payroll, and you'll make more than four dollars, know what I'm saying?"

I didn't respond.

The passenger saw that I was frightened.

"Kid," he said, "what the hell you shakin' for? We ain't gonna hurt you. Now come over to the window, or I'm gettin' out and drivin' my foot up your ass."

I quickly walked up to the driver's window. "That's better," the driver said. "Look, kid, we're gonna put you on our payroll, and you get some information for us, it's simple. Information, a hundred bucks. You can quit this slave paper route and spend some money on a girl and get laid, capeesh, kid?"

"You got a girlfriend, kid?" the passenger asked.

I shook my head.

"What?" the passenger wondered, "you ain't got no girlfriend?"

"How old are you, kid?" the driver asked.

"Fifteen."

The passenger leaned toward the driver, "Fifteen and he ain't got no girlfriend. Kid, you a paesano?"

"A what?"

"A paesano," the driver said, "Italian."

"Oh, no, I'm Irish."

"Oh, shit, that explains it, an Irish prick, no wonder he ain't got no girlfriend.

The driver turned and asked, "You ever been laid, kid? Ever get a blow job?"

I shook my head.

"All right," the driver said, "we're puttin' you on the payroll and if you give us what we're lookin' for we're gonna give you a hundred bucks and bring a little bella ragazza with us in the backseat."

"A what?"

"A girl, kid, you stupid or something?" the passenger hollered.

I didn't respond.

"Kid," the driver said, "you know about them murders the other night?"

"Ah, yea, everybody does."

"All right," the driver said, "Now, we've heard that there were some kids near the house when them people got whacked, capeesh? You hear anything about that?"

I shook my head.

"We want the names, kid," the passenger said. The names of the kids who were near that house. And if you give us the names, we're gonna a give you a hundred bucks and bring a nice little puttana with us, and she'll give you anything you want."

"Hundred bucks and a blow job," the driver said, "how the does that sound to you, kid?"

"Ah, I guess all right."

The driver turned to the passenger. "He guesses all right, ah fungolo, we should find another kid."

"No," the passenger said, "if we do, we have to waste him. Let's first see what he can do."

The driver turned back to me. "All right, we'll give you a few days, see what you can do. We'll catch up to you by the end of the week. And kid, if you try hidin' or runnin' away or tellin' anybody about this, we'll chop you up in pieces and feed you to the fish in that river over there, capeesh?"

"Well, I replied, "sure, I guess. But what were these kids doing, just walking by?"

The passenger leaned forward and yelled, "THEY WAS PICKIN' CHERRIES, KID."

"We should get another kid," the driver said, "this kid's stupid."

"No," the passenger said. "Kid, give us a newspaper."

"Oh, I'll be short if I do."

"Kid," the driver said, "if you don't,' you won't be short, you'll be fuckin' dead."

I quickly went to the wagon and got a paper and passed it through the window. The driver zipped up the window and sped off.

As I watched them drive away, I had only one thought: *Holy shit.*

CHAPTER 6

Help on the Way

After the conversation with the men in the white Caddy on Jefferson Street, I took a different route home. Usually, I avoided Fairview Avenue because it wasn't on my paper route, and the street is very steep. But something told me to go home that way. Call it a sixth sense. Halfway up Fairview I looked across the Curry's property and could see the front of my house on Ashland Avenue. Parked out front was a detective's car.

Every kid on the Hill recognized a detective's car. No way did I want to speak with detectives. I pulled my wagon into a clump of grass at the edge of the Curry's backlot and waited. After a few minutes, two men emerged from my house, got into their car, and drove away. I paused briefly, making sure they were gone, and then started through Curry's lot to my house. I was nearly through the tall hedges and into the lot where Billy's father parked construction vehicles when Billy shouted to me from his father's garage.

"Yo, Ronny, wait up."

As he approached, I could see the shit-eating grin on his face, like he'd just discovered how to build a gas-free engine.

"Hey, I knocked on your door a while ago," Billy said, waiting briefly to catch his breath. "Your mother said you were on your paper route.

You and your boys were in those cherry trees when the Otts got killed, weren't you?"

"Oh, I don't think so." But Billy could see I was lying, so his wry grin grew wider.

"Don't bullshit me, Ronny," he said. "Detective Frost called my father the other night, wanted to know where I was on the night of the murders. My father told him I was in the garage, helping him with an exhaust pipe."

"Did you go for the cherries, Friday, like you were gonna?" I stupidly said, trying to get Billy off the subject.

He grunted. "You kiddin?" he said. "No kid in his right mind would go there after the murders. But you were there Thursday, weren't you? Because I told you we were going Friday, and you and your fart-bird friends went Thursday to steal the cherries first and saw the murders, didn't you?"

My blank stare and open mouth gave Billy his answer.

"Goddammit I knew it," Billy howled, his grin lighting up his face. "Goddammit, I knew it. You seen them Otts killed. That's some shit. I'd give anything to have been in those trees that night."

"You would?" I asked

"Fuckin-a," Billy said, "You and your fart-bird friends are in the middle of the biggest thing to ever hit the Hill. Goddammit it, right there. Son of a bitch."

"But what if the killers are looking for us, what's so great about that?"

"Are they?" Bill asked, suddenly becoming serious.

I nodded.

"Holy shit, how do you know that?"

"Right after the murders," I explained, "we were making our way home, and I saw a white Caddy on Springfield like they were looking for us. Just about an hour ago that same Caddy stopped me on Jefferson and offered me a hundred dollars and a blow job if I got them the names of the kids who were in the trees."

"No, shit, what did you tell them?"

I shrugged. "Didn't tell them anything. I gave them a paper, and they left. They said they'd give me a few days and if I told anybody, they'd cut me up and throw me into the Schuylkill."

"Do you remember what they looked like?" he asked.

"Sure, the driver had really thick glasses, you know, the kind people wear when they can't see shit."

Billy was beside himself. He looked off in the distance, thought a few seconds, then said, "Ronny, you need help with this. There are plenty of guys on the Hill that can help you. This is bigger than just the four of you."

"Should we tell the police?"

"Fuck no. Those men in the Caddy you talked to are the mafia, you ever hear of the mafia?"

Billy didn't let me answer, which was good because I never heard of them.

"Frosty told my dad that he thinks it was a mob hit, you know, something the mafia would do. Those Italians in South Philly, they're crazy. They kill people for looking at them funny. If you go to the police, you and your fart-bird friends' pictures will be all over the newspaper, and you can kiss your skinny asses goodbye."

"So, what do you think we need to do?"

"Let me talk to some guys. We'll think up a plan. Meanwhile, you, Gary, Mickey, and Pete lay low. Try to avoid that white Caddy and if they do corner you, tell them you're workin' on the names and need a few more days. Give them some bullshit story. But whatever you do, don't run. They'll shoot you in the back."

"Okay. Thanks."

"Oh, and don't tell anyone about this. If you tell people I'm helping you then I'll chop you up and throw you in the river," he said.

I nodded. "No problem. But Bill there's something else."

"Yeah, what?"

"Running from Otts' place, Pete left his shoe in the tree and his sock in the middle of Mary Waters Ford Road. And there's more, Pete's shoes are old fashioned. Gary calls them dago shoes. He said they crush grapes in them."

Billy's mouth dropped open. "You're shittin' me now. Now's not the time to joke, Ronny, I don't think that's funny."

"No, it's the truth. Pete walked home, shoeless."

"Jesus Christ, Ronny, you guys fucked up." Billy rubbed his chin like he was thinking. Then he said, "Well, either the cops got it or the mob. I'm not sure what's worse. The cops won't chop you up, but your pictures will be in the papers, and the mob will chop you up. So, I don't know; it's probably 50-50. But one thing's for sure, you've got to lay low."

I nodded again. I was glad to have Billy's help. He had a lot of contacts on the Hill. He knew all kinds of kids. With that, Billy turned and walked back toward his garage — occasionally looking back over his shoulder and shaking his head — and I continued home. I put my wagon under the back porch and went inside. My mother was in the kitchen. She told me about the detectives.

"They first asked me where you were on the night of the murders," my mother said, as I entered the kitchen. "I asked them why they wanted to know that. They said there were kids in the vicinity that may have seen something and asked me if I still had the clothes you wore that night. I said I already washed them. But they were in the cellar still in a pile next to the washer."

Now my mother, with her strict Baptist upbringing, never lied. But for her five kids, she'd walk through hell in a gasoline suit. Besides, she wanted to make sure she wasn't giving me up as the killer.

"Are the clothes still there?" I asked.

"They're in the washer now. They were filthy, and the shirt you wore had cherry stains on it. The pants are ruined, covered with burrs and stickers and mud, and their torn. What's going on, Ronny?"

"Mom, all the kids pick cherries. That doesn't mean we saw somebody get murdered. You know the cops like to pick on us Hill kids. If they can't find the real killers, they'll blame us."

"Maybe so," she said, "but if you saw anything, you need to say so."

"Okay, Mom."

"Oh, something else, Ronny. Just before they left Mr. Lochran showed me a shoe. He asked me if it was yours. I said no. Tell you the truth it looked similar to the shoes Pete wears, but I didn't say anything."

"Mom," I said, "Thanks."

Fear gripped me by the throat. *Oh shit, they got Pete's shoe. Probably his sock, too.* This was getting worse, and now I had to deal with the South Philly guys who killed people for lookin' at them funny.

"Oh Ronny," my mother said. "Detective Lochran wants you to check around the Hill and see if any of the kids know who might have been picking cherries that night. I told him, 'Sure, Ronny would be happy to do that. I invited them to stop in again in a few days. He said they would.'"

"Oh," I said, "that's just great mom. Thanks."

"And Ronny, you got to pick up in your room."

CHAPTER 7

The Video Game

How to Make Carp and Catfish Bait

Take about four cups of cornmeal + Mix with water and molassses + Mold into a ball about softball size

Bring to boil and simmer for twenty minutes + Tie up in old t-shirt and store in refrigerator + Put glob on a fishhook

In 1964 the kids who lived in Belmont Hills didn't have cell phones, laptops or desktops, and they surely didn't play video games. Technology back then was a rotary phone and if you were lucky a color television. For us, the Hill was one giant video game, but it had to be played outdoors and with other kids. The Hill video game came equipped with sizable patches of woods, streams, hills, large backyards, a river, and enough stuff for us to do that we didn't have time to get into trouble. Nothing changed when the sun went down; we just did things in the dark.

We were rarely tied down, and we lived most of our childhood years free, to be creative, go where we wanted, and how late we stayed out. At no other time in our lives would we be as free as we were in the summer of 1964.

We camped in Smithy's or Croyles' woods or followed the railroad tracks along the river through the Flat Rock Tunnel to Valley Forge National Park, about a 20-plus mile hike. There were no camping and no fires signs, but we did it anyway. The Schuylkill River was less than a mile trek down the hill, and there we fished for catfish and carp. We never ate the fish we caught but took them beneath the El in Manayunk and sold them for dimes and quarters. Skippy showed me how to make carp bait from cornmeal mixed with molasses. It was a homemade invention, and the carp loved it. We fished from the rocks in the middle of the Schuylkill, visible upstream from the Green Lane Bridge.

In the early sixties, the river was a fishing wonderland. We waded through shallow parts of the river out to the rocks and cast out into the current. Using homemade sinkers to keep the bait down — carp and catfish are bottom feeders. When the tip of the rod jiggled, a carp or catty was tasting the bait. The big carp and catfish put up a great fight. In the afternoon, on hot days when the fish stopped biting, we stripped down to our underpants and dove into the river before going home or into Manayunk to sell our booty. We often walked along the railroad tracks and through the Flat Rock Tunnel to fish and swim at the foot of the Flat Rock Dam. It was a great place to build rafts, too, and float the slow water on the backside of the dam. No kid that I recall ever went over the dam.

In the woods, we organized war games that involved 10-15 kids. Three or four kids got a head start and then hid, the other lit out after them and tracked them down. It was our modern game of hide-and-go-seek.

Plus, there were the Phillies games. A half-mile walk to Manayunk, we boarded the 61 to Lehigh Avenue and transferred to the 54 which stopped at the Connie Mack Stadium gates. In the summer of 1964, the Phillies were one of the hottest teams in baseball, leading the league all summer until a disastrous nosedive. The team lost their last ten games of the season and didn't win the pennant.

We hung out at 'the dump,' which was what we called the township incinerator or landfill. We saw it as a place to get the wheels and axles that we removed from discarded baby carriages to build chuggies, a form of a go-cart or soapbox we raced down the hills. In the winter we removed doors from discarded refrigerators and stovetops and ran them down the snow-covered hills. But to us, the dump was more than a place to get wheels and refrigerator doors. We looked at it as our secret place, after all, who would hang out at the dump? We built underground forts there and used discarded appliance parts to fortify the floors and ceilings, lit by candlelight.

And football games. In the fall, starting when we were 15 or 16, we put a Hill team together to play kids from Manayunk, Roxborough, and Wissahickon. There were no uniforms, only a mixed bag of equipment. Some kids had helmets, or shoulder pads, maybe a few had football pants and if you were lucky, spikes — although most kids wore baseball spikes. The teams were organized without adult supervision and refereed by some of the older kids.

It was a special time and place to grow up in because it was sandwiched between Philadelphia's Manayunk and Roxborough, and Penn Valley and Narberth. We experienced all three aspects of life:

The city, country, and suburbs. We weren't rich, and we weren't poor. We weren't geniuses, and we weren't stupid, either. We weren't city kids nor were we Main Liners, not by a long shot. We were different. We were inbetweeners who spent one day in the city and the next day in the woods. One day on two city buses to Connie Mack Stadium, the next day hiking through the tunnel and camping at Valley Forge. We looked out for and stood up for each other, too. Just as Billy Curry did for us after we witnessed the Otts' murders.

We were free, free to roam Philadelphia and the woods surrounding the city, with no adult supervision and nobody telling us what to do.

The kids from the Hill were organizers. We learned to do stuff together without supervision and ninety percent of the time everybody got along. What Billy said about getting help made perfect sense. Instead of organizing a football team or a war game in the woods, Billy would get kids together to organize a defense against an outside threat, the mafia. If we could arrange camping and fishing trips, put baseball and football teams together, then figuring out how to get rid of mobsters would be a cinch.

CHAPTER 8

The First Meeting

Billy knew that individually, the kids on the Hill were street smart. Billy figured if he could put those smarts together — criminal creativity together — we'd be a much stronger force. So, Billy set up a meeting.

"This is the CIA. You know what the CIA is?" he asked. Most kids didn't so Billy explained it. "It's a secret organization to put some hurt on the bad guys, and that's what we're going to do. Secret means keep your mouth shut."

Billy had about 20 kids show up ranging from 14 to 17, and of course, us, the four boys who were in the cherry trees. We met at the cinder garage on Highland and Ebenezer. Besides organizing stuff, stealing things, fishing and camping, running and hiding from the cops, and being total pain-in-the -asses, the Hill kids also loved to bust balls and jumped at any opportunity.

The meeting was a fielding ground for kids to bust about one's mother, alcoholic father, queer uncle, body features, hair, and manner of speech. And, the nicknames. The kids on the Hill were great at making up nicknames. We had the Howler, Fuggie, the Ground Crew, Thor, Sex Machine, Jerk Off, Stinky, Wash My Hands, Prowler, Dirty Neck, Lard Ass, and many others. Billy brought the meeting to order and outlined the situation with the cherry stealing homicides and the mafia. When he finished, it became the opening day of ball busting season, and Skippy started it off. "Ronny, can I go in with you? You get the hundred bucks, and I get the blow job?"

The room erupted in laughter.

"Hell, with that," Georgie said, "let em' keep the hundred bucks and get two blow jobs."

Another explosive round of laughter.

Billy, smiling, let the joking go for a while then brought the meeting to order again. "All right, all right, enough joking," Billy said, "we need some ideas. I don't want to hear blow job again. I think you guys are obsessed with that."

"Can we use cull-ling-us?" Frankie asked, "how do you say that word, cunn-lingus?" Another explosion of laughter followed that.

"Frankie, if you ever ate Wash My Hands, she wouldn't wash her hands, she'd take a bath," Richie said, which prompted more laughter. Wash My Hands was a legendary girl who lived under the El in Manayunk. She loved to go to the backseat with boys. When finished, she'd say, "Ow, I've got to wash my hands. Can we go somewhere where I can wash my hands?" Every kid on the Hill claimed to have been in the backseat with Wash My Hands. Was she real? Probably not, but it sounded good. And if a kid wanted to prove his manliness? Well, ask Wash My Hands.

"Does anybody have any ideas?" Billy shouted. "Or I'm out of here, right out that door." Billy was frustrated, but the boys were having fun. Soon enough, an idea surfaced.

As the laughing died down, a lone voice rose from the group. It was Georgie Scavello. "Got to get rid of the mob guys first, that's our only chance. With them gone Pecker and the boys can go to the police."

Silence followed his remarks. It was good that Georgie spoke first, his opinion carried weight. There was maybe a thirty-second pause when Johnny Ciarlello, another respected voice, asked: "You mean, knock them off?"

"No," Georgie responded, "that's not what I was thinking, although that's possible. I was thinking to make it so they wouldn't want to set foot on the Hill again. Then the cops could take over."

"Yea," Bobby added, "who owns the Hill, them or us?"

"Damn right," Billy said.

"I know a little bit about the mob," Johnny cautioned, "they're killers. They don't scare easy, and there'll be more where they came from."

"I think Johnny's right," Roger added.

"Georgie," Roger said, "what about if we keep them at bay and away from the cherry boys while they go to the cops? If they're runnin' away or chasin' us, they can't be trying to knock anybody off."

"Yea and besides, that would be fun," Skippy gushed.

"I hear what you're saying, keep them on the run," Georgie added. "What do you think about that, Johnny?"

Johnny was in deep thought. After a brief pause, he said, "Yea, that might work, but it will be dangerous. We can't get within shooting range of them, and they can't know who we are, or they'll hide out and wait to get us coming from or going home."

"Well, shit, I ain't scared of them," Georgie said. "I think we can put our minds together and give them what they're not expecting. We can fuck them up."

"I like where this is going," Billy said. "Georgie, have anything in mind to start us off?"

"Yea, I do, Bill," he said, "I got an old Dodge that still runs. We can use that to start things off."

"But that car doesn't have headlights," Gary said.

"Yep, but the bitch runs, it'll take them on a ride they'll never forget," Georgie responded. "Pecker, it's a top-secret car, that's why it doesn't have headlights."

"What do you mean, top secret?" Billy asked.

"Shit," Georgie replied, "if it ain't got headlights, you can't see it at night, can you?" Laughter followed.

"Yep," Skippy cut in, "could be that it's a junker, too."

"You mean get them to chase you," Johnny asked. "How will you do that?"

"You could hit them from behind at night," Frankie suggested.

"Or I can piss on their door and then run and jump in your car; they'll chase us for sure," Skippy interjected. More laughter. You could count on Skippy to come up with and follow through on something different

"I like that idea, Skippy, now you're thinking like me," Georgie said.

"Then what," Billy asked," so what if they chase you?"

"What's that road in Penn Valley where the creek runs over it?" Chuckie asked.

"You mean the ford over Old Gulf Road," Roger replied. "You can pick it up off Haggy's Ford."

"Georgie, you bring them across that creek, and there'll be a nice surprise waiting for them," Chuckie said. Then everybody started talking. Billy looked over at me and winked.

"All right, everybody can't talk at once," Billy shrieked. "Georgie, when can you pull this off?"

"Ah, let's see, should be right away. How about tomorrow night?" Georgie inquired. "We have to plan it out, and we can do that this afternoon and tomorrow. We need to plan on who will be dropped off at the creek and who will be in the car. Skippy has to be in the car because he's the door pisser."

"Should they go to the police now?" Dirty Neck asked after the laughter subsided.

"I don't think so, not yet," Billy said. "Let's go after them, first."

"Oh yea, Billy, we're gonna go after them," Georgie said.

"Goddamn," Billy hollered, "let's get to work. Georgie, pick the kids you want with you in the Dodge and who will remain at the creek. This first one is on you."

Georgie didn't reply, but with a wry grin, he just nodded. Suddenly, a kid yelled, "Shit, who the hell farted?"

"Jesus H. Christ, that's Skippy," Gary said, "I'd recognize that stink anywhere." Skippy, with a twisted grin, shrugged his shoulders. Skippy amused himself by sickening kids with a stench so disgusting they had to get away.

"Hey," Skippy bellowed, laughing, "I couldn't help it, a rat crawled up my ass and died. Where's everybody going?"

CHAPTER 9

The Mob

In 1964 two essential forms of unexpected phenomena occurred on the Hill: first, Georgie acquired a 1948 Dodge junker for $35 and hid it behind the old school and church on Jefferson Street. Second, the Beatles arrived in the United States and became superstars. These two acts of unexplainable wonder influenced the success of Georgie's mission.

How so? Louis "Cock-Eyed Lou" Fratto, and John "Johnny Sausage" Barbatto didn't know about Georgie's junker, of course, but they did read the *Daily News* and were aware of the Beatles. "Bunch of punk-ass queers," Sausage called them.

"Yeah," Cock-Eyed Lou replied, "but they probably get laid every night."

"Cock-Eyed, how can you get laid when you're a queer?" Sausage replied. "That doesn't make sense, know what I'm sayin?'"

"Oh, no," Cock-Eyed argued, "many of them queers are acey-deucy, don't forget."

The two hitmen were sent to the Hill by the South Philly mob boss, Angelo Morello, boss of the bosses, to identify the four snotnose kids who were eating cherries witnessed the murders. But it wasn't just to identify them. The next step was to whack them. It was the South Philly mob that killed the Otts, the sweet couple on the Hill everybody loved and who rarely, if ever, called the cops when juvenile delinquents stole their cherries. It was the kind of job that was just right for the two aging mobsters.

The truth was, Angelo was unhappy about the work Lou and Johnny were doing. Lou's eyesight had gotten worse during the last several years, and some of the other hitmen refused to work with him for fear of getting shot. Not by an assailant but by Lou. Johnny Sausage's mind was going bad — "half fuckin' senile," the other hitmen said — and he was forgetting important things like which job he was working on and where he parked his car. Key concerns when you're a mob hitman.

Several times Little Nicky had to take his keys from him and find his parked car on the street in South Philly. So, the thinking was that the job of whacking four kids was just right for them so they could retire after a successful job. "Come on, they're 15-year-old kids, for Christ's sake," Little Nicky said, "how hard can it be? My mother-in-law could do the job, boss." So, Angelo divvied it out to Lou and Johnny with the last-minute advice of, "Don't fuck it up." The two hitmen got into Lou's Caddy and drove to the Hill, looking for the snotnose kid witnesses.

The kids assigned to ride with Georgie were told to meet him at the old church and school parking lot on Jefferson Street at 7. He said he kept the '48 Dodge there. The car looked like an old battleship, weathered and worn; tired looking, as if it was soon to draw its last breath, waiting for the final tow to the junkyard.

Its backseat windows were stuck open — permanent air conditioning, Georgie called it — and the front windows he said worked sometimes, but not most times. The tires were big and looked mean, with white threads visible on the sidewalls, with more cracks than Chinese drywall.

Skippy was the last to arrive, and he stunned us as only Skippy could do. He had a Beatles' haircut. Skip's dad was a hairdresser — his business called Styles by Val'— and he had a shop right in the house.

He helped Skippy get the Beatles' look. As far as records indicate, it was the first Beatle haircut on the Hill, and it was a beauty.

Pete: "What is that?"

Gary: "Jesus H. Christ."

Mickey: "Is that a wig?"

Georgie: "Ha, ha, ha, goddamn, Skippy, you're some shit. Where the hell did you get that?"

And me? I just smiled. Nothing Skippy did surprised me.

Skippy? He had his usual, famous crooked grin, loving the hell out of shocking everybody. Something else we noticed about Skippy, he jumped around and held his crotch like his pants were on fire.

"Skippy," Georgie asked, "what the hell's wrong with you?"

"Nothing, George," Skippy said, "just got to piss, that's all. Been savin' it. Can we hurry up and get going?"

"When was the last time you pissed?" Mickey asked him.

"Ah, probably yesterday afternoon," Skippy said. "Listen I don't want to have to piss and can't do it. Besides saving it up is better, it'll stink more."

"All right, then," Georgie said, "let's get a move on before Skippy wets his pants."

Laughing, and trying not to sit next to Skippy, we piled into the Dodge. We knew that with Skippy and Georgie in the car, we were in for a fun night. There were six of us — Georgie behind the wheel, Mickey and Pete in the front seat, and Skippy, Gary and me in the backseat, which seemed larger than a double bed.

The car had an old musty smell, like something from the attic, most likely from the rain that came through the stuck-open back windows and turned moldy on the seat and floor. Georgie told us not to worry about it; it will air out, he said, once we get going. Skippy told George he'd like to borrow the Dodge for a date. "One of them Manayunk girls," Skippy said, "we wouldn't have to move to the back seat." Georgie just nodded and grunted.

"Not crankin' it up yet," Georgie proclaimed, "waitin' to know where that Caddy is. Besides, the gas gauge ain't workin,' so I'm not sure how much is left. I think there should be plenty, though."

"George," Mickey asked, "when was the last time you gassed it up?"

"Never have, Mickey," Georgie said, "Never have. Do it when I need to."

We sat quietly in the darkness thinking about how Georgie would know he needed gas — with Skippy jiggling around and holding his crotch — and waited. Georgie told us he kept the Dodge at the church instead of at home because his father didn't know he had it, which made sense. It'd be tough explaining why you owned a car when you were too young to drive. Eventually, a car pulled up in front of us. Chuckie got out and came over to the driver's window. "The sons of bitches are sittin' up on School Street," Chuckie said.

"Which way they facin'?" Georgie asked, his face contorted, like John Wayne talkin' to a horse thief.

"Toward the school," Chuckie replied, "if you go up Lyle you can come in behind them. We're heading out to the creek."

Georgie nodded, then said, "We should be there in about an hour. Then he turned to us in the back seat, "That is if I can get this hussy to run," and he laughed.

"Okay, see you," Chuckie said, and he left.

"Let's get this mother rollin.' Let's crank it up," Georgie announced.

Georgie turned the key, and the engine coughed and sputtered. He turned it again. Nothing. He pumped the gas pedal and turned the key and the engine roared to life. "That's it, baby," he yelled, "wee-ooh, knew you wouldn't let me down." Suddenly the car began shaking, and the engine quit. Smoke coughed out the exhaust pipe, and a light breeze carried it into the car through the stuck-open back windows, gagging us in the back seat. Even with the engine off the car shook for another ten seconds.

Georgie tried to start the engine again, but the motor clicked and didn't turn over. "Shit," Georgie screamed. "Shit, shit, shit." He reached under his seat and brought out a big ass wrench like a steel-worker would use to loosen a giant nut on the Walt Whitman Bridge. Georgie flung open his door and got out. Skippy and I opened the back doors and got out too because everybody wanted to see what Georgie was going to do with that big ass wrench.

CHAPTER 10

Georgie's Junker

Owning an automobile in 1964 before you were old enough to have a license was not uncommon on the Hill. But it wasn't the norm, either. Most kids waited until they turned 16, passed the test for a license, and then went car shopping. Junkers were around and available, and if they ran for just a few months, that was okay, too. To most kids, driving it around for a few days was worth 15 or 25 dollars. Some kids owned more than one car and parked them on different streets around the Hill. No one had insurance —

we didn't even know what that was — and had little or no money for gas or repairs. Kids like Skippy — mechanically able — could get a car and fix it, then either keep it or sell it and buy another one. The driving motivation for most kids on the Hill to own a car, of course, was girls.

By the time we got to our junior year at Harriton High School, the urge to own a junker had become stronger. The girls we pursued didn't live on the Hill but in communities like Villanova, Bryn Mawr, Narberth, and Gladwyne. You couldn't walk or take a bus to those places, only drive. Inevitably, some parents spent sleepless nights when a kid from the Hill pulled into the driveway of their Villanova mansion in a beat-up '56 Chevy. Or '48 Dodge junker.

So, Georgie kept his Dodge at the church-school on Jefferson Street where on occasion he would take it for a spin. It was perfect for helping out the kid witnesses because Georgie didn't care what happened to it, and if it stopped running somewhere, so what? He'd leave it and maybe never go back. That wasn't uncommon on the Hill, either. But his Dodge had a sick generator, at least that's what Georgie thought, and he had a unique way to talk it back into rehabilitation.

He went to the front of the Dodge and lifted its hood, a massive piece of metal that covered the engine. It was all he could do to get it up, bending at the knees and extending his arms straight up, like a weight lifter.

"Ronny, Gary, get over here and hold this mother," Georgie commanded. We quickly did but could barely hold it up. "Mickey, Skippy, help them, weaklings," Georgie added. It took all of us, including Pete, to hold the hood up so it wouldn't crush Georgie. Then, Georgie hammered away at the motor with the big ass wrench.

"The generator, goddamnit," he said, as he pounded a round black metal object, which looked like a miniature loaf of bread. "Got to wake the fucker up." Sparks flew off the generator as he beat it. "Okay, that ought to do it. Drop that monster prick."

No one moved. "I said drop that monster, you deaf?"

56

Thankfully, Mickey said, "Okay, on the count of three, everybody let go of the hood and jump back. Ready? One, two, THREE…" That '48 Dodge hood dropped like the jaws of a sea monster bent on decapitating an arm or leg. It hit with a metallic bang so hard the car shook, and a few old crows took off from a nearby tree.

"This car is something? Huh, huh? Mean machine. Okay, everybody back in."

We scampered back in the Dodge as fast as we could, fearful of getting left behind. Georgie got back in and turned the key. Nothing. He turned it again and got the same clicking sound as before. Pounding the generator with the big ass wrench didn't work. We looked at Georgie. "What are we gonna do now?" Mickey asked.

"All right," he hollered, "don't worry, plan B, everybody the hell out."

Once again Skippy and I flung open the back doors and got out quickly. "Here's the thing," Georgie said, "we're gonna give it a push. Then I'll get in and pop the clutch when the mother is rollin'. When you see me get in you get your skinny asses in fast," he said, "or else you'll get left behind and miss all the fun. And don't let one of them tires roll over your foot. I ain't takin' nobody to the hospital until after we fuck over them mob guys." I looked down at the rear wheel, maybe four inches from my foot, and quickly jumped back.

Even though the car was on a downward slant, we had to rock it. It seemed like the junker had been sitting a while because the tires didn't want to move. They were probably comfortable where they were and didn't need the aggravation of coming out of retirement. Georgie called out the commands: "Forward, back, forward, back, one more time, forward, keep pushing, keep pushing, come on bitch move."

Miraculously, the big old junker with the giant tires and shitty generator began to creak forward. "Not yet, not yet," Georgie yelled, "keep pushing, push, push, okay, NOW."

He opened the front door and jumped in. Laughing, Skippy dove into the backseat, and we all did the same, piling up on each other, while the back doors swung back and forth like the bar doors in 'Gunsmoke'. The Dodge rolled out onto Jefferson Street, and Georgie cut the wheel in time to miss two parked cars while we struggled to close the back doors — first cousins to the car's hood in size, weight, and movability. When the Dodge got rolling, Georgie jammed the shift on the column into second gear and popped the clutch.

The car jerked forward, and we went flying. The motor roared to life sounding just like, as Georgie had earlier described it, "the biggest, loudest fart you ever heard." The engine coughed out thick black smoke that stunk, so the fart comparison was accurate. It rolled down Jefferson half-heartedly, as if it had better things to do than cart around six 15-year-old enthusiastic, thrill-seeking hooligans.

When the car leveled out on Jefferson Street, Georgie hit the gas. It took off. An old guy who was crossing the street ahead of us had to run out of the way. Skippy and Gary were hanging out the back windows yelling at people and laughing. Georgie drove the Dodge through the stop sign on Ashland without touching the brake — "not sure how good they work, got to save them" — and up the hill to Lyle Avenue, smoke billowing out its ass like it had a blowtorch inside the exhaust pipe. It backfired going up the Lyle hill, which sounded like a cannon shot at Picket's Charge. Halfway up Lyle I watched a mother frantically grab a toddler on her front porch and hurry inside.

We eventually got up onto School Street. Georgie managed to get the car into third before he applied the brake and drop it back down into second. And there it was, just as Chuckie said, "The sons of bitches are sittin' up on School Street." The white Caddy with the big ass tail fins, its lights on and idling as if it was waiting for the Dodge junker with six maniacal kids — four who were the snotnose witnesses — to come out and play. Georgie crept up behind it — that is, if a 1948 black Dodge with giant tires and squeaks and groans coming from every movable part and with smoke billowing out its ass

— could creep. I'd say Georgie got about three car lengths from the Caddy and slammed on the brake. We went flying in the back seat. "Yep, they work," Gary yelled.

"Hey, Paul McCartney," Georgie roared, "you ready to piss?"

"Oh yea," Skippy yelled, "Jesus Christ let me out."

"Go to it, man, go to it," Georgie yelled.

Gary stepped out onto the street and held the door open like a chauffeur would for some downtown big shot. Slowly but surely, Skippy walked toward the white Caddy; he paused, looked around, and looked back at us. With his right hand, he grabbed his crotch and bent over, trying to keep the pee in a little longer. It was as if he was teasing us. We watched in disbelief, our eyes wide open, knowing we were about to witness something we could tell our grandchildren. Or we were going to watch Skippy get shot, which was okay with us either way.

He strolled up to the driver's door, turned, and like he was standing at the urinal inside the boy's room at the Roxy Movies, bent his knees a little and opened his zipper.

Slowly, he pulled 'it' out.

He held 'it' with his left hand, and with the knuckles of his other hand, he rapped on the driver's window. Skippy looked back at the Dodge and grinned, again, that crazy grin that only Skippy could do.

We swear to this day we heard him yell out in joy with the feeling of relief as he experienced a total pee-gasm, which Skippy later said was equal to and even better than the other gasm. Of course, we didn't believe him.

Then he pissed like a racehorse.

CHAPTER 11

The Chase

The Cadillac Eldorado was one of the first Caddy's to introduce power windows in 1960. The mob favored power windows because the car's inhabitants could shoot quicker, rather than have to wait and roll the windows down manually. The bosses didn't go for shooting through glass, which resulted in expensive window repairs. Besides, the shattered glass particles were evidence.

That coupled with Cock-Eyed Lou being the driver of the White Caddy and that he inherited his nickname because cataract operations in the sixties were akin to running a scalpel over the eyeball to get the lens clear. Sometimes it worked and sometimes it didn't. It all gave Skippy the opportunity of a lifetime. Look, Cock-Eyed Lou's eyes were messed up. Sometimes when he wanted to look up, his eyeballs looked down and vice versa. Plus, the glasses he wore would've made the bottom of Coke bottles look like thin ice; thus, his street name Cock-Eyed Lou.

So, when Lou looked out the car window and saw Skippy, he said to his partner Johnny Sausage, "Hey Sausage, get a load of this shit, we got the lead queer Paul McCartney standing here by my window. Let's see what the fuck he wants." Then Cock-Eyed Lou reached for the power window button even as his colleague Johnny Sausage yelled, "NOOOOOOOOOOO."

It was too late. Skippy was halfway through his release on the Caddy's door and feeling good about things when suddenly an irresistible opportunity appeared before him: the window zipped down. Skippy had plenty of pressure left, so he did what any red-blooded kid from the Hill would do; he applied tilt. He arched his back and lifted 'it' up, so the power stream first hit Cock-Eyed Lou in the face. Then Skippy applied transversal guidance — an engineering term meaning he pissed to the left and directly on Johnny Sausage's lap.

Georgie, quick to see what happened, didn't waste time. He shouted, "Oh, shit, no," and threw the Dodge into first and popped the clutch so fast the Dodge laid rubber and squealed like it had got dipped in the fountain of youth. The three boys in the backseat were pushed back against the seat with such force they were lucky not to require neck braces. Skippy, seeing and hearing the Dodge accelerate, had only one option. With the Dodge roaring like it just came out of the showroom, Skippy grabbed the side of the back window and door handle and dove into the stuck open back window. But he didn't quite make it. Hanging half in and half out, and as Mickey said later, "with his pecker swinging freely in the summer breeze and leaking from a premature interruption." Georgie, seeing Skippy half in the Dodge, stomped on the gas and took down the stop sign with the car's massive right fender as he made the right turn at Elmwood and School.

Cock-Eyed Lou and Johnny Sausage, incensed beyond belief after getting pissed on by Paul McCartney, got out of the Caddy and got off three shots. Two embedded in the trunk and the third zipped through the rear window, exiting out the windshield just below the rearview — luckily hitting no one.

As a side note: Two weeks later, Georgie made $15 by parking the Dodge at the old church school again and charging kids a dime to see the three bullet holes. Georgie told the paying customers that it was John Dillinger firing his sub-machine gun at the Dodge, even though Dillinger had been dead 30 years. To a kid, their response was, "No shit. Can I touch it?" For that Georgie charged another nickel.

Gary and I grabbed hold of Skippy and pulled him in the car. Cock-Eyed Lou and Johnny Sausage got back in the Caddy, and the chase was on.

Skippy, laughing, and lying on his back on the floor, hollered," I'm not finished pissing, I got some left."

"Cap that pipe," Georgie yelled, "and who told you to piss on them?"

Skippy, laughing, said, "I couldn't resist it, I couldn't resist it."

"Yea," Georgie hollered, "now they're shootin' at us, goddamnit."

Now, Georgie had some mean-ass drivin' to do. He gripped the wheel with both hands and applied total concentration out the windshield. For Georgie, this was his moment of fame. He was driving like a lunatic and cared little about hitting things, including other cars and people. He didn't care what happened to the Dodge, and he was determined to beat that Caddy to the creek no matter what.

Georgie didn't have a lot of driving experience. Well, make that none. The car was a monster, and he had to quickly learn how to take corners, pass cars, and stay on his side of the road, which he rarely did. The Dodge was outclassed and outdueled by a much younger and sexier model, the '64 Eldorado. Georgie wasn't sure how much gas was in the tank because he'd never put gas in, and the gas gauge didn't work, anyway. Plus, the Dodge burned oil, the main reason for the thick smoke that billowed from its exhaust pipe. Therefore, not only did the car have no headlights and taillights — and by this time it was dark — thick smoke trailed the Dodge and engulfed the Caddy making Cock-Eyed Lou's eyesight even worse.

Cock-Eyed Lou and Johnny Sausage had guns and with their windows down took potshots at the Dodge. A lucky shot could have gotten Georgie. But because of the smoke, they had to shut the windows for fear of gaging to death. The Caddy gained in the straightaways but lost at the curves. Georgie went across lawns, through lights and stop signs, into fences and over anything in his way. With Lou's bad eyes and thick glasses, things went unseen until the last second, when Sausage would scream out, and Lou would jerk the wheel. Sausage kept blessing himself, praying to his deceased mother, and kissing the Italian crucifix he wore beneath his shirt.

It was at this point that Georgie decided not to take the usual route to the ford at Mill Creek, where Chuckie and his boys were waiting. For whatever God only knows reason, Georgie decided to take the chase through Ardmore, and head to the creek from there.

"Georgie," Mickey called out, "where are you going, this ain't the way."

"We're gonna have a little fun," Georgie said, "and shock the shit out of them rich old biddies shopping at Strawbridge's. Now you boys hold on and watch Georgie work." Gary and Skippy were still hanging out the back windows laughing and yelling at people.

Georgie managed to make it to Montgomery Avenue when disaster struck. Pete, sitting in the front seat next to Georgie, said, "George, what that's light blinking light on your dash."

"What," Georgie replied, "I didn't see nothing, Petey, what are you talkin' about?"

"There it goes again," Pete said.

"Wait, put your finger on what you saw blink," Georgie said, weaving in and out of traffic on Montgomery Avenue, getting honked at with no headlights and driving over the line and into opposing traffic.

Pete reached over and held his finger on the dashboard.

"Holy shit, you sure?" Georgie hollered.

By now, we were up in the back seat, looking over the front seats at the dashboard.

"What is it?" Skippy asked.

"It's the gas gauge," Georgie said. "Petey saw it blink."

"Twice," Pete said, "there it goes again."

The Dodge jerked forward — sort of sputtered, a split-second loss of power, then backfired and jerked again.

"Oh shit," Georgie said. "Oh shit, no."

"They just came onto Montgomery," Gary said, looking out the back window, "they're about a quarter-mile behind us, but they're coming on fast."

"George, where are you going?" Pete called out.

"Hold on fellows…."

CHAPTER 12

'Outta Gas'

No one said Georgie was a great driver. No one said he was a lousy driver, either, but one thing was for sure: he had some gonads. But Georgie made a calculated mistake. He decided to go through Ardmore because, he said, he wanted to scare the ladies coming out of the department store, Strawbridge and Clothier. He hated that store. That decision made the trip longer, but in reality, it may have saved our asses because there weren't any gas stations along the shorter route. Sure enough, with the white Caddy closing in, the Dodge coughed and ran out of gas.

As we approached Strawbridge's at Ardmore's Suburban Square, rolling on momentum after doing 80, the store was closing. Shoppers came out holding packages and saw the old Dodge approaching. It certainly gave them pause. At that point, with still plenty of momentum left, Georgie attempted a U-turn. As he did, the Dodge — with no headlights and kids hanging out of the windows — jumped up on the sidewalk and right into the shoppers. The U-turn was successful, but the Dodge scraped the side of the Strawbridge's building, leaving a broad strip of black paint that took the Strawbridge's people weeks to eradicate — it happened years before the graffiti removal era.

As people scattered, the Dodge straightened out, and still had momentum left to continue slowly up the sidewalk. Cars on the street honked at us like it was V-day. The sidewalk looked like a tsunami had passed. Sweaters, shirts, golf shoes, and neckties littered the pavement. As I looked out the back window, all I could think of was Alcatraz, Sing-Sing, and Rikers Island: where would we end up?

Finally, the Dodge stopped on the sidewalk. Georgie yelled, "Everybody out."

We couldn't have gotten out faster. We were inclined to run, but not Georgie. "We need to get a can of gas at that Esso," he yelled, sensing his companions were ready to bolt. "Gary, go get it, man, go get it."

Gary took off with Skippy and me behind him. The Esso was a block and a half away and Gary, easily the fastest of us, got there with a lead. Except, he didn't know what to do. But Skippy did. Skippy could steal wool from a cotton factory, so he ran past Gary right into the gas station garage. Five seconds later, he came out with an empty gas can grinning like a barracuda. But we encountered two significant problems. One, none of us had money except me from my paper route, and I had already spent it on sodas and Tastykakes. Two, none of us knew how to operate a gas pump.

The gas station man looked out the office window and saw three kids at the gas pump — this was long before self-service gas stations. He opened the door and yelled, "Hey, what the hell are you doing? Get away from that pump."

Skippy frantically turned every lever on the pump, trying to get gas. He found the right gear because gas shot out of the nozzle like it was a fire hose. Nobody thought to take the cap off the can, so I got down on one knee and worked at it. Except I didn't know which way to turn it; was it right to open or was that to close? I knew I had to find the answer fast because the man in the office opened the door and charged. I finally got it to move and spun it open, and Skippy jammed the nozzle in.

The gas station man was right on top of us, and Gary, pretending he was a linebacker in a game against Roxborough — that was his position, after all — slammed into the gas man and they both tumbled to the ground. The much older gas man was momentarily stunned. Gary got to his feet, and Skippy tossed the gas nozzle, and we took off. A crowd had surrounded the Dodge on the sidewalk when Skippy arrived with the gas can. No one knew the location of the car's gas tank since Georgie had never gassed it up. We desperately examined the outside of the vehicle. Georgie hustled to the front to lift the hood when a man standing nearby said, "It's not there."

Georgie froze. "Where is it?" he shouted.

"That's for me to know and you to find out."

"Tell, me goddamnit, or I'll throw you out in the street," Georgie replied.

"No reason to get contentious," the man said.

"Speak English. Where is it?" Georgie hollered.

"I believe some of you boys are the cherry stealers, am I right?"

That froze us like ice sculptures. No one spoke, we gaped at the man, who Georgie nicknamed 'the mysterious man.' He was average size, smart looking, with rimless glasses, slightly balding and dressed in a tieless suit. He stood watching us with his arms folded.

"You're wondering how I know that? Don't worry, I'll tell you in good time. Now, you boys have to get going. Hear the sirens in the distance? But it looks like the mobsters may beat the cops here. I could be wrong. Care to make a bet."

"Mister," Georgie yelled, "we don't have time for this shit. Where is the gas tank?"

"Wait," Gary said, "how do you know about the mobsters and us?"

"Oh, I know, Gary," the man answered. "I know all about you. I'll be visiting you soon enough."

"He'll be visiting us in Sing-Sing if we don't get out of here," Pete yelled.

"You're right, Pete," the mysterious man said. "Try looking behind the letters and numbers."

We scanned the car, dumbfounded and speechless. Suddenly, Mickey cried out, "Behind the license plate."

Mickey was the first to get there. He pulled the license plate back, and there was the gas pipe. Meanwhile, the Caddy passed us going in the opposite direction and went to the next light. Skippy poured the gas into the tank and tossed the can onto the sidewalk. We piled back into the Dodge. The police sirens were getting closer. Georgie pumped the gas and turned the key, and, after enjoying a brief nap, the Dodge roared to life.

Skippy yelled out the back window to the mysterious man. "You know who I am?"

"Skippy," he replied, "I know all of you, and in time we'll get to be good friends."

"Georgie," Mickey said, "who was that guy?" hoping Georgie knew him.

"Damned if I know," he answered. "Some mysterious guy. Don't worry; we'll never see him again."

Georgie drove the Dodge off the sidewalk and onto Montgomery Avenue. Gary, the official Caddy watcher, hanging out the back window, said the Caddy was right behind us.

"Georgie," Mickey yelled, "you got to turn around and go down Mill Creek Road." Without a word, Georgie cut the wheel and drove into another wild U-turn. Cars honked around us as if the first V-day was just a rehearsal.

The Dodge went over the curb and up on the sidewalk. Georgie cut the wheel, and the Dodge spun back onto Montgomery Avenue as the Caddy passed going in the opposite direction. And that's when we saw the police lights. Georgie stomped on the gas and drove through the red light as the honking got louder.

"Georgie, slow down," Pete screamed, "you won't make the turn."

Turning right onto Mill Creek Road, Georgie wasn't close to making it. The Dodge went up over the curb and took down a row of hedges, and just missed a fire hydrant. Busting through a white picket fence, it went over a beautifully landscaped lawn and across a driveway and nicked the back of a parked Mercedes. He steered it back onto Mill Creek Road after crushing the other end of the white picket fence. The Dodge drug part of the fence behind it for a mile.

"They just turned on to Mill Creek and are coming fast," Gary yelled.

"Come on, baby, come on," Georgie hollered, his foot pushing the pedal to the floor. "A little further, a little further."

"I'm going through this light," Georgie yelled, "hold on, boys."

To miss a truck in the intersection, he steered to the other side of the road and took out a no parking sign before he got the Dodge back under control and back into the right lane. Still, a football field or two away from the ford, Georgie pressed the gas to the floor. The Dodge picked up speed as it headed for the stretch. The ford in the road over Mill Creek came within eyesight at the end of a straight stretch of road.

"There it is," Pete yelled.

All Georgie had to do was maintain his speed and veer slightly to his left to make the creek.

"Slow down," Skippy yelled, "you'll miss the ford."

"Shit if I will. Here we go. Whoa…"

CHAPTER 13

Ford in the Road

The kids on the Hill had fantastic imaginations when it came to screwing people over. They may not have been A-students at school, and many barely got by, but with some noteworthy exceptions, most of the kids from the Hill saw school as another notch on their social agenda. Nevertheless, if schools had given diplomas for screwing people over, competition for summa cum laude on the Hill would've been fierce.

It was a typical summer day in the mill town of Philadelphia's Manayunk, maybe a 20-minute walk over the Green Lane Bridge from the Hill. Manayunk, or Manaiung, the Lenape word for river, had not yet become a haven for bars, restaurants, and impossible parking. There still were visible signs left from America's industrialization boom in Manayunk, specifically in textiles and manufacturing. Manayunk was still 20-plus years away from becoming "revitalized" into a chic town with an arts festival.

"Can I help you, fellows?" the salesman politely asked.

"Yes, sir," Chuckie responded, "I'm looking for a bureau for my room. My dad told me to pick one out, and he'll come by tomorrow to get it."

"Well, by all means," the clerk replied, "they're over here in the next room. Let's see what we can find for you."

They were at a furniture store in downtown Manayunk and Chuckie, Richie, and Frankie were bucking for summa cum laude. There was a half-dozen mannequins inside the store sitting and standing.

"Ah, excuse me, sir?" Richie asked, "do you have a restroom I can use while Chuckie buys a bureau?"

"Certainly, son," said the salesman. "Around the corner there, and down the stairs."

"Okay, mister, thanks," Richie replied. The clerk didn't notice that Richie had too much clothing on, especially for a lovely warm day in July. The salesman bought into the bureau purchase story nicely and focused on making a sale. Once in the bureau showroom, Chuckie became a knowledgeable buyer.

"Now, I like this one," Chuckie said, "but can you tell me how much square footage it has?" thus giving Richie, on the way to the men's room, time.

"Certainly," the clerk replied, "let me get the catalog. I'm sure it will be listed there."

"Yeah, that'd be good," Chuckie said, as he looked around, making sure no cops were in the store.

Frankie and Richie walked swiftly into the dining room area, where three lovely mannequins sat displayed as a family eating dinner. Frankie grabbed one from the table and dragged it down to the restroom. Richie stripped and dressed the mannequin in the clothes he wore over top of his other garments. When Richie finished, he snuck upstairs and out of the store.

Several minutes later, Frankie and the dummy walked arm and arm headed for the door; the problem being they had to walk through the bureau showroom. It was about that time when the salesman got suspicious about Johnny's true intentions of buying a bureau.

"Chuckie," Frankie said, holding the mannequin just right to make it appear as if he and Richie were leaving the store, "we'll be outside."

"Right," Chuckie replied, "I'll be right out."

Now Richie, Chuckie, and Frankie might have struggled in history class, but in screwing people over at the Manayunk furniture store,

they were worthy of extra credit. Completely outmatched, the salesman had graduated from Germantown High School, where there
were no awards for screwing people over. Shooting people, sure, there
were majors and minors in that. The salesman, however, wasn't a
complete moron. Most human beings in their right minds, especially
a furniture store guy, could tell the difference between a mannequin
leaving the store and a real person.

"Ah, excuse me," the salesman said, sensing something funny
about Frankie and the mannequin, "can you stop, please, I'd like a
word with you."

Frankie — holding the fake Richie — scampered for the door.
Chuckie sprinted right behind him, pushing the salesman out of the
way. The salesman followed, and when he got outside, he saw them
running up Main Street carrying the mannequin.

"Come back here with that," the clerk bellowed, "come back here,
or I'll call the police." Turning and charging back inside, that's what
he did.

The three of them — make that four counting the dummy — ran
up Main Street. The boys figured by the time the police arrived, they
could make it across the bridge and down a side path to the bank on
the Hill side of the Schuylkill River.

Then they'd follow another path up behind Baffas' bar, and come
out onto Jefferson Street, where they had diplomatic immunity. They
were correct in their escape assumption and successful in screwing over the furniture store people. Now all they needed was a bike,
which they stole from a yard where people didn't put things away.
Next, they needed some rope or cable, which they got at night from
a construction site on North Washington Avenue. The Hill boys were
fast workers — this was all completed in less than 24 hours.

Perhaps this could put the Hill in the book of records. But most likely not. The Book of Records indicates that the smallest woman alive was 24 feet, 7 inches. She married the tallest man, 15 feet, six inches. There's also the bubblegum record, where a guy blew the most massive bubblegum bubble ever, without his hands or feet and released it into the atmosphere. It landed on the moon. Be that as it may, there's nothing in the book of records about stealing a mannequin. There's nothing about the speed of a car hitting a ford in the road, either: a '48 Dodge junker with six hoodlum kids inside. But there should be.

All of the dots in the story connected: The Dodge, the mannequin theft, the chase, and six crazy kids in the car that rumbled down the stretch toward the ford crossing. It was the perfect example of Hill kids working together, although it never made the book or records, it surely was criminal creativity.

"Georgie," Pete yelled, "slow the hell down."

"The fuck with that, Petey, just hold on," Georgie bellowed, "everything's under control."

None of us thought so, but what could we do? We were merely occupants in the '48 death coffin barreling at a high rate of speed toward the ford in the road. The water from Mill Creek flowing over the road was merely six inches, no match for the two-ton Dodge junker. As Georgie made his approach, leaving the Caddy in the dust, Skippy, Gary, and I were up on our knees and holding onto the backs of the front seats, our heads down, bracing for the hit. In the front seat, Mickey and Pete extended their legs and pushed their feet into the floorboards; curled up on the front seat, afraid to look.

Georgie grasped the wheel tightly, his eyes wide open, tongue extended out of the corner of his devious smile. He glared at the oncoming water as if he was playing chicken with an 18-wheeler. The impact didn't stop the car, but it sure slowed it down. Waves of water burst through the stuck open windows drenching us in the back seat. Had it been any other car, a lighter one, perhaps, it might have rolled.

But not the Dodge. It hit the water like it was reenacting the Allied invasion of Italy.

Georgie managed to keep control of the steering wheel and get the car up the little incline above the creek. Water poured out of the Dodge from every imaginable crack and opening for the next twenty minutes. All eyes focused on the Cadillac approaching the creek.

Cockeyed Lou at the wheel of the Caddy and his ruthless passenger Sausage never saw the Dodge junker hit the water nor did they know the creek was there. How could they? Chuckie and his boys removed three warning signs above the ford. The street lights were taken out, too, with a few well-aimed rocks approximately two hours before the Dodge made its beach landing.

"Lou," Sausage said, "something doesn't look right."

"Ah, it's just dark," Lou replied. "I'll turn on the beams."

Immediately Sausage screamed, "Watch the bike."

Lou, seeing a kid on a bike in front of the Caddy — Sausage later said, "Madone, it came out of nowhere." The bike-riding dummy certainly did pop out of nowhere, when Johnny and his boys pulled on the ropes attached to the bike from opposite sides of the road. It popped up in front of the creek. Lou saw it good with his high beams on.

He immediately tried to avoid hitting the bike-riding mannequin by jerking the wheel to the left and into the nails. Johnny and his boys had placed two-by-fours along the right and left sides of the road. They figured when Lou saw the bike-riding mannequin; he'd steer to the right or left to avoid it. It became a bigger problem because the boys drove fifty ten-penny nails through the two-by-fours, which gave them the appearance of anti-tank obstacles leftover from Normandy.

It wasn't pretty.

The Caddy ran over the two-by-fours at a good clip and plunged into Mill Creek, where it stopped. Sausage opened his door and saw the creek running across the floorboards of the Caddy with four flat tires.

"Jesus Christ, you blind bastard," Sausage screamed.

"Va' a farti fottere," Lou answered, reaching for his holstered gun.

"Lou, wait," Sausage said, "there's a fish in the car."

"Where," Lou said. "he'll be a dead fish."

With that, Lou fired a shot at the creek flowing through the car.

"Jesus Christ," Sausage hollered, "You'll shoot me in the foot, be careful with that Goddamn thing you blind bastard."

Lou, sensitive about his eyes, had had enough.

"Out of the car, you sausage mother prick, out of the car. You're dead."

Both men climbed out of the car and into the creek, holding onto to the doors.

"Where are you?" Lou yelled. "Call me a blind bastard; you're fuckin' dead."

We were up at Georgie's Dodge maybe twenty yards away on Dove Lane watching. We saw Lou slip and fall into the water, which carried him downstream. How far downstream nobody knew, because we never saw Lou again. Sausage, seeing Lou floating away, got himself to the road and walked out to Old Gulf Road. He flagged down a car, threw the driver out at gunpoint, and drove back to South Philly.

We piled happily into Georgie's Dodge and returned to the Hill, wet, tired, and hungry.

CHAPTER 14

The Second Meeting

The second meeting of the boys, held at the cinder garage, wasn't as well attended as the first, but it was more fun. Nearly sixteen kids showed up, all in a light mood. We were victorious over the white Caddy, which we supposed had gotten towed out of the creek, but nobody knew for sure. Nor did we care. I figured since the threat was over, I could go back to my paper route.

I figured wrong.

The fun didn't last long when the door to the garage opened, and a man entered. Only six kids in the garage had seen this man before.

"You want something, mister?" Billy asked.

Gary looked at Georgie, who looked at Skippy. Pete said, "Oh shit." Gary said, "Jesus H. Christ," and Mickey turned white as a sheet.

"I think you got the wrong address, mister," Johnny said.

"Oh, I have the right address, all right," he responded. "And I believe I have the right boys here. I remember them from the sidewalk in Ardmore."

"Yeah, I remember you," Georgie remarked. "So why are you sticking your nose into this?"

"State your business, mister, or get out," Billy told him.

"Okay," he said, "but first I want to know if you've heard of this saying? Fell in shit and came up smelling like roses?"

No one spoke. No one laughed. Probably because we'd never heard that expression before. We heard 'shit or get off the pot,' but not that one. We looked uneasy as we exchanged glances.

"So, what's that mean?" Billy asked him.

"Well," he said, "four of you, the four that were in the cherry trees, fell in shit. Meaning, you saw something that you shouldn't have, two nice people get murdered."

"How do you know that," Pete asked, "somebody tell you?"

The mysterious man ignored Pete's question. "Then some more of you got involved in the chase with that old black Dodge. As a result, the fellow they call Cock-Eyed Lou got swept downstream and drowned. And the other fellow, Johnny Sausage, had a nervous breakdown."

"A nervous, what?" Richie asked.

"It means he went nuts," Mickey said.

"Holy, shit," someone hissed.

"So now more of you fell in shit. And guess what, you came up smelling like roses."

"I pissed on their car, and they came after us," Skippy told him.

"And we set it up, they went into the creek," Chuckie said. "We gave them a little nudge."

There were more than a few chuckles.

"Just curious," he replied, "how did you get them to drive into the creek?"

Georgie, remembering what the mysterious man told him on the Ardmore sidewalk, said, "That's for us to know and you to find out, mister."

The mysterious man laughed. "Well," he said, "I'll tell you one thing, you kids have balls. What do you call this neighborhood, the Hill?"

No one spoke, we were worried. We didn't know who this guy was and if he meant us harm. Most kids were looking at Billy to make a decision.

"Mister," Bill said, "the door's right there. Don't let it hit you in the ass on the way out." Under normal circumstances, Billy's comment would have drawn a room full of laughter. But not then, we were distracted.

The mysterious man ignored Billy's comment and said, "Now, you boys here never heard of the Genovese family of New Jersey, I know that. You probably never heard of the Angelo Morello family of Philadelphia, either, have you?"

No one answered.

He paused a minute and continued. "These two families have been at war with each other for quite some time. The people who got murdered that night on Mary Water's Ford Road – a murder which four of you witnessed — were the grandparents of Vito Graziano's godson, Salvatore," the mysterious man said.

He had a captive audience. He paused briefly, perhaps to allow his words to sink in, and continued.

"If Angelo Morello could, he'd put a bullet into Vito Graziano and end it. But Morello can't get to Mr. Graziano or any of his top people. So, he picked the Otts. Sometimes the La Cosa Nostra will target family members. So, the Otts got targeted."

"What do you mean, mister? What's Coss Nostra?" Georgie asked.

"It's La Cosa Nostra, son," he said. "It's the mafia — a family of crime. Also called organized crime. They eliminate their enemies by killing them."

"Are you part of the Cosa Nostra, mister?" Gary asked.

"Yes, I am Vito Graziano's consigliere. That means I am his attorney and advisor, and he has sent me here to follow your efforts."

"Follow our efforts?" Johnny asked, "why?"

"Look," he affirmed, "you four are witnesses to a mafia murder. That puts you in grave danger. Angelo Morello sent those two men who chased you to the creek to kill you. But they failed. Not only did they fail, one drowned and the other had to be put away."

"He drowned?" Skippy said. "It was only a creek."

79

"When you forced the car into the creek, Lou, the driver, who was old, got swept away and drowned. That means your troubles doubled: witnesses to a mafia killing and killing a top official in the Morello gang, Cock-Eyed Lou."

"We didn't mean to kill them," Frankie said, "It was an accident."

The mysterious man chuckled. "Mr. Morello won't think of it as an accident. You boys did something to make that Caddy go into the creek, and you ruined the lives of two made men."

"Well, what's going to happen now?" Billy asked, nervously.

"The Morello mafia family has a killer named Porky Bananas," he explained. "He's most likely responsible for over 50 murders ordered up by Angelo Morello. Porky is smart and ruthless. My guess is Angelo Morello will send Porky to take care of you, and by the way, Porky will kill the six of you pretty easily. One at a time, slowly and deadly."

"Jesus H. Christ," Gary said.

"Will Mr. Graziano help us?" Pete asked.

"Mr. Graziano is a private man," he replied. "He would usually send a hitman to stop Porky Bananas, but he won't now since you boys are involved. That'll bring too much attention to the Graziano family. Besides, other families who don't want a war will be upset if Mr. Graziano got involved. Those families could side with the Morello gang in Philadelphia if he did."

"So, he won't help us at all?" Skippy asked.

"I wouldn't say that, Skippy. You have me to ask for advice and consultation at no charge. Mr. Graziano thinks that's a generous offer. Through me, you have the eyes and ears of Vito Graziano."

"Sort of like a coach," Gary said. The mysterious man smiled and nodded.

"What about if we go to the police," Johnny asked, "would they protect us?"

"It doesn't matter if you go to the police. That won't take away Mr. Morello's curse on you. Sooner or later he'll get to you.

"You said you would advise us," Billy said, "so what should we do?"

"Well, you're off to a good start. I'd do what you've been doing. Give Porky Bananas a run for his money. But it won't be easy. He's not as dumb as Cock-Eyed and Sausage."

"So, do we have to hide?" Georgie asked.

"I don't think so, not now. Who's the one with the paper route?"

"That's me," I answered.

"You've had contact with Cock-Eyed and Sausage. They would've reported that. I'd say you would be the first one Porky will come after. And he won't put you on the payroll; you can be sure of that. He'll torture you until you've ratted everybody out. That might take him ten minutes. Once he has names, he'll come after the rest of you one at a time."

"Jesus H. Christ," Gary said.

"The only way you could keep serving your papers is to dress up like a girl. Porky Bananas has a thing about not killing or hurting women. That would be a liability but not in the mafia. There aren't many women in La Cosa Nostra."

"What do you mean, mister," I asked, "dress up like a girl?"

The mysterious man smiled and said, "If you want to stay alive."

"Ronnie, you got to do that," Skippy said. "That's no problem. I've got two sisters so I can steal some of their clothes. What size bra do you take, Ronny?" With that, the room erupted into laughter.

"That's right," the mysterious man said, "you have to take this lightly. That's how you will stay alive. Laugh. Have a good time. I watched you when you had that old car stuck on the sidewalk. You were in a tight spot, but you didn't panic. You had a good time. That's what you've got to do now."

"What's your name, mister?" Johnny asked.

"You've been calling me mister, so let's leave it at that," he said.

"How often will we see you, mister?" Frankie asked.

"Whenever I think you need me," he said. "I'll be watching you. I'll be checking in. If I think you're making a mistake on something, I'll show up. Just like I did in Ardmore.

"By the way, do you know what they call Porky Bananas in the underworld?"

No one answered.

"The ball-ripper," he said. "Before he kills, he likes to cut off the victims' balls while they're still conscious. Then he stuffs them in the victim's pockets. When the police check the victim's pockets and find his balls, they'll know who the killer was. It's Porky's trademark."

"No, shit," I said, then I gulped.

"Ronny," Pete said, "you've got to wear that thing you wear to protect your balls when you're catching."

"Yeah," Skippy said, "you can wear it under your skirt," and again the room exploded into laughter.

"Fuck," I complained, "it might be funny to you guys, but it's my balls at stake. I don't want them stuffed in nobody's pockets."

The mysterious man, laughing too, said, "Well, good luck, boys. I'll see you around."

With that, he turned and left the garage.

CHAPTER 15

Skippy

Besides their collective creative geniuses, some of the kids on the Hill did quirky things. Skippy was one of the best. Anytime the Hill kids hung out with Skippy, they had to be ready for fun. He never looked for trouble, but if it found him, he met it head-on. He was a typical tough kid from the Hill and a card-carrying summa cum laude member in the bust your balls division.

He also was at the top of the class in quirkiness. For example, Skippy could open his mouth, put the tip of his tongue on the roof of his mouth, and spit saliva droplets from beneath his tongue. And he did it silently, free of any spitting sounds to give him away. You could be talking to him, and he'd open his mouth slightly, and suddenly you'd be hit with saliva droplets. As you wiped off your face, you'd complain, "Skippy, cut that shit out." He could do it to some kids and tell them it was raining, and they'd believe him. I don't know how he did it; he tried to teach me once, but I couldn't get it to work.

In addition to the spitting, there were his world-famous, cesspool-like-smelling-farts. The better ones he called "silent but deadly." Let me tell you, they were the worst smelling farts imaginable, and kids who got downwind of them weren't happy. He said a rat crawled up his ass and died, and that was a pretty fair description. He was with Gary, Pete, Mickey, and me one afternoon eating at the Roxborough Diner counter when he let loose a silent but deadly. It stunk so bad they kicked the five of us out and as we left the other patrons were pretty pissed off. One accused us of "releasing stink gas." It wasn't stink gas; it was Skippy. They called the cops, but by the time they arrived we were well on our way to that hilly neighborhood where we had diplomatic immunity

A rat had crawled up his ass and died.

So, it surprised no one that Skippy was the first kid on the Hill to introduce and perfect the bird whistle. It was a wafer-thin reed-like piece slightly larger than a quarter that he put beneath his tongue. Annie's store was the first on the Hill to sell them. When he blew across the reed, it sounded just like a bird chirp. He had different reeds for different birds. He became an expert at bird sounds. One day on the way home on the school bus, Skippy let loose with some bird chirps that quickly caught the bus driver's attention. Once Skippy discovered he was annoying someone, it drove him to par excellence.

"I said who's tweet tweetin' in the back of the bus?" Casey, the driver yelled, looking into the giant mirror above him. I turned and looked back at Skippy, who was sitting upright with that wry grin on his face — the smile he perfected growing up on the Hill. I knew then and there that Casey was in for a rough ride. The thing was Skippy could tweet all he wanted without moving his lips, so nobody could tell who was "tweet tweetin.'" But I knew because I was at Skippy's house the afternoon he purchased one at Annie's store and tried it at home. Through practice and perfection, several days later, he became a master tweeter.

"Now I'm going to ask one more time, who's tweet tweetin' in the back of the bus?" Skippy then let out with the most beautiful robin concertos one could hear on an April morning near the green fields of Galway City — while he casually gazed out the bus window. Speaking of Galway, the bus driver Casey was an Irish immigrant and had a heavy Irish brogue.

Casey volleyed back. He slowed the bus down and pulled it closer to the curb. With the bus barely moving he looked into the big mirror again and hollered, "Now I know some kid is chirping like a bird, or we have a bird on the bus (that's how good Skippy was), so I'm a gonna ask one more time, who's chirp chirping?" This time Skippy answered with a warbler's call. He knew the names of each particular chirp. But Casey went advantage up when he stopped the bus and threw everyone off, girls included. Thirty-some kids had to walk about a mile back to the Hill. Everybody was pissed at Skippy, who loved every minute of it and considered it double whipped cream on top of the banana split that everybody got thrown off the bus.

Skippy was a good friend to have so it surprised no one that he was the first to offer help to his pal, Ronny. But with Skippy, you never knew if it came from his heart, or if he was setting you up to bust your balls. It could've been both. He took me home and told his mom and dad that I had to serve my paper route dressed up as a girl. Skippy had great parents, and they helped me with only one simple question: "Why do you have to dress up like a girl to serve your newspapers, Ronny?"

Before I could open my mouth, Skippy told them I had lost a bet playing cards in the cinder garage and had to do this as a result. His parents bought it, although I think they had their suspicions. Nonetheless, they helped out. Since Skip's dad was a hairdresser, he had a couple of old wigs lying around. His mom got out a box of his sister's old clothes — probably what they were saving if they had another kid.

Skippy insisted we have a dress rehearsal, and it was my first clue that yes, he was busting them. But that was okay with me, with Skippy I was used to that. Skip's dad was on the floor laughing and his mom, who called Skippy, "Skipper," said, "Skipper, you made his breasts too big, take out some of the newspaper." Skippy was on the floor laughing, alongside his father.

Skippy's mom gave me a shopping bag for the dress-up clothes and some lipstick in case, she said, I wanted to "look sexy." I was all set. I couldn't get dressed up at home so Skippy's father said he would leave the garage door open a crack and I could get dressed there whenever I wanted. That worked because the branch — what we called the garage where we picked up our newspapers — was a wagon ride straight down Springfield Avenue from Skippy's house.

The first day I was nervous. I had plenty of kids staring at me, but I dressed up so well nobody knew who I was. Sure enough, on the second day, the fun and games ended. When I took a paper into the 201 Bar on Jefferson, the bartender asked me if I was Ronny's sister. Or his girlfriend.

I shook my head. Back then, it was rare to see a girl serving newspapers, so every bar patron had to check me out. A man at the bar got off his stool and approached me. He wasn't from the Hill, and he was plenty mean looking. *I bet he could crush a watermelon with one hand,* I thought. He was wearing a business suit and a funny hat. His black necktie wasn't tied like most people tie them. It was open, probably, because he had such a thick neck. His fat hands were big, too, but it was his eyes that were so noticeable: they never blinked like most people's eyes do, and they were bigger than normal eyes. You were drawn right to his big eyes.

"Where's the paperboy?" he snarled at me.

Getting dressed up at Skippy's, it never occurred to me that I might have to speak. I didn't want to blow the whole thing and get my balls cut off by opening my mouth. But a thought popped into my head. I remembered watching a movie at the Roxy Theater where the cavalry and Indians met inside a teepee for a powwow. The Indians didn't know how to speak American, so they used sign language. It was pretty simple: Me (I pointed at my chest), I bowed, (then pointed at the man) here, not him (I pointed outside). Anybody could do it. It was like the game people played where you had to act out a something and people had to guess what it was.

The man repeated his question. "Where's the paperboy?"

So, I did the same thing, using the Indian signs: *He – not – here - just - me.*

The man took a step closer and asked again. And again, I gave the He –not-here-just-me sign language. He tilted his head like he couldn't figure it out. I was beginning to think that this guy wasn't the brightest lightbulb in the closet.

"Ah, sir," the bartender said, "I think she can't speak and is telling you in sign language."

"Huh?" he gushed, as he looked at the bartender then back at me, his mouth partially open.

Slowly, a smile appeared on his face. He bent a little, and his smile disappeared. His eyes narrowed, and he tilted his head, sort of like what a dog does when it can't figure something out.

"Sorry," he said. "So sorry."

He told the bartender to get me a soda. He led me over to a table to sit down. He told the bartender he was getting his car so he could help me deliver my newspapers.

"Oh, that's so nice of you, sir," the bartender crowed. "I'll keep her here until you pull up outside."

The man left and a few minutes later returned. When I finished my soda, he motioned with his hand for me to follow him outside. He parked in front of the bar. He put my wagon in the trunk and the newspapers on the backseat. With his hands, he motioned that he would take the papers on his side of the street, and I would serve them on the other side.

We finished serving my papers in record time. After we finished, he wanted to take me home. I nodded, but no way was I going to show him where I lived, and besides, I was dressed up like a girl. So, I had him take me to Skippy's house, where he dropped me off, and I waited until his car drove away. I went into the garage and changed. I left the garage and started for home. On Ashland Avenue, a car pulled up alongside me. The driver reached across the seat and rolled down the window.

"Ronny," he whooped excitingly, "stop I want to talk to you."

It was the mysterious man, who said he'd show up when he was needed.

"I was following you today on your paper route, and I saw you come out of the bar. Do you know who that was who helped you serve your papers?"

87

I shook my head.

"Jesus Christ, Ronny," he said, "that was Porky Bananas, the mafia killer. And he helped you serve your papers? What the hell...," he said, shaking his head.

"Look, we need to talk about this," he stammered. "Get your friends together and meet me tonight at the old church on Jefferson Street, you know, where you kids hang out. I'll be there around 9 o'clock. Make sure you're there, Ronny."

As he drove away, I thought, *no shit, that was Porky Bananas? He wasn't a bad guy.*

CHAPTER 16

Walls Closing In

I heard the car doors, so I went to the front bedroom window. The detectives were back. *I got to get out of here*, I thought. I looked around the room for a place to hide. *Under the bed? No way.* I went into the hallway and saw the panel-door to the attic in the ceiling. I quickly climbed up on the hall banister and reached up for the attic panel and pushed it open. I nearly lost my balance but held onto the attic trim. It saved me from tumbling down the stairs. I pulled myself up and into the attic. It was dark and hot. I slid the panel back into the grooves. It was the perfect place to hide. I could hear them talking in the living room.

"Hi Dot," detective Lochran said. "Tom?" It was a Saturday afternoon, and my father was home. "How's the bus business, Tom?"

"It's still there," my father replied. "Damn PTC, without the union we'd be working for free."

"Is Ronny around?" detective Frost asked.

"I believe so," my mother replied. "Ronny," she called, from the bottom of the steps. "Ronny are you up there? Come down; the detectives want to speak to you.

I stayed remained in the attic; didn't move a muscle. Sweat rolled down my face.

"I don't understand," my mother said, "he was up there a minute ago. Let me look."

I listened as my mother climbed the stairs and went into my room. *I bet she looked under the bed*, I thought. "Ronny?" She went back downstairs. "That's strange," she said, "I could swear he was up there. Maybe he's outback." She went to the backdoor and opened it. "Ronn-ney. Ronn-ney," she called, then came back inside.

"I don't know, detectives, I could've sworn he was upstairs in his room. Guess he slipped out."

"That's okay, Mrs. Costello," detective Lochran said, "we just wanted to let you all know that we've found the boys who were in the trees the night of the Otts' murders."

"Those poor people," my mother said, "and there were boys picking cherries and saw the murders?"

"That's right," detective Frost said, "please tell your son we have them in custody. We'll be holding them as accessories to the crimes since they refused to come forward."

"How did you find them?" my father asked.

"We picked them up, and they confessed," Lochran replied. "they're in jail right now."

What bullshit, I thought.

"Oh, my," my mother said, "are they in trouble?"

"Yes, they are, ma'am," Lochran replied, "big trouble, for not coming forward. You see, it's every citizen's duty if they see a crime, to report what they see. In this case, they didn't, and so they'll be in jail for a while."

Yeah, tell me about it, I thought, still sweating it out in the attic. *We come forward and end up dead when Porky Bananas cuts our balls off.*

"They should have reported it," my father said. "They deserve to be locked up."

"Will you please tell Ronny that we have them?" Frost asked.

"Oh, certainly," my mother remarked. "He'll be relieved. He was worried that you might have thought that you were looking for him and his friends."

"Why is that, ma'am?" Lochran asked, "did he say something?"

"Oh no, but mothers can tell, that's all."

"Do you think Ronny was in the trees and saw something?" Lochran asked.

"No, I don't think so. Besides, you say you have the boys, right?"

"Yes, ma'am," Frost answered. "Please tell Ronny we'd still like to talk to him. We'll come back around this time tomorrow."

"You can be sure that he'll be here," my mother answered, "No problem."

"Good day, ma'am. Tom."

And they left.

I could hear my mother and father talking after the detectives left. I made sure I heard the car doors close and the car pull away. I slid the attic panel back and climbed down. My father was telling my mother never to volunteer information to detectives because they'll twist it all around. I went downstairs.

"Mom, were you calling me?" I asked.

"Ronny," my mother said, startled. "Yes, the detectives were here and wanted to speak to you. Where were you?"

"In the bathroom," I answered.

"No, you weren't, the door was open when I went up for you."

"Oh, I was probably on the way or something. I'm going out; I'll be back maybe for supper. See you."

"Ronny wait, why don't you want to talk to the detectives?"

When I got outside, I saw Billy waiting for me on the sidewalk.

"Ronny," Billy said, "I saw the detective cars, we need to talk. Take a walk with me."

I followed Bill across the street and into his father's garage.

"That guy who showed up at our last meeting," he said, "I don't think we can trust him."

"Why not?" I asked Bill.

"Somebody said something to my father about him, that he's connected to the Philadelphia mob."

"Philadelphia mob?" I said, "I thought…"

Billy cut me off. "Right, that's what he said. But someone told my father they recognized a Philadelphia hitman come out of the cinder garage. He said he'd been seen a few times on the Hill, before and after the Otts' murders."

"Maybe . . ."

Bill cut me off again. "Exactly," he said. "Maybe that's Porky Bananas."

"Holy shit," I stammered, "then who was the guy in the 201 Bar?"

"What guy?"

I told Billy what had happened in the bar and how this guy had helped me serve my papers. Then the mysterious man, the one who showed up at our meeting, stopped me and told me that it was Porky Bananas who helped me serve my papers."

"That's bullshit," Billy said. "The guy who helped you, have you seen him before?"

"No," I replied, "never. He was nice, but he looked mean. Then the mysterious man…"

"Ronny, you and your boys, need to hide out somewhere.," Billy said. "Is there somewhere you can go until things cool off? You got the detectives closing in on one side and the mafia on the other."

"There's the dump," I answered, "we can go there."

"The dump?" he asked, slightly surprised. "The township rubbish place on Woodbine?"

"Yeah, we go there to get stuff, and we meet and hang out there."

"I knew you and your friends were fucked up," Billy said, puzzled, shaking his head. "Jesus Christ, who hangs out at the dump? Isn't the cops' shooting range right next to the dump?"

"Yeah," I said, "but we don't have to worry about that. The cops never go through the dump; they figure who'd hang out there, with all the rats and shit. And besides, we get our lead there."

"What do you mean, what lead?"

"There're sand mounds behind the targets, so we dig out the bullets and melt them down to make sinkers for fishing. Skippy showed me how to do it."

"Whoa, wait. You steal the bullets at the cops shooting range and make sinkers? Shit, Ronny, you get caught doing that, and your ass is grass."

"We do it at night, so if we see headlights, we can easily run to the dump. But cops don't police the range; they figure who'd be crazy enough to steal shit where they shoot. Talk to you later, Bill."

"Jesus Christ," Billy snickered, laughing, and shaking his head.

"Bill," I said wearily, "I got to get moving. The detectives are checking shoes, and we've got to get Pete's. If they get his we're dead."

"Shoes?" Billy sputtered, again surprised. "What shoes? What are you talking about?"

"Don't you remember?" I inquired, "I did tell you. When we were picking cherries and saw the murders, we took off, and Pete left his shoe and sock there at the Otts' place. The detectives have his shoe, and they're trying to find the kid whose other shoes are similar. They've been to everybody's houses except Pete's. So, we're meeting there now to get his shoes and hide them somewhere."

Billy looked at me in disbelief. "Yea, I remember now," he said, shaking his head. "But why all of his shoes?"

"They all look the same" I jabbered. "Gary calls them dago shoes. If they see one shoe, then they'll know the shoe they have is Pete's. So, I got to get going."

"Ronny, what are you going to do with Pete's shoes?"

"I don't know," I answered, "maybe bury them at the dump."

Laughing, Billy said, "Well, shit, he's got to have shoes to wear."

"Yea," I said, "maybe he can wear the pair he has on, and we'll hide all the others."

"What about his socks?" Bill asked. "You gonna bury them at the dump, too?"

"Oh," I replied, "I didn't think about his socks. I don't know; we'll have to talk about that. But I got to go. I'll talk to you later."

"Ronny," Billy called out, "you sure the dump is the best place to hide, with the cops next door?"

I stopped and turned around. "Yea," I said, "we don't have to worry about that. The cops never go through the dump; they figure who'd be crazy enough to hang out there, with all the rats and shit. Talk to you later, Bill."

"Jesus Christ," Billy snickered, laughing, and shaking his head.

PART TWO

CHAPTER 17

Hiding Evidence

July 2, 1964
Belmont Hills

By the time I got to Pete's house, a detective's car parked out front. A block away, Mickey yelled from Myers' store. Gary and Pete were there, too.

"What are we doing here?" I asked, "we've got to get Pete's shoes before the cops do. Let's go."

"They're already there," Gary said. "You're too late. Where the hell have you been?"

"With Billy Curry," I replied. "I'll tell you later. Let's get Pete's shoes."

"The cops are there," Mickey said. "We're too late."

"My bedroom window is on the Highland side, across from the bar," Pete said. "Maybe we can get in there."

"That's it," I suggested, "let's try it."

"Wait a minute," Pete said, "if my father catches us, he'll kill me. We won't have to worry about that banana fuck, or whoever."

"Maybe your father's talking to the detectives," Gary said, "that may give us time."

"He'll be distracted," Mickey said.

"Come on, dipshits," Gary snapped, "it's worth a try."

We left the store and went down a side ally that led us to Jones Street and came up alongside Pete's house. We were in luck. The detectives were still in his living room as Gary said later, "Talkin' that dago shit." But we hit a problem nobody expected. The window was locked.

"Ah, hell," Gary said. "Let's break the window."

"No way," Pete said, "go break your own goddamn windows."

"They might hear that," Mickey said, "that's no good."

"Wait a minute," Pete said, "Isn't that Joey heading up the street to go home? If we can get him, he can go to my house and tell my brother to unlock the window."

"Great idea," Gary said. "I'll get him." Gary took off and flagged Joey down. Joey, of course, wanted to know why we wanted to go through Pete's window with two detectives in the living room. Gary didn't have the reputation as the Hill's biggest bullshit artist for nothing. Like Pete told him, "You're so full of shit, your eyes are brown." Gary concocted a bullshit story that Joey believed. In this case, the brown eyes paid off.

Gary returned, and we waited by the window. Pete's brother, five or six years younger than Pete, also liked to bust balls, especially Pete's. And this was his shining moment. He came to the window cocky and smart ass. He held all the cards, and he knew it.

"Paulie," Pete softly yelled, "open the goddamn window."

Paulie pretended he didn't see us; he moved his head left and right like we weren't there.

"Paulie," Pete yelled, "open the goddamn window, or I'll kick your ass."

Paulie looked down. "How much is it worth to you?" he shouted through the glass.

"Come on," Pete said, "I'll give you my unopened baseball cards. You can have the gum, too."

Paulie thought it over, then unlatched the window and lifted it.

"Petey," he said, "the detectives want to talk to you. Mom is upset, and dad wants to kill you. Why do you want the window open? Where are the unopened baseball cards? They better still have gum."

"Paulie," Pete yelled, "get my shoes and throw them out here. Get every goddamn shoe, don't miss one."

"That's additional," Paulie said. "The unopened cards opened the window, but for the shoes, that's more."

"How about a kick in the ass," Gary said sarcastically, "how about if I do that?" Paulie didn't hear him or at least acted like he didn't.

"All right," Pete answered, "I've got two dollars on my bureau under the baseball magazine. You can have it."

Paulie left the window and returned. "What do you want your shoes for?" he asks.

"Never mind," Pete demanded, "just start throwing them out."

Sure enough, Paulie threw out Pete's shoes. He threw them everywhere — over our heads, to the left, and the right. We ran after them. All we saw were shoes flying out at a time.

"Don't miss any," Pete yelled, "don't forget my baseball spikes."

Paulie appeared at the window and looked down. "That's it," he said.

"Did you look under the bed?" Pete asked him.

"Yes," Paulie answered, "I got them all."

"Now Paulie," Pete said, "I need you to get all my socks and throw them out."

"Oh shit," Paulie responded, "no way. What's it goin' to be next, your stinkin' underwear? I'm not touching your socks."

"Paulie," Pete hollered, "I told you I don't want you cursing, or I'll kick your ass."

"Go ahead," Paulie responded, "and I'll tell Dad about the shoes, and he'll kick your ass. And then you'll get arrested. All of you. What did you do this time, anyway?"

"Paulie," Pete spat, "this is important. You've got to get my socks. Just grab them all and throw them out here. There won't be anything else."

After a few seconds, socks came flying out the window.

"Jesus H. Christ," Gary muttered, "how many of these dago socks do you have?"

We gathered the shoes and socks up into a pile.

"What are we going to do with all this?" Gary asked.

"Ronny," Mickey asked, "don't you serve the paper to the 201 Bar? Go get us a box."

"Sure," I said. "I'll be right back."

I took off across the street to the bar. I overheard Pete tell Paulie to close the window and get out of his bedroom. Inside, the bartender told me my girlfriend was a real hit with one of the customers. "He even helped her serve your papers," he laughed, "do you believe that?"

He got me a box from the storeroom, and I bolted out the door. That's when I saw him. He was standing next to a telephone pole part way up Highland. He might have been watching Pete's house and saw the detectives. It was Porky Bananas, the same guy who helped me serve my papers. But he didn't recognize me. He, of course, didn't know that I'm the paperboy. I was just another kid.

"Hey," he shouts, "come here, kid. I need to talk to you."

Suddenly, the two detectives came out of Pete's house.

"Ronny," one yelled, "there you are, we want to speak with you. Come over here."

I took off across the street, carrying the box to the bushes where Pete, Mickey, and Gary were hiding. Bananas saw me go in the bushes, but I don't think the cops did.

"We're up shits creek," I said.

"How so?" Mickey asked.

"See that guy up Highland," I asked.

"No," Pete said, "don't see anybody."

"Well, he was just there. Porky Bananas. He was standing right next to that telephone pole. Now he's not there."

"You sure you weren't drinkin' the sauce in the bar? Gary asked.

"I'm not shittin' you," I said, "Bananas was right there. And the two detectives came out of Pete's house, saw me and yelled."

"Hey Ronny," detective Frost again yelled from Jefferson Street. He was on the corner next to Pete's house. "Where'd you go?"

"Shit," Gary says, "let's back down this bank and see where it goes. Maybe we can come out on Jones Street and run from there."

"What about my shoes and socks?" Pete asked.

"Got to leave them here, nobody will find them in these bushes," Gary said.

"…the fuck," Pete said. "What if it rains."

"Pete," Mickey said, "there's a slight overhang at the bottom of your house, here. We'll slide the box underneath. That'll protect them."

That's what we did. Quietly, we moved down an embankment and into another yard, one with a barking dog. When we got to Jones Street, Gary said, "Let's go down to Leedom, we can hide in Johnny's yard. If not, we can work our way toward the railroad tracks and out to the Flat Rock Dam.

"Through that tunnel?" Pete asked. "I'm not going through that tunnel."

"You will if Porky Bananas is about to cut our balls off," Mickey argued.

"Come on shitbag," Gary said, "grow some balls. I'll go through that tunnel blindfolded.

Pete just shook his head and murmured, "How'd I get into this shit?"

CHAPTER 18

Top of the Tunnel

We hid in Johnny's yard watching the street. We could also see some of Jones Street. The detectives were closing in. Running and hiding was one thing; lying to the police about a murder was another. We had to avoid the detectives at all costs. Plus, Billy told me not to run if the mafia approached me, and what did I do when I saw Porky Bananas? I ran for the bushes alongside of Pete's house. It wasn't long before the detectives' car came down Jones Street and turned onto Leedom. We watched the detectives make a U-turn and go back. Even so, they were driving slowly, looking for me.

"They're both from the Hill," Mickey said. "They'll figure out where we'll go from here. They're not stupid."

"They can send the cops to both ends of the tracks," Gary hissed. "At the dam and behind Baffa's. Then close in. We'd eventually have to come out either end."

"No, we don't," I responded, "there's another way."

"I'm not going through that goddamn tunnel; I know that," Pete said.

Pete was leery of the tunnel and rightly so. It was about the length of a football field, maybe longer. Inside it was dark, pitch-black dark in the middle. If a train came, which had happened to us several times, you could either run for it and beat it out; or, plaster yourself on the inside wall and let it pass. The word on the Hill, however, was tried to let it pass, it could suck you under the wheels. Then the rats would eat what's left of you. Next day, kids said, there'd be no trace of you; like you disappeared in thin air.

Nobody questioned how kids knew that. Nevertheless, it helped make the mystique of the tunnel scarier. Most kids do that the first time. I did, so I didn't blame him; it's creepy in there. In the middle, all you can see is a tiny light at each end. There are noises, too; made by rats and other animals like raccoons and possums. And the animals don't like kids disturbing their sanctuary. The rumor mill said there are animals in the tunnel that have never seen daylight. It all added to the fear. The trains that went through were freight trains. Hence, they were long and slow, so if you got stuck inside, you were there a long time.

"We don't have to go through," I explained, "one time Skippy and I went out to fish the dam. We were just inside the tunnel when a train came. So, we got out, hid in the tall grass near the entrance, and waited. After it passed, we went through.

"On our way home," I said, "we went over the tunnel instead of through it. It was a pain in the ass because there's no path, just straight up. But at least I found another way to get past the tunnel without going through it.

"On the top of the tunnel," I continued, "we went through the woods and came out behind Welsh Valley Junior High. From that point, there are multiple ways to get back to the Hill. How about if we try that, and see for ourselves?

"That's good to know," Mickey said. "You just made me think of something, Ronny. If we go that way, to the top of the tunnel and through the woods, we can go home on Woodbine through the dump. Remember that fort we built there last summer? I bet it's still there."

"Yeah, the Alamo, what about it?" Gary asked.

"It'd be a good hiding place," Mickey said. "Nobody's going there to look for us. And if I remember, nobody can tell it's a fort unless they are standing on top of it."

"Jesus Christ," Pete complained, "now we're going to hide in a dump? What the…"

"We got to hide somewhere," Mickey said. "Better to hide somewhere where nobody goes. The dump's perfect."

"Yea, perfect, my ass," Pete complained.

"I don't think the detectives will find Pete's shoes," I stated. "So, we can leave them there for a while."

"Better not rain, goddamnit," Pete added.

"If it rains it'll clean them shoes up," Gary said, "and those dago socks. Then again, maybe nothin' will clean them fuckers up."

"Bite my ass, Polack," Pete volleyed back. "Your feet stink, too."

"Okay, let's go," Mickey said, "we'll go down to the tracks and head toward the tunnel."

That's what we did. From Johnny's yard, we followed a path to the train tracks. We followed the tracks toward the tunnel, frequently looking back for that big train lamp — what kids called the one-eyed monster — which scared the shit out of plenty of kids. If we saw it, we'd cut and run to hide in the overgrown weeds on either side of the tracks. We couldn't get seen by the train engineer because he would contact the train police to report kids on the tracks. The train police would come either on foot or in one of those little cars that ride on the tracks. Then you'd get arrested for trespassing. They didn't want any kids on the tracks.

When we got to the tunnel entrance, we stopped and decided to climb over it, rather than through it. But it was no easy climb. We had to cut a path through stickers and dense brush. It was a steep uphill climb. Eventually, Pete muttered, "Who's goddamn idea was this?"

Finally, we got to the top. It was surreal. We could see for miles. Nearly exhausted and covered with sweat, burrs, and stickers, we sat and rested.

"Look at this," Gary said, "what a view."

"Nobody would find us here," I said.

"Ronny," Mickey asked, "there's a guy on the tracks, coming toward us. See him?"

"Yeah, I do, barely, but I can see him."

"Who is he?" Gary asked.

"I don't know," I answered. "Wait a minute; I think it's Porky Bananas."

"You're shitten' me," Gary spat. "Are you sure?"

I nodded. "Yea, pretty sure," I said. "Yeahh, he walks just like him. Yeah, that's him, I'm positive."

"Do you think he's following us," Pete asked.

"Jesus H. Christ," Gary said, "no he's on a hike for the Boy Scouts. What do you think he's doing, dipshit?"

Pete flipped Gary the bird and said nothing.

"Pete," I said, "yeah, he followed us, all right. But Billy Curry said he might not be the Bananas killer. Anyway, he must have seen us go down Leedom and into Johnny's yard. Then from there to the tracks"

"Damn," Gary barked, "he must have been right behind us."

"Doesn't matter," Mickey added, "he'll never get up here, and if he does, by some miracle, we'll be at the dump."

"Maybe we should wait and see. If he does come up here, we'll throw him off," Gary offered.

"Gary," I stammered, "he's a mean looking mother. We don't want to screw with him."

"How'd Poland get their asses kicked so quickly," Pete said, "I guess they didn't have the Thor," (what we called Gary).

"Fuckin-a," Gary said.

"Let's go," said Mickey, "let's not wait around and find out. Let's get to the dump."

We cut through some thick woods and underbrush and came out in the Penn Valley neighborhood behind Welsh Valley. It was

definitely easier going through the tunnel than over it. But we discovered the top of the tunnel. If we ever had to hide out somewhere,
it'd be there. It was perfect. Besides, we got Porky Bananas off our ass.
He'd never be able to climb up the side of the tunnel like we did.

Never.

CHAPTER 19

The Dump

The Hill kids recycled long before there was recycling.

In the early sixties, people who lived in Lower Merion Township, which included the Hill, had trash pickup once a week. Appliances, bikes, baby carriages, and rolling tables on wheels, were picked up separately. When the trucks got back to the township incinerator, which we called the dump, they separated the garbage and trash from the appliances. They dumped the rubbish into an open building. There, a giant claw — moving on a track attached to the ceiling —scooped up the garbage and dropped it into a blazing furnace. The burned debris was moved from the furnace to a landfill about 100 yards away. There it sat smoldering until it cooled off. Next to the smoldering rubbish, they piled the appliances.

Most people didn't give the trash and garbage processes a second thought. But we did. We saw people's junk as opportunities. Consider this: In Belmont Hills, there were numerous steep hills: Ashland, Highland, Price, Jefferson, Springfield, the end of School Street, Lyle, and the granddaddies of them all, Fairview and Rockland. Most kids on the Hill discovered the challenge of the hills early, like maybe 7 or 8, and started with a wagon or sled. But by age 12, that was child's play. We wanted other ways to zip down the hills — something that provided more thrills.

It started with the invention of the chuggie. Some brilliant kid from the Hill invented it, but nobody knew who. It was similar to a go-cart or soapbox derby car, and the dump played a big part in its assembly. It had one basic design. First, the chassis: a board or plank, about six-foot-long, ten inches wide, and two inches thick. A pair of axels fastened to a two-by-four at the front and back.

Kids either used their feet or hooked a rope or a chain to the front two-by-four to steer. Later, as we got smarter, we went to junkyards in Manayunk and got steering wheels and other parts.

We got wheels and axels for the chuggie from the pile of appliances, including baby carriages, and strollers. A significant find was a baby carriage in top shape with good wheels. We removed the axels with a hacksaw and hammer; pulled out the cotter pin and removed the wheels. Besides wheels and axels, kids used their imaginations and found other stuff at the dump, like a hood, fenders, or rear-end.

When winter arrived, and snow and ice covered the hills, kids wanted a faster ride than a sled, and again we found it at the dump. Refrigerator doors were the best. Refrigerator doors, stripped of the handle and logos and insulation, were difficult to steer but sped down the hills at top speed. Kids experimented with other kinds of appliance parts, too, like a stovetop or a hammered out and greased up trashcan lid.

Eventually, we built forts at the dump. We used parts from the appliance pile to structure the foundation, basement, and walls of a two- or three-room, candlelit fort. By the time we witnessed the Otts' killings on Mary Waters Ford Road, we knew the dump inside, out. The summer before we worked on the mother of all forts; one you couldn't spot from a distance, since it was underground. At the Woodworth's in Roxborough, we found a toy periscope. So, we got it — not saying how — and brought it home. We took it apart and figured how to make it longer and better. We had several in the fort, which allowed us to watch the dump from inside.

We named our dump fort the Alamo; influenced by Disney's Davy Crockett series. But our Alamo was invisible. This was the "cold war era," so we built the Alamo as a bomb shelter, in case the Russians attacked. Centrally located between Croyle's woods, Centennial Road, the Flat Rock Tunnel, the Schuylkill River, the train tracks, and the Hill, the dump was perfect for us. We had numerous escape routes and could vacate the Alamo and dump when under attack.

We had good reason to move to the Alamo. The two detectives were hot on our trail. Plus, we weren't sure if Pete's brother Bobby managed to get every sock and shoe out of the window. If he missed one, then the cops could've had a match that led directly to us. We'd be picked up at our homes and made to confess. Sure, we'd be famous, and our photos would be on the front page of the newspapers. Shortly after that, Porky Bananas would cut off our balls and stuff them in our pockets.

And the dump was the perfect headquarters. Sure, it had a few rats, but Skippy and I wiped out most of them the year before with a BB gun and a .22. It was impossible to eliminate all of them; they multiplied as fast as rabbits. We had to lay low, which also meant I couldn't serve my papers. I got a kid to take over my paper route and told him to make sure nobody cut his balls off.

"I'll serve them for you, Ronny," Chuckie said, "ain't nobody gonna cut my balls off. They can't run that fast."

By the time we got to the Alamo from the top of the tunnel, we were tired, thirsty, and hungry. It was early afternoon, so, Mickey snuck out the dump road to Woodbine, and the store on Jefferson Street, without being seen. He returned with sodas, Tastykakes and a pack of Newport. We tidied up the Alamo and found some candles to lite. We figured, at least we planned to, when it got dark enough, sneak home to get more supplies and sleeping bags. What we didn't anticipate was having an unexpected and unwelcome visitor so soon.

CHAPTER 20

Three Days

Detectives Frost and Lochran entered the Lower Merion police headquarters on a warm July afternoon. The desk sergeant, Zip Roberts, immediately notified them that the Captain wanted to see them.

"Yeah?" Lochran asked, "what about?"

"Beats me," Roberts said, "I think it's above my pay level. I'm not in the stratosphere like you two."

"But you don't have to ride around looking for killers," Frost to him.

"Hmm, that's true," Roberts replied, "but you don't have to put up with all the inside bullshit, either."

"You're a damn good Sergeant," Frost spat.

"Yeah, fuck you too," Roberts replied.

The detectives laughed and approached the Captain's office. Captain Tolan spotted them and waved them in; he was on the phone. When he hung up, he sat down in his desk chair and said, "Gentlemen, how's the Otts' investigation going?"

"All right," Lochran said," as the detectives exchanged glances.

"What have you got so far?" Tolan asked, "You get the witnesses, yet?

Lochran still looking at Frost replied, "Not yet, we're working on it."

"Loch," the Captain countered, "look at me when you talk, not him. Shit, he's not your Captain, I am."

Lochran nodded and said to the captain, "No witnesses yet, but we're on it."

"What the hell," the Captain demanded, as he sat back in this chair and locked his hands behind his head, "we're talkin' about kids in some goddamn trees. Huh?"

"That's right," Frost responded, "and because they're kids, we don't want to make a mistake."

The Captain folded his arms and looked around the room. "Well, let me tell you a few things. First, we're getting all kinds of shit about this, that it's taking too long. You get eyewitnesses to a murder handed to you, and it's dragging, going nowhere.

"Secondly, the bosses upstairs tell me maybe I should remove you from the case because it's on the Hill; therefore, you two are soft on it. They want to know why you haven't brought in kids to put pressure on them. It's a damn good question. So why haven't I seen any kids in here?"

"Sure," Frost shot back," you want kids in here we can bring in a ton of em.' Hell, we can have 50 here tomorrow afternoon. We're not dragging our feet. That's an insult. When we bring kids in, they'll be the kids who witnessed the murders."

"What about the mob?" the Captain asked. "Mob guys have been spotted around Belmont Hills. If they get to those kids before you do, we might not have witnesses. We'll have two dead elderly citizens who never gave anyone shit and four dead kids. Then we're fucked."

"Come on, Captain," Lochran volleyed back, "half the Hill is Italian. Mob guys are always around there. We can start pickin' them up too, then the real killers will go underground, and we're screwed."

"We think we know who the kids are," Frost said.

"What," the Captain spat, "that shoe and sock bullshit?"

"It's not bullshit," Lochran shot back. "My neighbor's father came from Italy, and his shoes were similar to the one we found at the murder scene.

"So, what did you come up with?" the Captain asked, "at the kid's house?"

"The parents are Italian," Tolan said. "They don't speak much English, and the father doesn't take any shit. He wouldn't let us into the kid's room."

"He wouldn't let you?" the Captain said, as he threw up his hands. "What the Christ are we running here, a charity?"

"Look," Lochran countered, "they're witnesses, not the murderers. And they're kids. What did you want us to do, arrest the father? Bring him in here? Then the Hill people are against us and wouldn't give us shit."

"All right, all right," the Captain shot back. "You've got three days. If I don't see the kids in here, you're off the case. Both of you can go back to the Hill and investigate broken streetlights. Maybe you can catch those kids. So, what's the kid's name with the shoe?"

"Pete," Frost replied.

"All right, if I don't see Pete and his Italian shoes in here in three days, guess what, you're off the case.

"You guys got to bust their balls a little," the Captain lectured. "Grab their asses and get em' in here. They're witnesses to capital murder, for Christ's sake. Either that, they're not witnesses, and you two are chasing some shoe that will make us the laughing stock of the state."

Frost went to comment, but the Captain stopped him. "No, no discussion here. What's today? Tuesday. You've till Friday, and I want to see Pete and his asshole friends from the Hill in that integration room. Got it?"

Both Lochran and Frost nodded.

"All right, get out of here and do your job."

The two detectives got ripped new asses, as they like to say. It wasn't nice. It wasn't meant to be. Everyone in the police headquarters knew it, too, because when the detectives walked back through the main room, it suddenly grew quiet. Even the typewriters stopped.

"Shit," Frost said, "everybody is staring at us."

"Fuck em," Lochran said, "let em' stare."

When the officers got to the parking lot, they stopped to talk and enjoy the afternoon sunshine that warmed their faces. Frost spoke first. "What do you think, Loch?"

Detective Lochran scratched his head. "Well, we've got to bring Pete in by Friday, or we're up shit's creek without a paddle, partner."

Frost nodded. Then said, "Let's go get him."

Fourteen miles from the Lower Merion police station on Lancaster Avenue, in Ardmore, sat another headquarters. In a storefront at McClellan and Moore Streets, in the heart of South Philadelphia, twelve men were seated around a table. At the head of the table was Angelo Morello, the boss of bosses, the Gentle Don. Usually, Mr. Morello was calm; he's not the excitable type; he's the Gentle Don. But the boss of bosses was outraged. He gripped the edges of the table, and the men saw his knuckles turn white — they exchanged silent glances. The boss just got the news that Cock-Eyed Lou had drowned while he and Johnny Sausage chased the old Dodge. Inside the Dodge were the four snotnose kid witnesses.

Under doctor's orders, Mr. Morello breathed slowly and deliberately through his nostrils as he was told to do. But he was struggling. "Cock-Eyed Lou had been a capo for what, twelve years, Nicodemo?"Mr. Morello asked. Nicodemo 'Nick the Builder' Amuso nodded and grunted. Mr. Morello smiled.

"And Sausage, remember at the Italian festival after the Columbus Day parade. With the mention of Columbus, more than a few of the men blessed themselves in the Italian-Catholic tradition. "Johnny Sausage ate so much sausage," the boss went on, "he puked his guts in the pew at St. Monica's during the Columbus vigil. All over the mayor's shoes. And somebody said, 'Johnny, madonn, don't you chew the fuckin' sausage?' Cause there was whole sausages sittin' on the mayor's shoes."

The men around the table nodded and laughed, still exchanging nervous glances.

"So, what happened to Johnny Sausage?" Mr. Morello asked.

Thomas 'Tommy Sneakers' spoke up. "He had a nervous break-down, Angelo."

Mr. Morello, still clutching the edges of the table while his knuck-les got whiter, nodded.

He said, staring at the table, "We send two good men to that little shithole town, what do they call it, the Hill? Fuckin' little shithole town. Two made men chasing kids in some old beat-up car and one is dead; the other is at the nut farm. I would like someone to explain to me how that happened."

"Boss," 'Jimmy the Lapper' quipped, and he too was staring at the table. "We fucked up Angelo."

Mr. Morello nodded. "We fucked up," he fumed. "Bunch of snot-nose kids and we fucked up. Joey, what day is today?"

Young 'Little Joey' Martino, not at the table but an onlooker in a chair against the wall, quickly responded, "Tuesday, sir," he said.

Mr. Morello took his right hand off the table and, with his palm up, asked for Ralph Polizzi's piece. Polizzi took the .38 from his vest holster and placed it in his hand. The Gentle Don grasped the gun and emptied the bullets onto the table. He picked up one bullet, placed it into the cylinder, snapped it shut, spun the cylinder and put the gun on the table.

"Joey says it's a Tuesday," Mr. Morello snapped, as he looked over at Little Joey. "By a Friday, if we don't have-a four snot-nosed kids either floating in the Delaware or buried in the swamp grass behind-a the airport, then-a we're coming back to this table. I'm passing this-a gun around, and every one of you losers will spin the cylinder, put the gun to your head, and pull the trigger.

"We'll go around the table, and each of you will get a turn until one of you is lying dead on the floor. Gentlemen do I-a make myself clear."

The eleven men responded, nodding, "Yes, sir, very clear."

After the meeting, Nick the Builder took Anthony 'Tony Potatoes' Ianniello by the arm and said, "Tony, leave Bananas on the job, but we got to add some of our best people. Add Crazy Phil 'Bomb Bomb' Ruggiero and Harry 'The Hunchback' Battaglia. Tell them we're lifting the pay to 25 grand each. Also, tell them if those kids aren't dead by Friday, they can find a job at Sears Roebuck, capeesh?"

"You want Crazy Phil back on the streets so soon, after whackin' them old people?" the Builder asked.

"The boss is upset," Potatoes said, as he patted Nick on the back, "he wants to go all out. Them rules is out the window. Oh, and one more thing, keep Salvatore the Golfer Napoli ready and Tommy Sneakers, too. Sort of like in the bullpen."

Nodding, the Builder said, "I get it, boss, I'll get right on it."

CHAPTER 21

Buck Ass Naked

It was a few hours before dark, so we waited in the Alamo. When it got dark, we'd break up, and each go home our separate ways. One of us would draw less attention, we figured, than four of us together. We also agreed to go through yards and back streets and stay away from the main roads on the Hill. It was a warm Tuesday afternoon in July, with some ugly rain clouds in the distance.

"Whoa, wait a minute," Mickey said. "There, he is again. He's coming up the dump road. See him? Isn't he the one that was following us on the tracks?" We moved to a barrier in the fort where we could look out over the burnt rubbish and appliances and down the dump road.

"Oh, shit," I said, "yea that's him. That's Porky Bananas."

"I thought you said the mysterious man was Porky?" Pete asked.

"That's what Billy told me," I responded.

"Jesus H. Christ," Gary said, "how the hell did he get here? Did he follow us?"

"He must have," Mickey said. "Look closely at him. What's he holding?"

We stared, not sure what to do. "I think it's a bottle," I said.

"I think he's drunk," Gary observed. "Yeah, that's what it is, I think he's drunk."

"Sure, looks that way," Pete said.

"He's not just drunk," chided Mickey, "that mother is stone drunk."

"I'll be goddamned," Gary said. "He can just about stand up."

We watched him drain the bottle and throw it into a pile of trash.

"Whoa," Mickey said, "he almost fell."

Suddenly, Porky took two short steps forward and fell flat on his face. He was out. He lay there, motionless.

What do you think we should do?" Pete asked.

"Let's go find out who he is," Gary said.

"You're shitten me," Pete growled, "he'll shoot us. Maybe it's a trick."

"Give me that hammer over there, Ronny," Gary said. "If you pussies want to stay here, fine. But I'm going to look him over, and if he gives me any shit, I'll nail him with the hammer."

Among the four of us, Gary was by far the toughest. The thing was, I never saw him in a fight like I've seen other Hill kids, and I saw lots of fights. Gary was a quiet tough, and nobody challenged him. He crawled out the front opening of the fort, got in a crouch and carefully slow-walked toward Porky, holding the hammer menacingly in his right hand. We followed him. I picked up a pipe near the appliances for insurance. When we got down to Porky, we dropped down on our knees around him.

"Pecker, what do you think," Mickey asked.

"He either passed out from the whiskey, or he's dead," Gary replied. "Either way, he won't bother us."

"I hope not," Pete said.

"Let's try to roll him over on his back," Gary instructed.

He was a big man. It took all of us to turn him over, and we didn't get it on the first try. We had to rock him. Gary spotted the gun in his chest holster. He reached in carefully and lifted it out: then stuck it in his pants.

As Porky laid unconscious, we started in on a serious conversation.

"Look," Mickey observed, "he's got white shit coming out of his mouth."

"His breath stinks, too," Pete noted.

"What about a wallet," I asked.

"Damn," Gary said. "We should have thought of that when he was on his stomach. Want to turn him over again?

"I got a better idea," Mickey said, "let's pull his pants down."

"Well?" Pete said, looking at his feet, "we better take off his shoes first."

I got one, and Pete the other. We struggled with the laces but untied them and pulled his shoes off. "His feet smell like my ass," Gary said. "All right, I'll undo his belt."

After Gary unbuckled his belt, he pulled the zipper down, and he and Mickey slowly shimmied his pants down. Once they got them past the knees, it was easy. "Here's his wallet," Pete said.

"Keep it," Gary insisted, "we'll look at it later. What about his shorts?"

"His underpants?" Pete asked. "Have lost your mind?"

"We got his pants, his wallet and his gun," Gary muttered, almost to himself. "If we get his shorts, where's he gonna go? He's ours then. We can go back to the Alamo and watch him. See what he does."

"We've got to roll him on his back again," I said.

Again, we rocked and turned him over.

"All right, you take em' off," Mickey said.

"Me take them off?" Gary shot back. "Why me?"

"It was your idea," Pete said.

Gary looked down at Porky's shorts. We all did, but no one was first to make a move. No one said a word.

"All right, you assholes," Mickey said, "here goes."

Mickey grabbed Porky's shorts by the waistband and pulled them down to his knees and then slipped them off his feet.

"Here," Mickey said, "put them with his pants."

"Nobody look at his pecker," I said, "but if you do, he's got Thor beat by ten miles."

"Told you Italians don't need to eat cherries," Pete said.

"Shit," Gary said, "he ain't got me beat."

"Fine, then," Pete shot back, "pull down your zipper, and let's compare."

"We ain't got time for that shit," Gary rebuked, "are you nuts?" Pete laughed.

"Want to take everything back to the Alamo and watch him wake up?" I asked.

"Wait," Mickey said. "We're taking his shoes, socks, pants, and underpants. If he wakes up, he can wrap his shirt and jacket around to hide his pecker. So, we need to take everything."

"What if he goes straight up that bank and finds us," Pete asked.

"That's doubtful," Mickey said, "but if he does, we got his gun so what's he gonna do?"

"All right," Gary said, "let's take the rest of his shit off."

That part was easy. I wrapped everything in his suit jacket and curled it up into a ball, then tied the sleeves around it.

"Wait," Pete instructed, "I got an idea. Where do you think the nearest payphone is?"

We studied Pete. Slowly but surely it sunk in.

"You aren't as dumb as you look, you son of a bitch," Gary howled, a smile on his face.

"You think we should call the cops?" Mickey asked.

"Yeah," Pete answered, "they get him, and that's another one down."

"Anybody know what time it is?" I asked.

"How's that have anything to do with his?" Mickey asked.

"The guy working the trash claw in the incinerator," I answered, "maybe he'll call the cops."

"Who?" Gary asked. "George?"

"You know him?" Mickey mumbled.

"Shit yeah," Gary said, "that's George Ferraco. He lives on the Hill. He's a good man, said he would give me a reference if I applied for a township job. You assholes don't know half the guys I know."

"That's because you blew half of them," Pete taunted.

"No," Gary responded, "you're mistaking me for your mother."

"Well, he must be a loony if he'll give you a goddamn recommendation," Pete guffawed, then pushed up his glasses.

"Alright, enough of that shit," Mickey said, "we don't have time for it. He wakes up, and we're screwed. Gary, can we go up there and you ask George if he'll call the cops?"

"Sure," Gary answered, "and he won't rat us out to the cops, either."

Suddenly, Porky grunted and then farted. White shit was pouring out the corners of his mouth again.

"Jesus H. Christ," Gary said, "his breath stinks."

"His breath?" Pete said, "did you smell the fart?"

"Yea," Mickey replied. "He's got Skippy beat."

"Who the fuck are you?" Porky asked, blinking his eyes. "What the fuck's gonin' on here?"

"Let's go," Gary said, "Ronny's got his shoes. Pete, the wallet? And I got his gun."

"Where we goin'," Mickey asked.

"Up to the incinerator," Gary declared, "follow me." He got up and ran up the dump road toward the incinerator. We followed him.

"Hey, you mother fuckers," the man yelled, "where you goin' with my pants. Come back here, you little pricks. I'll kill every one of you."

"Tell it to the cops," Mickey yelled over his shoulder.

We high tailed it up the dump road. We could hear Porky yelling, calling us every Italian and American name he knew. He was sitting up on the dump naked as the day he was born.

"What happens if this guy isn't there?" I yelled.

"Don't even think it," Mickey bellowed.

When we got to the side of the incinerator, the man who worked the trash claw, the one Gary said was George, was closing the place up.

As we approached him, Gary howled," George, can we talk to you?"

The man turned to face us. "Sure," he said, "come on in fellows. How you doin' Gary?"

CHAPTER 22

Time to Run

"George," Gary said, slightly out of breath, "we're in trouble and need your help."

"What's the problem fellows?" George asked, "how can I help? Here, let me get this door down, and we can sit inside and talk."

George dropped the door down — sort of like a giant garage door —that was attached to the building's ceiling. It sealed off the building so no one could enter or see us from the outside. "Here, take a seat on these chairs here," he told us, "I've been collecting them from the throw-aways. What seems to be the problem?"

We started right in. We told George about seeing the Otts' murders from the cherry trees. We told him about the cops and how we'd get our balls cut off if the cops caught us and made us testify. We told him about the mob chasing us in Georgie's car. We explained about Porky Bananas and that he was down on the dump road naked as a jaybird.

"These are his clothes," I said, "he's completely naked."

"And look," Gary said, "I got his gun. That proves he's a killer."

"Holy cow," George said, "so you were the boys in the trees. That's some shit, fellows. You're certainly in a pickle."

"Can you help us out, George?" Gary asked.

"Hell yea, Pecker," George said, "you boys came to the right man. You can count on me. Hell Gary, you know what they say, once from the Hill always from the Hill."

"Great, George, thanks," Gary said.

"Listen," George said, "if you boys want to hide out here, I can put you in a storage room downstairs, or better yet, I can take you one at a time to my home, and you can stay in the basement until this thing blows over."

"No, George," Gary said. Gary was the first to pipe up, but we all were thinking the same thing. "We don't want to get you in trouble. If you hide us here, you could lose your job, and if you take us home, you and your family would be in danger from the mob."

"Well," he said, "I don't mind, and like you fellows, I'm not afraid of the mob or the cops," he laughed. "I guess that's how you get growing up on the Hill, right fellows?"

Relaxing a little now after stripping Porky, we smiled and nodded. We felt better. But we were starving and hadn't decided our next steps.

"So then, what do you fellows have in mind?" George asked.

"Well, first, can you call the police and report a naked man on the dump road. And ask them to pick him up?"

"You got it," George said. "But you fellows need a lead before I do, so they don't pick you up, too."

"I think we need to head out of here, but we can't go home. If we go home, we're screwed." Gary said.

"Let's go to the top of the tunnel," I sputtered.

"You mean the Flat Rock Tunnel?" George asked.

Gary nodded.

"You mean we're not going home?" Pete asked, "what's up with that shit?"

"Pete," Gary said, "after the cops pick up that Porky prick, they might put two and two together because that asshole might tell them he got stripped by kids. Besides, we don't know if they got any of your shoes or socks. So, I'm sayin', if we try to go home, the cops will get us. They're probably watching for us now."

"Ronny," Mickey inquired, "why the top of the tunnel?"

"It's perfect," I said, "a great view of everything. We can see down the tracks on either side and the river. We can see for miles on the expressway. Anybody that comes after us we'll see and be long gone. It's a great place to hide out."

"I agree," Gary said. "We can't go home. Petey, open his wallet, let's see who he is."

Pete took it out of his back pocket and opened it. "Holy shit," Pete said, "look at the money." We counted $300. Pete then pulled out his license. "George L. Romano," Pete said. "He lives on Tasker Street, where's that?"

"Don't know," Mickey said. "Ronny, you ever hear of it?" I shook my head and said, "Beats me. But we've got about two hours before it's dark, so we've got to decide quickly on where to go."

"Wait, there's another card here under his license, it says AA member, wonder what that is?" Pete asked.

"Oh?" George chipped in, "if you're a member of AA, you have a drinking problem. I suppose that's why the fellow passed out."

"Makes sense," Pete said. "And here's another card, it says something about contact in case of an emergency. Says the contact person is Angelo Morello of South Philadelphia."

"Let me see that, Pete," George said. He took the card and studied it.

"Oh yeah, this guy is a card-carrying member of the Philly mob," George commented. "He's an important one, all right. Fellows let me have his clothes and wallet. Pete, you take the money out, you fellows might need it for supplies. I'll tell the police I found it on the side of the dump road. They'll figure he was so drunk he stripped himself."

"Thanks, George," I said.

"And Gary," he continued, "you better give me that gun. You fellows don't want to get picked up carrying a gun."

"Sure, George," Gary said, "here."

"Now look," George said, "you fellows need to get going. And you'll need some provisions right away. Here's what I'll do. I'll let you out the main door there, and you head out toward Woodbine Avenue. Stay away from the dump road. Then go down Mary Waters Ford Road toward Centennial.

"But watch for cops coming to the shooting range; if you see them, ditch to the side and hide. Once you get to Centennial, hide in the woods there, near Mary Waters Ford. I'll give you a ten-minute lead and call the cops. I'll say that I was leaving and saw this guy half-naked on the road.

"When I get home, I'll throw some blankets and sleeping bags in the trunk; then I'll go over to Carl the Butchers on Ashland and get you boys something to eat."

"Thank you, George, that's great," Mickey said. "Petey, give George half the money for the supplies."

"Thank you, fellows," and he laughed, "funny using the mafia money for food. But that's fine with me if you want to. Now," he continued, "once I have everything, I'll come down to Centennial Road to about where you will be hiding and beep three times, short beeps, 'beep, beep, beep,' like that.

"You boys come out, and I'll open the trunk and give you what you need, and then you can make your way to the tunnel. Only thing I ask if you do get caught you don't mention my name."

"George," Gary said, "they can cut my balls off, and I won't tell them you helped us. Never do that."

"If they can find them," Pete guffawed.

We laughed. It felt good to laugh.

"Now," George said, "one more thing. I don't want to know where you boys are hiding, because if I'm picked up, I don't want to lie and get in trouble. If I don't know, we're all better off. We need a way to communicate so we can talk to each other. Every night, on the way to my home on Jones Street, I'll swing down Mary Waters and turn onto Centennial Road. If you need to talk to me, be out on Centennial Road, and I'll pull over.

"Or, you can come up from the tracks to my home on Jones Street and pound on the back door. Just make sure it's dark, so nobody sees you. Okay?"

"George," Pete said, "how can we thank you?"

"You want to thank me, Petey?" George said, "you boys stay alive."

Nodding, we exchanged nervous glances.

CHAPTER 23

Thank God for George

We did what George Ferraco suggested. It was sound advice. Still not quite dark, we left the dump on Woodbine and went down Mary Waters Ford. We were prepared to dash into yards and hide if a car approached. We were nervous as a cat in the bathroom. It was scary. Luckily, we saw neither car nor person on the roads. We turned on Centennial Road and immediately went into the woods far enough not to be seen but able to see the road. There we waited.

"Those mob guys are going to be pissed," Pete said. "They'll come at us with everything they have."

"We took care of three of them," Gary replied. "How many more do they have?"

"Enough," Pete said. "Trust me enough."

Pete knew more about the mafia than any of us, his family coming from Italy. Even in the town he came from, he said, there was a mob presence. "They'll keep coming at us until we're all dead," Pete warned, "I can't see any way out of this shit. Even if the cops arrest them all, they'll eventually get out. Look at Porky; we know he wasn't the killer, so he'll be out of jail by the end of the week."

"They have expensive lawyers," Pete continued, "that will cover their asses. What we did to him he'll never forget until he's dead."

"Or we're dead," Mickey remarked.

Pete's words put us into a sorrowful mood. We sat silently in the woods, listening to the sounds of the night animals coming out and rustling the leaves leftover from the fall. There was a partial moon that broke through passing clouds and stars twinkled in the night sky. Headlights caught our attention, and we followed them as they turned onto Centennial Road and stopped. We listened for the three short beeps.

Without speaking, we got up and went down a bank through trees toward the headlights. As we came onto the road, George got out and opened the trunk.

"When I turned off Jefferson to go down to Jones Street, a detective's car and two patrol cars were sitting on Jefferson in front of Petey's house," George told us. "So, I went back out to Jefferson, and a police car was out front of Gary's." I wasn't sure where Ronny and Mickey lived, but I bet police cars watching there, too."

"Oh, shit," Pete fumed, "were they in my house or just outside?"

"Couldn't tell, Pete," George said, "I didn't want to appear too noisy and draw attention. After all, they know I work at the dump, and they know I reported that fellow on the dump road. But I made sure I wasn't followed to the store or to here. I also borrowed these sleeping bags because I only had one. And I got a couple of extra blankets, although I don't think you'll need them tonight. It's pretty warm."

"Thanks, George," Mickey said. "We appreciate it." The rest of us also chipped in with thank yous.

"I also borrowed this knapsack, and I put the food in from Carl the Butcher's. There's lunchmeat, rolls, cheeses, some pepperoni, a whole bunch of Slim Jims, some Tastykakes, some candy and what not and four bottles of Coke. You boys won't go hungry tonight or for a few days. There's a bottle opener in with the food."

We thanked him again.

"You boys look kind of down," George quipped, "not like you were earlier at the trash furnace. Keep your heads up; this isn't over yet."

We thanked him again. "Now you boys will need to be resupplied in a few days or so. If I keep going to stores and driving down here, somebody will get suspicious. Tomorrow the Mrs. and me will go shopping where we always do, and I'll buy a lot of groceries. Store em' at my place.

"Then one or two of you come down the tracks and sneak through the yards on Leedom and Jones and come into my backyard. I'll leave a cooler on my back porch and fill it with groceries. When you need more come late at night, empty the stuff from the cooler into the knapsack, and I think you'll be fine."

"Great, George," I said, "thank you. If you hear of anything that might help us will you put a note in the cooler? We'd be interested to know what happens to Bananas."

"Of course, Ronny, good idea. We can communicate that way, that's good. I'll put in a newspaper if I think it has something for you."

"George," Pete asked, "you know my father. You mind stopping in to talk to him and my mother? Maybe he knows something, too."

"Of course, Pete," George replied, "I will. I don't think the cops will bother me if I stop in to visit your folks. I'll let them know you're all right."

"Maybe you shouldn't tell them where we are, though," Pete suggested, "you know my father. He might come looking for us."

"I'll handle it, Pete," George responded. "Now look, you boys know where you're going? Know how to get there?"

"We do George," Gary said. "We'll talk it over. From here we'll probably cut through the woods. We've done this before but never at night."

"Yeah," Mickey added, "there's some moonlight. I think we'll be fine."

"Okay, fellows," George added, "be careful. I put a small flashlight in the knapsack. I don't know if you want to use it, but at least you have it."

We shook hands and headed toward Mary Waters Ford. We had a tough hike ahead of us — difficult in the day, but much harder at night. We stayed along the edge of the woods until we got to the top of Mary Waters Ford, then we cut into the woods toward the tunnel. We hardly spoke and mostly pointed in the direction we wanted to go. We tried to be quiet, but that was nearly impossible at night in the thick woods, with four of us.

Several times deer bolted out either directly in front of us or off to the side; scared the shit out of us. We heard other animal noises as we trudged along. We eventually came to a clearing, and that opened things up direction wise. We sensed we were near the top of the tunnel. We came across a small field that appeared dry with tall grass, and we decided to bed down there, waiting to get to the top of the tunnel in daylight.

We rolled out our sleeping bags on the thick grass and crawled into them without speaking. Exhausted, we were asleep within minutes.

CHAPTER 24

More Powerful than God

Equipped with a steel armor-plated roof, doors, and sidewalls, the white stretch limousine turned off Strada Provincial 234 and headed for southern Italy. It meandered along Contrada Gidora and carefully and slowly maneuvered around the sharp curves of the hill country of the Italian Province of Calabria. Twenty miles away, standing along the side of Strada Provincial 248 was a man dressed in odd clothing which didn't seem to fit.

He wore old, calf-high boots covered with dust from the gravel road out of Luzzi. He wore a grey felt hat with an extra-wide brim. With both hands, he held a large beat-up black canvas bag that looked as if it came off a 1940 TWA flight. It was long enough for golf clubs. Mr. Randazzo was a humble and unassuming man who avoided attention at all costs, and he never played golf.

Not one to be late, Mr. Randazzo of Luzzi, Italy, a small village just east of the Fiume Crati River and nestled near the top of a mountain, waited patiently for the limousine. Unable to navigate the narrow and steep road up to Luzzi, the limousine driver had instructions to pick up Mr. Randazzo, also known as il Tasso, the Badger, on highway 248.

Eventually, two headlights appeared like a pair of asteroids in the night sky and cut through the early morning mist. They grew bigger and brighter as the limousine slowed and pulled up alongside Mr. Randazzo.

The driver quickly got out and came around the car and opened the door. Mr. Randazzo tipped his hat and got in. The driver offered to take the large black bag, but Mr. Randazzo's cold stare made him think otherwise. Mr. Randazzo placed the canvas bag on the backseat next to him. The limousine turned around and began the six-hour drive to the Leonardo da Vinci airport in Rome, where Mr. Randazzo boarded an overnight Pan American flight to Philadelphia.

Another limousine, this one black without the steel armored doors, pulled up in front of the District Courthouse on Montgomery Avenue in Narberth. Three men got out. Two wore $3,000 custom-tailored, Burnello Cucinelli suits from Boyd's; the other wore dungarees and a black leather jacket.

The expensive suit wearers were South Philadelphia lawyers who specialized in defending associates of La Cosa Nostra. So confident, one carried a duffel bag containing a shirt, pants, underwear, shoes, and socks. The lawyers knew every trick in the book and even tricks they invented on the spot. The leather jacket and dungarees wearer was Harry Hunchback Battaglia, a well-known hitman for the Morello crime syndicate. He carried a nine mm Browning in a chest holster, and a Luger stuffed into a holster above his fanny, and two .32 pocket pistols, one each in ankle-strap holsters beneath the cuffs of his pants. The three men walked side-by-side up the steps and through the courtroom doors. They were instructed to sit in the gallery until their case came up.

Shortly after ten, the judge requested the representatives of Mr. George L. Romano take their seats at the defendant's table. The two men in the custom-tailored suits moved to the front, left side. The Hunchback remained in the gallery. The Montgomery County Assistant District Attorney was seated at a table opposite the defendants. Shortly after 10:15, George L. Romano, also known as Porky Bananas, was brought in a side entrance handcuffed and wearing an orange jail suit. He sat between his two attorneys. He looked over his shoulder and nodded at the Hunchback.

"Mr. George L. Romano," the judge stated, "you were arrested for a sexual misconduct crime of indecent exposure and public drunkenness, how do you plead, sir?"

The slick lawyer to Porky's right stood and addressed the judge.

"Your honor," he said, "may I approach the bench?"

The judge nodded, and the prosecutor joined the two slick lawyers at the judge's bench. "Your honor," the slick lawyer said, "this is not a sexual misconduct crime. It's not a crime involving my client. My client was brutally attacked and stripped of his clothing by four ruthless juveniles. They not only stole his clothes but his wallet and money, too. He has the bruises to prove it."

The young DA started to interrupt, but the lawyer held up his hand while still focused on the judge. "A hammer was found near the site of the encounter as well as a lead pipe, and there is proof that both were used on my law-abiding client. Therefore, your honor, we believe the case should be thrown out."

"Law-abiding client?" the DA muttered.

"Mr. Stager," the judged said to the assistant DA, "do you have any evidence to the contrary?"

"Well no," he said. "But we need some time…."

"You've had several days to investigate," the judge said, "I'm throwing this case where it belongs, in the trash. Do you have clothes for the defendant, gentlemen?"

"Yes, we do, your honor," the slick lawyer said, "and thank you, sir. It's good to see there is fairness in your court."

"Case dismissed," the judge announced as he pounded his hammer down.

As the slick lawyers walked past the assistant DA, one said, under his breath, "Better keep your mouth shut sonny-boy, or somebody will shut it for you."

"Your honor," the DA complained, "he just threatened me, he can't get away with that."

The lawyer turned and looked at the judge, "Your honor, I merely asked him to be more prepared. I believe my colleague here heard what I said."

"Goodbye gentleman, this case has been dismissed. Mr. Stager, may I have a word with you in my chambers?"

Several miles away, a couple didn't arrive in a limousine but walked up the hill from their home on Jones Street to a corner house. A police car was sitting out front. They opened the gate and walked toward the front door; an officer got out of the police car.

"Excuse me," the officer said, "can I ask the purpose of your visit here?"

"Really?" George Ferraco said, "we're visiting our neighbors, Bruno, is there suddenly a law against that?"

"No, sir," the officer replied. "Do you live in Belmont Hills?"

"We live on Jones Street, the third house down," Mrs. Ferraco pointed out. "You must have seen us walk up the hill."

The officer nodded. "Okay, ma'am," he said, "sorry to bother you."

"No bother at all, officer," George Ferraco said.

George knocked on the door.

A stocky young boy around 10 opened the door. "Yeah, can I help you?" he asked.

"We'd like to speak to your dad," George replied.

"Sure," he said," wait just a minute. I'll get him."

After a few minutes, Mr. Bruno came to the door. He looked at the couple but did not speak."

"Mr. Bruno," Mr. Ferraco said, "we'd like to come in and speak to you and Mrs.Brescil about your son, Pete."

"What about him?" Mr. Bruno replied.

"We'd like to come in and not discuss it out here," George told him.

Mr. Bruno stared at them for a few seconds looked over them to the police car, and said, "Please come in."

Once inside, Mrs. Ferraco introduced herself and her husband to Mrs. Brescil; who was seated in the living room. Mrs. Brescil nodded and welcomed them. She appeared upset.

"What about my son, Petey?" Mr. Bruno asked.

"Do you know he was one of the four boys in the trees outside of the Otts' home who witnessed the murders?" Mr. Ferraco asked.

"Ah, maybe," Mr. Bruno replied, "and maybe not."

"You don't have to worry about us, Mr. Bruno," Mrs. Ferraco said, "we are on your son's side. We are here to let you know what's going on."

"What makes you think I don't know what's going on?" Mr. Bruno asked.

"It's not just the police after the boys, but the Philadelphia mob, too." Mr. Ferraco said. "Are you aware of the mafia? he asked.

"Mr. Ferraco," Mr. Bruno chuckled, "I brought my family here from Italy, from the Province of Calabria, where the mob is more prevalent than in New York, and you have to ask me if I know about the mafia? The question is not good."

"I didn't mean to insult you, Mr. Bruno," George said. "The boys are hiding, and they are safe. They think if they turn themselves in, the mafia will get to them and kill them."

"Please," Mr. Bruno said, "have a seat. I will tell you."

"Where is our son?" Mrs. Brescil asked.

"Mrs. Brescil," Mrs. Ferraco answered, "George gave the boys his word that he would not reveal their location. "If he does, they may never trust him again. All we can tell you is that they are safe."

Mr. Bruno nodded, "I feel that I can trust you, too," I've seen George on the street. I know he is from here. A week ago, long before the police arrived, a man stopped me outside. He told me about the cherry trees and the boys. He said they were in great danger from the Philadelphia syndicate.

"Now," Mr. Bruno continued, "there is a mob war between the Philadelphia and New Jersey families. We had these many times in Italy. This man said he was helping the boys, but they disappeared because they didn't trust him."

"Do you know who he was?" Mrs. Ferraco asked.

Mr. Bruno held up his hand and asked her to wait.

"This man asked me if I have any underworld contacts in Italy," Mr. Bruno explained. "I told him that my brother knows the underworld Mafioso in the Calabria Province near our home town of Luzzi. The man said if I expected to see my son again, that I should contact my brother. So, I did."

"Are they prepared to help you?" Mr. Ferraco asked.

"Yes," Mr. Bruno said, "they are sending a representative."

"And what will this representative do," he asked.

"There has been a lot of bad publicity about the mafia in Italy," Mr. Bruno explained. "The families there have been laid back for a while. They have reduced their public activity. But these families also want to keep their hitmen busy, so they don't turn soft. The Sicilian mafia is the most powerful family in Italy. They have a man feared by all mafia families not just in Italy, but in the world. He is never called by his God-given name, but by his family name."

"And what is that," Mrs. Ferraco asked.

Mr. Bruno looked down, then slowly looked up at Mrs. Ferraco and said, "He is the Badger, Giovanni Randazzo."

"Why the Badger?" she asked.

"Because," Mr. Bruno replied, "this man can dig escape tunnels so quickly, that he is called the Badger. This Badger is not just a digger, not just an escape artist, but a killer, too. In Italy, the Badger is more powerful than God."

CHAPTER 25

Dago Red

We woke just after dawn in the field near the top of the tunnel. We got out some of the food Mr. Ferraco gave us and made sandwiches and shared a bottle of Coke.

"Hey, ass wipe," Gary said to Pete, "don't lip it."

Pete stuck his tongue inside the opening of the bottle and twirled it around. "How's that shit," Pete needled.

"Jesus Christ you're ignorant," Gary said.

"We learned that from the Polack's," Pete said, "who wanted to blow us all the time."

Gary chuckled, and gently stabbed Pete in the side with his open hand and said, "Smartass."

"What are we gonna do?" I asked.

"I don't know," Pete said, "it's a good day to pick up some girls and bring them up here. Wash My Hands would probably come."

"Is that come or cum," Mickey asked.

"Hell," Gary directed to Pete, "she'd want a man, not your little prick."

"That leaves you out," Pete said.

Mickey looked at me and smiled. We knew we were getting over our doldrums from last night and getting back to normal.

"We should make a campsite on top of the tunnel," I said, "one that can't be seen from a distance, but we should have paths that lead to lookout points so we can see who's coming."

"We need an escape route, too," Gary said, "where we can get out of here if somebody comes."

"Is that come or cum," Mickey said again.

"Shit, Merk," Gary said, a nickname he often used with Mickey, "is that all you think about?"

"Yeah," Mickey said, "what's wrong with that?"

We laughed. It felt good to laugh.

"Go jerk off," Pete said, "it'll pass."

We laughed again.

"You know all about that," Gary shot back at Pete, laughing.

Pete laughed, too, and said, "I wouldn't talk if I were you." He guffawed and pushed his glasses up.

We lay back in the grass, watching the puffy clouds drift across the blue sky. The sun was peeking above the trees, and we knew we had our work cut out for us. I looked over, and Gary had a straw of grass in his mouth, his hands clutched behind his head, staring at the sky. Pete and Mickey appeared as if they were falling back to sleep.

"Let's go," I said, "we need to get to the tunnel." We weren't far from the tunnel, so we packed up and trudged through the dense brush. The top of the tunnel was a mass of stickers and thick weeds, mostly Sumac trees with bright red plumes. No paths existed because nobody ever went to the top. Hell, besides the railroad people and the Hill kids, nobody ever went through the tunnel, either.

As experienced fort builders, so we knew what to do. We worked that day, clearing light stuff from the top of the tunnel, but we needed tools. Mickey and I decided that during the night, we'd sneak back to the dump to find some tools we had hidden in the Alamo. It was the only way we could cut through the thick brush.

"While you two birds are there," Gary suggested, "why don't you stop and see Bobby Wilson. He has a pair of police binoculars. We could see much further."

"Yeah," I said, "that would be smart. Bobby's father is a cop."

"Oh, yeah, I forgot that," Gary said.

Pete guffawed uncontrollably, "You dipshit, why do you think he has police binoculars?"

"Shut up, ass-wipe," Gary countered.

We all shared Pete's laugh.

After midnight, Mickey and I left for the dump, and Gary and Pete went down to the tracks in the opposite direction and headed toward George Ferraco's backyard. Any headlights Mickey and I saw immediately drove us into hiding. Cops would grab two kids being out so late. We had to move slowly and carefully. We dug up an old box inside the fort that had another hammer, a saw, a hacksaw, a hatchet, several knives, a small shovel, and a pickaxe. We had forgotten we left so many tools there. We put most of the stuff in the knapsack; the one George Ferraco gave us. We backtracked the way we came. Gary and Pete had returned from their expedition first. They had another supply of food. Plus, a note George put in with the food. They hadn't read it. We gathered around our flashlight and unfolded the paper.

"Fellows," it read, "things are happening you should know about. At the top of Mary Waters Ford Road, about where you cut into the woods, there is an old road. It only goes about 50 yards or so, but I checked it out, and I can drive in on it. We can't be seen there from Mary Waters Ford. The night after you find this note, I will go to that road and park. You should be able to find me. I'll be there around 11 p.m. See you then." George Ferraco.

"That's tomorrow night," Mickey said, "eleven. Ronny, your watch still running?"

"Yep," I said, "it's a Boy Scout watch. A good watch."

"Boy Scouts," Pete remarked, "now there's some ass-wipes."

"What do you mean," I said.

"Come on, Ronny," Pete said sarcastically. "The only reason to be a Boy Scout is to get at the Girl Scouts; in the woods, at night, no doubt," and he laughed. "Can I join the Boy Scouts?"

"Okay, we'll go tomorrow night," Mickey said.

"Do you think all of us have to go?" Gary asked.

"Yeah, Pecker," Mickey replied, "I think all of us should be there and hear what he has to say in case we need to make some decisions. It's all woods to get there so it shouldn't be a big deal."

The next day we worked clearing the underbrush and making two paths that led to either side of the tunnel. On one side we could see the Flat Rock Dam, and on other, we could look down the tracks almost to the Hill. We also made two escape paths that took us down either side of the tunnel. At dusk we went down one of our escape paths and crossed the tracks and took a dip in the Schuylkill River, cooling off and using the bar of soap George gave us. We decided the next time we washed up we would do it at night. We figured we could be seen in the river from the expressway and even across the river from Manayunk.

We left for our meeting with George around 10. We're getting used to the terrain. We stayed off the logging road until we saw headlights come up Mary Waters Ford and turn. Light flashed through the trees. When the lights went out, we headed toward the car. George was leaning against the front of the car when we arrived.

"Hello, fellows," George said, "good to see you boys again."

We thanked him for helping us and getting us food.

"Pete," George said, "me and the Mrs. visited your mom and dad. Hell, your dad knew more about this than we did. But they're fine, and your mom was relieved to hear you are safe, at least for the time being."

"Does my father want to come and kick my ass," Pete asked.

"No," George chuckled, "but he did ask if I knew where you were."

"Did you tell him," Pete asked.

"Well if I did, Petey, he'd a been here already," George joked. But we knew it wasn't a joke.

"Thanks, George," Pete said quietly, "appreciate that. What do you mean he knows more about this than you?"

"He told me some fella stopped him on the street and told him about everything. The fella suggested your dad get in touch with someone near your hometown in Italy. A mafia-type guy. So, your dad called his brother in Italy, and now there's some mafia fella named Giovanni coming here. You know anyone named Giovanni, Pete?"

"No," Pete responded, "but I know my uncle over there knows a lot of people. He helped us get here. But who the hell told my father?"

"I wonder if it was the mysterious man?" Mickey asked.

"The guy told your father that he was talking to you kids, but you disappeared on him. Said probably you stopped trusting him."

"Yea, that's the mysterious man," Gary said. "Who else would know all about this? Hell, he knew everything, even our names."

"Sounds like the one," George said. "Your dad said this fella was tall."

"Yea, that's him," Mickey said. "That's the one."

"Why did you decide not to trust him?" George asked.

"A friend of ours on the Hill said he might be Porky Bananas, the naked drunk guy on the dump road," I muttered.

"Oh, that's another thing," George said, "the fella from the dump road got out of jail and is free as a bird. That's not good news for you boys. He's gonna be lookin' for you. Oh, before I forget, Pete, your father asked me to get this to you."

George opened the passenger side door and grabbed a bag off the seat. He handed it to Pete, who immediately opened it.

"Shit," Pete jabbered, "it's three bottles of dago red. Son of a bitch."

"I thought that would cheer you boys up," George said.

Pete looked prouder than a peacock. "My father never gave me dago red; I always had to sneak sips."

Suddenly, a pair of headlights came up Mary Waters Ford and slowed down by the old road. Then it sped away. We watched the lights through the trees, and they turned around again and came back down Mary Waters Ford. The headlights slowed up by the old road entrance and stopped.

"Oh, shit," George said, "what's this? Boys, get behind the car here."

From inside the car, a flashlight flickered onto the old road. Then it swept through the trees and back like the driver was looking for someone. We heard the car door open.

"You mother fuckers are dead," a voice yelled. "Deader than a fuckin' doornail. I'm gonna cut your balls off, stuff them in your mouth, and watch you bleed to death; you rat bastards. I'll be back." Then he got back in the car, and we watched the headlights slowly continue down Mary Waters Ford and disappeared.

"I've got to get out of here," George said, a bit upset. "You boys go back to the tunnel. Be careful."

"George," I said, "how did he know where we are? Did he see the note?"

"No, I doubt that," George said. "He followed me and stayed back far enough, so I didn't see him, and he followed my lights and saw me turn onto this road. He probably had his headlights off. It's an old trick at night. If it were daylight, we'd be dead now. He must be afraid to come into the woods."

"Which means he'll be back first thing tomorrow," Gary said.

George turned and looked at Gary. "You can count on it. You boys ought to think of leaving tonight or at daybreak tomorrow."

With that, George got back in his car and slowly backed out the old road. Mickey yelled, "George, be careful."

George didn't answer, and we headed back to the tunnel with the dago red.

CHAPTER 26

Another Murder

We stayed up talking after our meeting with George, and we drank the dago red. We assumed it was Porky Bananas who yelled from the road because he said he'd cut off our balls. We were worried about George, but there was no reason for Porky to attack George. He had nothing to do with any of this, but as Mickey pointed out, he helped us, and that may be enough.

The more wine we drank, the braver we got. Gary suggested we don't stay in one spot but move around, change locations every couple of days. Hopefully, he said, that would keep Porky off guard. We discussed leaving just before daylight and going back to the Alamo.

"I don't know," Mickey said, "Porky knows about the dump. He could go there next."

"But he didn't see us in the fort," I offered, "for all he knew we walked up the road and found him. He might not expect us to return there."

"Yeah, I agree with Ronny," Pete insisted, "especially after tonight. He might concentrate on the woods here for a while. When he gives up, we can move back to the tunnel."

"What do you think, Pecker?" Mickey asked.

"I'm leaning toward the Alamo," Gary said, "If he catches us there, we can run to the shooting range, the incinerator, or back down to Centennial Road and into Croyle's woods. We got choices."

"He may stay away from the dump after gettin' arrested there," I argued, "but if he does go there unless he saw us come out of the fort, he'd never find us."

"When we came out of that fort," Pete explained, "he was out cold. He never saw us until after we stripped him. Besides, we can easily outrun him."

"Okay," Mickey stated, "it's the fort then. We get up first thing, leave our stuff hidden here, and go to the fort."

"Can we stop for breakfast on the way?" Gary asked.

"Wouldn't that be nice," I said.

We drank the rest of the wine and got out some cheese and rolls and crawled into our sleeping bags.

I was the first one awake. It was daylight. We were supposed to get up before sunrise, but we were tired and drank the wine. We overslept. I started waking up the other three.

"Shit," Mickey spluttered, "what time is it?"

I looked at my watch. "Seven-thirty," I said.

"We were supposed to be up sooner," said Gary, "let's pack up and get the hell out of here."

"You still want to go?" Mickey inquired. "You don't think it's too late?"

"We can still do it," Gary insisted, putting on his sneakers, "let's go. Put the food in the knapsack. I've got to piss and then we're off."

We covered our tools with the thick brush we cut and loaded up with the knapsack and sleeping bags. We cut across the field and into the woods.

"Let's be as quiet as we can," Mickey warned, "if he comes early, we don't want to run into him. But if we do, run like hell for the tunnel."

We nodded in agreement.

We trekked into the woods toward the dump, trying to be quiet. I figured we were getting close to the old road where we met George. Pete stopped, and he may have saved our lives.

"Wait a minute, goddamn it," Pete warned, "I've got to take another piss."

"Jesus Christ," Gary said, "you got weak kidneys or something? Come on we ain't got all day."

"This will just take a minute," he said, "I'll piss right over here."

While we stood and waited, I thought I heard something. I scanned out in front of us and saw movement. "Sshh, wait," I whispered, "I hear something."

"Yeah, I'm not fallin' for that shit," Pete hissed, "good try."

"No, be quiet, there's somebody out in front of us," I said. "Let's go to those sumac trees. Lay down in there."

We moved quickly to the trees with Pete bitching and moaning about not finishing his piss. We lay on our stomachs after putting the knapsack and sleeping bags behind us. We lay there and watched the woods.

We heard them before we saw them. Two men and the one in front leading, holding a gun, was Porky Bananas. I didn't recognize the other man. He wore a black leather jacket and jeans. The two were not used to walking in the woods and were making a racket. The one in the leather jacket swore after he ducked from a sticker branch Porky grabbed and let go. They were coming not exactly at us but just off to our left, close enough to see us if they suddenly changed direction.

"Should we run?" Gary hissed.

"No," Mickey whispered, "not yet."

Porky Bananas stopped and scanned the forest in front of him. He said something to the man behind him, but we couldn't hear. They took a few more steps and got closer to us. The man behind Porky, the one in the leather jacket, reached behind his back and pulled out a gun. He crept up behind Porky, raised it, and fired a shot into the back of Porky's head. Porky dropped to the ground. The man looked around, then down at Porky, lifted his gun and fired three shots into Porky's back. He took a step around Porky and scanned the woods. We tried silent breathing, trying not to move. The killer reached around with both hands and put his gun away. He gave the woods one more look, then turned and walked back toward Mary Waters Ford. After about five minutes, we thought we heard a car start.

"Go ahead," Pete whispered, "say it, you Polack prick."

"What, Jesus H. Christ?" Gary asked.

"Shh, not yet," Mickey said. "Maybe he's tricking us. Let's wait."

We lay there maybe ten more minutes until Mickey said it was safe.

"Jesus H. Christ," Gary said, "how many murders can you see in a lifetime?"

"What are we gonna do?" Pete asked.

"I don't think we should go to the dump," I said, realizing we were now getting in deeper.

"Let's go back to the tunnel," Gary stammered.

"What about Porky?" I asked. "We just gonna leave him there?"

"How about if we drag him out to the street and let a passing car find him," Gary suggested.

"No, not good," Mickey offered, "the cops will see he was dragged and will follow our tracks to the tunnel. Then we're screwed. Besides, I think you can get in trouble fooling around with a dead body."

"Or trying to change the scene of a murder," I added, "I saw that on Perry Mason."

"How about if we let George know," Gary said. "Then he can call the cops."

"We're gettin' George involved in this too much," Mickey warned. "If he reports this, the cops may lock him up, and he'll get fired from the township job. We can't do that."

"Well, what can we do, then?" Pete asked, "just let him lay there and rot?"

"Who the hell was the guy that shot him?" Gary asked. "A mob guy? Why would one mob guy shoot another?"

"It happens all the time," Pete said. "Usually that's all they kill unless you saw something."

"Like three murders?" I inquired.

"Yes," Pete said, "like three murders."

"I don't know," Mickey said, "but we've got to get the hell out of here. The guy in the back jacket may come back or somebody else."

"Let's go," Gary said, "let's go back to the tunnel. We can talk about it and come back tomorrow."

That's what we did. We gathered up our gear and headed back to the top of the tunnel.

CHAPTER 27

The Bird Killer

The door opened, and a striking young Italian woman with a pen and pad in her hands came out. "Louis, Mr. Graziano will see you now," she said, smiling at the man who sat by the exit door.

"Thank you, Maria," Mr. Regina said, and he walked across the plush carpeting, entered the room, and closed the door behind him.

The older man who sat behind the desk and wore an expensive Italian custom-made suit got up quickly. "Louis, it's great to see you," he said. "I hope I haven't kept you waiting long."

"Not at all sir," Mr. Regina said, "I got to watch the eye candy out there."

Mr. Graziano chuckled, "Yes, indeed, yes, indeed; I know what you mean. Sit down over here, please."

"Thank you, sir."

Louis Regina, consigliere for Vito Graziano, Don of the Newark, NJ, based mob, was always amazed at the strength and power of his boss. Amazingly handsome, even in his eighties, with thick grey hair and sharp blue eyes. Louis found Vito Graziano to be one of the kindest and gentlest men he's ever met. That caused the downfall of many of the Graziano family enemies, who took the soft-spoken Don for an easy mark. Louis Regina knew Vito Graziano was the furthest thing from an easy mark. Mr. Graziano took the chair next to Louis. "What's been going on in that town you've been visiting? What do they call it, the mountain, or something?"

Louis smiled and said, "It's not quite a mountain, sir, more like a hill. The kids there call it the Hill."

"And how are they doing?" Mr. Graziano asked, "the kids there?"

"Well, sir, surprisingly well. At least they're still alive. They're gritty kids. They've got some balls."

"You're doing a great job there, Louis, I thank you for that. The Morello people haven't caught up to them yet?"

Regina gave his boss an update regarding the car chase and Porky Bananas' arrest and embarrassment."

"The kids banded together with other kids on the Hill, and they keep moving around," the consigliere explained.

"Amazing," Mr. Graziano beamed, "although I doubt that Mr. Romano is long for the world."

"I don't know for sure," Louis said, "but I agree with you. After what he pulled at the trash dump, Angelo Morello will get rid of him."

Mr. Graziano nodded.

"There's one other thing, sir," Louis said. "One of the boy's fathers has contacts with the Sicilian family in the old country. The Sicilian's have sent Giovanni Randazzo over to help the kids. He's on his way in now."

Mr. Graziano, his elbows resting on the arms of the chair, his hands folded together beneath his nose, stared intently at his consigliere and said,

"Yes, 'il Tasso,' the Badger? Is he here yet?"

"I received a call from Tony Milano in New York. As you know sir the Gambino family keeps close ties with the old country."

"Yes, Louis, Tony the Wolf would know. Is il Tasso coming into New York?" Mr. Graziano asked.

"Tony said no, that he's flying directly to Philadelphia."

"When?"

"Thursday," Louis added, "the Wolf asked that I meet him and make arrangements for him. I, of course, said I would talk to you before I do that."

"That's why you are a good attorney, Louis. This is alarming. The Badger is evil, a psychopath, plain, and simple. I can't believe the Sicilians would send him for this. Is he coming over on the side of the kids?"

"One of the boys who witnessed the murders is the nephew of people in the Calabria Province."

"Do you know where?"

"Yes, sir, the small mountainous village of Luzzi."

"Sure, my Rosa's people are from near there. Okay, Louis, this changes everything. You may think this killer is on one side, but he will flip over and kill you before you figure him out. But you can't figure him out. Nobody can. He does not show which side he's on until he starts killing, and once he starts, he doesn't stop.

"Pick him up as requested, Louis, keep close tabs on him, everything he does. Give him all the information you can about the boys, the Morello's, everything. And be armed. I know you don't like that, but I'm ordering you to. Keep me informed every step of the way. I'll have Maria put your calls into me immediately, no matter who I'm with. Maybe I underestimated this thing."

"Yes, sir."

"And keep visiting those boys, keep close tabs on them, as well. I don't want this thing blowing up in our faces."

"Yes, sir. The boys have been avoiding me lately. Not sure why," Louis said.

Mr. Graziano stood. Louis did too. "Well, you know how to fix that, Louis. I'm counting on you."

"Yes, sir."

Mr. Graziano took Louis's hand to shake and pulled him closer to slap his back. "Good luck, Louis, and keep me informed."

"Yes, sir."

"Oh, Louis, one more thing," Mr. Graziano said. "the Badger, he's not only a cold-blooded killer, but he's also a digging maniac. The Sicilians usually used him for bank robberies, kidnappings, and any job where they need a digger and a killer rolled into one. He's small and quite muscular — a powerful human being.

"He's the one that got to the rat Oscar Flats before he testified against the Sicilians. The Federals in Italy kept Flats in solidarity confinement in one of Italy's worst prisons. He had five armed guards watching him in his cell 24 hours a day. The Badger dug under the prison walls and right up beneath Flats' cell, where he stuck a bomb in the heating vent. By the time the bomb went off, blowing Flats and the guards to hell, the Badger had gone back out the tunnel and was drinking wine in a Naples whore house.

"Don't ever get in his way, capeesh?"

"Yes, sir, I'll be careful," Louis replied, holding the office door open.

"Did Tony the Wolf tell you anything else about him?" Mr. Graziano asked.

"Nothing, sir."

Mr. Graziano motioned for Louis to shut the door. "Couple of more things I know, Louis. He speaks only in two-word sentences. That's it, never a sentence with more than two words. He doesn't carry guns he carries axes. He's deadly with them."

"Does he speak English, sir?"

"I believe so, if you call two-word sentences, English. Anyway, good luck Louis, remember call if you need me, and have your .38 with you."

"I will sir, thank you," Louis said as he walked out the door.

Louis went to his car in the parking lot. He sat for a while, thinking about his next move. *I'm going to have to bring the digging psychopath to the boys. That's who he's coming for. Sicilians wouldn't waste his time unless it were something big. And this is big. I'm not sure even Vito Graziano understands what's at stake. But I do, and I've got to see this thing through. Too bad those kids will end up living short lives.* Louis started the car and headed for the New Jersey Turnpike.

By this time, the four of us had left the tunnel and headed into the woods to find Porky Bananas' body. "You sure it was around here?" Mickey asked."

We neared the old road where we saw Bananas get shot. We decided we just couldn't let his body rot. We were going to carry Bananas out of the woods and dump him on Mary Waters Ford. Hopefully, someone will see him there.

"Yes, right here. Look there's blood all over these pine needles and shit," I said

"Brain shit," Mickey said. "Disgusting brains all over here. He blasted him in the head. Look, skull parts and brains all around here. It's the place, all right."

"So, what happened to him? How come he's not here," Pete asked.

"Well, he didn't get up and walk away, that's for sure," Gary said.

"Jesus Christ," Pete snapped, "he got his brains blown out, you think he walked away?" Then Pete did a belly-laugh.

"Hey, blow me, dago," Gary said. "Maybe he just got wounded."

"Wounded?" Pete exclaimed, laughing uncontrollably. "His brains are all over these leaves."

"Pete, keep it down," Mickey warned. "They may be still around here."

"Wounded," Pete repeated, "fucking wounded."

"Come here you prick," Gary barked, as he tried to get Pete in a headlock, "now your brains are gonna be here, too."

"What brains," Mickey said.

Pete shoved him away, still laughing.

"All right let's go," I said, "we're done here. Let's go back to the tunnel."

Pete stomped along, "Wounded," he laughed, "he got wounded, his brains all over the ground. No wonder the Germans took Poland in three days."

"Eat me, you ignorant prick."

It made Mickey and me smile to hear Gary and Pete back breaking each other's balls like before. As we made our way through the thick woods, it reminded me of another ball breaking time we had walking through the tunnel.

It wasn't too long ago when we took Pete through the tunnel for his second time. Though apprehensive, he went through with us. It's always creepy going through the tunnel, but Pete took it like a champ. We were three quarters through with no train in sight. As we approached the end, a big bird, I think maybe it was a crow or raven, sat on the tracks just ahead of us. Gary picked up a stone from between the rails and tossed it at the bird to, as he said, to scare it away. It was a throw that missed its mark because it hit the bird on the head and killed it. Gary was physically and emotionally upset.

But for Pete, it was an opportunity to bust some balls.

"Jesus Christ, Polack," Pete hollered, "you killed the damn bird."

"I didn't mean to," Gary replied, obviously upset. "Jesus H. Christ, I didn't mean to," he said as he ran over to the bird. The rest of us did, too. As we hovered over the bird, Gary was on the verge of tears.

"Why'd you kill him," Pete asked.

"It was an accident, I didn't mean to kill him," Gary pleaded.

Pete did a belly-laugh. "The shit winds are blowin' again," — Pete sometimes referred to Gary's bullshitting as the shit winds. Then another belly-laugh.

Gary stomped away from the bird, heading toward the tunnel exit. "Believe what you want," he said, "but I didn't want to kill it."

The rest of us followed. Pete continued to harass him as we made our way down the tracks. "You didn't mean to kill that poor bird, so you threw a rock right at his head, sure Pecker, we'll believe that."

"Eat me, you four-eyed prick," Gary retorted.

"Ronny, what are you grinnin' at?" Mickey asked as we trekked through the woods, heading back to the top of the tunnel.

"Oh," I responded, "just remembering the time Gary threw the rock and killed the bird. Pete broke his balls all the way home."

I looked over at Mickey and he was grinning, too. For Mickey and me, it took our minds off things. We saw Porky Bananas get shot and we saw who did it. At least that's another mob guy out of the way. But surely more will come. By the time we got to the top of the tunnel, we were hungry. We'd most likely need a food run to George's tomorrow night, I said. We sure could use some more of the dago Red. Gary asked Pete if he could go home and get more. "What, have you lost your mind," Pete responded. That answered that. When we got through the woods and back to the top of the tunnel, we had unsuspected visitors.

CHAPTER 28

Undercover

Back on McClellan Street in South Philadelphia, the boss of bosses, Angelo Morello held another meeting with the under-bosses. It was Friday morning, and Angelo predicted that if the snotnose kids weren't in the river or buried behind the airport by Friday, he would pass a gun around and the underbosses would play Russian Roulette. This time Mr. Morello was calm.

"Last-a time," he said, "I said we would play the Russian game if the snotnose kids weren't whacked. Maybe I was a bit excited. You can rest-a easy, no gun will be passed today."

"Nickodemo, can we-a have a report-a on that Porky Banan-as?"

Nick the Builder, looked around the table, smiled, and said, "He's with the fishes, boss."

"Which-a da river is it, Nickodemo, the Schuylkill or the Dela-ware-a?"

Nick the Builder, again with a warped and sardonic grin on his face, replied," The Delaware, boss."

"That's-a good, that's-a real good," Morello said, "that's-a better place to catch-a da fish and not as polluted. Porkie will have-a nice-a home there."

Nodding, the bosses chuckled. They knew the boss of bosses wouldn't pass around a gun to play Russian Roulette. If he did, he could wipe out his command structure. They're used to the boss go-ing off the table. But today, he was back on it.

"Nick tells-a me we got Crazy Phil 'Bomb Bomb and Harry-a 'The Hunchback' on the job. This-a good, this-a real good. So what's the plan boys?"

The eleven men exchanged glances before Tony Potatoes spoke up.

"Boss," he said, "as you so elegantly and specifically pointed out, we got The Hunchback and Bomb Bomb on their trail; right this minute as we sit here. But for insurance purposes, we also got Tommy Sneakers ready, too, cause you know, these are fuckin' kids. Ain't one of them outrunnin' Tommy Sneakers."

Tony Potatoes paused and watched the bosses around the table smiled and nodded in agreement. Then he continued. "We also added Salvatore 'The Golfer' Napoli. If one of them mother fuckers gets on a golf course — cause, you know, kids like to play golf — Salvatore will wrap a nine iron around each of their necks. All, this, just for insurance, so to speak."

The men around the table nodded and voiced approval to Tony Potatoes' plan. Two or three were heard saying, "Good job, Tony, damn good job."

Tony Potatoes sat back in his chair and smiled, confident of a well-proposed plan.

"All right," Mr. Morello said. "keep-a me informed every step of the way."

Tony Potatoes nodded and said, "Of course, boss, of course."

"Alright," the boss of bosses said, "let's move-a on to further business."

Meanwhile, it was Friday deadline, too, at police headquarters in Ardmore when Frost and Lochran walked through the main doors on their way to meet with the Captain. As expected, they were on-edge and grouchy.

"Well Jesus Christ," the desk sergeant Zip Roberts, declared, "Look who just walked through the doors. Elliot Ness and Sherlock Holmes."

"Hey," detective Frost said, "go fuck yourself, you prick."

"Well, shit, fellows," Roberts replied, "I thought you were gonna have the whole thing solved up by Friday." Roberts looked around and then said, to no one in particular, "It's Friday, right? isn't today Friday?"

Frost stopped. He could feel Lochran grab the sleeve of his suit jacket. "Why don't you kiss my ass," Frost said.

"We went and got that conference room all cleaned up for you boys," Roberts teased, "we even got candy and shit there. That's what those Hill kids like, right? Hey, didn't you two grow up on the Hill?"

Frost started to go back after him until Lochran grabbed his shoulders, "Come on, Butch, ignore the asshole." He pulled Frost back toward the captain's office.

"I'm just trying to help, that's all," Roberts called out, smiling.

The Captain's door was open, and he waved them in. "Shut it," he told them. Then said, "Sit."

"Look," he said. "I know this isn't easy for you two. Trying to find four kids hiding out on the Hill is like trying to find a dingleberry up your ass. Don't think I don't know that."

"So, you're taking us off the case?" detective Lochran asked.

"No. No, I'm not," the Captain answered, "but there are new orders from the top'?

"Yeah?" Frost replied.

"Butch," the Captain huffed, "take a breath. Relax. We're all in this together. I get pissed on from upstairs, and I piss on you. That's how it works. Don't think I don't know you two are busting your asses."

"What new orders Captain?" Lochran asked.

"We feel pretty certain," the captain went on, "that the Otts' murders were the work of the mob."

"Why would the mob want to kill the Otts?" Frost asked.

"You know how the mob operates," the Captain replied, "some convoluted bullshit about disrespecting someone and then wiping out that someone's grandparents. Something like that. They're animals. Anyway, the Philly cops have picked up on it and contacted the Commish. They want us to protect the kids who witnessed the hit, and at the same time, catch the killer."

"Exactly what we said earlier in the week," Frost pointed out. "We think it's doable because the killers will be in close to the kids."

"Yea," the Captain replied, "but if the killer gets to the kids before you two get to the killer, goodbye kids."

"I sent two detectives to question a guy who was picked up drunk on at the township landfill," the Captain revealed. He's a made hitman of the Morello gang in South Philadelphia."

Both detectives sat up in their chairs.

"Wait," Lochran said, "he was picked up at the landfill next to the Hill?"

"That's right," the Captain said. "He was drunk and wasn't wearing a stitch of clothing. The DA couldn't make the charge stick. He claimed four kids attacked him, and the DA on the case was the assistant to the assistant and experienced as an Iowa whore. So, he walked."

"Why didn't you tell us about this?" Frost asked.

"I'm telling you now. We don't think there's a connection."

"Of course, there's a connection," Lochran gushed. "Shit, Captain, if he was a mob hitman, maybe he was after the kid , and maybe the kid witnesses attacked him."

"Or defended themselves," Frost added.

"He did claim getting attacked by kids, but it's all speculation and bullshit," the Captain rasped. "We think he was just a drunk pervert who ended up at the landfill."

"Do we still have him?" Frost barked.

"We couldn't hold him. We didn't have anything. He probably went back to South Philly."

"Goddamn, Captain," Lochran complained, "that might have been a key lead. Why didn't you contact us?"

"And what are you going to do?" the Captain asked, "get a hardened mob guy to spill his guts? I don't think so. You got…" And the captain stopped.

"Go ahead, Captain, you got what, four kid witnesses, and can't do anything with them?" Lockran steamed.

"Look," Frost said, "I want to tell you something about these kids. They're not normal kids. They're not scared of shit. And they got good instincts; they seem to avoid the mob guys at the right time."

"Yeah," Lochran uttered, "and us, too. We had one down on Jefferson Street, and he suddenly disappeared."

"That may be so," the Captain replied, "but they're still kids."

"Wait a minute," Frost said, "didn't we just tell you that on Tuesday?"

"All right, all right," the Captain answered, "what's now is now and Lochran, stop shaking your head. The thinking now is to pull the cars watching their houses. Pull back completely, and then you two become 16 years old again."

"Sixteen years old again," Lochran scoffed, "what the hell is that supposed to mean?" He looked at Frost and Frost shrugged.

"Ditch your detective car. Go on foot. You two know every hiding place in that town. You talk to people, people you've known for years. Find out where those kids are and join them. If you have to, camp in the woods for Christ's sake. Eventually, the killer shows up, and you grab him."

"Just like that," Frost mocked.

Frost turned to Lochran, lifted his hands, and said, "Of course, why didn't we think of that?" Then turned back to the Captain. "Okay,

I like that. Hell, I was just tellin' Butch here I wanted to camp out again and cook marshmallows over the fire."

"Yeah, right, Frost added, "we can skip stones on the river and climb trees again. Shit, Loch, do you think we can swim bare ass naked in the Schuylkill again?"

"Funken'-a Butch," Lochran rasped, "maybe we can get some of those girls in Manayunk to swim with us, bare ass naked, of course."

"All right, smart asses," the Captain smirked, "get the hell out of here and do your jobs."

"So, what you're saying," Frost said, "is go do your jobs the way you think they should be done? Isn't that right, Captain?"

"Use your resources," the Captain chirped, "go undercover. Get people on the Hill to trust you and join those kids and protect them. That's what I'm saying."

Both detectives rose to their feet. "We're out of here, Captain," Frost quipped, "come on Loch, let's go. We're off to be 16 again."

"Goddamn right," Lochran said, as the two detectives walked toward the office door. "Hey, Butch, can I hit cleanup?"

"Shit no," Frost replied, "you strike out too much, you hit eighth."

"I'll choke up," Lochran said, "you know, shorten my swing, you'll see."

168

CHAPTER 29

The Reunion

"**J**esus H. Christ." Gary hollered. "Look who's here."

"I'll be dipped in shit," Pete exclaimed. "Who left the woods door open?"

As we approached our campsite on the top of the tunnel, three kids from the Hill were there waiting for us: Billy Curry Georgie Scavello, and Johnny Ciariello.

"Well, aren't you a sight for sore eyes," I said. "How'd you know we were here?"

"Wasn't hard," Billy said, "Johnny said from his back porch he saw you a couple of times walking out the tracks."

"You guys don't sneak real well, do you?" Johnny quipped. "Just figured you'd be coming either here or the dam."

"So, we tried here first," Georgie concurred, "must say, your camp is impressive."

"Could you see it from the tracks?" Mickey asked.

"Hell no," Billy said, "not until we got right here. Right on top of it."

"This would be a good place to bring some babes; you'd never be seen," Johnny remarked.

We all agreed.

We were happy to see three Hill kids from our former past lives since we've been on the run. We were elated.

"Hey Pecker," Georgie said, "them under the El girls have been asking for you."

"They miss the Thor," Gary said, "can't blame em.' Tell em' I'll be back soon."

"We brought you some things," Johnny said, "Billy, give them the bag."

Billy picked up a shopping bag from the ground and dumped it on the grass. Tastykakes and sodas. Enough to feed and army. "This ought to do you for a while," Billy said.

"Jesus," Pete said, "you spent a lot of money."

"Negatory," Georgie replied, "can't say we exactly how we paid for them," and he laughed. We all laughed. We almost felt like the black cloud hanging over us had lifted, even for a short time.

"We brought something else," Billy said. "This tarp here which you can make a lean-to out of it. How the hell do you guys stay dry when it rains?"

"We don't," Mickey replied.

"Well, now you've got something," Billy said.

"Thanks, Bill," I said.

"Why don't you hang around," Mickey said, "we're gonna swim in the river."

"We didn't bring any bathing suits," Johnny said.

"Who needs bathing suits?" Gary asked, and we laughed again.

"Look," Billy said, "we need to talk about some things. Can we sit here?"

We sat down, and Georgie passed around the Tastykakes and sodas. Man did that stuff taste good. Georgie said he even stole a bottle opener. We were stuffing the Tastykakes in our mouths and washing them down with cream soda while Billy talked.

"You remember the mysterious man," Billy said.

"Yeah," Mickey replied, "the mob guy who is after us."

"No, not exactly," Billy explained. "I know I told Ronny that, but my dad got some wrong information. Turns out the guy is on our side."

"No shit," Gary remarked, "can he help us?"

"He stopped me on Price Street the other day," Billy went on, "said he needed to talk with me. I was ready to run, but he insisted I listen to what he had to say. Something just told me to hear him out."

"How do you know he's on our side?" I asked Billy.

"What he told us in the cinder garage," Billy went on, "that he works for mob guys in New Jersey, he says that's the truth."

"Yeah," I said, "and he told me to dress up like a girl to serve my papers, and it worked."

"Well," Billy continued, "he said his name is Louis something, I think Louis Vagina or something."

"Vagina," Pete gushed, and we all laughed.

"Yeah," Billy went on, "says he wants to have a sit down with us. He said you fart-bird's need his help, and if you don't get it, some mob guy will find you and kill you."

"Hey Georgie," Gary said, "better get that Dodge fired up again, we got to kill some more of them mob assholes."

"I had to hide it, Pecker," George replied. "Them cops were hot on my trail after we ran them old ladies off the pavement in Ardmore. Runnin' over their bras and shit. I found a pair of green panties up the exhaust pipe."

We roared with laughter. "We got to do that again, George," Gary beamed, "that was some fun shit."

"Maybe the next time Skippy will take a dump on their car," Mickey laughed.

"I got a better idea of how to get rid of them," Johnny said, "and if Georgie can't get his Dodge runnin' again, we'll do it."

"Okay," Billy interjected, "but let's finish the business we came out here for. The Louis guy wants to meet with you. How about if I see if he'll come out here."

"That's okay, Bill," Mickey said, "as long as you think he's on our side."

"Well," Billy conceded, "he convinced me of it. If it's okay with you fart-birds, I'll see if he can come out tomorrow."

"Pete, talking with a mouth full of Krimpets, mumbled, barely understandable, "We ca poosh hi ass of the tuel if he giv us any shit."

"Hey Petey," Georgie said, "give me another pack of those Krimpets you're stuffen' away. I'm hungry as a bear walkin' out here."

"Here," Mickey said, "take these cupcakes, too. They've got cream in them."

"We'll bring him out the tracks?" Billy asked.

"Maybe you should bring him to the old logging road at the top of Mary Waters Ford Road," Mickey suggested. "Less of a chance for anybody to see you."

"I agree," I said, "if you come out the tracks there're too many places the cops or the mob can spot you. We can take you back that way today, through the woods to the old road, and you'll see where it is."

"Shit, Ronny," Georgie said, "I know where that trail is. I'll take us home that way."

"You boys came out the tracks today?" Gary asked.

"Yeah," Johnny said, "from my house."

"Okay," Billy proposed, "how 'bout if we bring the Vagina man out tomorrow at noon. You sorry asses be out of bed by then?"

"Shit, yea," Pete said, "these assholes get up before daylight. They think their Davy Crockett or some shit like that."

"What time those dagos get up on Jefferson Street, Petey," Gary asked. "Probably suckin' down that wine by nine or ten."

"You can suck on this right here," Pete responded, then laughed.

"Holy shit," Billy sneered, "you shit-birds haven't changed one bit."

"Wait, Billy," I barked, "I thought we were fart-birds?"

"Ronny," Billy replied, "do I have to teach you everything? Shit follows farts, don't it?"

I lay back in the grass and laughed my ass off. We all did.

CHAPTER 30

The Odd Combination

L ower Merion detectives Tommy Lochran and Butch Frost weren't sure if they got promoted or demoted, but they undertook their new assignment with excitement. Walking the streets of the Hill brought back many pleasant memories for the two middle-aged detectives.

"Let's try the stores first," Butch Frost said, "that will get us warmed up."

Their mission was to — through the people on the Hill — discover where the kid witnesses were hiding out. So, with the advice of the Captain, the detectives ditched their car and took to the streets.

They turned off Ashland and ascended the short hill on Highland Avenue to a small mom and pop store at the crest of the hill. They entered through a front screen door and climbed the few steps into the store that was once the living room of the Ross home. The store was empty, so detectives stood quietly and waited.

Detective Lochran nudged his partner and motioned with his head to the mirror in the corner against the ceiling, leaned over and whispered in Frost's ear, "She's watching us now and listening to what we say."

Frost nodded and said, in the same hushed tone, "Let's fill our pockets with the penny candy and shock the shit out of her."

Lochran smiled and nodded.

After a few minutes, a grey-haired lady came through a curtain separating the store from another room.

"Yes," she said, "what can I do you for? Oh, la de da, I mean, do for you?" Then she laughed.

"Hi, Annie," Frost said, "it's been a while."

Annie leaned forward and studied the men's faces and said, "Oh my God I'll be dipped in Campbells Tomato Soup, look who it is? The long arm of the law.

Detective Frost chuckled and said, "How's it been, Annie?"

"Grab yourselves a couple of them Yoo-Hoo's out of that cooler, boys. Go ahead. it's on the house. Oh, wait, I'm not trying to bribe you or anything, am I?" she snickered.

Detective Lochran smiled. "That's okay we just want to ask you a few questions."

"Why, any of my boys in trouble?" she asked.

"No, nothing like that," Frost explained. "Do any of the younger boys on the Hill, Ronny, Mickey, Gary, or Pete, come in your store?"

"Nah," she said, "not too often. They hang out on Jefferson Street. Besides, they spend most of their time playing baseball and chasing the Manayunk girls, you boys know about that, right? Now I get most of my information by listening and watching. See that mirror up there in the corner? I can sit in my living room and watch who comes in, hear what they say, and especially what they take. Then I flush the toilet in the bathroom and come out and say, 'Sorry, I was in the bathroom,' while I was sitting there watching and listening the whole time."

Frost laughed, "You haven't changed much."

"Why do you think I keep the penny candy down here and the nickel stuff up here? Then I love to see their scrawny faces when I ring them up and charge them for what they five-fingered. You'd be amazed how fast that candy comes out of their dirty little pockets and back into the boxes. Next day different kids come in and do the same thing. So, what can I do for you two?"

"Did you ever hear them talk about where they go, where they hang out?" Lochran asked.

"Well darn yes, what kind of question is that? Do you boys have short memories? You know I know everybody's business. It's always the same places where my boys hung out and where you shining examples of crooked gone straight hung out, ain't it?

"It don't change much from one pack of kids to the next. The woods at the bottom of Mary Waters Ford, or the dump. The dump. Can't understand why these kids think the dump is a place to spend time. They go down on the tracks near the river and walk out through that tunnel, I've heard that mentioned a few times."

"Have you heard anything lately," Lochran asked her.

"Well, matter of fact," she said. "A few of them came in the other day. They went on a shopping spree. They had a knapsack with them and bought all kinds of stuff, mostly sodas, and Tastykakes. But they were smart they didn't say much while I listened and watched. I asked them what they wanted all this junk for, and they left faster than a cat can scratch its ass. They were up to something,' all right. What, do they think I was born milkin' a cow or something? Well, I ain't been, and I ain't when you two been in here as brainless snots, either.

"Who were those kids, Mrs. Ross," Lochran asked.

"What's with the Mrs. Ross poopy?" she asked. "You so high and mighty now you can't call me Annie no more?" Then she lowered her voice. "If I tell you they goin' up the river or something? I don't want to be part of none of that. Bad for business. The snotnoses won't come in here no more."

"No," Frost said, "we need to talk to them. They may have information we're looking for, that's all."

"Okay," she said, "one of them was the Billy kid. He don't come in here too much he's always workin' or fixin things. The other was the boy from that Italian family on Leedom. You boys know where Leedom is or do you stick to the highfalutin streets now?"

"No, ma'am," Frost said, smiling, "we grew up on the Hill, too, remember?"

"Huh," she cooed, "how can I forget? The third one was the boy just down the street. Come to think of it, kinda odd seein' them three together. Kind of like the Lone Ranger and Sally Star walkin' in here. Know what I'm sayin'?"

"What do you mean," Lochran asked.

"Well hells bells," she replied, "only thing Bill hangs around with is a toolbox. Get it? A toolbox? And the Leedom boy is a ball kicker. Everywhere he goes he's kickin' a soccer ball or bouncing a basketball. And Georgie, he don't hang around with nobody steady. I seen him with a lot of other kids. Never seen him with the ball hogger or the grease monkey. It was odd that's all I'm sayin. It was unusual seeing them all together, and I doubt if they just walked into my store by coincidence and decided to conduct a major heist, you think?"

"No, you're probably right," Lochran chuckled.

"Probably? I'm righter than rain, and that's all there is to it. So, now, do I get some big reward for this? Don't answer, I already know the answer."

"Thank you, ma'am," Frost said. "We appreciate your help."

"If you appreciate it so much, why don't you get those thieving vultures at the township to lower my taxes. Now that'd be appreciation. I turn my living room into a store, and they think I'm the next millionaire. If I'm so filthy rich, why do you think I turned my living room into a store so a bunch of dumb bunny kids can steal penny candy? Huh?"

The detectives thanked her again and left. Outside, Frost said, "Every kid on the Hill knew about her mirror and that she sat in the next room watching and listening. I could write a book on the creative way's kids got around that.

Lochran nodded. "When it comes to things like that, we're all creative genesis. But it was interesting what she said about the three not hanging around together. And what they bought, sodas and cakes, enough to fill a knapsack? Most kids don't do that."

"You're right, Loch," Frost said. "Unless they were helping out other kids. Georgie is just down the street, let's pay him a little visit."

Lochran nodded, and the two men walked five or six houses down Highland, crossed the street, and went to the front door. Frost knocked. After a few minutes, a kid opened the door.

"Georgie?" Lochran said, "How the hell are you?"

Georgie's mouth dropped open. The detectives noticed.

"What do you want?" Georgie asked

"Take it easy, George, you look a little worried," detective Lochran said.

"Not worried," Georgie replied, "taking a little nap, is all. You woke me up."

"Oh, Georgie," detective Frost said, "we're so sorry. Just wanted to ask you a few questions."

"Ask away."

"What did you want the Tastykakes and sodas for, the ones you got at Annie's?" Frost asked.

"Ah, shit," Georgie explained, "we were goin' on a little picnic. You, know, hanging out at Smithy's woods and havin' fun. Are you arresting me for that?"

"No," Lochran said, "we're wondering where you were going with all that stuff."

"It was a picnic," Georgie said. "We were just havin' fun.'"

"Just having fun, huh?" Lochran repeated.

"So, Georgie," Frost asked, "how come you went into that store with Billy and Johnny? You a soccer player now?"

"No, what, you crazy?" he answered. "I wanted Billy to do some work on my..." Georgie stopped in midsentence.

"On your what?" Lochran interjected, "on your black Dodge? The one you drove illegally through Ardmore, no headlights, reckless driving and scaring the crap out of Strawbridges' customers? You mean that one."

"Oh, that wasn't us," Georgie pleaded.

"Uh-huh," Frost said. "Guess that was somebody else with a piece of shit '48 Dodge. Lots of them around, right?"

"So, where'd you hide it?" Lochran asked.

"I didn't hide nothin'," Georgie remarked.

"Look, George," Frost said, "if you're trying help the four boys who witnessed the Otts' murders, that's admirable. But it's also against the law. You could wind up in jail for it."

"Why?" Georgie asked. "They didn't do nothin', did they?"

"They're witnesses to capital murder, and the police want them. That's enough right there to get you at least six months in a juvenile center."

"Come on," Georgie laughed, "I didn't do nothin'. I don't know where those guys are, and if I did, you couldn't get it out of me if you tortured me. Would you rat on your friends?"

"Georgie, it's not..." detective Lochran stopped in midsentence.

Police sirens. Not just one or two, but several, coming closer it seemed, from all ends of the Hill. Frost turned and saw two go by on Jefferson Street, visible from Georgie's front porch. They could be heard on Ashland, too.

The detectives took a step or two away from the doorway and listened.

"Jesus Christ," Georgie said, "somethins' going on. You two better go investigate, you're missin' it."

Frost pulled his portable Motorola police radio out of his back pocket. "Frost, here."

"Frost, it's the Captain. Where are you two?"

"We're at the intersection of Highland and Rockland on the Hill, captain."

"How fast can you get to the grocery store at Ashland and Price?"

"Yea," Frost responded, "Carl the Butchers. Running maybe eight minutes."

"Well run then, goddamn it. Get there as quick as you can — a robbery and kidnapping. Witness saw two men drag a woman out of the store and stuff her into the trunk. Get there now."

"Holy shit," Georgie exclaimed, "I'm small bananas compared to that. You guys better go."

The detectives ignored Georgie's comment as Frost stuffed the Motorola in his back pocket. He and his partner darted off running toward Rockland Avenue.

"Hey," Georgie yelled, "you better save some. It's not all downhill, you know, you old farts." Then Georgie laughed like he told a good one.

PART THREE

CHAPTER 31

The Flip

August 10, 1964
Belmont Hills

Our next meeting with Louis Regina was set to take place on the old logging road at the top of Mary Waters Ford. It was where we had met George Ferraco and near where we saw Porky Bananas get shot. It was dark, and the bugs and mosquitos were out in droves. We've had a lot of rain lately, and it adds to the misery of mosquitos; they seem to get worse after thunderstorms. We waited to see the headlights come up Mary Waters Ford Road. We were tired of living in the woods and had hoped Louis Regina could help us get out of this mess. We were starting to get on each other's nerves.

"Goddamn mosquitos," Gary barked, slapping away the big ones that encircled our heads. "How long do we have to wait here?"

No one answered. Mickey mumbled something about asking George Ferraco to get us bug repellant. Suddenly, headlights flickered through the trees and stopped. As the car turned onto the logging road, its headlights grew as it slowly moved toward us. When the lights went off, we approached the vehicle.

"Gentlemen," Louis Regina called out, as he got out of the car, "good to see you again." Johnny got out too and opened the trunk. He unloaded two boxes filled with jars of his mother's canned tomatoes and peppers.

We stood in the darkness, and Louis outlined the situation as he knew it. Slowly, we began to trust him, and we apologized for avoiding him. Then he told us about the il Tasso.

"He's from Luzzi?" Pete asked. "Must be a hell of a man."

"Shit," Gary added, "another dago."

"Gary be careful of saying that around the Badger," Louis cautioned. "He's protective of his country and people."

"What do you mean, Louis," I asked, "are we gonna meet him?"

"I've been thinking about this since I met with my people in Newark," Louis said. "I think we need a new plan and that plan is for me to bring il Tasso out here, out to your campsite to meet you. What do you think?"

"Shit yeah," Pete responded, "that would be okay with me."

"What about the rest of you," Louis asked, "what do you think."

None of us objected. We thought it would be cool to meet a mafia hitman from Italy called, il Tasso, as long as he wasn't hittin' us.

"How soon?" Mickey asked.

"Well, I have to pick him up tomorrow at the airport," Louis said, "maybe sometime after that. Maybe the next day."

"Will you bring him here, to this spot," Gary asked, "or to the tunnel?"

"Gary," Louis said, "I think it would be best to take him to the tunnel, in daylight, rather than stand here in the dark on this old road. That okay with everybody?"

"Yea," I replied, "but do you know the way to the tunnel and how to get to the top?"

"I'll bring them," Johnny offered. "They can park by my house, and I'll bring them out the tracks. That way I get to meet him, too."

"That's right, Johnny," Louis said, "I keep forgetting you're a paesano. I'm sure il Tasso will be happy to meet another countryman."

"Shit, Johnny," Pete said, "we'll get all the dagos from the Hill out here and have a party for him."

"Jesus H. Christ," Gary said, "give me a break."

"Okay, we'll clear a better path for you," Mickey said. "Go to the left side of the tunnel entrance, and you'll see a path straight up. I hope this guy can climb."

"He's pretty tough," Louis remarked, "I don't think you have to worry about that."

"Shit yeah," Pete added, "he's from Luzzi, isn't he?"

"Louis," Mickey asked, "just one more question. What's the purpose of our meeting him?"

We all noticed that Louis paused before he answered like he wasn't sure what the purpose was and had to think one up. "Well," he said, "I suppose he needs to know where you kids hang out, so if you need him, he'll know where to find you."

"Need him for what?" Gary asked.

"For protection," Louis shot back. "You got the cops and the mob looking for you. You might need his help sooner than later."

"Jesus Christ," Pete spat, "what the hell do you want, Pecker, a signed contract? The mob doesn't work that way. We're lucky to have him."

Gary fell silent but told us later that he was suspicious of Louis's intentions. Pete didn't want to hear it. He couldn't wait to meet il Tasso.

We watched as Louis backed his car out of the logging road. Louis drove back to the Hill and dropped Johnny off, then went to a nearby motel for the night.

CHAPTER 32

Buffalo Bill

Crazy Phil 'Bomb-Bomb' and Dominic 'the Hunckback' decided to not arrive on the Hill in a Caddy but instead drove a Chevy. "Phil," the Hunchback said, "we should get more money for drivin' around in a piece-of-shit Chevy, know what I'm sayin?"

"Yeah," Crazy Phil responded, "what can you do? Boss got the case of the ass, and we can't be complaining about no Caddy, Hunch. Got to do the job with this, that's it. Little Nicky said after what's gone down, a Caddy would draw attention."

"Okay," the Hunchback said, "but I ain't got to like it. Hey, there's a store on the right, pull up here while I run in and get a pack of Pall Malls. If they have them in this shit-ass town. Phil, you want anything?"

"No, but maybe I'll come with you and buy some candy or a soda. It's Saturday; stores are closed tomorrow."

"Better not park on this hill," Hunch said, "this town is like the Seven Hills of Rome, for Christ sake. Back down here a little and pull over on this side street."

As Crazy Phil backed the car down Ashland to make a right onto Price Street, a pickup truck came up behind them, and the driver laid on the horn. "Wait, Phil, goddamnit," the Hunch said as he reached inside his jacket for his gun, "stop the car, let me put a bullet in his head."

As Phil slammed on the brakes, the Hunchback flung open the door and started to get out. "Hunch," Crazy Phil hollered, "no, not now, get back in."

The Hunchback stepped out onto the street and yelled, "Hey, go around dickhead, or I'll put a bullet between your ears."

The truck sped around; as it did, the driver gave them the finger. "You see that," Hunch exploded, "Mama Mia, let's go after that no-good son of a bitch."

As Hunch got back in and closed the door, Phil said, "Hunch, take it easy. We got a job to do. We can't go after nobody until we whack them kids. Take it easy, will you? Get a hold of yourself."

"Madonn, we'll come back later and get that bastard, I'll remember that truck," Hunch growled.

"Easy, Hunch," Phil repeated. "Settle down. Forget about it. You need a smoke. Let me park here on this shit street, and we'll go in."

Phil backed the car further and then turned onto Price and parked. The two hitmen got out of the car and walked around to the store named Karl the Butcher's. They entered the store and walked to the counter where Karl and his wife Ruth were waiting on two customers. Carl, a big burly man, who, if he had a white beard, could've passed for the real Santa Clause. Ruth, who wouldn't be mistaken for a runway model, had streaks of white marbled through her back hair and had the nervous habit of wiping her hands on her apron every couple of minutes, whether she needed to or not.

Phil and Hunch waited patiently while Carl and Ruth waited on a man ordering a variety of food: rolls, lunchmeats, cheeses, candy, sodas, and Tastykakes. The man's wife came down from the toilet paper aisle and said," George, here, the kids will need these in the woods. God knows what they've been using up to now."

Crazy Phil looked at the Hunchback. Then he turned and said to the woman, "A-scuse a me lady, you taking that stuff camping or somethin'?' That's a whole lot of stuff, no what I'm saying? And all that toilet paper. Madonn, somebody got the shits or something?"

George Ferraco took the toilet paper from his wife and added it to the pile they were collecting. George and Carl the Butcher locked eyes, before Carl said, "Can I help you, gentlemen?"

"Well," Phil replied, "you ain't done waitin' on these people. I'm not buttin' in front of nice people like them. Wouldn't be polite now, would it? What did you say your name was?"

"I didn't say mister, but it's Carl, Carl the Butcher," he replied.

"Carl the Butcher?" Phil mocked. He laughed and hit Hunch with the back of his hand. "Holy shit, maybe I can get you a job where I come from, no what I'm sayin'? Carl the fuckin' Butcher, that's some name," then he and Hunch laughed again.

Phil straightened up a bit, and his smile disappeared. He pointed his finger at Carl and said, "Until then Goombah, keep your fuckin' mouth shut, capeesh?"

Then Phil turned back to the lady. "Ma'am, you says you is takin' this stuff to kids? Is that what I heard you say?"

"What she meant," George explained, "is that we are visiting our children and grandchildren, and we always take a care package."

"So, where them grandchildren live?" Hunch asked, suddenly realizing what Phil was thinking.

"Ah," George murmured, "we don't like giving our grandchildren's addresses out to strangers."

"Nobody's asking for addresses," Phil mocked sarcastically, "my friend is just asking where they live. Russia? Spain? Conshohocken? This shit, town?"

"Gentlemen," Carl asked, "is there something you want, cigarettes or…"

"Hey," Hunch scoffed, lifting his arm and pointing his finger at Carl, "I said, shut your mouth."

Carl slowly moved his hand down and fingered a meat cleaver hanging on a nail inside the edge of the counter. He glared at the two men.

"Now, lady," Hunch urged, as he put his hand inside his sports jacket indicating he was reaching for his piece, "my friend asked you a question."

Carl grabbed the cleaver off the nail and laid it gently on the counter in front of him. "Now I'm sure you gentlemen are well-armed," Carl said, "even so, I cut meat for a living and with two swings with this razor-sharp cleaver I can turn your arm into a shoulder cut, and on the backswing get the other one at the elbow for spareribs. So, before you pull out that six-shooter, I'd do some thinking. I might end up dead, but you'll be sucking your liquids from a straw."

Ruth meanwhile slipped unnoticed through the doorway leading to the store's storage room. She fumbled through the top desk drawer until she found the keyring with the key to the metal cabinet. Carl is a deer hunter, and he and Ruth own a cabin in the Poconos. They often locked up the store on Friday afternoon and went directly to the cabin. Therefore, Carl kept his hunting gear in the cabinet.

Ruth quickly put on Carl's bright orange hunting coat, hunting pants, and hat, then lifted his 30-30 lever-action Marlin rifle from the cabinet. She quietly snuck out the back door and hurried around the corner to the store's front entrance. Carefully, and as quietly as she could, she opened the door and slipped unnoticed into the store. On her tiptoes, Ruth snuck down the canned goods aisle and came up behind Crazy Phil and the Hunchback.

"Freezer," she yelled, pointing the Marlin at the two men.

Now Ruth never held a gun in her life and spent her time on the deck reading paperbacks while Carl trudged through the woods looking for a buck. She wouldn't know a bullet from a bestseller, and therefore the gun wasn't loaded. Nevertheless, Phil and Hunch didn't know that, and she sure looked like a hunter.

Both men turned to look, and Hunch said, "What the...who's this? Buffalo Bill?"

They were staring down the barrel of the Marlin, held by a woman who looked like she came out of a deer-stand in the Poconos.

"Ah, I think she means freeze, gentlemen," Carl proclaimed. "She spends a lot of time in the walk-in freezer. But she can nick the whisker of a possum at a hundred yards."

"Looks to me like she don't know how to hold it," Hunch quipped.

"Play me," Ruth shouted.

"Play me?" Crazy Phil snapped. "Play me?" and he turned and looked at Hunch. Hunch shrugged.

The front door opened, and a customer entered the store. Carl watched a beautiful young blond who he immediately recognized stroll down the paper goods aisle. She was the heartthrob of any man, short blond hair and a beautiful — Grace Kelly looking — face. The perfect combination of pretty and sexy.

"Dorothy Ann," Carl hollered, "get out of here; we're closed."

"I just came in to say hello," Dit announced, used to a more approachable Carl. So Dit joined the standoff party and chirped, "Ruth, is that you in the hunting stuff? You look so funny."

Crazy Phil reached and grabbed Dit's arm and pulled her to his side. "Hey, get away from me," Dit complained, "you're hurting my arm." At the same time, he pulled out his piece and put it to Dit's ear. "Now who's sucking on a straw, fat man?" Phil dared, as he looked at Carl. Hunch also pulled his gun out, and the standoff was now a hands-up.

"Ma Barker," Phil barked, "put down that pea shooter nice and easy. And you, fat man the hacker, lay down the meat ax. Everyone else, get your hands up, now."

"Ow, you're hurting my arm, ease up," Dit protested.

"You love it baby, and you know it," Phil said.

"Drop dead asshole," Dit fumed.

"All right, we're backing out of here just like the fat man said," Crazy Phil stated, "only we're taking Sweet Pea with us, and if anyone of you makes a move, I'll put a slug right in her ear. Got it?"

Hunch and Phil backed up the vegetable aisle with Phil holding Dit by the arm. When they got outside, Phil flipped Hunch the keys and told him to open the trunk. "In you go, Sweet Pea," Phil demanded.

Dit began kicking her feet and screaming for help. It took both of them to get her in the trunk and get it closed. Dit hit Phil with a solid kick on the side of his head. "Bitch," Phil cursed. With the trunk lid down, Dit was kicking her feet and swearing like a sailor. Crazy Phil and the Hunchback got in, and Phil turned the key. He stomped on the accelerator, and they took off down Price Street.

"Phil," Hunch yelled, as Dit kicked and screamed in the trunk, "where we goin'?"

Phil gripped the steering wheel tightly with both hands and stared angrily at the road. He shouted, "I don't know. I'll let you know when we get there."

CHAPTER 33

Nabbed

The two detectives ran most of the way to Carl the Butchers. Police cars blocked off Price and Ashland Streets. As they entered the store, they saw two detectives talking to Carl and Ruth and the Ferraco's. Next to Carl and Ruth sat an elderly couple. "Hey Mike," Tommy Lochran said to Lower Merion detective Mike Brennan.

"Loch, glad you're here. "

"What happened?" detective Butch Frost asked.

"About 1:30 p.m.," Brennan said, "two men came in the store and stood over there to get waited on. These folks were buying groceries and the men, both with heavy Italian accents, asked them questions about what they were buying. They got a little pushy and Ruth, the woman over there, Carl the Butcher's wife, snuck out the back of the store and came around through the front door with Carl's deer rifle."

"No shit," Lochran said. "Ruth did, huh? Would have loved to have seen that."

"Was the rifle loaded," Frost asked.

"No," Brennan replied. "She said she was trying to scare them away. Thought maybe they would leave after looking down the barrel of the Marlin 30-30."

"Would scare me away," Lochran stated.

"Then a young blond woman came in the store and back to the counter here, and one of the men grabbed her and pulled a gun. Both pulled their guns. They backed out of the store and took off with the blond. The older couple over here saw them leave the store from their front porch."

Lochran and Frost followed Brennan to the older man and woman sitting next to the bread rack.

"Ma'am," Brennan said, "this is detective Lochran and Frost. They'd like to talk to you."

The elderly couple had white hair and were in their mid-eighties; frail, yet spunky. Thin and a little bent over.

"Afternoon, ma'am," Frost said, "and you are…"

"The Thompsons," the man said, "Mabel and Bernie."

"You saw them come out of the store?" Lochran asked, "did you recognize the woman?"

"Yes," the woman replied, "Dorothy Ann from up the street. Everybody calls her Dit. She's an awfully nice young woman. One of them had a hold of her and pulled her along. She was putting up a good fight. Trying to get away from them."

"Did you see them put her in the car?"

"Not from our front window," Bernie answered. "They turned onto Price Street. But I hurried out on the sidewalk and walked down a little, and they were closing the trunk. She was screaming and putting up a pretty good fight."

"You saw her in the trunk?" Frost asked.

"I saw her feet kicking out of the trunk when he closed it."

"You didn't happen to get the plate number of the car?" Lochran asked.

"Oh no," Bernie replied, "my eyes ain't what they use to be."

"Okay, sir, ma'am," Lochran said, "can you write your name and address on this tablet? We may visit again if we have further questions."

"Certainly," Bernie said.

The three detectives walked over to where Carl and Ruth were talking to the other detective. Carl recognized Frost and Lochran. "I know these two fellows," Carl said. "Been coming into the store since they were kids. How are you, boys?"

"Carl, Ruth," Frost said.

"Looks like you had some trouble here," Lochran said.

"Loch," Carl responded, "them fellows were up to no good. Mean kind of men."

"Foul talking, too," Ruth groused.

"I think they would have gunned us all down and wouldn't have thought twice about it," Carl stated. "That's the kind of men they were."

"Have they ever been in the store before?" Frost asked them.

"No, never saw them," Carl replied.

Detective Lochran was watching George and his wife talking with the elderly couple. "Butch," he said to his partner, "isn't that the guy who works at the incinerator?"

Frost looked over. "Yea," he said, "Ferraco. George Ferraco. He was involved with the mafia guy they found on the dump road naked and drunk. He called it in. Let's talk to him."

"Wait, Butch," Lochran interjected, "he found the guy on the dump road?"

"Yeah," Frost responded, "I read the file."

"How far down on the dump road?" Lochran asked his partner.

"I think pretty far down, close to Centennial Road."

Lochran turned to look at his partner. "You can't see that far down the dump road from the incinerator."

"Yeah, probably right," Frost said.

"So how did he call it in if he can't see him?" Lochran wondered aloud.

"I don't know," Frost responded, "that's a damn good question. Let's go ask him."

As Lochran and Frost moved away to speak with George Ferraco, detective Brennan said, "Loch, Butch, we're out of here unless you want us to stay. Looks like it's in your ballpark."

"Mike," Frost said, "thanks. Good job here."

Frost and Lochran approached the Ferraco's. "George," Lochran said, I'm Tommy Lochran of the Lower Merion Police, and this is detective Frost."

"Oh, sure, fellows," Ferraco responded, "you boys are from the Hill, right?"

"That's correct, sir," Frost answered.

"How did the two men in here engage you in conversation," Lochran asked.

"They wanted to know what we were buying," George replied.

"Why would they care what you're buying?" Frost asked.

"Not sure," Ferraco replied. "Guess they through it was strange the stuff we were buying."

"So, what did you tell them," Frost asked.

"Ah," Ferraco said, "said it was for our grandkids."

"So was it for your grandkids," Lochran asked.

"Well, no, not really," Ferraco said.

"Why did you tell them that then?" Frost asked.

"Ah, not sure," Ferraco responded.

"This your stuff sitting on the counter?" Lochran asked.

"Yep, that's our stuff."

"George, didn't you report the guy on the dump road who was naked and drunk?" Frost asked.

"Yeah, that was me."

"Well, that's funny," Lochran added, "I'm not a hundred percent sure, but I don't think you can see down the dump road from the incinerator, can you?"

"Yeah, that'd be tough," Ferraco responded.

"So, who told you he was drunk and naked on the dump road," Frost asked.

"Well, I decided to leave that way. You know, go down the dump road to Centennial Road," Ferraco said. "Then up Mary Waters Ford."

"Isn't it a lot easier going out to Woodbine? The dump road is a rough, dirt road."

"Well, sure," he answered. "Sometimes, you know, you want a change of scenery."

"George, you're not trying to protect anybody are you?" Frost asked.

"No, no," he stammered.

"George," Lochran said, "I think we have a problem here. We want to take you out to Ardmore to ask you some more questions. You'll have to come with us, please."

"Are you arresting my husband?" Mrs. Ferraco asked.

"No, ma'am, not at all," Lochran replied. "We're taking him to police headquarters so we can sit down and discuss this kidnapping and some other issues we have."

"And what other issues would that be?" Mrs. Ferraco asked.

"We're not ready to discuss that now ma'am," Lochran said. "We'll have an officer take you home. Mr. Ferraco, please come with us, sir."

Detective Frost leaned in close to his partner and said softly, "Loch, we don't have a car, remember? We're undercover."

"Oh, yea that's right," Lochran chuckled. "We'll have an officer out front take him in, and we'll walk up to our car. Where is our car?"

"I believe it's in your driveway, Loch," Frost responded, smiling.

"Right, let's go."

CHAPTER 34

The Introduction

Hiding out from the police and the mafia on top of the Flat Rock Tunnel left us with long days and nights. We had no televisions, telephones, or stuff to read. So, we invented our own board game. We played it day and night.

The board game focused on the probability of the hitters on each team: I had the Phillies, Pete the Yankees, and Gary the Cardinals. Mickey never played, but he watched and made sure the probabilities were consistent.

The player at bat rolled four dice, resulting in 1,296 equally likely outcomes. Each card had different outcome possibilities.

Ken Boyer on Gary's Cardinals, for example, had a better chance of hitting a home run or extra-base hit, than Cardinal shortstop, Dal Maxville, a light hitter. On Pete's Yankees, Mickey Mantle had a much higher probability of hitting one out than Bobby Richardson.

I made up the number-combinations on each batter from newspaper box scores and baseball cards. Nobody ever questioned them. Occasionally I had to change the outcome possibilities if a light hitter like Maxville was hitting too many home runs. Amazingly, the numbers were similar to the real-life numbers.

We didn't have pitcher dice-probabilities. Even so, we kept pitching records and would bring in a relief pitcher if we had luck when he was on the mound. We were in the ninth of a good game when we were interrupted.

"Hey, we got visitors," Mickey, positioned to watch the tracks, yelled. We dropped what we were doing and joined Mickey at the lookout spot.

"Can you make them out?" Gary asked.

"I think one of them is Louis," I said. "Not positive but I think so."

"Yeah," Mickey said, "I think you're right. But who's the other one?"

"He walks like my father," Pete said. "Could he be the one from Italy that Louis told us about."

"Hope it's not your father," I said. "No, I don't think it is. They're coming closer. Pete, I think you're right. I've never seen him before."

"I hope this guy's friendly," Gary said.

"We're fucked if he's not," I said.

"One of us should go down and lead them up here," Mickey said.

"Good job for you," Pete pointed out. "You're on lookout duty, anyway."

Mickey got up and started down the path that led down the side of the tunnel opening. "Be careful," Gary said. "Don't be nervous."

Mickey stopped and looked back. "Shit, just going to meet a mafia killer. Why the hell should I be nervous?"

We laughed. Not a 'ha, ha laugh,' but an 'oh, shit kind of laugh.'

Mickey disappeared down the side of the tunnel, and we moved back to our campsite. We tried to tidy up if you can tidy up a campsite on top of the Flat Rock Tunnel that four 15-year old's made. It took an hour for Louis and the Luzzi hitman, the il Tasso, to get to the Hill. Mickey greeted them on the tracks and brought them up. We heard them before we saw them.

All eyes were on il Tasso. Strange looking guy. The first thing I noticed was his sharp eyes that darted around taking in each of us. He was small, but his hands were enormous. His neck was thick, and he stood in front of us with a look of confidence. But he appeared friendly, and when he locked eyes with Pete, he smiled, as if he had met Pete before. We stood there silently just taking it all in before Louis broke the ice on the hitman.

"I'm glad we had the chance to meet," Louis said. "Mr. Giovanni Randazzo here…" and Louis stopped. "Mr. Giovanni," Louis asked, "what should we call you?"

"Giovanni, of course," Pete offered. "That's what he's called in Luzzi."

Giovanni smiled and said, "America John."

There was a pause, and he said, "You Pete?"

"I'm Pete, John, from Luzzi. Born there and left with my family at age seven."

Giovanni put his bag down and walked toward Pete. He hugged Pete and slapped his back several times. We all swore we saw Pete wipe a tear away. He didn't admit it later, and in fact, he said his famous, "Get the fuck out of here." Even so, Pete pulled himself together and said, "John, this is Gary, and Mickey and this dipshit here is Ronny. We're glad you're here."

"Glad, too," John said.

"I'll take John to a hotel once you get acquainted," Louis said. "Take all the time you need."

John looked at Louis and said, "No leave."

We stood there, not sure what to say. I looked first at Pete, then at Louis. I sure as hell wasn't going to open my mouth, so Louis spoke first. "You want to stay here, with the boys?" He asked John.

John turned slightly and looked at Pete, then back at Louis. "Stay here," he said again.

"Well," Louis said, "we'll need to get you a sleeping bag and maybe a change of clothes…"

John stopped him cold. "Need nothing."

By this time, I was starting to get a feel of the situation, and I could see that Louis was handling him carefully. "Okay," Louis said, "whatever you like. The police are after these boys, and they could show up here at any time. I want to caution you about that."

"Va, fungool."

We exchanged glances. We could see that John said what he meant, if only two words at a time, and handled Louis; not the other way around. We had a famous hitman from Italy suddenly joining our camp. A guy who appeared to take shit from nobody. It was cool but scary. One thing was sure; Pete was happy about it.

On the other side of town, Crazy Phil took the City Line exit off the Expressway and merged into the exit ramp toward City Line Avenue. Dit was still kicking and screaming in the trunk. On occasion, the Hunchback shouted, "Shut up, ya crazy bitch."

"We're going to the Marriott," Crazy Phil said. "We're gonna put her in a room there and gag her and tie her up. You and me will get a room next door and try to figure this thing out. Whatever we do we can't let Angelo know we have her or we'll be buried alongside Porky Bananas."

The Hunchback looked at Phil, looked at the road, then turned back to Phil again and said, "You don't think he'll know when he hears about us takin' this broad? I mean, I'm sure it's all over the news. What else could we do, Phil? We had to take her."

"True," Phil said. "People get kidnapped all the time, I guess. He probably won't tie it to us. He'll think some sick assholes out after pussy grabbed her. That ain't us."

Phil turned into the Marriot Motor Hotel and drove to the far end of the parking lot where he stopped and turned off the motor. He turned to the Hunch and said, "Hunch, open the glove compartment and give me the muffler." Hunch removed the silencer from the glove compartment and handed it to Phil, who screwed it onto the end of his gun.

"You go get two rooms and come back," Phil instructed, "I'm gonna talk to this broad. If we got to whack her, we could dump her down in back of the airport."

"But we ain't got no shovels," Hunch said.

"Don't worry, we'll get 'em, now go get the rooms."

Hunch got out and headed toward the hotel. Phil followed him out of the car but went to the trunk. He bent over slightly.

"Hey," he said, "beautiful, we can do this nice-nice, or we can do this not so nice, it's up to you, sweetheart."

"Up, yours," Dit yelled.

"All right, all right," Phil said, "I know you're upset, gettin' thrown in the trunk and all. But I need to talk to you. I'm going to open the trunk and speak to you in a nice way, and all that."

"Drop dead," Dit yelled again. "My boyfriend gets ahold of you, and you're dead meat."

"All right, I can drive you down behind the airport, open the trunk and put a bullet in your head and nobody will ever find you. And we're done with the problem, capeesh? You ain't got no say in it if you know what I'm talking about."

No response.

"That's better. Now, you just walked in that store not expecting all this, and you got yourself in a shit jam. We don't want you any more than you want to be here, so we got to get out of this so both sides wins, capeesh?

"All right, I'm holding a gun, and I'm gonna slowly open the trunk. If you make trouble, I swear to God I'll shoot you right here and we'll bury you at the airport."

Phil reached inside his jacket and pulled out his gun. He slowly inserted a key into the trunk lock and turned it slightly, then some more until the trunk-lid latch clicked and the trunk popped loose. Slowly Phil raised the lid. Dit, laying in a fetal position, sat up and glared at Phil.

"All right, good," he said. "That's good cause I want us both to get out of this. I know you do too. We're both in a tight spot here. But if we work together, we can work it out without anybody gettin' hurt."

"Who the hell are you," Dit demanded. "And why the hell did you put me in this goddamn trunk?"

"Whoa, you got a mouth for a sweet lookin' babe. We got in a tight spot in that store, and you were our way out, is all."

"If I do what you say, then you'll shoot me anyway."

"That's not the case. No. Now, when my partner comes back, we're gonna walk in that Marriot you and me across the lobby, get in an elevator and go to your room. Nice and easy, no trouble, understand? Just like we're husband and wife."

"Get lost," Dit said, as she pushed herself toward the back of the trunk, "I'm not going to some goddamn hotel room with you as husband and wife, you think I'm nuts?"

"You're not going in the room with me, capeesh? You're going in your own room, and me and my partner will have a different room, all nice-nice. Nothin' sexual intended or nothin', we're not intended for anything like that."

"How do I know you're sayin' this shit just to get me in the room?"

"I'm asking you to trust me so we both can get out of this one. Here comes my partner."

"Got two rooms side by side," Hunch said, as he approached the back of the car. "You gonna trust her? If she goes crazy in the lobby, we're screwed."

"This is what you're gonna do, Hunch," Phil said. "You're gonna move the car. Get it as close to the hotel door as you can. You stay in the car with the motor running and leave the passenger door open a few inches. When you're in place, she and me will go in the hotel and walk across the lobby. If she tries any shit, I'm a gonna drill her with two shots, one in the head and the other in the back. I'll come runnin' out that door like a starvin' dog after the meat truck. You hear all this, Sweet Pea?"

"Yeah, I hear it," Dit said. "First you say you're going to treat me nice and next you say you're going to shoot me in the head. So how can I trust you?"

"No," Phil responded, "I'll shoot you in the head if you act up. Screaming or something. If that happens, I'll leave your brains all over the lobby. I can't afford to get caught by no police. I'm just telling you I mean business."

Dit looked away.

"Alright, Hunch," Phil said, "give me the room keys." Hunch handed Phil both room keys.

"All right," Phil said, "park the car near the door. Once we go through the doors, give us twenty minutes. If everything's quiet after 20 minutes, park the car and come up to the room."

Phil looked at both keys. "Come to room 801. Oh, and bring the supplies box, we'll need that, too." Phil looked at Hunch to make sure he understood. Hunch nodded.

Phil grabbed Dit by the arm and said, "Let's go, we're on Sweetpea. If you try to run, I'll blast you in the back and then in the head."

Dit and Crazy Phil walked side by side toward the hotel entrance. Phil held his gun inside his jacket. They watched Hunch park the Chevy just outside the hotel door. When they got to the entrance, Phil stopped.

"Okay, Sweet Pea, put your arm in my arm like we're, you know like we're intended."

Dit did what he said and then looked away in disgust.

"One move the wrong way, and you're dead. Here we go."

CHAPTER 35

"John Dig. You Dirt."

When detectives Lochran and Frost left the store, the detective Mike Brennan was waiting for them on the sidewalk.

"Loch," Brennan said, "the woman kidnapped in the store? She's the sister of one of the kid witnesses in the cherry trees. "

"You're shitten me," Loch responded.

"No," Brennan said, "the Captain got me on the radio and wanted me to tell you."

"Does he want us off the case?" Lochran asked.

"No, I don't think so," Brennan replied, "at least he didn't say anything."

"Thanks, Mike," Lochran said. "I appreciate you telling me."

"He did say," Brennan continued, "that he will talk to the newspapers and try to get them to sit on the kidnapping story. He said if it gets out and the kidnapper knows the girl is the kid's sister, it could put her in even more danger. But he said he didn't know how successful he'd be."

"Thanks, Mike. We're going out to headquarters now. I'm sure he'll speak to us about it."

"You got it, Loch," Brennan said, "good luck with this."

After making arrangements to take George Ferraco to Ardmore, Lochran and Frost walked up the hill to get their detective car in Lochran's driveway. Frost knew when Loch needed time to think, so he kept quiet. They reached the car and started for Ardmore. Nearly there, Loch spoke up."

"It'll hit the newspapers," Lochran said. "And when it does the mob will want to make a trade. Otherwise, they'll kill the girl. Do you know something? We got to bust the incinerator's guy's balls. He knows where those kids are."

Frost looked at his partner. "I agree with you. He's got to cooperate so we can get to those kids. If not, the mob controls the situation, and when that happens, people end up dead."

They remained silent for the rest of the ride to Ardmore. Upon entering the building, the desk sergeant was nicer. He knew when to keep his mouth shut.

"Want you fellows to know they have the incinerator guy in interview room one, but the Captain wants to see you first," he told the two detectives.

Lochran nodded, "Okay, thanks."

Two FBI agents were in with the Captain when Lochran and Frost entered the office. "Take a seat fellows," the captain said. "You boys know agents Watts and Hacket?" The four lawmen shook hands.

"Sure, how are you, gentlemen?" Frost said as they shook hands.

"Okay, so some things have changed," the Captain said. "We now got a kidnapping on our hands. If there's any evidence that the Dorothy Ann woman was taken across state lines, you guys are off the case, and the Bureau takes over."

"They won't cross state lines," Lochran said.

"How can you be so sure?" agent Watts asked.

"Look," Lochran said, "we got four boys who witnessed the Ott's murders hiding out someplace. We got a guy sitting in an interview room right now who may know where the boys are. And the mob has the girl. Once they find out she's one of the kid's sister, they're not going to leave the area. They'll stay here and try to scare them by offering a trade. Then they'll kill all five of them."

"How are they going to do that if they don't know where the boys are, either?" the Captain asked.

"We've worked on some mafia cases," detective Frost said, "we know a little about how they work. They'll move hard and fast. They want those kids whacked to protect their hitmen."

"We've worked on a lot more mob cases than you two," agent Hacket said. "In this situation, they don't have to work fast. They have all the cards. They have the woman, and you don't have the kids. Why do they have to be fast, here? They will find a way to use the woman to get what they want."

"So right now," Lochran asked, "there is no evidence of them crossing a state line with her?"

"That's right," the Captain said, leaning against the front of his desk.

"So, we need to get to the man in the interview room, if you don't mind," Lochran said.

The Captain unfolded his arms and looked at the two FBI agents. "He's right, gentlemen. All right get back to work. Let's solve this thing."

As they were about to leave, agent Watts said, "Look, while you work on the guy in the interview room, how about we help you with the girl. Just make some inquiries with our contacts in the under-world?"

"Fine with us," Lochran answered, and the two detectives headed for interview room two.

Back on top of the tunnel, we learned quickly how the Badger worked and began to understand his thinking.

"Need place," the Badger said.

We froze. "What's he mean, Pete?" I asked.

We were already getting a place ready for the Badger to sleep. We were also adjusting to having a stranger among us. We were a tight group of four kids, and now we had an adult in our midst; not just any adult, but a killer adult.

"Sure," Pete said, "you'll have your place here; anywhere you want it."

"No hide."

Mickey and Gary stopped what they were doing and joined Pete and me with John. "What's he saying," Gary asked.

"Not sure what you mean, John," Pete said

"Cops hide," he said again.

"We need a place to hide when the cops come; he's saying," Pete explained.

"Hide good."

"He's right," Gary said.

"Yeah, he is," I said, "but where? If the cops come, they'll be all over this area. I doubt there is…"

"Underground."

"Yeah," Mickey said, "that's brilliant. Good idea, Giovanni."

"Okay," Pete said," but where?"

"America Giovanni."

"Scavatrice di gallerie."

"What?" I asked. "What's he saying?"

"Wait," Pete cautioned. "He's telling us he's a digger."

"Il Tasso."

He's saying in Italy, he's called il Tasso. Right, John?"

John smiled and nodded.

"What the hell is L lasso?" Gary asked, "we can't understand this gibberish."

"Let me think," Pete said. "In Italian, it's some kind of animal."

John smiled. "Tasso Badger," he explained.

"Right," Pete remarked. "Il Tasso, the badger."

"A badger lives underground," Mickey said."

John smiled, then said, "John Badger."

"Jesus H. Christ," Gary remarked, "he lives underground?"

"Badger digger," John said.

"Where John?" Pete asked. "Where should we build a tunnel?"

"I show."

We followed John to the side of the tunnel. When we got to the point to go down, John stopped us.

"Halfway," he said.

"Halfway down the side?" Mickey asked.

John nodded. Then said, "Align tunnel." He made a motion with his hand, signifying that we dig in alongside the tunnel.

"Dig sideways," he said.

"How the hell are we gonna dig along the side of this tunnel?" Gary asked. "You can't stand up down there."

The Badger looked at Gary and smiled. "John dig," he said.

"What about the dirt," Mickey asked. "They'll see the dirt and know we dug a tunnel."

"John dig," he said. He paused and then said, "You dirt."

"He'll dig the tunnel," Pete said, "and we'll get rid of the dirt. But where John, where we can we put the dirt?"

"Dirt tunnel," he said, pointing down toward the tunnel.

"That's brilliant," Mickey announced. "We spread the dirt in the tunnel."

"John show."

We followed him down the side of the tunnel and into the opening of the tunnel. He motioned for us to follow him into the tunnel, which we did, walking on the ties and staying close to one another. We glanced over our shoulders and watched for the one-eyed monster. When we got halfway through the tunnel, he stopped. It was dark. We couldn't see our hands in front of our faces.

"Both sides," we heard him say.

"Against walls," he said.

"Spread the dirt against both the tunnel walls on both sides of the tracks," Pete said. "Is that right, John?"

"Right, Pete."

"Dark there."

"Okay," Gary chimed in, "let's get out of here. This place makes me nervous." No one argued as we followed John back toward the tunnel opening.

No one spoke until we were nearly out of the tunnel. "Brilliant idea, John," Mickey said.

"I dig."

"Take dirt," he said, pointing to us.

"Right, John," Pete said, "we take the dirt."

"How?" Mickey asked. "How are we going to get the dirt we dig halfway into the tunnel?"

"John dig."

"Okay," Mickey said. "You dig. Don't we help you?"

"John dig."

"John, you can't dig by yourself," Pete said.

"Badger," the Badger said, pointing to his chest.

"Okay," I said, "if that's what he wants to do."

"John show."

John started up the side of the tunnel. We followed him. He might be a badger, but he's a mountain goat, too. He climbed up the side so fast he was waiting for us at the top. We were out of breath, but John wasn't. He got his black bag and opened it. It was filled not with guns and explosives, but with digging tools. Digging tools and all kinds of axes, small, big, axes with long handles, and axes with short handles.

214

His digging tools were odd-looking, but we didn't worry, he knew what he was doing. We didn't see any handguns in his bag. Just digging tools and axes. He pointed to the tarp Billy Curry brought us and said, "Pete get."

The Badger was about to give us a lesson in digging a tunnel.

CHAPTER 36

"It's a Safe Bet."

Dit and Crazy Phil started through the main doors of the Marriott Motor Lodge with Dit's arm in Phil's. They looked more like father and daughter than husband and wife.

"Come on," Phil said, "play the part. Don't look so disgusted."

"I am disgusted," Dit said.

They got in the elevator, and Phil pressed the button for the fifth floor. They remained silent until the doors opened, and they walked to room 801. Phil used the key to open the door.

"All right, Sweetpea," Phil said, "sit down."

"You get out, first," Dit demanded, standing in the room with her arms folded.

Phil closed the door behind him and went to the room phone. He jerked the cord out of the wall and wrapped the wires around the phone, then dropped it in the trashcan. He parted the drapes and looked out. "You're not jumping, that's for sure," he said.

He sat on the end of the bed and waited until Hunch knocked on the door. He let Hunch in and latched the door behind him. Hunch gave Phil a bag and Phil dumped it on the bed. Then he pulled his gun out.

"What are you going to do with the rope and shit?" Dit asked.

"We're gonna tie you up so you can't escape," Phil said.

Dit got up from the chair. "Oh, no, you're not," she said, "you didn't say anything about that. You're not tying me up."

Phil lifted his gun and made sure the silencer was secure on the end of it. "I can kill you now and leave you here. He checked in with phony names. They'll find you here in a day or two. Is that what you want?"

"No," Dit answered.

"Then behave and let my partner tie you up. He won't hurt you. We'll bring you a sandwich when we return. You hungry?"

"Yes," Dit said.

Hunch tied Dit to the chair and used a pillowcase and rope to gag her. He was gentle. When he and Phil were convinced she was secure and couldn't get loose; they headed for the door.

"Okay," Phil said, "she ain't going nowhere. Let's go downstairs and get something to eat. Then we gotta find them kids. We'll whack 'em, come back here, whack her, and we're done with this."

"Phil, I got an idea," Hunch said. "When I was with Porky Bananas, he took me to a spot in the woods where he thought them kids were. We got out of the car and walked some, and I shot him dead."

"Hunch," Phil demanded, "what the hell, why haven't you mentioned this before?"

"I didn't think, Phil. I whacked Porky Bananas, and that was that. I forgot he said he swore them kids were there."

"Did you see the kids," Phil asked his partner.

"No, didn't see nobody. I looked around a little, then left. Next day I helped two dirtbags Angelo hired to move the body. They took it and buried it somewhere, you know, probably by the airport."

"Can you take me to that spot in the woods," Phil asked.

"Yeah, definitely," Hunch replied. "I been there twice. It's like an old shit looking road off the main road."

"Let's go," Phil said, you show me where that spot is."

"It'll be dark soon, Phil," Hunch said, "you want to wait until tomorrow? Besides, we gotta eat something."

Crazy Phil looked over Dit one last time to make sure she was secure, and said, "Let's go Hunch," Phil said as he opened the door, "you show me now."

～

The cops and the mob didn't know where the boys were hiding. But there was someone who did. That, someone, was sitting alone in an interview room at police headquarters. "George," detective Lochran said as he and Frost entered interview room two at Lower Merion police headquarters in Ardmore.

"Gentlemen," George Ferraco responded.

"This is not going to take long, George," detective Lochran began. "We want to know two things. First, do you know where the four boys are? And two if you do where are they?"

"Okay, look," George said. "I don't know where they are right this second. They could be in several places. I did help them. I bought them food and left food on my back porch for them to have access to."

"When you bought them food, George," Frost asked, "where did you meet to give it to them?"

"Down on Centennial Road," George responded. "It was late at night, and they came out of the woods. I don't know where they were. I just met them there."

"Where on Centennial Road?" Lochran asked.

"Just after you turn off Mary Waters Ford, maybe 50 yards," George replied.

"Did they come from the dump?" Frost asked him.

"I believe so," Ferraco said, "but I'm not positive."

"Where else have you met them," Lochran asked.

"At the top of Mary Waters Ford Road," George answered. "If you leave Centennial Road and go up Mary Waters Ford Road toward Penn Valley, at the top there is an old logging road. I met them there."

"You said you left food on your back porch," Frost said. "How did they get it? Did they use the streets?"

"No, sir," George answered, "they came from the railroad tracks."

"So, let me get this right," Lochran stated. "You met them at the top of Mary Waters Ford Road, off an old logging road, correct?"

"Yes," George answered, "that's what I said."

"And they used the tracks to come up behind your home on Jones Street to retrieve the supplies you left out, right?" Lochran asked.

"Yes, that's correct," George replied.

Lochran looked at his partner, then said, "From the point where he met them at the top of Mary Waters Ford, if you draw a straight line from there, you'll come to the railroad tracks."

"Right," Frost replied. "But they wouldn't be hiding out on the tracks; they'd be spotted by the train people who try to keep kids off the tracks."

"That's right," Lochran said, "but what about around the tunnel? On top of that tunnel, you can see pretty far. Then when you need food, you go down the tracks to George's house and get resupplied. Get on the tracks and go back to the tunnel."

"Is that where they are George, on top of that tunnel," Frost asked.

"It's a safe bet," George replied.

"George, have you told us everything you know?" Lochran asked.

"No," George said, "there's one more thing. Do you know why those boys don't want you to catch them?"

"Not sure," Lochran answered. "Are they afraid of something?"

"Yes, they are," George replied. "They have it in their heads that if you grab them, their photos will be in the newspapers and the mob will know who they are. They think that places them and their families in danger."

"But that might not be the case," Frost answered.

"Are you sure about that, detective Frost? Or are you just saying it because you've got a job to do?" George asked.

Frost motioned with his head to his partner, "Let's go, Loch. We've got work to do." Then he turned to George.

"Mr. Ferraco wait out in the main room by the Sargent's desk, an officer will take you home."

CHAPTER 37

The Escape

D it was deep in thought.

How was she going to escape? Phil and Hunch thought things through carefully but made two mistakes. First, they didn't blindfold Dit. Secondly, they spoke within hearing range of her, so she knew they were after her brother and his friends. The mobsters didn't care; they planned to whack Dit, anyway.

Dit could still see in the room. Enough light came through slots in the drapes, and once her eyes adjusted, she could make out most of the objects in the room. The Hunchback tied her to a chair and bound her hands together behind her back. He tied her feet and wrapped the rope around the base of the chair so she couldn't stand, then left her in the middle of the room. She discovered, by jerking her body in one direction or the other, she could move the chair, if only an inch or two. That gave her some mobility, but she was careful not to topple over. If she did, she was done. She'd never be able to get back up.

Although gagged, she could make noise, but it was more like a muffled hum. "Mm, mmm." For anyone to hear, they'd have to be standing right outside the door, and as far as she knew, there wasn't anyone right outside the door. Once, she heard a noise in the hall. She hummed, but the sounds went away. She spotted the water glasses on the desk, two of them together next to an ice bucket on a tray. She began jerking herself to the left and right, moving the chair closer to the desk. It wasn't easy. She moved maybe ten inches, and had to rest; she was tired, and her movement made the rope cut into her hands and feet. Each time she shifted her weight and moved the chair, she winced from the rope burns.

But she was moving. With perspiration burning her eyes and dripping off her chin, Dit continued to move the chair closer to the desk. She felt the sweat on her ankles; it soothed the rope burns and lubricated her ankles beneath the rope.

She could painfully wiggle one foot. With her other heel, she pried off her loafer, taking advantage of the sweat. It wasn't easy, and the rope burns hurt, but her shoe was loose, and it finally slipped off. The more she perspired, the more wiggle room she had with her right ankle. She wiggled her foot as hard as she could and tried to ignore the fiery pain. Slowly, the rope around her ankles loosened and gave her more flexibility. She wiggled her foot so much, she nearly passed out. It was coming; the ropes were loosening. Almost ready to give up, she jerked and pulled and twisted as hard as she could.

Don't stop, she told herself, *don't stop now. Come on, come on, keep pulling and twisting.* She felt the top of her heel slip above the rope. She pulled and twisted again. *Come on, come on.* Her heel was moving. She turned her foot, and she felt the rope move further down her heel. She pulled and wiggled, pulled and wiggled, then, "Yes," she screamed through the stuffing in her mouth.

It was free.

She laid her head back and tried to blink the sweat from her eyes. Her ankles burned as if someone held a match to them. She looked at the two glasses on the desk. She wanted to rest but knew she couldn't waste time. Any minute, they were coming back. She lifted her foot. When she saw her ankle, it frightened her — it was raw and bloody. She lowered her foot briefly, resting it, and then brought it back up. *You can do this*, she told herself. She held her foot up a few seconds and lowered it, again. She had to get her foot up as high as the desk. She lifted it back up and in one motion, swung her leg around and knocked both glasses to the carpet. She turned and looked down at the glasses and rested.

Dit knew what she had to do. Swiveling the chair around, she positioned it where she thought it would land when she toppled over on her right side. She rocked to the left and right. She closed her eyes and forcefully jerked her body to the right, toppling over and falling to the carpet. Her aim was perfect. Not only did the side of the chair smash one glass, it crushed them both, but the shreds of glass cut deeply into her right arm.

Laying on her side and still tied tightly to the chair, she jerked her body around until she positioned herself over the broken glass. She flipped the chair from her right side and onto her back, her hands and arms descending on top of the broken glass.

"Owww, shit," she cried, as the glass cut into her hands and wrists. In ghastly pain, she felt the pieces of glass with her fingers until she found a sizable chunk that she could hold. The rest was easy, but not any less painful. It didn't take long for her to slice through the rope and free first her hands, and then her arms. She grabbed the side of the bed and pulled herself back up to a sitting position. Using the same chunk of glass, she cut herself free. Immediately she ran to the bathroom and held her hands and arms under the running water. The pain was nearly unbearable. While the water eased the burning, she picked out as many of the larger shards of glass as she could; then wrapped a towel around her arms and headed for the door.

In the hallway, Dit ignored the elevator and spotted an exit sign that led to the stairs. *Those assholes won't come up the stairs.* Hurrying down eight flights of steps, she burst through the doors and into the lobby, running toward the hotel's main doors.

"Ma'am," a bellhop inquired, "are you okay?"

She stopped. "Oh, yes, I cut myself on broken glass. Do you have a dime? I need to call my father. He's a doctor, and he told me never to go to any other doctor but him."

"Well, I don't know," the bellhop replied, "I think maybe…"

Dit did her best impression of Grace Kelly and cozied up to the bellhop, "Oh, can't you please help me? You're so sweet. I know you are nice and will lend me a dime. I'll never forget it, I promise."

"Well, okay," he said, not being able to resist. He reached into his pocket, "here, take two dimes in case you dial a wrong number."

"Where's the pay phone?" Dit demanded, her tone changing abruptly.

"Right over there, ma'am," the bellhop said, pointing to a phone on the wall. "Want me to help you, dial?"

Dit ran to the phone and put in the dime. She dialed and waited. "Come on, come on…" she pleaded.

Finally, someone picked up, "Hello?"

"El," Dit shrieked, "it's Dit. You've got to help me."

"Johnny put out the trash, why don't you."

"All right, mamma," Johnny Ciarlello replied, "the trash men don't come until the morning. I'll put it out."

"Now," she demanded. "Time to put it out now."

"All right, all right, for crying out loud, I'll put it out now," he said.

Johnny went out into the backyard through the cellar to get the two trashcans in the back and put them out front. As he lugged one can toward the side of the house, a light caught his eye. It was a light down on the railroad tracks. He set the can aside and made his way to the end of his backyard where he could see better.

There were several men on the tracks with flashlights. Were they Conrail people checking out the condition of the tracks? He couldn't quite see, so he followed the little path that led down to the tracks. He went maybe ten yards and ducked behind a clump of tall grass. He positioned himself so that when he parted the grass, he had a clear view down to where the flashlights were moving in the dark.

No, he thought, *they're not train men, they're cops. Why would the cops be down here this time of night*? He decided to move down closer. Perhaps if he got closer, he could hear them. He moved down as silently as he could. Johnny got to within 20 yards of the men still on the tracks. He could barely hear them.

"I think right here is the best spot," one cop said. "We can see the mouth of the tunnel, but if we move back to this point," the cop explained, as he pointed down the tracks, "we can't be seen."

"So, you think we can stay hidden, yet still watch this side of the tracks," another cop said.

"Definitely," the other cop said. "And if they break this way, we can stay back and grab them as soon as they make this turn."

"I think Marty is right," yet a third cop added, "they will come down the tracks to here and cut up this bank to get up to Leedom Avenue and pointed to exactly where Johnny was hiding. He slowly pulled his hands away from the grass. He lowered his head to hear better.

"Well, they can't run to the woods," the first cop said, "so they will bolt in this direction, and we'll nab them."

They? Johnny thought. *They must be Mickey, Gary, Pete and Ronny. They gotta be they.*

Johnny watched the flashlights move up the tracks where the cops used a broader path to get to their cars on Jones Street. When he was sure they were gone, he went back up the path to his backyard and into the cellar.

"Ma," he yelled up the steps, "I'm going out for a while, be back later and put the trash out then.

Johnny's mom opened the basement door and began yelling down to him in Italian. Johnny went back out through the door, closed it behind him and headed for the tracks. He made sure the cops left. When he was sure, he went down to the tracks and headed for the tunnel.

CHAPTER 38

Broken Bones

As Crazy Phil drove toward the Hill, he turned and said to Hunch, "Hunch, turn on the radio, put on that KY whatever shit, you know news all the time."

"Yeah, Phil, good idea," Hunch said, "we'll see if there's anything on about us being in Carl the hacker's store, piece of shit that it was. We probably got bedbugs in there."

"Hunch, you only get bedbugs in bed."

"Yeah, yeah, I know," Hunch said, "you never know. I was just sayin' to my brother in law."

"Hunch, wait, shut up, here it is. Turn it up."

"*And the kidnapping is believed to be related to the husband and wife who were murdered in Belmont Hills several weeks ago. The police are still looking for four boys who allegedly witnessed the murders. The woman abducted is the sister of one of the boys…*"

"Mother fucker," Phil shouted and jerked the wheel of the Chevy nearly hitting an oncoming car head-on. Phil made a U-turn in the middle of City Line Avenue.

"Phil, watch it," Hunch yelled as he nearly hit another car. "Jesus Christ, mother of angels, I thought we was dead. Where you goin' now, Phil?"

"That broad is the kid's sister?" Phil hollered. "We've got her in our hands. This is it, Hunch, we've got her, we've got the kids. This whole thing is over, and we whack them kids and then whack her, and we collect our pay."

"And get back to drivin' a Caddy, but where you going now, Phil?" Hunch groaned, "I thought we was going in the woods to whack them kids."

"I'm goin' back to get that broad," Phil roared, "she'll lead us to them kids, Hunch. It's all over. We died and went to heaven, my friend."

Crazy Phil turned off City Line Avenue and sped up the ramp to the Marriott motor Lodge. He parked in the first spot he found open and he and the Hunchback fast-walked toward the Marriott's main doors. They boarded the elevator and Phil pushed button eight. He turned to his partner and said, "We've been handed a gift by God, almighty."

Hunch blessed himself and said, "Madonn, Jesus, Mary, and Joseph."

The two mafia hitmen hurried down the hallway, and Phil put his key in the slot and opened the door. He flicked on the lights, and said, "What the…. Where'd she go?"

"How could she have gotten loose, Phil?" Hunch asked as he pushed open the bathroom door. "Hey, Phil, look at the blood in the sink. What happened here?"

"Goddamnit," Phil scoffed, "she knocked those glasses off by the desk and broke them. Then she cut herself loose. Son of a bitch."

"She ain't been gone long, Phil," Hunch added. "Maybe we can still find her. She's probably on foot. Let's go, let's find the bitch."

Phil and Hunch ran back out to their car and sped out of the Marriott parking lot onto City Line Avenue. Phil drove up City Line Avenue maybe two miles and turned around.

"I don't see her anywhere," Hunch said, "what do you want to do?"

"We've got to back to South Philly," Phil stated," ditch this car and figure out what to do next."

Detectives Lochran and Frost were members of a hunting camp called Broken Bones, or, BB, as most of the members called it. It was nestled deep in the woods near the Pennsylvania Grand Canyon, called God's Country, at least that's how the sign read on Route 6. Once off the main road — six miles west and four miles south of the postcard-picture town of Wellsboro — the camp members traveled for another five miles on a rough, potholed filled dirt road that wound up through the mountains. The road dead-ended at a wooden fence chained shut by several padlocks with a sign that read:

Camp Broken Bones
No Trespassing

The two detectives were the only "flatlanders" in the camp. In most cases, flatlanders weren't welcome in a hunting camp made-up of experienced deer hunters. Broken Bones' rank and file hunters lived their entire lives within a 50-mile radius of Wellsboro. But detective Tommy Lochran had a cousin in the camp who invited him and his partner Butch Frost up to hunt in 1958 — not as members but as opening day guests. Hunting deer is just one reason for membership in a hunting camp. There are plenty of other activities: such as card playing, drinking, joke-telling — the dirtier, the better — farting and belching at will, eating with your mouth open, pissing off the porch, talking about women, and eyeballing through the stack of Playboy magazines piled up near the bathroom door. The fact that Lochran and Frost were Philadelphia detectives and could drink, cuss, spit, shoot, and tell jokes with the best of them, made them camp favorites and with that came an invitation for camp membership.

Besides, hunting camp was a pleasant diversion for the two detectives who made the six-hour drive to Broken Bones and left behind the complex problems of law enforcement. Most deer hunters entered the woods at dawn, found a good spot to sit — whether it be in a tree stand or hidden in what looked like "a good spot" on the ground — and waited. Eventually, if the hunter was quiet and downwind, deer might move through, allowing the hunter a decent shot.

The problem with that way of hunting was that deer used their moist, sensitive noses and sharp eyesight to detect danger. It a deer didn't like what it saw or smelled; it ran, without the hunter getting off a shot. Besides, the deer often bedded down in the thick brush and didn't move. Even so, many deer were killed annually in Pennsylvania by hunters who sat and waited.

But as members of Broken Bones, Frost and Lochran learned a new way to hunt: They drove the deer. At dawn, 15 or so hunters spread out across the top of a ridge. Several hundred yards away, seven "spotters" sat hidden and waited. The drivers drove the deer into the spotters, and if the drive was good, the deer ran through the woods like the little ducks at a boardwalk shooting gallery. Deer drives were so successful, most of the Broken Bones' hunters had their deer in a few days.

Therefore, it wasn't surprising that Lochran and Frost figured out a way to drive the four kid witnesses out from hiding at the top of the Flat Rock Tunnel. The same way they learned to drive deer at Broken Bones. Twenty-four hours after their meeting with George Ferraco, Lower Merion detectives Tommy Lochran and Michael "Butch" Frost, made a presentation at police headquarters: how they were going to grab the four boys who witnessed the Otts' murders.

Meeting in the "strategy room" in Ardmore, four detectives attended besides, of course, Frost and Lochran, and a half dozen uniformed officers freed up from other duties. Plus, the two FBI agents Lou Watts and Ben Hacket, who headed the Bureau's division of organized crime. If and when the boys or the blond woman people called Dit, crossed state lines, Hacket and Watts would step in and take over the investigation.

The Captain strolled to the podium with a slight limp from arthritis that had set in both knees — a degenerative problem that could get him a paper-shuffling desk job or an early retirement — and started the meeting. "Purpose for this meeting, gentlemen, is for all of us to get up to speed on both the kidnapping and whereabouts of the juvenile witnesses. As far as we know at this minute, the woman abducted in the Belmont Hills' grocery store is still missing. Plus, we still have no clues to where the four boys are. Therefore, I'm turning this meeting over to detective Tommy Lochran and his partner Butch Frost, who've been spearheading the investigation."

Tommy Lochran went to the podium while his partner fastened a map on two tripods to the right of the podium. Detective Lochran used a yardstick for a pointer.

"Captain," detective Lochran stated, "as of now we do have an idea where the four juveniles are hiding."

"Good," the captain hollered from the rear of the room, "how soon will they be in custody?"

Lochran ignored the question and started in on his presentation. "The four juveniles are residents of Belmont Hills, shown here on the map. We believe they could be hiding out in this area," he said, as he circled the tip of his pointer on the map. "This is the Flat Rock Tunnel, and we believe the juveniles are hiding here, possibly on top of the tunnel. Agent Watts?"

"If you think they're there, detective," FBI agent Lou Watts asked, "why don't you just go and pick them up?"

"It's not that simple, agent," Lochran replied. "These kids are cagey. They've grown up in the woods, and they're smart."

"They also think they're fighting for their lives," detective Frost added. "They believe if we catch them, their photos will be in the newspapers and they and their families will be in grave danger. Besides, this area here where they're hiding has both thick undergrowth and overgrowth. These kids know it like the back of their hands."

"The longer we play around like amateurs, the longer the boys stay hidden and the longer the Otts' case goes unsolved," detective Lochran added.

"Detective," agent Hacket asked, "I understand the woman that was abducted is the sister of one of the boys in hiding, is that true?"

"It is, agent," Lochran replied.

"Do you think the abduction is related to the Otts' murders and the juveniles on the run?" agent Watts asked.

"Yes," Lochran said. "But not intentionally. I don't believe the mobsters went into the store looking for her. We believe it was coincidental. They got into a situation in the store, and the woman walked in. It was just dumb luck."

"The Packers, owners of the store," Frost pointed out," have identified the two mobsters from file photos as two made men of the Angelo Morello organization in South Philadelphia. They're both killers, and we believe they're both hot on the trail of the four juveniles."

"Loch," detective Brennan, who helped interview the Packer's, said, "why do you think the boys are on top of the tunnel."

"A gentleman in Belmont Hills, Mr. George Ferraco," Lochran answered, "who operates the township incinerator, has met a couple of times with the boys and has given them food. He indicated that in his last meeting with them, they could be in the vicinity of the tunnel. And we agree with him."

"Mr. Ferraco last met with the boys here," detective Frost pointed out on the map, "on an old logging road, and believes the boys went east into the thick woods toward the tunnel."

"Our strategy," Lochran continued, "is to drive them out. From this point on Umbria Street in Manayunk, we can observe the top of the tunnel. If we come at them from this direction, the kids are going to run here, or here. Or across the expressway and into the river. Whichever direction they use, we can nab them."

"We believe," detective Frost said, using a ruler as a pointer, "if we station officers here, and here, and we come at them from this direction, they'll run right into our hands."

"Once we have the kids," Lochran added, "we'll go after the blond woman."

"If she's still alive," agent Watts said.

"Her best chance of staying alive," Lochran added, "is to be used as trade bait for the four kids. Now, the mobsters know they've been seen. So, they'll most likely go back to South Philadelphia to get another car. They may hide the woman in a room above a pizza shop."

"Or in a cellar," agent Watts added. "They're big on cellars."

"We're going to set this up Friday at sunrise," Frost said. "So, we need to do some careful planning."

"What do you need, Loch, Butch?" the Captain asked.

"We need uniformed officers stationed here and here," Lochran said, again pointing to the map. "We need radio communication set up here, in Manayunk, on both sides of the tracks, here and here, and down here, along the river."

The Captain, back at the podium, said, "You got it, detectives. Good work. Let's set this baby up. Any more questions?"

"Yea, there is something more," FBI agent Hacket announced, as he stood up. "This thing is bigger than four boys picking cherries and a woman abducted in a grocery store."

"How so, agent?" the Captain asked.

"The Bureau has done a lot of work monitoring the underworld families both here and abroad," Hacket stated. "Less than a year ago, the President of the United States was murdered. One theory is the President's murder was the work of the La Cosa Nostra."

"We've isolated certain crime families," agent Watts added, "that could have had their hands in the assignation: the Graziano family of Newark, the Gambino's of New York and the Morello people of South Philadelphia. We believe, and this is top secret and goes nowhere outside of this room, that if the mafia was involved, it could have been one of these three families or all of them working together."

"So?" the Captain asked, "what's that have to do with our investigation here?"

"We have evidence," agent Hacket replied, "good evidence, that the Otts had information relating to the Kennedy assignation, and may have been murdered because of what they knew."

"You're kidding," detective Lochran said, "the Otts were in their eighties, what could they have known about Kennedy's murder?"

"It's information we cannot reveal now, Mr. Lochran," agent Watts replied. "What I can tell you is the three families under investigation in the Kennedy murder have some tie in what you are currently investigating. These three families could be at war with each other, and it involved the murders of Mr. and Mrs. Otts."

"So, what does that mean?" detective Frost asked, "as far as the work we are doing with the boys?"

"It means, detective," agent Watts said, "that you could be dealing with a huge threat to national security and our people say it may even have ties to crime syndicates in southern Italy."

"There's evidence," agent Hacket continued, "that the La Cosa Nostra in Italy, namely the Sicilians, may already in some way have their foot in the door and are involved here."

"That's interesting, agent Hacket," Lochran said. "But why would the Sicilians want to get involved in a dispute between domestic families?"

"Look, detectives," agent Watts said, "we know you've put a lot of work into your investigation. But we want you to hold off on this full-scale approach like the one you just outlined. "

"It could turn ugly in those woods," Hacket added. "Some people, including law enforcement and kids, could get killed. We'd like you to sit on this until we're further along in our investigation of the Kennedy assignation."

The Captain interrupted several seconds of silence following agent Watts' remarks. "You're asking us to hold off? We have four witnesses to capital murder, and a woman kidnapped out from under our noses. Holding off is not what we had in mind. So, this Kennedy thing, is it just a hunch?" Or a theory, like a million other theories about the assignation."

"It's more than a theory," Hacket said, "we have people in the field who say they saw one of the top Sicilian's hit men board a plane in Rome. That's not a hunch."

"Maybe he was going on vacation, or on a trip to visit his sick mother," Frost offered.

"Sicilian hit men like the one we're talking about, the one called the Badger, don't go on vacations, detective," agent Watts replied. "When they go somewhere, it's usually to kill people."

"The Badger?" Lochran asked, "that's a hitman?"

"One of the best," agent Hacket said.

"We know you want to solve this thing," agent Watts pleaded, "but this is temporary. Things are going on we can't discuss here. A full-scale operation like this could hurt the work our agency has done. You need to trust us on this. It won't be for long."

"Gentlemen, "the Captain said, "I think we're done here. Loch, Butch, call off the operation but keep looking for the kids. Agents, can I see you in my office?

CHAPTER 39

Digging Machine

D it dropped her second dime into the pay phone at the City Line Esso and held the phone tightly against her ear. In the middle of the third ring, her friend Eleanor pick up.

"EL," Dit said, "I'm at the Esso station on the corner of Conshohocken and City Line."

"I'll be there as quickly as I can," Eleanor said, hung up the phone and grabbed her car keys. She sped down Highland Avenue, hung a left onto Jefferson Street and stepped on it toward Conshohocken State Road. Passing traffic and rushing through intersections — whether she had the light or not — El arrived at the Esso in less than 10 minutes. Dit ran out from the office, flung open the door and got in. "Okay," she said, "let's get out of here."

"Oh my God," Eleanor howled, "what the hell happened to your arms. You've got blood all over them,"

"Eleanor," Dit pleaded, "please, let's just get me out of here. I'll tell you everything when we get to your house."

"You don't want to go home?" El asked. "You want to go to my house?"

Dit gave her friend a look, and El pushed the pedal to the floor, and the car screeched out of the gas station.

On the Hill, the mob wasn't doing well. Already they lost three capos and unbeknownst to the mob; the kids had the Badger on their side. So, after losing Dit in the Marriott Motor Lodge, Crazy Phil and the Hunchback took off for their home turf, South Philadelphia. Their Chevy was dirty — too many people eyeballed it leaving Carl the Butchers on the Hill and at the Marriott, not to mention Dit, the Grace Kelly lookalike abducted woman who escaped.

"The boss wants to see you," Little Nicky told Crazy Phil, as they pulled in front of Nicky's house. "Leave the car here, I'll get rid of it."

Phil and the Hunchback walked somberly for two blocks to the boss's place on Snyder Avenue. They rang the doorbell, and thirty seconds later, the door opened.

"Mrs. Morello," Phil said, "we're here to see Angelo."

"Come in-a, come in-a please, it's-a gonna rain soon," Mrs. Morello said. "Angelo in-a the office, go on-a, go on-in a," and she waved the two mob captains down the hall toward her husband's office. Phil and Hunch walked nervously down the hall and stopped at the office door. They stared at one another for what seemed like ten seconds, and Phil said, in a soft voice, almost a whisper, "If he starts shootin,' you get him, hear?"

"Phil," Hunch said quietly, as he held out his arms and shrugged his shoulders, "it'll be okay. What a you gonna do?"

Crazy Phil turned and rapped on the door. "Come in gentlemen, the door is open."

Angelo Morello, boss of bosses, was seated behind his desk. The drapes were pulled shut in the three windows of the room. A small lamp on Mr. Morello's desk was lit, which illuminated his face and made him look even more sinister to Phil and Hunch.

"Shut the door gentlemen and have a seat."

Without a word, the two hitmen did as told.

"So, you had the blond woman, the kid witness's sister," Mr. Morello said, "so where did you bury her?"

Phil and Hunch exchanged glances, and Phil spoke first.

"Boss," he said, "she escaped. We had her tied up at the Marriot while we were headed out to whack them kids and she cut herself free. We looked for her but nothing. We don't know where she is."

Mr. Morello opened a box on this desk and took out a cigar. He bit the end off and leaned forward to spit it into a trashcan alongside his desk. He struck a match and lit it, then leaned back in his chair, drew in a deep breath, and slowly exhaled. The smoke, a whitish blue mix from Mr. Morello's exhalation emanated over Phil and Hunch's heads like the first wisp of smoke from a cannon shot.

"So," he said, "you had her in-a you hands and didn't think to watch her every second she breathed, no?"

"Boss," Hunch replied, "we didn't know at the time she was the kid's sister. If we had known it, we would've acted differently."

Mr. Morello nodded and drew in from his cigar again, holding it in his mouth for several seconds and exhaled. "This isn't your fault," he said, "so relax. It's-a my fault. I should have taken those snotnose bastards more seriously. Those pricks caused-a demise of three good, made men, Cockeyed Lou, Johnny Sausage, and Porky Bananas." He flicked the end of his cigar into a large, glass ashtray on his desk. "You have any idea of-a where these snotnoses is hidin'?"

"Boss," Hunch answered, "before I whacked Porky Bananas, he took me to a spot where he thought them kids was hidin'. It was in the woods and Porky told me he thinks they was headin' some place. Somehow Porky knew them kids went that way. But between me and you, I think Porky knew where they was headin.'"

More smoke filled the office as Mr. Morello sat back in his chair, listening to Hunch and licking the tip of his cigar. "Can you find that place?"

"Yeah," Hunch said, "that's why we left the dame in the hotel room. We was headin' for the woods to find the spot where I whacked Porky when the radio came on."

"And we heard she was the kid's sister," Phil said. "So, we went back to the hotel to grab her, and she was gone. Just like that, boss."

Mr. Morello swiveled in his chair to look away from Hunch and Phil in deep thought. He drew on the cigar again spilling even more smoke toward the ceiling. "If you was the kid's sister," Mr. Morello asked, "and you got stuffed in the trunk. Then escaped. What do you-a think your next move would-a be?"

Phil looked at Hunch. He slowly turned to face Mr. Morello and said, "Go warn your brother?"

Angelo Morello swiveled back in his chair to face Hunch and Phil. "There's another car waiting for you outside. Go back to that place in the woods and start looking, capeesh? Do it first thing in the morning. Not tonight. Get some rest and get out there when the sun comes up. Sneak-a through them woods, like you was kids again. Walk a little, then hide a little. Like Daniel Boone. Or the Lone Ranger. Them woods will tell you where them kids are. Do-a good job for me."

"Boss," Crazy Phil replied, "you can count on it."

The Badger didn't want to wait.

"Start now," he told us.

"It's nearly lunchtime," Pete said, "don't you think we should start tomorrow, you know, to have a full day to work?"

"Start now," the Badger replied.

Who were we to argue?

"I change." He got his bag of tools and began "changing."

The thing was, the Badger didn't change into anything; he just removed his clothes without putting anything back on. He stripped naked. We tried not to look, but it was impossible not to. Sort of a sneak look and a few glances, we could see that God awarded the Badger with a pretty sized cuckoo. Pete smiled and said, "Shit, we're all like that from Luzzi."

'Yeah," Gary said, "you're all bullshitters, too."

Pete belly laughed. "Jesus Christ, look who's talking?" And he did another belly laugh.

"Come here you dago prick," Gary said, trying to grind his fist playfully into Pete's stomach. "Oh shit," he said, "I forgot, better not let the groundhog hear me say that."

"It's not groundhog it's Badger," Mickey said, correcting his friend.

"Shit," Gary slurred, "in Poland we don't have no animals just men who can kick ass."

"Yeah," Pete said, still laughing, "you're so full of shit your eyes are brown. You do know that, don't you?"

"Holy shit, look at that," Mickey exclaimed.

It was the Badger. Standing naked before us, he had steel tools strapped to his elbows, knees, and ankles. They looked like cups, but with sharp edges, and when he moved, they seemed to move in unison. He had a light strapped to his head and a pad on his ass that he could sit on when he needed a rest. His cuckoo was just dangling freely.

"Jesus, John," Pete said, "are they your digging tools?"

"Digging machine," he replied.

"Jesus H. Christ," Gary said. "He looks like he's going to war."

"I am," the Badger replied.

"I told you us Italians don't have to eat cherries," Pete said.

After he instructed us what to bring, including the tarp, Billy Curry gave us for rainy nights. When he got about halfway down, he stopped and carefully began carefully pulling the weeds and branches back. His bare feet were dug into the dirt, holding him in place. From where he started working, it was a drop straight down of maybe 50 feet.

The last place someone would look for a cave. The four of us climbed down, holding on to the thick weeds and the short, small sumac trees, rocks, and anything we could grab and hold. He took some twine he had inside one of his digging cups and began pull-ing back the weeds and tying them together. He did the same with the small sumac trees and disgusting stickers and thorns. He gently cleared away a spot to start digging without disturbing the natural ground cover around the cave.

"Make natural," he told us.

We figured that he didn't want to damage the weeds and shrubs around the entrance of to the cave so nobody could find it. The Bad-ger called it a cave, but we looked at it as a fort, similar to the one we built at the dump.

"Where tarp?"

"Shit," Mickey said, "we didn't bring it down. Ronny, you're the closest to the top. Bring it down."

"Rope too," the Badger called out.

"Ronny," Mickey yelled, "bring the rope, too."

By the time I climbed up to the top of the tunnel, gathered up the tarp and rope we brought from the dump, then climbed back down, the Badger was getting impatient."

"Move faster," he called out.

We passed down the rope and tarp while keeping some of the rope behind, which he told us to do. With his feet dug into the dirt, he slipped the tarp under his heels to hold it. He looped rope through two holes at the other end of the tarp and brought the rope up and wrapped it around his shoulders. It looked like he was about ready to take a crap into the tarp, which bulged out from beneath his butt.

Then he started digging. He filled that tarp up in about 30-40 sec-onds.

"Jesus H. Christ," Gary called out. "He's a digging machine." But we hadn't seen anything, yet.

"Get tarp."

Holding on as our life depended on it — and it did — we slid down behind him and tried to get hold of the tarp.

"Give rope," he yelled at me, and I flung the extra rope at him.

He ran the rope through the remaining holes in the tarp which allowed him to draw up the tarp in a ball, filled with dirt, of course. He pointed at Mickey and said, "Over here."

Mickey moved in next to him, and the Badger draped the rope over his shoulder. He pointed at Gary and Pete and told him to "go bottom." They both slide to the bottom of the steep incline.

"Lower tarp," he told Mickey. The tarp was filled with dirt, and it was heavy. The Badger pointed at me and instructed me to "help Mickey."

From that point on, we worked like dogs. The Badger dug while we lowered the rope and carried the tarp into the middle of the train tunnel, emptied it by the wall mid-way through, and brought it back for Mickey and me to pull up for the Badger. But we were too slow. The Badger told the two "tarp men" to run it into the tunnel and run the empty tarp back. He also had us rotate, so we shared each job. After about three hours, the Badger stopped up and said, "Time water."

"Shit," Gary complained, "I'm dead. Is this heaven or hell?"

"Gimmie that water," Pete said. "I need it bad."

Even in darkness, we looked pretty weird — covered with dirt and sweat. The Badger limited us to two or three gulps each because he said too much, "Make lazy." Besides, we only had so much water in our camp. After a ten-minute break, we started again. We worked into the night lowering the tarp, taking it into the tunnel, and bringing it back empty — running the entire way. Digging wise, John Giovanni, the Badger from Luzzi, was a madman. In three-four hours he dug a cave — alongside the Flat Rock Tunnel — that was as large as a bedroom with two beds. The amazing part was that when he untied the weeds and stickers, it was impossible to find the cave.

"Yo," someone called from down on the railroad tracks, "yo, you guys up there?"

"Who's that?" the Badger asked.

"Not sure," Gary replied, then he yelled, "Who's there? Name yourself."

"Pecker, it's Johnny, Johnny Ciarlello."

CHAPTER 40

"Bunch of Queers..."

Two miles away, Dit was relieved to be back on the Hill. Growing up on the Hill is like growing up in a family. You meet other kids at an early age, and they become friends for life. Like Dit and Eleanor. Eleanor pulled in front of her house, and she and Dit quickly got out. They hurried inside, and Eleanor shut the drapes over the front windows. "What's going on, Dit?" she asked.

"I got kidnapped by a couple of jerks from the mafia," Dit explained. "They put me in a room at the Marriott and tied me to a chair. After they left, I escaped."

"Oh God," Eleanor said, "did they try to do anything sexual?"

"No," Dit replied, "I would have killed them."

"Well, thank God for that," Eleanor said. "We heard it on the news, and I was scared shitless, but they didn't say your name. I'm glad you're safe. You're going to the police, aren't you?"

"Not yet," Dit replied, "first I have to warn Ronny and his friends. Is there someone in the kitchen?"

"Georgie, is that you?" Eleanor asked.

"Yeah, it's me, Aunt El," Georgie answered.

"EL," Dit said, "I've got to talk to Georgie."

"Let's get to the kitchen, then," she responded. "We've got to clean you up, anyway. Look at your arms."

As Eleanor got out the first aid kit and the iodine, gauze, and tape, Dit told Georgie what happened.

"Jesus, Dit," Georgie said, "two detectives were questioning me on the front porch when they got the call about Carl the Butchers. We're glad you safe now."

"Thanks, Georgie," Dit said. "But the two idiots who grabbed me are after Ronny and his friends. I've got to find them. Any idea where they are?"

"Here, Dit," Eleanor said, "let me wash those arms in the sink, and I'll bandage them up for you."

"I know exactly where they are, Dit," Georgie answered. "They're hiding on top of the Flat Rock Tunnel. They move back and forth from the tunnel to the dump."

"I've got to go there," Dit responded. "I heard one of the mob guys say they know where they are. I've got to let Ronny and his friends know that the mob is hot on their trail."

"I'll take you there," Georgie said, "can you go now?"

"It's dark out there," Eleanor said. "Besides, her arms are still bleeding."

"If I wait, El," Dit said, "it could be too late. Those two assholes may be looking for them first thing in the morning. I've got to warn them."

"Well they won't go into the woods at night, that I can guarantee," Eleanor insisted. "If we get there in the morning, just as the sun comes up, that will be in plenty of time. Trust me on this."

"Okay, but how will we get there, Georgie?" Dit asked. "Do we have to walk on those railroad tracks down past Baffa's?"

"No," Georgie responded, "first thing in the morning I'll drive you up to the top of Mary Waters Ford. We can go in from there."

"What do you mean you're drive her?" Eleanor said, "you ain't even got a driver's license."

"Right," Georgie said, "I forgot about that. But how will we go, Aunt El?"

"Sometimes Georgie, I don't think you think at all," Eleanor said. "What do you think I'm going to do, let you walk? I'll drive you up there. I'm not afraid of mafia guys. I went out with one once, and he wouldn't pay for nothing. I had to pay for the Roxy Movies. For both of us.

"Okay, and you can wait for us by the Plymouth," Georgie instructed.

"Well, if you think I'm drivin' ya there," El replied, "and staying in the woods by myself, you got another thing comin'. They'll be sellin' whiskey on Sunday before that happens you can be sure.

"Dit," she continued, "tonight you sleep up in the middle bedroom. I'll get everybody up around four."

"Jesus, El," Dit said, "picking at the bandages on her arm, did you have to put so much iodine on?"

"Well, you want to live, don't you?" Eleanor said. "Don't want to get an infection, cause glass will do that."

"Right," Dit said, "thanks."

"Okay, then," Georgie said, "we'll all be ready by four, four-thirty."

"Thanks, Georgie," Dit said, "I appreciate this."

Johnny stayed with us for an hour or so and then headed back down the tracks for home. He told us he saw flashlights on the tracks below the embankment from his backyard. He said he overheard the cops planning some kind of network to watch the tracks. He said we better not use the tracks to go into George Ferraco's yard.

"They'll be hiding and waiting to grab you," Johnny said.

He promised to return in a day or two and bring us water and some food. We asked him to let George Ferraco know not to leave food on his back porch. We told Johnny we didn't need water because there's a small stream close by and it empties into the spring. We dip our buckets in the spring to get water.

Just after Johnny left, we went down to the Schuylkill River and cleaned up. Then the Badger made us clear up our camp at the top of the tunnel and bring everything into the cave. We tried to smooth out the grass to make it look like we were never there. The Badger was big on stuff like that. "No traces," he said.

Johnny saved our necks, and the Badger was right to have us dig the cave so we could move into it immediately.

～

The next morning, Georgie's aunt Eleanor drove Georgie and Dit to the top of Mary Waters Ford Road in total darkness. "Jeeze, Georgie," Aunt El said, "I told you we left too early. Ya can't see anything."

"I know Aunt El," Georgie replied, "but there was no traffic, so we got here a little early."

"Traffic?" his aunt replied, "hells bells there's never any traffic on the Hill, to begin with, so how'd we beat the traffic?"

"Here," Georgie replied, "slow down. The old road is right there. You just passed it. If you back up and approach it from an angle, your headlights will light up the road."

"That's a road?" Dit asked, "we can't drive on that thing."

"Simple," Georgie remarked, "pull in a little way from the road, and we'll leave it there. You don't have to drive far."

"Georgie's accustomed to driving junkers around," Eleanor said, "like the '48 Dodge junker, right Georgie?"

"I thought you didn't have a license," Dit said.

When Georgie didn't answer, Eleanor said, "Didn't think I knew about that, huh, Georgie?"

"Well, thanks for not telling anybody, Aunt El," Georgie answered.

"Oh, I get it," Dit remarked, "driving illegally. Nothing wrong with that, half the people on the Hill drive illegally."

Eleanor pulled the Plymouth up over the curb and onto the old logging road. She drove maybe fifty yards and stopped. She cut the engine.

"That's it," she announced, "that's as far as we go. The road is getting too rough."

"Okay," Georgie said, "let's go."

"Wait a minute," Eleanor said, "it's still too dark. We'll wait until the sun starts to come up.

Quietly, the three waited, as daylight trickled in like slow pouring cream in coffee. Georgie spoke up first. "Okay," he said as he grabbed the door handle, "time to go."

The sun was peeking out over the Delaware River, creating a beautiful orange haze. The city's pollution was not yet visible — give it time — but if you stood long enough and sucked in the air, you could fill your lungs with the petroleum, gasoline, diesel fuel, and heating oil fumes drifting off the Point Breeze oil refinery and carried over the city by a light eastern breeze.

"Mmm, ah, wake up and smell the roses."

Eastbound traffic was backed up from Girard Avenue to the Conshohocken curve. A disabled vehicle in the westbound lane near Manayunk had traffic creeping and crawling like cheetahs in tall grass stalking a lame wildebeest in the savannah.

Crazy Phil and the Hunchback had gassed up their new car — this time a Buick, which made the Hunchback remark, "Yo Phil, we look like two businessmen, ridin' around in a fancy Buick. Which corporation you work for?"

"Goddamn, traffic," Phil remarked. "Makes my balls ache."

"Phil, what-a you gone-a do?" Hunch replied.

Phil veered over on the berm and gunned the Buick's engine passing cars and trucks and sped off the Belmont exit. Driving up through the Hill and passing Carl the Butcher's, Phil said, "I'd like to stop here and put a slug in that fat butcher's ass."

"You wanna do it, I'm game," Hunch said.

"Naw," Phil said, "the old man would have a bird."

At the top of Ashland Hunch had Phil turn on Highland and then turn left on Jefferson. "At this stop sign, go right," Hunch told his partner. "This is Mary Water's Ford Road, stay on it, and I'll tell you where to slow down."

"Mary Shit's Ford," Phil said, "who ever heard of a street named that."

"Bunch of queers live on this Hill, Phil," Hunch remarked, "you know that, and I know that."

"All these forests drive me crazy," Phil said. "Goddamn bears and shit in here."

"All right, Phil," Hunch pointed out, "slow down here. There should be an old road to the right up here. Yea, yea, stop, there it is. You can back up and pull in this road."

"That's a road?" Phil asked, "look s like some cow path."

"Phil," Hunch said, "there ain't no cows in these woods. There're on the farm, standin' out in the field eaten grass and shitten' all the time."

"Yeah," Phil answered, "it still don't look like no road."

"Pull in, we have a shit car anyway," Hunch said.

As Phil cut the wheel and pulled into the old logging road, Hunch yelled, "Wait, what's that car doing there? There's a car parked up ahead. How'd that car get there?"

"Same way we did," Phil responded, "somebody drove it."

"Who?" Hunch asked.

"How the fuck would I know," said Phil, "I'm pullin' up behind it."

Hunch reached inside his jacket and pulled out his piece. Slowly, driving over ruts, rocks and small tree branches, Phil pulled up behind the late model Plymouth. He cut the engine, and he and his partner got out. Phil also pulled out his gun. The two of them walked around the Plymouth and looked it over.

"What do you think?" Hunch asked.

"Not sure," Phil answered, "but if the kids are in that direction," he said, pointing to the east, away from Mary Waters Ford, "could this car be connected to them? Somebody here to help them?"

"Yeah, I bet," Hunch reasoned. "I bet that's what it is."

"Where'd you pop Porky Bananas?" Phil asked.

"All right," Hunch said. "We came up this road about to here. Then we walked this way, maybe fifty feet, and I came up behind him and put one in his head. He fell about here."

Phil ambled over and moved the leaves around with his toe. "No signs of anything," he said to Hunch.

"It's been a while, Phil," Hunch replied, "fuckin' bears probably licked up his blood and shit. Next day Angelo send some boys to take away the body and bury it someplace nice."

Phil looked at Hunch. "Someplace nice, huh?" he said. "Like in a pit behind the airport?"

"Yeah, could be," Hunch said, smiling. "A nice place."

"Come on," Phil instructed, "let's walk this way. See what we can find. Maybe we'll run into them kids, and better yet, we'll find the people with this car, and they'll lead us to them kids."

"Just so we don't get lost, Phil, we can't have that, these woods is scary."

Phil didn't respond, and the two of them began walking in the direction of the Flat Rock Tunnel."

CHAPTER 41

Dit and the Badger

At the tunnel, Dit, Eleanor, and Georgie finished their meeting with the boys and the Badger. Dit told them that the two mobsters that grabbed her were on their way to the tunnel. She said they could expect them any day. "Yeah, but probably in the daylight," Georgie said, "I don't think they have the balls to come at night." Georgie also told them over the last couple of days he's seen police cars on Jefferson and Jones Streets. If they're down on Jones Street, Georgie said, "they're either harassing George Ferraco or planning to come up the tracks.

"Or both," Gary observed.

The three visitors were impressed by the Badger. "Holy shit," Georgie remarked, "he's something else. I bet he can kick some ass."

"Ronny," Dit said, "he keeps staring at me. Why does he keep staring at me?"

To which the Badger remarked, "Dit beautiful."

"Yeah, just what I need," Dit said, "a relationship with a mafia killer who digs holes."

"Dit dinner," the Badger said.

Everybody laughed except Dit.

"Dit," Georgie said, "maybe you could take him to the dump for a bite."

Everybody laughed again, except Dit.

Dit said, "I think it's time to go. "It's getting late, and we should be on the road."

"Come back," the Badger said.

Dit didn't respond, and with everyone laughing and making cracks, the three of them headed back to Eleanor's car. Ronny yelled, "Thanks, Dit, love you."

"Be careful," she replied. "Come home when you can."

Crazy Phil and the Hunchback had begun their trek down the logging road, stepping carefully around rocks and tree limbs. Eventually, the road ended. It emptied into a small path that cut into the woods.

"What's this?" Phil asked. "What happened to the road?"

"Don't know," the Hunch said. "I thought it would go all the way."

"All the way where?"

"To them kids," the Hunch answered. "I thought it would lead us to them kids."

"Did you try it?" Phil asked, "did you check it out?"

"No, after I whacked Porky, I left."

"Oh shit," Phil pleaded, "now we don't know how to get there? You're kiddin' me, Hunch."

"Look, Phil," the Hunch explained, "them people from that Plymouth most likely came this way, then went onto this path. Maybe the path leads to them kids."

"All right," Phil said, pulling out his piece, "let's do the path. Anything moves shoot it and ask questions later."

Phil and the Hunch weren't good in the woods. They've never been in the woods except at funerals at West Laurel Hill Cemetery on the edge of the city. "You know," Phil would say, "he was buried at that cemetery in the country," meaning West Laurel Hill. One-time Phil played golf at Walnut Lane golf course in the city — the only reason he played was to whack the guy he was playing with, and after he killed him, he just left, leaving the clubs, bag, and the dead body on the seventh tee. He referred to Walnut Lane as "in the mountains."

"Jesus Christ," Phil complained, "these woods are a pain in the ass. We'll be covered with ticks by the time we get back."

"These woods have ticks?" the Hunch asked.

"All woods have ticks, Hunch," Phil replied. "That's why they got woods, so there'd be a place for ticks to bite us and suck all our blood, those mother fuckin' tick bastards."

"You think they got bed bugs in here, Phil," Hunch asked.

"Shit yea," Phil replied, "this is where they come from looking for beds to sleep in."

Georgie was leading his aunt and Dit through the woods back to the Plymouth — which, by the way, Georgie knew like the back of his hand — and as he walked, he was thinking up and verbalizing different places Dit and the Badger could have dinner. "Maybe," Georgie said aloud, "he'll build you an underground cave and put romantic candles in it and a table and two chairs for your dinner."

"Just keep your eye on the way back, Georgie," his aunt Eleanor said.

"And for dinner, he could get you a couple of dump rats," Georgie teased.

As soon as Georgie got those words out, they came to a clearing and right into Crazy Phil and the Hunch. "Uh, oh," Georgie stammered.

"Phil," Hunch yelled, "there's that blond broad." Then Hunch pulled out his gun and fired a shot at her.

"No, Hunch," Phil hollered, "we want her alive."

"That's them," Dit yelled, "the mob guys."

"And they're shooting at us," Georgie screamed.

Georgie turned and reversed his direction telling the two women to follow him. He led them over a small ridge and out of sight of the two mobsters. He led them into a grove of thick pine trees and stopped. "You two go back to the tunnel and warn the boys. I'll lead these two away from the tunnel. Go now."

"Okay," Dit said, "which way."

"See that little clearing next to those big trees?" Georgie asked.

"Yes," Eleanor replied, "we go there?"

"Go right into that clearing and then just follow your nose," Georgie explained. "It's a few hundred yards beyond that clearing. Hurry, they're coming."

"Be careful, Georgie," his aunt Eleanor yelled. With that, Dit and Eleanor ran toward the clearing.

But it wasn't fair. Georgie knew the woods; he knew where the creek came in, where the clearings were, the location of the ridges and hills, and where the main roads sat. Everything. Phil and the Hunch were scared of the woods but more afraid of what was in the woods, like ticks and bears. They were also were afraid of getting lost. So, they moved slowly, deliberately, giving Georgie a considerable advantage.

Georgie circled them, allowing the two killers plenty of room, especially after getting shot at. He could hear them as they moved through the thickets and brush. When he got to their left, he moved in closer, and when he got within range, he bellowed, "Oh no, there they are. Let's go this way, girls."

"Phil," Hunch yelled, "over there, I saw them."

Now Phil saw that he and his partner had left the path and were in thick woods. But he lost Sweet Pea once he wasn't about to lose her again. He wanted to kill El and Georgie and take Sweet Pea back to South Philly.

Therefore, he was willing to take chances. But off the main path, the two mobsters were clearly out of their league.

"Phil," Hunch yelled, "stop a minute, one of those goddamn thorn branches' hit my eye. Shit. I can't open it."

"Rub it," Phil answered, "we can't stop now, or we'll lose them."

So, Hunch with one eye and Phil half crazy about getting Dit back, moved into dense brush. Hunch was slowing Phil down. Every few minutes, he had to stop. His eye hurt, and it was swollen shut. Hunch became a liability to Phil and Phil knew it.

"Hunch," Phil insisted, "find yourself a good spot to sit until your eye gets better. I'll go on ahead to get that crazy broad. Keep your gun ready. If you hear shootin', get up and walk toward the shots. I'll find you."

"Alright, Phil," Hunch replied, "don't leave me here."

"I'll be back, Hunch," Phil said. "Don't you worry."

Dit and Eleanor ran into a clearing and along a row of pines, straight to the top of the tunnel. They yelled for the boys, who were still on top of the tunnel getting their tools ready for another dig. So was the Badger.

"They're back," Dit yelled, "they're back, the two mob guys who grabbed me."

"Where?" Gary asked.

"Back that way," Eleanor said, "we ran. Georgie is trying to lead them away. They shot at us."

"Jesus H. Christ," Gary stammered, "shall we go get them?"

"No go," the Badger said, as he rushed to his black bag and zipped it open. He wrapped the rope they used to lower the tarp filled with dirt around his waist. He lifted out what looked like a white piece of canvas and several axes. "Stay here."

The Badger ran into the woods, running through the clearing and into the dense brush.

PART FOUR

CHAPTER 42

The Final Week

August 1964
Monday, 9 a.m.
New Jersey Turnpike

Louis Regina cut his speed to 45 considering the heavy rain on the New Jersey Turnpike. He was on his way to Philadelphia to check in on the Badger and the kids. Mr. Regina, consigliere for Vito Graziano, Don of the Newark, NJ, based mob, was just past the Elizabeth exit of the turnpike when the flashing lights caught his eyes in the rearview.

The lights were a half-mile back but caught up quickly and lit up Louis's car like a boardwalk merry-go-round. *What the hell is this?* The police car pulled up on his back bumper and then backed off. Louis glanced at his speed. He flicked on his turn signal and slowed down and pulled onto the berm and stopped. Louis looked at his side mirror and saw more flashing lights approach. He watched a New Jersey state trooper get out of his car and walk toward him.

It was still raining buckets when the trooper walked up to his window, bent slightly and looked in. Louis rolled the window down. "Mr. Louis Regina?" the trooper asked. Water ran off the state trooper's hat in streams onto his raincoat, the door, and sprayed Louis's face.

"Yes?" Louis replied. At least two more state police cars pulled up. Their lights caught his eyes, too, and he shifted them to the side mirror and back to the trooper. "I guess you want my license and owner's information?" Louis asked as he reached for his wallet.

"That won't be necessary, sir," the trooper insisted. "Keep both of your hands on the steering wheel, please." The other troopers also got out of their cars and came up on both sides of Louis's vehicle. One watched through the windshield.

"Are you carrying a firearm, sir?" the trooper asked.

"Yes, officer, I am," Louis replied.

"And where is that firearm, sir?"

"In a belt holster on my left hip," Louis said.

"Very slowly I'd like you to reach over with your right hand, grab the firearm with your thumb and first finger, and pull it out slowly. Hold it up so I can see it, keep your other fingers away from it, and hand it to me. Can you do that, sir?"

Louis, his hands on the wheel, stared out the windshield.

"Sir?" the trooper said.

As the consigliere for the Newark mob, Louis was no dummy when it came to police matters. As its attorney, he advised the boss and caporegimes (capos) on how to handle police matters, especially if you were arrested or involved in a traffic stop. Louis knew this situation was unusual. The trooper knew him without asking for identification. Plus, at least three other state police cars pulled in for backup.

"Mr. Regina," the trooper said, "I know who you are, and I know what you might be thinking. If we wanted to kill you, we would have done it already and placed a gun in your right hand. That is your shooting hand, is it not, sir?"

Louis turned and looked at the trooper. Several seconds elapsed before Louis said, "What do you want, officer?"

"As soon as I have your firearm, sir, I will tell you what I want."

Without taking his eyes off of the state trooper, Louis unzipped his jacket with his right hand and felt for his gun. He pulled it out of its holster like the trooper said, with his thumb and finger. He lifted the Smith and Wesson .38 straight up.

"Alright," the trooper said, "now hand it here."

He moved his right arm toward the open window, handing the gun over, and watched as the trooper gave it to another trooper behind him. The officer leaned back down.

"Sir," he said, "I'm going to pull out in front of you, and I'd like you to follow me. The other troopers will block the right lane for you to pull out safely."

"Where are we going, officer?" Louis asked.

"About two miles down the turnpike there's a Howard Johnson's. Follow me into the parking lot and park your vehicle alongside mine. Exit your vehicle and follow me into the restaurant."

The trooper didn't wait for Louis to answer. He turned and walked back toward his car. Louis started the engine but remained until the police car drove off.

Louis Regina followed it.

~

Monday Mid-Morning
Top of the Tunnel

For a small, muscular guy, the Badger moved through the woods with the ease of a bobcat. He was a natural and quickly moved around obstacles; he sidestepped low hanging branches, bounded over rocks, leaped over a small spring, quickly cut around downed tree branches, and zipped between the pines and hardwoods. The Badger moved several yards and stopped. He crouched and scanned the woods; he moved again, amazingly quiet through dead leaves. He frightened a rabbit that bolted from a log he nearly stepped on.

As the Badger moved through the woods, he watched and listened. His eyes scoured through the trees in front of him and on both sides. He started to move again but froze. He didn't see anyone, but he heard a noise. Leaves rustled, and a twig snapped. He moved slightly to his left; then forward a few feet. To the left again.

It was just in front of him. He could smell it and hear it. He moved a few more feet and crouched again. He parted several branches of a tree. There it was. He sat alone, his back toward him. Sitting and watching the woods; he lifted his hand and dabbed his eye with a handkerchief. A handgun lay on the leaves beside him. The Badger moved around a downed tree and got closer. He undid the rope around his waist. Looped it and moved forward. The Badger quietly moved in behind him.

Fast and furious, he leaped forward and twirled the loop around him and tightened it. Quickly, he wrapped three more loops around Hunch's upper torso, preventing the use of his hands and arms.

"Who the are you, you son of a bitch," the Hunchback howled. The Hunchback could feel the power in the Badger's hands and his hot breath. Without answering, the Badger grabbed the hanky and stuffed it into Hunch's mouth. He kicked away the handgun. He dragged him over to a thin maple tree and with more rope secured him to the tree. He pushed the hanky in further until Hunch gaged. The Badger stood back and observed his work. He quickly cut a shorter piece of rope and wrapped it around Hunch's ankles.

The Badger pointed his finger and in a low voice said, "Don't move," Hunch's eyes, wide as donuts, for he had never seen anyone like the man in front of him. As quickly and silently as he came, the Badger moved on to find Crazy Phil.

∾

Monday Afternoon
New Jersey Turnpike
Howard Johnson's

Louis Regina had no idea what the New Jersey State Police wanted. Thoughts raced through his mind. Maybe somebody got whacked at the restaurant, and they needed an ID. Perhaps they had a rat Louis knew, and they wanted him to rat, too. Or maybe they had evidence that could tie him to a murder or two — not as the trigger-man, no, Louis Regina was rarely the trigger-puller. But he was the voice and the brains behind the Newark mob, which made him as guilty. Louis knew about everything; when it happened and how. He never defended the capos in court; he was too valuable for that. He was the man behind the scenes; he was Vito Graziano's, right-hand man. Perfect for the FBI to grab.

The truth was, on a rainy night when the road was slick and visibility poor, and the wipers struggled to clear the windshield, Louis had no idea what they wanted.

As the trooper ordered, Louis pulled in and stopped. Several other police cars followed them into the Howard Johnson's. *I guess so I can't escape,* Louis reasoned, and he smiled. Louis got out of his car and went around to open the trunk. But he stopped and yelled to inform the trooper that he was getting his raincoat. The trooper nodded.

Louis held the raincoat over his head and followed the trooper into the restaurant. The other troopers remained in their vehicles. Inside the restaurant, Louis followed the officer around the sit-down counter and back to a corner table where two men sat waiting. They wore suit and ties, and at first glance, Louis figured they were either lawyers or the FBI. He was, of course, right on the second guess.

They stood as Louis and the trooper approached. "Mr. Regina," the first agent said as he held out his hand, "I'm agent Watts, and this is agent Hacket. We're both with the Federal Bureau of Investigation."

"Let me guess," Louis said, "assigned to organized crime."

Watts smiled. "That's right, how'd you know?"

It was a joke, of course, and Louis replied, "Well, I figured you weren't assigned to domestic disputes."

Both agents chuckled. "I'll be right over at this table," the trooper said, "in case you need me."

"That won't be necessary, officer," agent Hacket said, "we're good here. Thank you for delivering Mr. Regina."

The trooper gave Louis a dirty look and said, "All right, but I'll be outside, just in case."

"The long arm of the law," agent Watts said. "They keep our streets safe."

"Do they?" Louis asked.

"Well," Hacket answered, "they're supposed to."

"Mr. Regina, would you like a burger, some coffee, a banana split?" agent Hacket asked.

"Coffee would be delightful."

"I'll grab the waitress when she comes by," Watts said.

"So, you gentlemen didn't invite me here to have coffee."

"No," Hacket said, "their coffee is okay, but it's not that good."

"Keeps the 18-wheel driver's awake at night," Watts added.

"Mr. Regina," Hacket said, "we know you work for Mr. Vito Graziano of the Newark mob."

"We don't call it a mob, it's a peaceful organization."

"Sure, it is," Watts said. Both agents smiled.

"You've been seen in the Philadelphia area several times in the past month," agent Watts said. "You want to tell us what that's about?"

"Last I checked, gentlemen, it's still a free country. We have some business interests in the Philadelphia area."

"Would those interests include four kids?" Hacket asked.

"Four kids, who witnessed two murders?" Watts added.

Louis shifted a little. Accustomed to answering difficult questions; he sat back in his chair. The waitress saved him.

"You gentlemen want to order?" she asked.

"Coffee, please," Watts said.

"Look, Mr. Regina," agent Watts continued. "We know you've had contact with the boys. What we don't know is why. Why would the Graziano organization be interested in those kids.?"

"Unless," Hacket added, "your organization was somehow involved in the murder of Mr. and Mrs. Otts."

Louis smiled. "Well," he said, calmly and with a spark of humor, "I can't exactly ask for a lawyer, now can I?"

It worked. The two agents chuckled. "Well you can, Mr. Regina," Watts said, "but you've got one right here, and he's a good one."

"I guess you mean me," Louis said, smiling, "and I guess it's a compliment."

Louis sat up and clasped his hands out in front of him on the table. "Look," he continued, "you know these organizations quarrel sometimes. And sometimes people die when they quarrel. This isn't one of those times. There is a disagreement between the Graziano and Morello organizations."

"Over the Otts' murders?" Hacket asked.

"I won't get into that now. That question is out of line. If you have proof that ties the Graziano organization to the Otts' murders, I'd like to hear it. Otherwise, it's not for me or anyone in the organization to answer or comment on that."

"Is there anyone else helping the boys, Mr. Regina," Watts asked. 'Or is that out of the discussion, too?"

"Yes, the boys have someone protecting them, but I can't comment on that, either.

"Here's the thing," Louis continued, "the boys want to cooperate with the authorities. But they can't or won't as long as the killer remains free. They believe if they go to the police, their photos will make the newspapers and the killer will target them."

"We can protect them," Hacket said.

"You and I both know, agent," Louis said, "that isn't foolproof."

"Do you know who killed the Otts?" Watts asked.

"I do not," Louis replied. "I have an idea, but that won't get six inches in court. I, nor anyone in the Graziano organization knows who killed the Otts."

"But do the boys?" Hacket asked.

"You know the answer to that agent. Otherwise, we wouldn't be sitting here."

"Help us find the boys, Mr. Regina," agent Watts said, "they can ID the killer from file photos, and we'll grab him. The boys pick him out of a lineup and tell a jury what they saw. It's the American way."

"Dead is the American way, too, agent," Louis replied.

"Okay gentlemen, here you go. Lots of creams and sugars on the plate."

"One other question," agent Watts said, "which organization killed President Kennedy?"

CHAPTER 43

The Cave Jail

Late Monday Afternoon
Top of the Tunnel

"Ronny," Dit barked. "Why are we standing around here? We're all going to get killed. I think we should go down the tracks, go home, and call the police."

"And then get killed," I answered, "and probably you, too. Look, if we go to the police our pictures will be in the papers and the South Philly mafia will come for us. At least this way they don't know where we are."

"Listen," Dit said, "you've got to listen to me. At home, we can stay hidden better than here."

"They haven't found us yet," Mickey offered.

"Not yet," Dit said, "give them time. They're ruthless. They'll never stop searching for you. What are you going to do live your entire life on top of this tunnel?"

"Sounds good," Gary said, "we won't have to go to school. What more could we want?"

"And we've got the Badger from Luzzi, Italy, protecting us. If we go home, we won't," Pete pointed out.

"You mean that nut case?" Dit questioned. "Oh, he's just great. He's killed so many people, what's a few more. Maybe when he's done, he'll kill us, too."

"The Badger?" Pete said. "Shit, no way."

"I think Dit's right," Eleanor said. "This is no place for you kids to live. You better listen to her."

"Uh-huh," I said, "we have the perfect place. We have a cave you haven't seen yet."

"What do you mean, cave?" Dit asked.

Just then, Georgie came busting through the woods, yelling, "Get in the cave, get in the cave…"

"Where's the Badger," Pete asked.

"I don't know," Georgie said, "isn't he here?"

"No," Gary answered, "he went after the mob guys. When Eleanor and Dit got here, he took his axes and went into the woods. You didn't see him?"

"Hell no," Georgie replied, "I lost the mob guys, and double backed this way. I didn't know the Badger was coming. I would have stayed out there, watch him kill those dipshits with an ax."

"Georgie," Aunt Eleanor said, "we think everybody should go home and let the police handle this. You can't stay out here on top of this tunnel anymore."

"What?" Georgie said, disgusted at his aunt's suggestion. "No way, we're winning this thing."

"Nobody is winning, Georgie," Dit said, "they're living out here in the wilderness on this tunnel. Sooner or later the mob will find them."

"Either that or the cops," Mickey said, interrupting Georgies' Aunt Eleanor. "Maybe if we play our cards right," Mickey continued, "we can get the mob and the cops here at the same time and let them shoot it out."

"Wait," Pete yelled, "here comes the Badger now."

"And he's got the two mob guys," Dit screamed. "Those are the men that kidnapped me."

"Jesus H. Christ," Gary said."

"Holy shit," Mickey exclaimed, "that's the guy who killed the Otts, the one on the left, and the other guy, in the leather jacket, he's the one who shot Porky Bananas in the woods."

"I'll be dipped in shit," Pete exclaimed. "the Badger has them both."

~

Early Monday Evening
Howard Johnson's
New Jersey Turnpike

Louis Regina stared straight into the eyes of FBI agent Ben Watts. An attorney's mind races when faced with difficult questions. But a mob attorney speaking to the FBI has to look relaxed and confident, even though the question is challenging. A wrong answer could prove damaging. To get a temporary delay, a confident attorney will say that he didn't hear the question or didn't understand it. That bought anywhere from 30 seconds to a minute — good thinking time.

Stirring his coffee and adding more cream, Louis said, "I'm sorry, what did you say?"

That bought 30 more seconds, even though Louis heard the question clearly, and another ten seconds to stir his coffee. That's 20 more seconds of thinking time.

"Which organization killed President Kennedy?" Watts asked again.

Still stirring, Louis looked up and said, "Wait, you said who killed President Kennedy?"

"No, not who," agent Watts said, "which crime family in New York, Newark, or Philadelphia, or all three together?

Louis placed the spoon on the saucer next to the cup, lifted the cup and took a sip — calmly like he was sitting by himself. He could feel the eyes of agent Benny Hacket bearing down on him as he sipped his coffee and stared at agent Watts. He dabbed his mouth with the napkin and said, "How the hell would I know anything about that?"

"Oh, we think you know plenty about that," Hacket said.

"And that's why the Graziano family has an interest in protecting those kids hiding out somewhere in Philadelphia, isn't it, Mr. Regina? What was so important about the Otts' murder that the Graziano family got involved?"

Louis pulled on his shirt sleeve, making sure it was even with the end of his suit jacket. He adjusted his cufflinks as if he was somewhere else. Hacket reached down and with his open hand swept Louis' coffee cup across the table, and it smashed on the floor.

Hacket got right down into Louis' face. "Listen, Goombah," he said, "if you know something about President Kennedy's murder, you better come clean now."

Louis looked at his cup and coffee on the floor and said, "I'm not Italian; I'm French Canadian."

"I don't give a fuck if you're the Pope," Hacket said, "you know the ties Walter Otts had with the major families. He was the best goddamn tailor out there, and all the Don goombah assholes wanted him. Including Angelo Morello. Otts ends up dead, and Morello's gorillas are out there trying to snuff out four boys just beyond wetting their pants, to shut them up. You and some psychopath from the Sicilians end up helping them. Now, what's going on?"

"Not sure," Louis replied, "maybe he made Angelo's cuffs too long."

Then agent Watts took over. "You can joke all you want, but if we catch you near those kid witnesses, you're going to San Quentin or Sing, Sing."

"You mean I'll get a choice?"

"You son-of-a-bitch," Hacket said, "don't you have any patriotic feelings about the United States? The President of the United States was murdered, and you sit there being a smart-ass."

"Look, gentlemen," Louis said, "read the newspapers. Everybody has an opinion on who killed Kennedy. Some think the Martians did it."

"Did your boss Vito Graziano have any prior dealings with Jimmy Hoffa and the Teamsters?" agent Watts asked.

"Of course not," Louis stated. "You boys know we weren't involved with the unions. Not the Teamsters, anyway. Morello had his head so far up Hoffa's ass it began to smell good. And here you are banging on me about the Kennedy assignation. Why aren't you knocking down the doors of the Genovese capo Tony Provenzano or the guy in New Orleans? No, you're busting my balls, and you want answers from me."

"Walter Otts heard something," agent Hacket said, "he knew something about Kennedy. You know it, and I know it."

"I don't know shit, and neither do you," Louis answered.

"So, Morello sent a thug to murder the Otts," Watts said. "To keep them quiet. He didn't figure on the kids in the trees. We wouldn't have taken notice if you and the psychopath from Italy weren't involved."

"But you can forget about using the kids as a wedge against Morello; we know where they are, and we're about to grab them. They'll be in police custody soon."

"And that's why you're in my face," Louis said, "you think we're the link to the big mystery. Let me ask you this agent, why aren't you in Angelo Morello's face?"

"Because we need verification from you as to why you're involved. Unless you're heading a Boy Scout troop we don't know about; there's no way a consigliere such as yourself is in the woods helping those kids."

"Maybe my boss liked Walter Otts," Louis said. "And maybe the Sicilians liked him too. And maybe we don't like Angelo Morello and his organization. So, you add that up, and that's why we're helping those kids."

"Or how about this," agent Hacket offered. "Maybe your boss and the people in Italy liked Kennedy so much; they're striking back at the Genovese's and Morello's?"

"Maybe," Louis said. "Okay, let's say your addition is better than mine. Let's say Vito Graziano and the Sicilians wanted to strike back at Angelo Morello for killing the Otts. Whether it was over Kennedy or not, it still comes back to this. You should be in their face, not mine.

"You've got the wrong dog in the hunt, gentlemen."

~

Tuesday Just Before Noon
Top of the Tunnel

Even before Dit and Aunt Eleanor showed up, and the Badger captured Crazy Phil and the Hunchback and brought them back to camp, the four of us realized that we were in the presence of some-thing special. Royalty, if you will, if killers have royalty. And digging, he's always digging. If we went down the tracks at night for food, or searched the woods behind us during the day, the Badger had another tunnel dug. He told us we needed them because if the cops found one tunnel, we could escape in another. He also said he could work faster alone. He said on his jobs — we took that to mean when he's whack-ing someone — he always worked alone.

The Badger said when the police, come, we can't run away from the tunnel because that's what they want. He said they'd be waiting no matter which way we ran.

That was a lot to say when you only speak two-word sentences. We could also sense that the Badger liked us, especially Pete. That's good because no way would we want the Badger not to like us. The Badger especially loved Dit, but she wasn't interested in the Italian, maniac killer. Dit said he gave her the creeps.

The Badger didn't use a lot of words. He said actions are better than words. When he captured Crazy Phil and the Hunchback, we could see the fear in their eyes. The Badger roughed them up. Purposely, on the way back to the tunnel, the Badger took them through the thickest and roughest terrain.

"That son of a bitch there killed the Otts," Gary said, pointing to Crazy Phil.

"That's right," Mickey offered, "and this one here killed that mob guy we found drunk at the dump. Shot him in the back of the head."

The two mobsters glared at us, wishing, willing themselves to get free. Silence us for good. You could see it in their eyes. To them, we were a one-way ticket to getting fried. But with the Badger present, they'd never try. The Badger dug a special room for Phil and Hunch. It was on the riverside of the tunnel. They were lowered down by rope to a cave only a mountain goat — if there were any mountain goats around — could find. The Badger sat the first one, Phil, on his ass at the edge and wrapped rope around his waist. The Badger climbed down the side and got into the small cave."

"Send now," the Badger yelled.

Phil pleaded for his life with grunts and groans, undetectable through his gag. Mickey, Pete, and I grabbed the rope. Gary placed his foot on Phil's back and pushed him off the side, then joined us to help lower him down. When the Badger yelled, "Stop now," we dug our heels in and held on. The Badger reached out and pulled Phil into the small cave. He yelled, "Pull rope," and after we pulled the rope up, he yelled, "Next one."

The Hunchback was ready to shit his pants. Gary wrapped the rope around his waist and tied it. Sitting on the edge, he looked straight down, maybe 200-300 feet. Shaking his head and pleading through undetectable grunts and groans. But his eyes spoke plenty. Gary looked back. "Ready?" he asked.

"Go ahead," Mickey said. Gary put his foot on the Hunchback's back and pushed. We lowered him down until we heard the Badger yell.

"Goddamn ingenious idea," Pete said. They can't escape down there." Pete was continually praising the Badger. We didn't say much because he was right, and we figured it was the Italian thing between them. It killed Gary, though, that he couldn't shit-talk Pete. At least not with the Badger around. But Gary was as much in awe of the Badger as any of us.

"Oh, they can escape," Mickey pointed out. "But they'd be dead if they try."

The Badger didn't need help coming back up. For him, it was a piece of cake. Dit, Eleanor, and Georgie returned to the Hill. The Badger didn't want their car left on the old dump road — a signal to the police, he said. Besides, the Badger was protective of Dit — didn't want anything to happen to her. If the police came and grabbed her, the Badger would go nuts. The Badger gave Georgie the keys to mobsters Buick and Georgie parked it on a street in the 'Heights.' Eleanor drove back to the Hill.

Dusk rolled in as the sun dropped. We enjoyed the beautiful weather; we've had our share of rain. Thanks to Billy, we used the lean-to to stay out of the rain at night. During the day we got wet and stayed wet. Homesickness also set in. It was an August Friday evening, and we've been in hiding too long. Most Friday nights we'd be chasing girls under the El in Manayunk or "Ridge riding," what we called a car full of us riding up and down Ridge Avenue in Roxborough looking for girls — or hanging out at the church-school on Jefferson Street.

We might have had an American Legion baseball game at Narberth or Ardmore. I'd be warming up Russo or DiCicco, and Pete would be hitting ropes around the field. Gary had been complaining that his baseball hat was uncurling his blonde curls, the curls girls love to rub their hands through. He swore the hats would make us bald.

Maybe we'd be in the grandstand at a Phillies game at Connie Mack Stadium, sneaking down to the good seats. Or down the shore. We walked the boardwalk in Wildwood, trying to pick up girls. We placed fifty-cent bets against each other in the shooting galleries or knocked down stuff with a ball or beanbag. We'd throw a football around on the beach or had a beach football game against kids we didn't know. No, instead we were on top of a stinkin' tunnel in the middle of nowhere. It was hot, and the mosquitos were all over us. Even bug spray didn't work. But we felt the end was near, that either the mob or the cops would find us, and we still hadn't decided which was better.

We began playing cards by a flashlight in our cave with the Badger watching over us like a mother hen. Gary and Pete trading insults, or whose mother did what. It wasn't late when we heard a voice down on the tracks.

"Yo, Gary, Pete, you guys up there?"

"Who's that?" the Badger asked.

Gary moved to the edge of the tunnel and looked down. "Yo," he yelled. "Is that you, Johnny Ciarlello?"

"Wel, it ain't Santa Claus, Pecker."

CHAPTER 44

A Digging Fool

Tuesday Afternoon
Lower Merion Police Headquarters, Ardmore

Desk sergeant Zip Roberts was ready to bust some balls at Lower Merion police headquarters in Ardmore. It was part of his job. Nobody took it personally. If fact it was part of the joy of reporting for duty — sparing with Zip.

"Yo, look who it is, the Lone Ranger and Tonto. You got the cavalry ready to capture those kids?"

Detectives Tommy Lochran and Butch Frost found it pleasurable to take shit from Zip. "No," Butch replied, "we're gonna turn in our badges and get bullshit desk jobs like you."

"Besides," Lochran pointed out, "they're probably with your mother, you know…," and Lochran made whistling sounds and wiggled his fist near his hip.

"Uh, oh," Roberts chirped, "listen to this. Once from the Hill, always from the Hill. The captain wants to see you two. The two G-men are with him. They want to know about your cavalry operation, so maybe they can copy it to catch kids smoking in the boys' room."

"Smoke this," Frost said, as he turned and grabbed his crotch.

"Hey," Roberts yelled, "I mentioned the boys' room and look what you grab. That's an automatic mental response from jerking off in the boys' room. That's proven."

"Learned from you," Lochran yelled.

Agents Hacket and Watts were indeed in the Captain's office. They stood and gave their customary handshakes.

"Sit, fellows," the captain barked, "we need to go over some things."

After Lochran and Frost took their seats, the Captain asked for a rundown on the kid witnesses.

"They're on top of the tunnel," Lochran said, "there's no doubt about that, but so far we haven't seen them there."

"There are some things you should know about, detectives," FBI agent Watts said. "These kids are right in the middle of a mob war."

"And it's gone international," agent Hacket added.

"Oh, yea," Frost replied, "you told us about that the last time, about how the Otts knew something they shouldn't have about Kennedy. One of the many theories out there."

"It's not just a theory," Watts said, "it's what the Federal Bureau of Investigation is leaning on. That the mob was involved in the President's murder."

"And the Otts knew about that? Come on, agent," detective Lochran said, "I think the theories about the Cubans or Russians make better sense."

"You're right," agent Hacket said, "the mob was tight with the Cubans in casino gambling and drugs. When the Bay of Pigs failed, the mob took it out on Kennedy."

"Walter Otts," agent Watts continued, "was a tailor and a damn good one. His clientele consisted of the heads of La Cosa Nostra."

"Which ones? the Captain asked.

"Pick one," Watts said. "They all employed him, and they fought over him. Our theory is that he heard something he shouldn't have, and for that, he and his wife were gunned down."

"The Philly mob?" Frost asked.

"Right now," Hacket answered, "I'd say yes."

"There are two individuals involved with the boys that you should know about," agent Watts said. "The first is Louis Regina, the consigliere for the Newark, NJ, crime family of Vito Graziano. The second is a psychopath killer who works for the Sicilians in southern Italy,"

"The first one," agent Hacket added, "we know he is involved. We picked him up on the New Jersey Turnpike the night before last."

"Is he in custody," Lochran asked.

"No," Watts replied. "We could have arrested him for witness tampering, but the guy's a lawyer, and it would've been hard to make it stick."

"Besides," Hacket said, "we know who he is, and we can watch him. If you gentlemen can't come up with the kids, we can grab him again and force him to tell us where they are. He's s a reasonable guy for a mob lawyer."

"What about the second guy, the one from Italy," the Captain asked.

"That one you don't want to mess with," Watts replied. "Our people who watch the La Cosa Nostra in Italy say he boarded a plane in Rome for Philadelphia. Now we doubt he's a Phillies fan, so why is he coming to Philadelphia? His name is Giovanni Randazzo, the Badger."

"We believe he was picked up at the airport by Regina," Hacket said. "We don't know all the pieces, but it doesn't make sense."

"What doesn't make sense," Watts added, "is why the Sicilians would send a killer to America to help four boys."

"In Italy, namely Sicily," Hacket said, "the mob is ruthless. Much more than here. They're better organized and have more control over the courts and police.

"The Sicilians loved Kennedy, and they loved Walter Otts. So, what we are describing to you detectives isn't farfetched," Watts said.

"Holy shit," Frost replied. "Who would have thought. So, you think Regina and this Badger fellow are with the boys?"

"We've searched high in low around the Philadelphia area for Randazzo and came up with nothing. But we know he's here because he was on the flight."

"If he is with the boys," Lochran asked, "will he protect them?"

"Detective," Hacket said, "think of him as a wild, vicious dog. If he feels attached to those kids, he will come after you; you can be sure of that."

"And he has no respect for police and law and order, "Watts said, "the fact that you are detectives mean nothing to him."

"Why do they call him the Badger?" Lochran asked.

"Our contacts in Italy," Hacket said, "say he's a digging fool. He can dig tunnels and caves within hours. He's been tied to several bank heists in Germany, France, and Switzerland. Once, he tunneled into the gruesome Italian Bologna prison and sprung three Sicilian mobsters inside. Then dug another tunnel on the other side of the prison to get out — while the cops and guards were waiting at the other end of the first tunnel. Fooled the shit right out of them."

"Goddamn," Lochran exclaimed.

"He's been known to bury himself alive to escape capture," Watts said, "and walk away on the other side of town."

"Holy, shit," Frost said. "and you think he's with those kids?"

"Well," Hacket observed, "if you can't find them, start looking underground."

"Take your safeties off your firearms," Watts said, "if this guy attacks, you won't have time to pull your gun and click off the safety. You pull your weapon and start shooting. Immediately."

"Shoot for his head," Hacket said, "his skin is like that of a wild turkey. Ever hunt wild turkeys?"

"Sure," Lochran said, "plenty of times. You can hit them with a 12-gauge, three, four times, and they'll get back up and run because the shot didn't penetrate their tough skin."

"Shoot for the head, gentlemen," Hacket said. "He is lightning fast and strong as an ox. He'll gouge your eyes out and bite off your nose before you even see him. Are you armed with shotguns and do you have snipers?"

"They do now," the Captain said. "Loch, Butch, are you ready for this?"

"Oh, yeah," Lochran said. "He doesn't scare us. We grew up on the Hill, remember?"

∽

Monday Evening
Newark, New Jersey
Trattoria Resturant

Immediately following Louis Regina's meeting with the federal agents at the Howard Johnson's on Monday evening, a little after dark thirty, Louis made a phone call from a payphone at the restaurant. Then he took the New Jersey Turnpike north to Newark. His one call was to Maria Esposito, secretary to Vito Graziano, Don of the Newark crime family.

The rain continued to beat down on his windshield as thoughts ran through Louis's mind like wine at an Italian wedding. It didn't take him long, but he wasn't the first there. As Louis turned onto Monroe Street and passed the small Italian café called Trattoria, Vito Graziano's Ford Galaxy sat out front, the driver behind the wheel. Two men — Mr. Graziano's security guards — in raincoats and hats pulled down, stood on either side of the doorway, hands in their raincoat pockets. Louis continued down the street and parked a half a block away.

As he got out, he pulled his raincoat collar up and walked up the sidewalk. Without a word, one of the security guards opened the door, and the other one nodded. Inside, Mr. Graziano was seated alone at his favorite table in the corner. There was no one else in the restaurant. As Louis approached, Mr. Graziano stood.

"Louis," he said, as he stuck out his hand. They shook, and Mr. Graziano embraced his consigliere; he slapped his back once or twice. They both sat.

"Tony," Mr. Graziano called out softly to the restaurant's maitre d', owner, and only waiter. Trattoria catered to the Newark mob and offered the wine and pasta Mr. Graziano preferred. "Please get my friend a glass of Chianti."

"Certainly, Mr. Graziano," Tony replied. "Mr. Regina, how are you, sir?"

"I'm fine, Tony, thank you," Louis replied.

"I suppose those boys are still in hiding," Mr. Graziano said, "they've held out well, wouldn't you say?"

"Extremely well," Louis replied. "But it may be coming to a close, and we need to discuss my role in it."

"How do you mean?" Mr. Graziano said.

"Last night on the Jersey turnpike to Philly, I was pulled over and taken to a Howard Johnson's to meet with two FBI agents. They have a theory that Angelo Morello killed Walter Otts because Otts overheard information about Kennedy's assignation."

"Okay, then our plan is working," Graziano replied. "Any involvement of the CIA?"

"No sir, I haven't picked up anything."

"Good, how about Jack Ruby, any mention there?"

"Nothing."

"Good, the FBI knows nothing then," Mr. Graziano said firmly, "they're just reaching for straws. Some shirt and ties are brainstorming ideas. They bought into our plan perfectly. The CIA will let them run with it knowing it will lead nowhere."

"As long as Ruby continues to keep his mouth shut," Louis added.

"Mr. Ruby is solid. The entire scheme rests on his shoulders. He has too much to lose by flipping now. Lyndon Johnson will leave our Cuban hotel and gambling interests alone. I'll let the New York families know what's going on. Good work, Louis."

"Thank you, sir. I am concerned about one thing. The agents let me know that they know the Sicilians sent Randozza."

"Of course," Mr. Graziano said. "They want to watch and see what you'll do. I bet they even took your gun."

Louis chuckled, "Now I know why you're the boss."

"You're wise to stay away from the boys. Do the boys know the police know where they are?"

"I don't think so. After our meeting, I plan to go down to the Hill and find a kid who will tell them."

"Be careful," Mr. Graziano said, "if they find you involved, they'll arrest you for witness tampering whether they have proof or not. They can hold you six months during an investigation."

Louis nodded.

"What I'm most concerned about are the boys," Louis explained, "and I know you are too. If the police get their hands on them, it could spell trouble for us. With the Sicilian hitman with them, it could be a huge problem down the road."

"Louis," Mr. Graziano said, "I understand your concerns. Things could get out of control if the boys survive. You think the police are closing in on them?"

"Yes, sir."

Mr. Graziano looked at his watch. "It's two a.m. in southern Italy. Eight o'clock in New York. I'll go back to my home and try to get Tony the Wolf in New York. See if he can set me up with the Sicilians by phone on Wednesday. Count on coming to my office first thing Wednesday morning, Louis."

"Yes, sir," Louis said.

"Maybe we can get the Badger to make his move before the police come. The only person who can do that is Carmine Di Pesa, head of the Sicilian La Cosa Nostra. Carmine sent the Badger over here as a favor to me. Let me see if Tony the Wolf can get us together on the phone, fast. If so, I may need you at my side tomorrow during the call."

"Of course, sir," Louis said.

Mr. Graziano stood. He held out his hand. "Louis, I'll see you on Wednesday. Thank you for your good work on this."

"It's a pleasure, sir," Louis replied. They shook, and Louis got two more slaps on the back."

"Oh Louis, you might want to stay someplace off the turnpike for the next few nights, rather than at home. The feds may be watching your house."

Louis nodded.

Mr. Graziano stopped before he reached the door and turned toward Louis. "Louis, your car keys please," he asked.

Without question, Louis retrieved them from his pants pocket, got up, and handed them to Mr. Graziano. "Tony," Mr. Graziano said to the waiter, "please get Louis another glass of Chianti."

"Certainly, Mr. Graziano," Tony replied and went into the kitchen.

"Relax a bit, Louis," Mr. Graziano said, "have another glass of wine. You have a lot on your shoulders. There will be a .45, and a chest holster on the seat of your car. Your keys will be beneath the floor mat. Check your trunk, too."

"Thank you, sir."

At the restaurant door, one of the security guards, holding the door open, said," Mr. Graziano, your car is ready, sir."

With that Vito Graziano walked through the restaurant door toward his Ford Galaxy.

CHAPTER 45

"With his dinky out?"

Wednesday Afternoon
South Philadelphia

Angelo Morello leaned back in his chair and looked out at Snyder Avenue. He wanted a cigar, but the doctor told him three a day. "That's it, Angelo, three a day." *Vaffanculo. What does he know?* Angelo can't think straight unless he has a smoke, so he reached and opened the lid to the beautiful cedar cigar box on his desk. It was a gift from the Vatican, with a short note signed in ink by Pope Saint Paul: Angelo, Dio vi benedica (Angelo, God bless).

Angelo picked out a cigar, one of those long, thin jobs from Tuscany. It looked like an eight-inch dead snake. Most people wouldn't guess it was a cigar, but an overgrown Slim Jim that's been in the sun too long. Not one of those fat stogies like the hoodlums roll down on the plantations. These handmade Garibaldi beauties were rolled by artisans not far from the cradle of the Renaissance, in a little town called Lucca.

Angelo knew about Lucca. He's been back to the old country seven, eight times. Sat in the shade on Main Street with the old men and played bocce when the sun set, and the air got cooler.

"Ah, I made a great shot, no?"

"No, no è fuori, non va bene, mi morki il culo grasso, ha, ha, ha," (No, no it's not good, it's too wide, you bite my fat ass, ha, ha, ha). It was doubtful that the old men in Lucca knew who they sat in the shade with as they smoked cigars and eyed the young Lucca women shopping on the square. Doubtful they knew he was responsible for over 25 murders. "He has the business in America," was all they said.

He smelled it, rolled it around in his fingers, and smelled it again. Held it out in front of him. He kissed it and whispered, "*Mio dio, meglio, ha un odore migliore di una puttana francese*" (*my God, smells better than a French whore*). He opened his middle drawer and took out the cutter, snipped off the end cap, and placed it in his mouth. Next to the box was a small lid-less, four-inch-long box of striking matches.

With a swift hand — he could do it in his sleep — he struck the match and lit the Garibaldi, waved the match several times, then dropped it in the glass ashtray. With the cigar placed just so in his mouth, he did his customary inhalation — three, four times quickly, drawing the smoke through the cigar and into his lungs. He blew the smoke upward and watched it billow across the ceiling and down his office walls.

Now he could think. He swiveled his chair around again so he could gaze out onto Snyder Avenue and enjoy the sweet fragrance of the cigar. And think.

A tap on the door disturbed him.

"What?" he said, as impatiently and angerly as he could.

"Angelo, non fumare piú ne hai abbastanza" (no more smoking, you've had enough).

"Vaffanculo donna," Angelo answered, "ho bisogno di pensare." (Fuck off old woman, I need to think). She mumbled something as she walked away, but Angelo was deaf to it.

Those kids, those punk, wet nose sons-a-bitch kids threaten to bring down his empire. How so? The other bosses watched closely. Particularly Newark and New York. Thorns up his ass most times, anyway. They laughed at him. He could hear them. Hear what they said. Hear their snickering. *Shit, they may even be helping the snotnose bastard kids in some way.* That thought made him inhale again. *If I find out, I'll kill the bastards.*

290

The Newark and New York bosses told him to leave the Otts alone. "Angelo, why create trouble? Forget about it. Concentrate on the drugs and whores, the numbers. Fix a few baseball games. Those Otts will be dead soon naturally, you know, drop-dead on their own account. *Shit, they will. They'll have us all in prison.*

Nobody tells Angelo Morello his business. He pulled the cigar out of his mouth and watched the smoke ease out of the tip. It immediately reminded him of the sexy belly dancer he knew at that restaurant, with the dark eyes and big tits. What was it called? Non ricordo piú la merda, he said under his breath (can't remember shit, anymore). She could move her body like… Middle East. That's-a it, Middle East-a Restaurant. He put the cigar back in his mouth and smiled. *Not so goddamn senile, after all.* But enough of that. He had thinking to do. Important thinking.

Little Joey. The name dropped into his brain as if it was sent from the Holy Mother of God, Mary. Little Joey. The kid was hungry. Just like Angelo was hungry fifty years ago on the streets of Rome. He sucked in the smoke. He held it there, ten, maybe twelve seconds, then collapsed his chest and slowly and quietly exhaled, sending more smoke into the room. *Middle East-a goddamn restaurant.*

He looked at the phone. *Go ahead. Do it. Trust your instincts. Trust Mary, the mother of God, pick it up Angelo, pick it up.* He stared at the phone, then quickly reached for the phone, picked it up, and dialed a number.

"Nicky," he said, speaking softly into the phone. "Bring-a Little Joey here to see me as soon as you can. And bring-a the two boys who picked up Porky Bananas' body in them woods. Bring-a them, too.

"Call Tommy Sneakers and Jimmy Whispers. Put them on high alert and have them stay put. That's right. That's-a correct. Then bring Little Joey and them two boys to see me now. Right away."

With that, the Gentle Don hung up. He smiled, and thought, *Middle East-a goddamn-restaurant.*

~

Thursday Morning
South Philadelphia

Nicky did precisely as his boss said. It didn't take him long to round up Little Joey and the two low-level gangsters who picked up and then buried Porky Bananas. To these mobsters, when the boss says now, now means now. But a now followed by a right away means drop what you're doing. Nicky rapped on Mr. Morello's office door.

"Come in-a."

The two-low level gangsters who picked up and buried Porky Bananas body near the airport were scared shitless. En route, they asked Nicky why Angelo Morello, boss of the bosses, wanted to meet them. Nicky enjoyed busting their chops a little. "Don't worry," he told them, "if the boss wanted to whack you, you'd be fuckin' dead now. He wouldn't be invitin' you to his home."

And then he added, "Unless he wanted to shoot you himself." Then Nicky laughed. The two low levels turned white. "Take it easy, take it easy," Nicky said in between laughs, "I'm just pullin' your chains."

Little Joey sat in the front seat. He wasn't sure why he was invited either, but Joey felt that the boss liked him. At meetings, he would ask for his advice. The boss always praised him. "That's a-good, Joey. You gentlemen take notice, this-a kid's on his way up." Nicky didn't dick around with Little Joey. He winked at Joey and said, "I think the boss has somethin' good for you, know what I'm sayin'?"

Angelo watched closely as the four men entered his office. As they took their seats, Angelo immediately picked up the nervousness in the two low levels. He didn't mind busting a few chops, either.

"You," he said, "what's-a you name?"

"I'm Carmen."

"And you, what's-a you name?"

"Rosy."

"Rosy? That's-a girl's name, Rosy. How come-a you got a girl's name?

Rosy looked at his shoes. "I don't know, Mr. Morello, I was just given it."

"By who," Angelo asked, "by you mama?"

"No, sir. I fucked up, er, sorry. I beat up a couple of kids in the schoolyard, so they gave me that name."

"Well, if you beat-a shit out of kids, how come they give you-a that name? That'd be a name if you pussied out."

"Well, I guess my face was red, kind of."

With that, Angelo laughed heartily, which made him cough, which is why Mrs. Morello didn't want him to smoke. Sometimes she saw him spit blood on the sidewalk.

After he composed himself, he said, "That's a good one, a good one." Nicky was laughing too, and Little Joey was smiling and shaking his head.

"You two boys," Angelo said, "you have promise in my organization. You did-a good job picking up and burying Porky Bananas. Good-a job, good-a job."

"If you get picked up," Angelo continued, "you tell the police that Porky died of a heart attack while jerking off-a near a tree, understand-a?"

Little Joey smiled again and Nicky, his arms folded in front of him, looked out the window and chuckled. They knew what was coming.

"Rosy, what-a you tell the police?"

"That he was jerking off and he died of a heart attack," Rosy answered.

"With his dinky out?" Angelo asked.

Rosy looked scared and looked at Carmen.

"Why you-a look at him when I'm talking to you?" he asked Rosy.

"Yeah, with his dick out."

"Was it a big one or little weenie?"

"It was okay, about average," Rosy answered.

With that, Angelo laughed and coughed, spitting out blood. "About average," and he laughed and coughed some more.

When Angelo Morello finished his hearty laugh, he wiped his face with several handkerchiefs. His men noticed the bloody hankies when he stuffed them in his pocket.

"Boss," Nicky asked, "you okay? Can I get you something? A glass of water or something?"

Angelo Morello scoffed. "How bout a good piece of ass, you got-ta that handy?" The men in the room chuckled. It was a nervous chuckle. Little Joey looked nervously at Nicky.

"Boss," Nicky asked, "you want us to do something. What can we do for you?"

"Joey," Angelo said, "you-a ready for-a your first-a big job?"

Little Joey sat up in his chair. "Absolutely, boss," he said.

"That-a good, Joey. You-a going to be-a star. You-a take these two men here, Rosy and-a, I don't know the other name. They will show you where they picked up Porky Bananas in the woods. Then, you get-a Tommy Sneakers and-a Jimmy Whispers. And you go back to the spot in the woods. Look around. Go-a here and there. And you-a find them kids and take care of this-a problem once and for all. Can you do that, Joey?"

"You got it, boss," Joey said, nodding.

"Boss," Nicky asked, "what about Crazy Phil and the Hunchback? Are they both still after the kids?

"Ah," Angelo replied, "they-a pain in my ass. I don't know where they are, haven't heard-a from them. Maybe they're dead. Who knows? But Joey's in charge now. He's in charge of the whole god-damn-a thing."

"All right, boss," Joey said. "We'll get started on it right away."

Nicky looked skeptical. It's not often a boss will give out a job that's been assigned out. Highly unusual. Nicky didn't like it.

"Boss," Nicky asked, "what happens if Joey runs into Phil and the Hunchback in the woods? Maybe they got something going, and Joey, Tommy, and Whispers stumble in their way?"

Angelo slammed his hand down on his desk. "Va' a fare in culo," he yelled. "You do as I say-a. No questions. No answers. I'm-a tired of all this shit. Be a man, goddamn it. Do as the boss says or you get the hell out."

"You got it, boss," Joey said. "Consider this done. Those kids are fuckin' dead."

"That's-a my boy," Angelo yelled. "That's-a why you is in charge. Now go-a and don't come back until them-a kids is all buried next to Porky Bananas. We'll have a nice-nice funeral."

And then he started laughing and coughing.

Thursday Afternoon
Belmont Hills

Tommy Lochran took time off Thursday afternoon to clear his head regarding the kid witnesses hiding. He had put long hours into his work and wanted to spend time with his wife. Therefore, he was at home having a late lunch with Delores. When detective Lochran ran into difficult "detective problems," he usually turned to her.

"Listen, something is bothering me, and I'd like to get your opinion," Lochran said to Delores, in between bites of tuna salad on rye.

"No," she mocked, "something is bothering you? I couldn't tell." Then she smiled. "The boys hiding out?"

He nodded, took another bite, then said, hardly understandable when he talks with food in his mouth — which Delores dislikes — "Eu don to wet hurr."

She shook her head, smiled, and said, "Why don't you finish chewing, and then let me know what you just said?"

Lochran smiled. Took a sip of his iced tea — another thing Delores disliked, drinking with food in his mouth — swallowed, cleared his throat, and said, "Sorry. Born and raised on the Hill."

"Yeah," Delores said sarcastically, "and never left."

Lochran smiled and gulped his iced tea, then said, "To answer your original question, I'm worried about the four boys getting hurt in a police raid."

"Have you spoken to those boys?" she asked.

He was about to take another sip and stopped. He put his tea down and looked at his wife. "No," he said.

"Well, instead of driving them out like deer," she said, "why don't you just go and talk to them?"

"They're hiding, I can't," he said impatiently.

"Oh, come on," his wife replied, "you can't find four 15-year old kids? You find rapists and murderers. We're talking about children hiding there. Let's say Shane was there, what would you do?"

"Lochran studied his wife's face, then said, "I'd go get him and kick his ass." Then he winked.

"Duh," she answered. "Instead of taking the FBI and the entire Lower Merion police force, not to mention the Staties, why don't you go talk to them like a father? I'm sure you will charm their socks off."

"They're probably not wearing any socks; they've been in the woods for nearly two months."

"Loch, maybe you're making a mountain out of a mole hole. Maybe all you have to do is speak to them and then call off D-day."

Lochran wiped his mouth with his napkin. Pushed away from the table and reached over and retrieved his jacket from another kitchen chair. He folded it over his arm and said, "Maybe you should be the detective, here. I'm going for a ride."

She smiled. "Don't shoot them, Loch."

He mockingly scratched his cheek with his middle finger and said, "Love you, sweetheart."

"Love you too, Loch, be careful. Oh, Loch, be home for dinner?"

Detective Lochran stared back at his wife, and she laughed. That was his I don't know response. Lochran went out to his car, pulled out of the driveway, and headed for Mary Water's Ford Road. He was minutes from the old logging road at the top of the hill. When he got there, he pulled over and decided not to park on the old road. He pulled away and went to the top of the hill and parked on a side street.

He got out, locked his car, and walked back down to the logging road.

CHAPTER 46

"...Search Up their Asses"

Thursday Afternoon
Newark, New Jersey

When Louis Regina entered the outer office of crime boss Vito Graziano, Maria sprang from her seat and quickly opened the door into Mr. Graziano's office. She smiled at him, and he returned the smile. Mr. Graziano was seated at his desk. He got up, and they shook hands; no back slaps this time.

"Have a seat, Louis," he said. Then he picked up the phone.

"Maria," he said, "put the call through now, please. That's right. Good, thank you."

He hung up. "It will take a few minutes for the call to be set up. Maria will put Mr. Di Pesa through to us via the speaker. It's a new method that we haven't tried before, but I'm sure it will work fine. Maria is not only beautiful, but she's also very good at these sorts of things.

"Carmine Di Pesa lives in Corleone in southern Italy and is head of the Corleone clan of the Cosa Nostra. The Badger works for him." The tap on the door interrupted Mr. Graziano's explanation.

"Sir, I have Mr. Di Pesa on hold," Maria said.

"Thank you, Maria," Mr. Graziano replied. "Can you check to make sure the speaker is on and working?"

"Yes, sir," she answered. She took the speaker on Mr. Graziano's desk, lifted it, and turned it on. "It will be fine, sir."

"Thank you, Maria." He waited until she closed the door behind her.

The conversation was in Italian, in which both Vito Graziano and Louis Regina were fluent.

Mr. Graziano leaned forward slightly and said, "Mr. Di Pesa, are you there, sir?"

"Yes, I am here, Vito," the speaker barked, 'but please, I am Carmine."

"Carmine," Mr. Graziano said, "we have a little situation here where I may need your help. But first, I want to thank you for sending Giovanni Randazzo to America. He has been a great help."

"I have sent my best; he can solve any situation that exists."

'He's been protecting the four boys who are hiding out from the police. He has done a marvelous job."

"The police will never catch them."

Mr. Graziano looked at Louis, though for a few seconds, then leaned back into the speaker. "The police are closing in on the boys and Mr. Randazzo..."

Mr. Di Pesa interrupted, "Do not worry Vito, the Badger will never be found. The police will even search up their asses and not find Giovanni. How long has he been with the hiding boys?"

Mr. Graziano looked at Louis. Louis paused for a moment, then held up the four fingers of each hand and mouthed eight weeks.

Mr. Graziano nodded and leaned forward, "Eight weeks," he said.

Di Pesa chuckled, "Oh, don't worry Vito, by now he has had time to dig underground and prepare for any onslaught. I bet to you the finest case of Chianti and cheese from our Sicilian farms that the police will not even smell his farts."

Mr. Graziano and Louis stared at each other, speechless for 20 seconds, and Mr. Graziano replied, "Would there be any way, Carmine, that he could be instructed to move forward on this?"

"What?" Carmine replied, "What do you mean? He can never be instructed. He can never be stopped from carrying out his work. Never, as you say, in a million years. He is a gift from God, and even God cannot tell him what to do. Are you unappreciative of this gift, Vito? Only an unappreciative one would speak in this manner."

"Carnine," Mr. Graziano replied, "I am most appreciative. It is a wonderful gift, one that I can never repay."

"Then don't ask such foolish questions, Vito, it does not bode well for your leadership in the stink hole Newark. When the Badger is finished with his job, he will be done and return to Italy. Appreciative the gift you have and don't waste my time."

With that, Carmine Di Pesa hung up.

"Carmine, are you still there, sir? Are you there?"

Nothing. Mr. Graziano looked pale. He clicked off the speaker and sat back in his chair. He stared at the bookcase on the left side of his office and said, without looking at Louis, "Louis, I think you need to join the Badger and the boys and try to move things along."

"I can do that boss," Louis replied.

Mr. Graziano turned slightly and looked at Louis. "Maybe you can get the Badger to do his job," he said, "and take care of business."

With that, they both stood and shook hands, and Louis left the office. Within a few minutes, he was on the turnpike, headed south to Philadelphia.

~

Thursday Afternoon
Heading to the Tunnel

The two low-level mob guys who buried Porky Bananas in the swamp by the airport took Joey to the Hill to find the spot where they retrieved his body. Little Joey was driving his T-bird and was impatient.

301

"Thought you knew where it was," Joey said, "I mean shit, come on."

"The street," Rosy said, "I can't think of it. It had some cunt's name."

"Some cunt's name?" Joey said. "What the....? Here, let me pull up next to this jagoff."

Joey pulled over next to a man walking on the sidewalk and put down his window, "Yo, come here a sec. We're looking for a street that has a cunt's name. Can you help us out?"

The man smiled and shook his head. "Some cunt's name?" he asked.

"Yeah, that's what I said, you got shit in your ears or something?"

"Let me think. Could it be Mary Waters Ford?"

"Yes, that's it," Carmen yelled from the back seat. "That's fuckin' it."

"All right," Joey said, "where can we find this street?"

"See that stop sign up there," the man asked, "that's it. Turn right, and you're on it."

Joey drove up the hill and made a right onto Mary Waters Ford Road.

"All right, all right, just follow this for a while," Carmen said.

"You're the brain trust of you two, I can tell," Joey said.

"Now follow this road," Carmen said.

"What else can I do? I'm on the fuckin' road, ain't I?"

They dipped down the hill past Centennial Road leveled out and started up the hill. Both Carmen and Rosy were glued to the passenger side windows looking for the old logging road.

"Slow down a little; it's coming up."

Little Joey didn't like working with the two low-levels, but they knew where Bananas got whacked. The boss of bosses concluded that the kid witnesses weren't far from that spot. Besides, the boss hadn't heard from Crazy Phil and the Hunchback. They could've gotten lost in the woods, or they were dead, for all he knew. So, the boss concluded, this had to work.

"Slow down, it's right in here."

"Fuck that shit," Joey yelled, "I'm going slow enough."

"All right, stop, stop right here," Carmen hollered.

Carmen and Rosy got out of the car and walked a few yards up the old logging road. They were sure this was the road the Hunchback told them about — where they could find Bananas' body.

"Joey," Carmen yelled, "come with us up this road."

Reluctantly, Joey got out.

"What," he said, "is this the place?

"Up here," Rosy instructed. They walked maybe 20 yards into the woods. Carmen and Rosy poked around a little just off the road and figured that was the spot. Even if it wasn't, they were going to say it was because they knew Little Joey would have whacked them on the spot.

"Right here," Carmen said. "Off this road maybe 40 feet or so. That's where we found the body."

Joey looked around. He looked in the woods, and he made some mental notes about how far from the cunt road they were.

"You're sure," Joey said. "No bullshit here, you're sure this is the spot?"

"Completely positive," Carmen said.

"Completely positive," Joey said, repeating and mocking Carmen. "All right let's get back to the car. We're going back."

As they returned to the car, Joey thought about whacking the two low- levels, but it was broad daylight, and he'd be returning to the spot with Tommy Sneakers and Jimmy Whispers. How good would it look with the two low-levels lying dead on the road? Anyway, the boss didn't order it, and if the boss wants to whack them, there'll be a better time and place. They walked back to the car and Joey made a U-turn and headed back to South Philadelphia.

Friday 4 a.m.
Belmont Hills

Delores Lochran let the phone ring for several minutes before hanging up. She redialed the number. Finally, Frost picked up.

"Hello?" he said, wiping the sleep from his tired eyes.

"Butch, it's Dee."

"Dee? what's the matter, Loch sick?"

"No, but do you know where he is?"

"No," Frost replied, "he took yesterday afternoon off, and I'm scheduled to pick him up around seven. Something wrong?"

"We had lunch together yesterday, and I suggested he go and talk to the boys that are hiding. When he left, he didn't say for sure, but I assumed that's where he was going."

"Yea, that sounds like Loch. So?"

"He didn't come home last night."

"Wait. What?"

"He didn't come home last night, and I'm worried. He usually tells me when he'll be out all night."

"Holy shit. You sure he went after the boys?"

"Well, he didn't say that, exactly, but I could tell the boy's thing was bothering him, so I suggested he try to talk to them. I could see where his mind was. I'm sure that's where he went."

"All right, calm down, and sit tight. I'll look for him, and I'll get back to you sometime this morning." Then Frost hung up.

He changed quickly, strapped on his gun, and headed for the driveway. He went up Springfield, crossed over to Ashland, went up the hill and turned right onto Highland. He gunned the engine and pulled up in front of Georgie Scavello's house. Leaving the motor running and the door open, he went up on the porch. With a closed fist, he pounded on the door. Once, then twice, then a third time before he heard a female voice inside yell, "All right, all right, what do you want?"

"Eleanor." Frost hollered, "open up. It's Butch Frost of the Lower Merion police."

She opened the door and said, "Well hell's bells, I don't know no other Butch. What is this, Nazi Germany? You come here at this time of the day?"

"Where's Georgie?" he demanded, his voice rising to a near yell.

"Take it easy, where do you think he is, he's in bed, I'll get him…"

Frost walked through the doorway bumping Eleanor as he went by, went to the bottom of the stairs and hollered, "Georgie, get your ass down here, NOW. He better not go out the window or I'll shoot his ass."

"Jesus Christ, take it easy," she said, "what'd he do this time? Murder somebody? Kill your dog? You cops are getting' awful pushy lately."

Frost waited impatiently at the bottom of the stairs and again yelled,

"Georgie, come on, hurry up."

"Jesus Christ," Eleanor pleaded, "it's still dark, can't this wait until morning?"

As she finished the sentence, her nephew came down the steps. "All right, all right, I'm here. What's the problem?" Georgie asked.

Frost grabbed Georgie by the arm and said, "Get in the car, now. NOW." He shoved Georgie out onto the porch.

"Where are you going?" Eleanor asked. "Where are you taking him? I'm going to call the cops. Oh, wait, you are the cops."

Frost didn't respond. He got in behind the wheel and sped down the steep hill of Highland.

"Where are we going?"

"You're going to show me where the kid witnesses are."

"The fuck if I am. I'm not rattin' on my friends."

Detective Frosts slammed on the brakes at the bottom of Highland. "Listen, Georgie," he yelled, "my partner is in the woods, and I've got to find him. You tell me where they are, or we're getting out of this car, and I'm kickin' your ass."

"Frosty," Georgie said, "I ain't scared of you. You can take the cap shooter you're carrying and put it to my head. I still won't rat on my friends. So, go fuck yourself."

Frost continued up Jefferson Street to the stop sign at Mary Waters Ford Road. "If your partner is in the woods, then his car must be there, right?" Georgie asked. "If so, you can see his car and start from there, and I haven't ratted them out."

Frost turned onto Mary Waters Ford Road and sped toward the old logging road. He looked at Georgie. "Well shit, you aren't as dumb as you look," Frost said. When they got to the logging road at the top of Mary Waters Ford, Georgie told him to stop.

"Back up," Georgie instructed, "and then turn the car as if you are going up the logging road, but don't go on the road. If Loch's car is there, you'll see it."

Frost followed Georgie's suggestion. When the headlights lit up the road, there was no car. "Nope, he ain't here," Georgie said.

"Oh, no, he's here somewhere," Frost said, "he's here all right."

'Wait," Georgie said, "back out, and continue up the hill."

"Why," Frost asked, "where are we going?"

"Just drive," Georgie said, "I want to check something. Go on; his car could be up there."

Frost followed Georgie's directions, and when he got to the top of the hill, Georgie instructed him to turn right, which he did. As soon as the car straightened out, Frost could see Lochran's car parked further down the street. He pulled up behind it."

"All right," Georgie said, "let me out. I'm done here."

"Oh no," Frost demanded, "you're coming with me. I know you know these woods. You're a walking map."

"It's not goin' happen, Frosty," Georgie said. "I found your partner for you, and now I'm leavin'. If you want to shoot me, go ahead." With that, Georgie opened the door and got out. Frost did, too. He watched Georgie walk away. Frost figured he was right; he did find Loch's car. Frost locked his vehicle and then strapped on an ankle holster and put in it a small .32 caliber. By the time Frost got back to Mary Waters Ford Road, Georgie was out of sight.

Detective Frost walked down the hill to the old logging road and started in to look for his partner. Dawn had arrived, and Frost could start to see in the woods. Once the road ended, he cut to the left and into the thickness of the deep woods.

CHAPTER 47

Tommy Sneakers

Friday, 7 a.m.
South Philadelphia
Melrose Diner

It was a warm Wednesday morning when Little Joey picked up Jimmy Whispers and Tommy Sneakers in front of the Melrose Diner on Broad Street. Joey pulled into the Melrose parking lot and cut the engine. He got out and opened the trunk and Jimmy and Tommy each placed a large duffle bag in the trunk. Jimmy Whispers got in the front and Tommy Sneakers in the back. Joey headed up Broad Street toward the newly opened Vine Street Expressway. Still, partially under construction, Joey crawled in one lane to the Schuylkill Expressway to Belmont Hills. He exited at Belmont and went up the hill and on to Mary Waters Ford. He drove to the spot where the two low-level mob men Rosy and Carmen took him.

"Yo, boys," Little Joey said, "check out the name of this street," as he pulled over and slowed down. It was Friday afternoon, and they were headed to the old logging road he hoped would lead them to the snotnose kid witnesses.

Jimmy Whispers leaned over toward Joey, so much so he was only several inches from his ear and softly said, "Mary Waters Ford Road."

"That's right," Joey said, "and you know how we found it? Dumbfuck Rosy Trattalonie said he couldn't remember the name and could only remember it was a cunt's name. Do you believe that? I had to pull over and ask some schmuck where's a road that's a cunt's name."

"What were you doing with Looney Trattalonie?" Tommy Sneakers asked.

Tommy Sneakers wore sneakers everywhere. Never would you find Tommy wearing shoes. Once when he was 14, Tommy and three friends robbed a store on Passyunk Avenue in South Philly. Frankie Fingers tells the story the best because he was there. "We go into this clothing store on Passyunk," Fingers said, "and Tommy takes a pair of sneakers right off one of them fake models. You know, the plastic jobs. I mean, it's broad daylight. We didn't know he was gonna steal anything. All of a sudden, the store alarm goes off. So, we take off. We run out of the store and start up the sidewalk. Tommy comes out of the store with a brand-new pair of Converse sneakers, real beauts, they were. All of a sudden, he plops down on the sidewalk. I turn around and go back and scream, "Tommy, …the fuck, the cops are comin."

It's like he don't even hear me. It's like he's sittin' on his front step without a care in the world. So, I go back and grab his shirt collar and say, "Tommy, we got to get out of here."

"Got to lace them up," Tommy hollered back. "Best sneaks I ever had, but I got to lace them, Frankie."

Sirens are coming down Passyunk, and people are standing around watching, know what I'm sayin? And Tommy ain't movin', he's sittin' there, still lacing them up, and now them cops are out of their cars, and on the sidewalk. Finally, I yell, "Tommy, here they come." So, I take off. I look back and Tommy's right behind me in his new sneakers, with the white laces flopping around, see? Tommy runs right past me, runnin' his ass off. Them sneakers made him Jim Thorpe. I never seen nobody run that fast. Then some cop dives and tackles me on the sidewalk. I got all banged up. He's cuffing me, and I look up, and Tommy is about four blocks away running. He's gettin' away. I thought, *son of a bitch.*

"Tommy never took those sneakers off. He wore them for about six years before they fell apart. He wore them to school, church, everywhere. Even when he got laid, he didn't' take them off. Around the neighborhood, guys would ask, 'Tommy, why'd you sit down on the sidewalk when you was stealing them sneakers. And Tommy'd say, '…the fuck, what kind of schmuck do you take me for?' You think I'm stealin' sneakers that don't fit?'

In South Philly, he was forever Tommy Sneakers."

Little Joey continued his explanation to Tommy Sneakers and Jimmy Whispers. "Looney and his pal Rosy picked up Porky Bananas body in the woods and buried it," Joey said. "So, the boss figures the kid witnesses are in that area of the woods. I had the two bozos' in the car to show me the spot."

Will we have to bury these kids?" Sneakers asked.

"No," Joey replied, "I don't think so. Since those two nitwits know where the woods are, I think the boss will send them back to clean up the mess."

"Good," Sneakers said, "cause I don't like burying no kids."

Joey slowed down. "All right, here's the road right over here. Yeah, that's it, I'll pull up here, and we'll go in a little bit."

Little Joey pulled up on the old logging road and went in about 25 yards. "This is as far as I'll go. I don't want to get stuck back here and have to get towed out. It's still pretty wet."

Joey got out and popped open the trunk. He watched as Jimmy Whispers unraveled a large cloth bag that contained a 16-gauge pump shotgun, about two and a-half-feet long. Joey was trying to look over Tommy Sneakers' shoulder to see the guns. "What are they?" he asked.

Tommy turned his head and told Joey their nine-balls.

"Nine balls," Joey said, "what's that?"

Tommy reached and took a nine-ball and brought it around to show Joey. "It's a pump sawed off. It fires .33 caliber balls, nine per shot. They're double ought buckshot. Ain't it a beauty?"

"Holy shit," Joey exclaimed, "can I hold it?"

"No, you can't hold it," Sneakers said. "It's loaded. You want to hold one go to a gun store."

Jimmy Whispers turned and leaned into Joey's face and said, "They don't have them in gun shops. They're special made."

"How many shots does the thing have?" Joey asked.

"Six," Sneakers said, "pumped rapid fire. If you need any more, you'll be dead."

"Wait," Joey said, "what just fell out of there?"

"What, you writin' a book on ammo or somethin'?" Sneakers asked. "They're baseball grenades. You can throw these little sons-a-bitches like you're throwin' out some stiff at home plate."

Whispers turned again and said into Joey's ear, "Cept with these fuckers you kill the catcher, umpire, and anyone else within 50 feet."

"Goddamn," Joey said, "how many of them you got?'

As Whispers handed Sneakers four and stuffed four into his pockets, Sneakers said, "Enough."

Then Whispers lifted two chest holsters which he gave to Sneakers, who looped them over his head. Whispers handed him two big-ass .45s that Sneakers stuck into the two holsters, one on each side of his chest.

"Jesus Christ," Joey exclaimed. "That's the biggest gun I've ever seen."

Whispers leaned closer to Joey and said, "Just make sure you're never on the receiving end."

Finally, Whispers lifted a Thomson submachine gun out of the bag and handed it to Sneakers.

"Jesus Christ," Joey said, "Jesus fuckin' Christ."

Sneakers laughed, then said, "We done with this dog and pony show, kid? Haven't you seen guns before? What are you carrying?"

"Oh, this .38. I keep it in a belt holster."

Whispers looked at Sneakers, and they both laughed. Then Whispers slammed the trunk shut.

Now this being Joey's first command and the fact that he was with two veteran mob captains, Joey wanted to impress. Like in all jobs, the two made guys, Whispers and Sneakers, would tell everybody how Joey did in his first assignment. When Nicky first contacted Whispers and Sneakers about doing the job under Little Joey, they refused. But Nicky told them the boss requested it, and he was in a highly pissed off mood over these kids. "If he fucks up," Nicky said, "you can take over."

Standing on the logging trail, the mobsters checked their weapons and ammo. "We see any kids we start shootin," Joey said. "We can't let them get away this time. Jimmy looked at Tommy, but neither said a word. "We'll head in this direction," Joey instructed.

Jimmy moved up closer to Joey and whispered, "How do you know it's this direction?"

"That direction is the direction the old road is headed, Jimmy. Just makes sense."

Again, Jimmy looked at Tommy, but neither said anything. By this time, it's well into mid-afternoon. Soon the logging road ended, and Joey had to decide which way to go. He decided it should be off to the left. He said that's what his instincts told him.

Sneakers asked him how often he was in the woods.

Joey laughed and said, "Like, never."

Whispers shot Sneakers another look. The trio veered to the left. It was way past dinner, and the sun was setting. Jimmy Whispers approached Joey and whispered, "It's getting late; I think we should start back." Joey nodded, and they turned around and headed back to the car. When Joey gave a bunch of shit to Rosy and Carmen, that was one thing. But he wouldn't do it to Jimmy and Tommy. They'd drop his ass right there and wouldn't think twice about it.

Joey suggested they find the end of the logging road and start back. The problem was, they couldn't find the logging road, and the sun had dropped considerably. The shadows were long.

"Joey," Tommy Sneakers said, "you said you knew where to go."

"I know," Joey replied, "it's here somewhere. Let's look in this direction."

They veered off again in another direction, and it didn't take a lot of brains to realize they were lost. It would soon be dark. They were fucked. Jimmy got close to Tommy and said, "This kid doesn't know which way's up." Tommy nodded.

The daylight was slowly creeping away, and the trio stumbled over rocks and fallen trees. They were moving like turtles trying to find the logging road. At this point in the early evening, it would've been impossible to find the road, even if they walked right onto it. Finally, Tommy spoke up. "Look, Joey, we're not going to find the car in the dark."

"Well we got to," Joey replied, concerned about his rising reputation in the Morello syndicate. "We got to find it."

Jimmy took Joey by the arm and this time, instead of leaning in close, he pulled Joey toward him. "We're gonna stay here for the night and start again in the morning when we can see." It wasn't a suggestion. He released Joey's arm and pushed him away, a sign that he wasn't pleased. The two experienced mob men were pissed that Joey had them spending the night in the woods.

Whispers leaned into Sneakers and said, "Does this count as fuckin' up?"

"Fuckin'-a," Sneakers answered.

"Find a tree or a bed of leaves and try to get some sleep," Tommy said. "In the morning we'll spread out and cover more ground, which is what we should have done today."

It took Little Joey a couple of hours to get to sleep. Not because of the mosquitoes and hard ground but thinking about how he can't let Tommy Sneakers take over in the morning. Losing control of a job is the second worst thing a mobster can do. The first, of course, is getting your brains blown out.

CHAPTER 48

Hill Kids Unite

Friday, 9:30 a.m.
Ashland Avenue

Billy drove his go-cart across Ashland and into his grandmother's driveway and stopped. Ronny's mother was weeding the rock garden in front of her house. "Mrs. Costello," Billy said, "how are you?" As Billy got off the go-cart seat, he looked up Ashland and saw the detective's car sitting on Ashland near Maple Avenue.

"Oh, hi, Bill. How's your family?"

"Okay, Mrs. Costello, any word about Ronny, yet?"

Ronny's mom dropped a clump of weeds into a bucket and said, "Nothing. We are so worried. Dit had made contact with him and said he's fine, but she won't tell me anything more. Have you heard anything?"

Now Billy, of course, knew that the kid witnesses were atop the Flat Rock Tunnel. He didn't know about the mobsters and the Badger. *Shit,* he thought, *I let this get away from me.* Billy had been busy the past month helping his father restore a bulldozer motor in his garage. He was also learning how to operate a back-ho. Even so, he wasn't spilling his guts to Mrs. Costello until he knew more about the kids and if they were safe.

"Mrs. Costello let me see what I can find out. I'll ask around," he said.

317

"Billy, you're such a good boy," Mrs. Costello remarked. She went back to pulling weeds.

"Thank you, Mrs. Costello," he said.

Billy walked back to his go-cart in his grandmother's driveway and started it back up. Just as he did, Dit came out of the house.

"Billy," she said, "I need to talk to you."

Billy turned the engine off and got off his go-cart as Dit approached him. "I don't want my mother hearing this, all she'll do is worry."

"I won't tell her," Billy said.

"I know that. Listen, there's a lot more going on. You're aware that I was kidnapped at Carl the Butchers."

"Sure," Billy said, "everybody knows."

"They were mafia guys from South Philadelphia, and they were looking for Ronny and his friends. I think they went out to the woods near the tunnel to look for them."

"Oh, boy," Billy said.

"Plus, some crazy guy is living with the boys."

"Crazy guy?" Billy remarked.

"Yes, he's protecting them, but I don't trust him. He looks evil; I would have stayed out there if it wasn't for him. I couldn't stand to look at him."

"What do you think I should do, Dit?"

"What if you rounded up all the kids on the Hill and took them out there. You know, create a big scene. Maybe then you could get Ronny and the boys out of there."

Billy looked away. Then he turned to Dit and said, "I don't know. We could get some kids killed."

"I don't think so," Dit said. "They can't kill everybody."

Billy nodded. "Thanks," he said. "Let me think about it."

Billy went back to his go-cart, started it, and turned it around. He stopped at the edge of the sidewalk. *Should I or shouldn't I,* he thought. *Screw it.* He gunned the engine and turned out onto Ashland Avenue and started up the hill. He was moving pretty good for a kid without a license. He turned onto Highland and sped down and pulled over in front of Georgie Scavello's house. After he turned off the motor and yanked on the emergency brake, Eleanor Scavello came out of the house. She was on her way to the store.

"Eleanor," Billy asked, "is Georgie home."

"No," Eleanor said. "That crazy Frost detective came this morning and dragged him out of bed. It wasn't even light, yet. Took him out to the tunnel to find the boys. I don't know what's going on. I'm worried stiff. I have to get to the store." And she walked away.

Billy sat on his go-cart, thinking. It sounded like Ronny and his friends' needed help, and Billy only knew one place to get it — the kids from the Hill.

"Hey, Billy, what's going on," Richie Pompizzi said, as he came out of his house across the street. "Like your cart, looks like the one they use at Connie Mack Stadium."

Billy smiled. "Yeah, I've heard that before."

"Looks like something is on your mind, Bill. What's wrong?"

"I need to round up some kids, Richie," Billy said. "I need to do it fast."

"What for? You got to push some giant truck?" Richie asked, then chuckled.

"No, nothing like that. Pete, Gary, Mickey, and Ronny have been hiding out by the tunnel."

"Yeah, I know," Richie cut in, "Mr. Turtle our American Legion coach is pissed. We can't win any games without them. What do you want these kids to do, Bill?"

"If we could get a lot of kids, then we'd go out to that tunnel and make sure Pecker and the boys are okay. Maybe even take over and get them out there. What do you think, Richie?"

"Sounds good to me," he said. "I can ask Mr. Turtle if he can get the kids from both teams, you know, the big team and little team. There are lots of kids who will do it; I know there are."

"All right, Richie, let's work on this. We'll ask every kid to meet tomorrow, Saturday, at the firehouse. Let's see how many kids we can get. I'll drive down and see if Johnny Ciarlello'is home. After you talk to Mr. Turtle, go up to Madison Avenue, there are some kids up there. Ask Skippy to get more kids."

"What time tomorrow morning at the firehouse?" Richie asked.

Billy thought for a few seconds, then said, "Seven. Seven tomorrow morning."

"I'm on it, Billy," Richie replied. "Let's go. We can do this."

◈

Friday, 10 a.m.
Top of the Tunnel

The Badger seemed irritated. He stood slightly apart from the boys looking out into the woods, scanning as if he heard something. It was a warm afternoon, just after several days of heavy rain which left the foliage thick and the ground soggy.

"Giovanni," Pete said, "do you hear something?"

The Badger had been telling the boys that he could feel something was up. He was sure that somebody would find the two mob guys he had in the cave jail missing. Then send people to find them. And there were also the police, who surely would come looking for the boys. The Badger couldn't understand why they haven't been here by now. But he was unfamiliar with policing in America. Maybe, he thought, they move more slowly here.

"Someone woods," he said to Pete.

Pete walked up to the Badger's side. The three other boys, hearing what the Badger had said, move in closer, too. "Did you hear anything? Mickey asked. The Badger didn't answer. Pete noticed his nose twitching, like a dog trying to test the wind."

"Someone woods," the Badger repeated, and he pointed.

"Do you want us to go into the woods and look?" Pete asked.

"No, cave," the Badger said.

"I think he wants us to get in the cave," Ronny added.

"I go," the Badger said.

"We want to go with you," Gary suggested.

"No cave."

"We better listen to him," Pete said, "and get in the cave."

We followed the Badger down the side of the tunnel into the main cave. He then showed us two more caves or tunnels; he had dug.

"Wait," Ronny asked, "you dug these by yourself?"

"Yes, tunnels," the Badger said.

"What did you do with the dirt?" Mickey asked. "There's no dirt outside."

"Dirt, woods," he said.

"No shit," Gary remarked. "How did he do that by himself?"

"Giovanni, Badger," the Badger said, smiling.

He crouched down in front of one tunnel. "To woods," he said. Then he went to the other tunnel located in the main cave about ten yards from the entrance to the first tunnel. "Tunnel, dam," he said, again smiling.

"Jesus H. Christ," Gary remarked, "that's unbelievable."

"Tunnels, escape," the Badger said, pointing to the first tunnel and then to the second one.

"How do we know when to use them, Giovanni," Pete asked, "and which one to use?"

Still, in a crouch, the Badger looked at Pete and said, "Split up."

"Jesus Christ," Gary remarked again, "he's unreal."

"No Polack," the Badger told Gary, then he chuckled.

"Guess he told you, dipshit," Pete said, laughing.

"Yeah, all you Dagos are alike," Gary said. To which everybody laughed, even the Badger. The Badger took several axes out of his bag and what looked like a pair of white overalls.

"With me," the Badger said. We followed him out of the cave and up to the top of the tunnel. "Stay Here." With that, he started into the woods. Suddenly he turned around and said, "Visitors come," and he pointed toward the cave.

"We'll go to the cave and tunnels," Pete said, "don't worry."

The Badger smiled and disappeared into the woods.

CHAPTER 49

"Control Woods!"

Friday Mid-Morning
Near the Tunnel

Detective Frost was no stranger to the woods. He's hunted deer and turkey in Potter and Tioga Counties. He's tracked wounded deer over long stretches of dense forests into ravines, across creeks, through fields, sometimes finding the wounded animal, sometimes not. This wasn't much different. He figured that the tunnel was to the east, in the direction of the sunrise. So, he kept the sun to his right as he quietly moved through the woods. Just after crouching low and stepping into a grove of young white birch trees, he thought he heard something.

Trying to stay in the grove of trees, he moved to the edge, where a small meadow of reed grass swayed slightly in the light morning breeze. The ground was wet. At the end of the tall grass, he parted it, and there he was, detective Tommy Lochran, maybe twenty yards away. He was crouched over a creek, dipping water out with his hand. Frost smiled. "Well, how long have you been lost," he called out.

Lochran spun around, and recognizing the voice replied, "Who says I'm lost?"

"Well shit," Frost said, "you've been out here all night, and half the day, your wife worried half crazy, you got dirt all over you, and you haven't eaten. That spells lost in my book."

"I don't know what book that is, partner," Lochran responded. "You can learn a lot both day and night creeping quietly in the woods. You know that."

"So, what'd you learn?" Frost asked.

"Those kids are on top of the tunnel. Somebody is with them, probably that Badger nut. Then suddenly they all disappear; likely into some underground tunnel. Then they reappear. When I was watching them, I snapped a twig, and the Badger heard it. Don't know how he did; they were a football field away."

"Why didn't you take them?" Frost asked.

"Too risky," Lochran replied. "The Badger fellow is supposed to be crazy, didn't want to risk the kids getting hurt. Besides, I learned more just watching. I bet you didn't notice the T-bird parked on the old logging road."

Frost chuckled, "Hell no," he said, "I was looking for your sorry ass. Who's that? Early morning lovers?"

"No," Lochran replied, "unless you consider the mob early morning lovers."

"How many?" Frost asked.

"Three, and they're roaming around lost in these woods. It doesn't make sense because it seems like a kid is giving orders to two mob killers. And they don't like it. They're arguing, and the two pros seem ready to shoot the kid."

Frost chuckled. "Loch, I'll give it to you, I don't care what everybody says about you, you're all right. But we need to get out of here. I'm parked right behind you."

"Not leaving, partner," Lochran said. "I'm staying here today and tonight."

"I didn't hear you say that. Come on; we've got work to do."

"Not going, Butch, I'm staying here. I've got the lay of the land, know where the kids are, the mobsters and the crazy Badger. You and me can work this out."

"Loch, you can't be serious. You can't stay here in these woods."

"Why not, we use to. Remember?"

"Loch, what the fuck. Have you lost your mind?"

"You need you to tell Dee I'm fine and not to worry. You can get me a sandwich and leave it on the hood of my car. I could use a double barrel sawed off, and a box of shells. Leave it beneath the car inside the right front tire. Do you have your ankle holster and .38 on?"

"You're fucking serious. I don't believe this."

"If you do, leave it with the shotgun. Make sure the clip is full."

"Where the hell are you going to sleep tonight?"

"Where I slept last night, in a pile of leaves, good buddy."

"Do you want me to leave a blanket for you?"

"No. It'll be warm tonight like last night. But you've got to talk to the Captain. Have him call off the federal agents. You and I can handle this. He'll be pissed, and the agent assholes won't like it but tell them to go fuck themselves. You and I are handling this."

"What do you want me to do?

"After you deliver the guns, go home," Loch told his partner. "Come back in the morning and park behind my car. Wait there for me."

"What about the mobsters?"

"I'll handle them unless they kill each other. I'll drive them toward the tunnel, and if I'm lucky, the Badger will go after them. If he does, I'll find the kids underground and take them down to the tracks."

"Are you sure about this?"

"Hell no, but if we want to keep the kids alive, it's the best plan."

"Okay, I better get a move on. I have a lot to do."

"And you better not fuck up."

"Listen to this. At least I didn't sleep in the woods."

"There could be a lot of worse things."

"Yea, I know, you learn a lot sleeping in the woods, right?"

Friday, 3 p.m.
The Woods

Tommy Lochran was feeling good about himself. He spent the night in the woods and felt he had a good fix on the terrain between himself and the three mobsters. For all Lochran knew, one of the mobsters could be the Otts' killer. *High probability of that*, he thought. Therefore, he decided to stay close to them. Maybe he got a little too close. They made noise that chased the animals. An occasional deer bolted from their location and ran past Loch. An occasional crow caw, another marker that the mobsters were nearby.

What Lochran didn't know was that the Badger was stalking the mobsters, too. Lochran figured they were just over the ravine. He decided he'd watch them for a while, then just before it got dark, double back toward his car to get what Butch left for him. The ground was still soggy from nearly a week of rain, and he was wearing loafers. He climbed slowly up to a steep ravine — which would give him cover and be high enough for him to watch the mobsters.

Almost at the top, his foot caught on a vine. He tried to dislodge it and he rolled and tumbled down the side of the ravine. His fall not only made a racket, but he hurt his ankle. When he stopped rolling, he reached down and straightened his leg. Pain shot through his leg, particularly from his right ankle. He couldn't move his ankle, and the pain was alarming, so much so that he knew it was either a severe sprain or broken. His legs were caked with mud as was his hair, hands, and face. He instinctively reached inside his sports jacket for his gun. He was in trouble. The pain in his ankle grew with every move he made. He tried to sit up. He looked around. Little did he realize that the fall most likely saved his life.

He heard a noise behind him: leaves crunching, twigs breaking, then he heard," Well look what we got here. You got a shotgun trained on your head Mr. policeman, so if I were you, I'd toss that six-shooter about as far as you can."

Lochran figured they must have heard him fall and came up around behind him. He flung his gun away and tried to turn his body around so he could see them, but the pain shot up through his leg. From what he could hear and sense, all three were behind him. "Now you can do the same with the peashooter on your ankle," the voice said.

"I don't have an ankle gun," Lochran responded. "That's the only gun I have."

"Pull your pants up nice and easy, so I can see," the voice said.

Lochran tried reaching down to his knee to pull up his pant leg, but the pain rippled through his body. "Owww," he yelled and lay back. "I can't. I think my ankle's broken. I can't reach down to grab my pants."

I've got a Tommy on you that'll cut you in half, understand?"

"Yea, understand clearly," Lochran responded.

Tommy Sneakers then slowly began to move off toward Lochran's left and got behind an oak tree. He looked out from around the tree, and Lochran saw him. He stepped out into plain view, holding the Tommy with both hands out in front of him.

"Oh, yea, looky what we got here. A slimy, slippery fuck of a law-man. He gonna look nice buried with them kid rats down by the air-port swamp." Jimmy said something but of course nobody heard it. Little Joey was told to stay back for precautionary measures, but the real reason was that neither Sneakers nor Whispers trusted him or figured he was worth a damn.

Lochran thought he saw movement off to Sneakers' left. Maybe his mind was playing tricks, he reasoned. As Sneakers bent over to grab Lochran's weapon, a figure came out from behind a tree. It was the most godawful figure the detective had seen in law enforcement. The Badger had on his war suit: A white, full-body suit, with a white hoodie, with white gloves and what looked like a gas mask. He was carrying a long-handled, bloodstained ax. There were blood spots on his white bodysuit, still wet. like he recently ax-murdered some unfortunate soul. Several short-handled axes dangled from his belt.

"Don't move," The Badger said.

"Who the fuck are you?" Sneakers asked.

The Badger looked over at Sneakers and said, "I'm death."

Jimmy Whispers recognized that there was something different with the man standing before him holding a big-ass ax. But Jimmy had one thought, *where does he keep his guns, up his ass?*

Suddenly, Little Joey, holding his .38 with out in front of him, appeared on the other side of the detective, and said, "...the fuck, this Halloween, or something?" Little Joey then fired off three shots at the Badger. One winged him on the meaty part of his upper arm, but the other two missed.

In a flash, the Badger reached his right hand behind him, brought an ax up over his head and whipped it at Little Joey, hitting him in the middle of his forehead. Joey dropped to his knees, the ax embedded deep in the middle of his forehead, blood gushing down his face. He muttered, "The, fuck." Then fell flat on his face.

"Holy shit," Jimmy Whispers whispered.

Sneakers stood frozen, unable to think, unable to speak. Lochran lay on his side and studied the Badger. Lochran figured him for the crazy hitman from Italy. The Badger scanned the ravine around him. He turned a little, trying to look behind. He said, "Control woods," and banged his closed fist against his heart. And as quietly and mysteriously as he appeared, he disappeared into the woods.

Whispers walked over to Sneaker's side and said, "What the..."

"Keep your gun on him," Sneakers told Whispers, pointing to Lochran.

About two stone's throw away, up in a tree in an old deer stand on higher ground, another pair of eyes watched. Georgie Scavello was lying across four pieces of rotted pine boards nailed between two maple branches about 30 feet above the ground.

"*Holy shit*," he thought. He lay still, not wanting to move, and tried to follow the Badger through the woods, but he could only for a few seconds before the Badger disappeared.

Jimmy Whispers went up to Sneakers and said, "We got to waste the cop now."

Sneakers turned to Lochran, "You're dead, you do know that, and by your own gun."

Lochran tried to sit up. He knew Sneakers had to kill him. It's funny how a man's mind thinks when he accepts death. Some scream and cry and beg for their lives. Some get giddy and crack jokes, and some accept it, figuring on a better next life if there is such a thing. Lochran managed to sit up. The pain in his ankle was intense, but what's a little pain when you're knocking on death's door. Lochran had been chasing criminals all his adult life; he wasn't going to kowtow to one standing a few feet away holding his .45.

Jimmy Whispers moved closer to Sneaker's ear and said," Maybe we can use him to get the kids."

"See if he knows where the kids are," Whispers offered, "tell him we'll let him live if he tells us where they are."

Sneakers looked at Lochran.

"I know exactly where the kids are," Lochran said. "Do you? In these woods, it'll take you days to find them if you ever do. I guarantee you the cops will be here by tomorrow afternoon looking for me. You got lost easily today. It will be dark soon, what makes you think you won't get lost again. If you want to kill me, go ahead. But if you want to kill those kids, you need me to show you where they are."

"Shut up, copper," Sneakers said, "I'm trying to think. Shut the hell up." Then he turned and quietly said to Whispers, "He can't walk, how's he gonna show us?"

"Tell him we won't kill him if he shows us."

Sneakers turned to Lochran and said, "All right, tell us where they are, then. Draw a map in the dirt and show us. You do that, and I won't kill you."

Lochran knew he was lying. As soon as he drew a map for them, Sneakers would fire a shot into his head and two into his heart. Lochran's life depended on what he said next.

"Impossible," Lochran said. "You've never been in the woods. It's not like you go up one street and turn left on another. Even if I drew you a map, one slight misstep and you're lost again. I grew up in these woods, played here as a kid. I tracked you for several hours, and you never knew it. You were roaming in circles. Besides, those kids went underground, and you'll never find the tunnels, either. Once you have them, you can kill anyone you want.

"Some other things you need to think through. Who the hell just killed your partner? Where'd he go? And how long do you think it will be before he kills you. He was sent here from Italy to protect the kids. No, I have to show you where those kids are first thing in the morning. It will give you a little time to get out of here."

Sneakers stared at him briefly, then turned to Whispers. "What do you think?" he said.

"Whoa, wait, why can't we grab them now?" Sneakers asked.

"It will be dark soon," Loch said. "We'll never find them at night, and once it's dark, we can't move through the woods."

Whispers leaned in. "What he says makes sense," Whispers said, "if he's lying, we'll shoot his brains out. These woods make me nervous. Maybe he can take us to them kids."

Sneakers nodded, then turned toward Lochran. "How do we know you're not lying, like some lying scumbag cop?"

"I give you my word," Lochran pleaded, "I'll take you to the kids at sunrise."

There were some big holes in detective Lochran's offer. The biggest being why would he take Sneakers and Whispers to the kids if he gets his brains blown out when he does? The two mob hitmen were smart enough to see that but what other choice did they have? If they whacked him on the spot, they would have to navigate through the woods on their own. They tried that today and failed. Moreover, the monster-looking hitman from Italy scared them shitless. Who was he and how soon will he be back?

"You're banged up, how you gonna walk?" Sneakers asked.

"If you can help me find a tree limb, I can use it as a crutch," Lochran said.

"What if you lead us back to the car?" Sneakers asked. "Jimmy and I can sleep in the car, and you can sleep in the woods. How 'bout that?"

"It's best we try to get closer to the kids now, while we have some time. If we go back to the car, we'll have longer to go in the morning. You want to grab those kids just after daylight and get out of there."

Whispers nodded. "Let's do it. These woods make me crazy; I can't tell one goddamn tree from another. And who the fuck was the hooded freak? Let's use him to get them kids and get back to South Philly."

"All right," Sneakers said, nodding. "We'll get you a tree branch and help you up. But you got to stay with us."

"No problem," Loch said. "Let's get started."

CHAPTER 50

"Whose Deal Is It?"

Early Friday Night
Belmont Hills
Leedom Avenue

It was more or less like any other night on the Hill. Louis Regina parked his car on Leedom. He turned off the engine and sat watching, glancing into his rearview. Except for a dog occasionally barking off in the distance, and the muffled sound of children playing on Jefferson Street, it was a usual dark-thirty evening. Regina had to be careful that the FBI or police weren't watching the street. Up on Jefferson, just two blocks away, Louis saw the car with two men in it, obviously watching Pete's house.

At the Howard Johnsons the night before, the FBI agents told Louis that if they catch him trying to make contact with the boys, they will arrest him for witness tampering. They also refused to give him back his .38. Said they needed to check to make sure it was registered to him, which was bullshit but there was nothing Louis could do. Vito Graziano left another gun on his car seat, so he was good to go.

Louis sat for 30 minutes before he cracked his door and stepped out into the street. He wasn't sure which house was Ciarlello's, but he knew it was one of two houses set back from the street. So, he picked one. Louis stood a minute and watched the street behind him. He turned and knocked. The door cracked open, and an older lady peered through the crack. "Is this the Ciarlello residence?" he asked. The lady responded in Italian, so Louis figured it was the next house. He went next door and knocked there, too. He waited a minute and knocked again. Finally, the door opened, and there stood Johnny Ciarlello.

"Johnny," Louis said, "do you remember me?"

"Ah, no," Johnny said, "but whatever it was I didn't do it."

Louis chuckled. "No," he said, "at the meeting in the cinder garage, I came and spoke with the kids there."

"Wait a minute," Johnny said. He clicked on the front porch light. "Oh yea, now I remember. The mysterious man. Sure. Sorry, it's dark."

"No problem," Louis said. "Johnny, can you do me a favor and turn off the porch light?"

"Oh, sure," Johnny replied.

"Look, Johnny, I need your help."

"Sure, what is it?"

"I got stopped by the feds the other night," Louis explained, "and they wanted information on the boys at the top of the tunnel. I didn't give them anything. But while they were interviewing me, they let it slip out that the local cops, the Lower Merion police, know where they are hiding and are planning to raid the tunnel and drive the kids out."

"No shit," Johnny replied. "Ah, what did you say your name was?"

"It's Louis. Louis Regina. The boys know me. I've been out to the tunnel."

"It's dark but if you want me to take you out to the tunnel tonight, just let me get my shoes on."

"All right," Louis said, "hurry up. I've got to get out there." But Johnny didn't hear him he was already up the stairs to his room to get his sneakers. After several minutes he came back down and joined Louis on the front porch. "Come on," he said, "I parked up the street. We can drive out there."

"Look," Johnny said, "I don't want to tell you what to do, but it'll be a lot faster if we go down to the tracks and walk there. Maybe a mile, a mile-and-a-half, is all."

Louis turned and looked out at the street. He bit his lower lip and said, "Is my car safe parked there?"

"Hell, yeah," Johnny said, "very safe. We don't even lock our doors down here. It's safer than shit."

"Okay," he said, "let's go. Lead the way, Johnny."

Louis followed Johnny around to the back of the house. They went down the path through bushes and high weeds to the railroad tracks. Then straight to the tunnel. It wasn't an easy walk — tough walking on railroad ties, double tough at night. Plus, they kept turning and looking back for the one-eyed monster or listening for the little honk of the diesel horn. When they got to the tunnel, Johnny yelled out to the boys, "Yo, are you up there? We want to come up."

Inside the cave
Top of the tunnel

Inside the cave, the boys used two flashlights to play cards. They were also listening to the Phillies game on Ronny's transistor radio. The Phillies were in first place, and no double murder was going to keep the boys from the game.

"Wait a minute," Mickey said, "did you hear something? Turn off the radio. I heard someone yell."

"You sure, Merk," Pete said, "I told you to clean the shit out of your ears."

"How can I with you blowing me all the time?"

"You're mistaking me for your mother," Pete shot back.

"No, I heard something, too," Gary added.

Gary laid down his cards and got up. He went to the cave entrance, parted the vines, and looked out. "Jesus H. Christ," he said, "it's dark out there, can't see shit."

"Yo, you guys up there?"

"Is that you, Johnny Ciarlello?" Gary yelled.

"It ain't the Easter Bunny, Pecker," Johnny yelled back.

"I'll go down and get him," Gary turned and said, "don't anybody look at my hand."

"Fuck no," Pete said, "what do you take us for, we don't do shit like that. What's wrong with you?"

As soon as he disappeared through the cave entrance, Pete picked up Gary's cards, looked at them, then passed them to Mickey, who looked and passed them to Ronny, who also looked and gave them back to Pete. Pete laid them down, just like Gary had them. He reached down to the cards again and parted two of them. "There," he said, "now they look good.

"He didn't have shit," Pete remarked amusingly. "He's the biggest bullshitter going."

"Yo," Gary yelled from outside the cave entrance, "we got two visitors. I'm bringing up Johnny now."

"Two?" Mickey said. "Who's the other?"

"Don't know," Gary said," maybe it's your mother."

As Gary helped Johnny part the vines covering the entrance and Johnny stepped into the cave, Gary went back down to get Louis.

"Jesus Christ look at the size of this thing," Johnny remarked. Did you guys dig this?"

"Well, yeah, sort of," Mickey said, "with a little help from our friend the Badger."

"It's bigger than this," Mickey said, "there at two tunnel entrances in the back, we'll show you tomorrow. And there's a jail cave next door. Next door and down a little."

"Jail cave? Johnny questioned, "what the hell's that?"

Mickey was about to answer, but Gary brought Louis through the entrance. "Louis," Johnny said, "look at this cave, ain't it something?'"

"Fellows," Louis said, "it's good to see you all still breathing. Where's the Badger?"

"Oh," Gary said, "he's not here. He heard something this morning and went out in the woods looking. He told us to stay in the cave."

"He didn't come back?" Louis asked. "Did you look for him?"

"Listen," Pete said, "he can take care of himself, trust me. A few days ago, he brought us the two killers. We got them next door in the cave jail."

"Two killers, what two killers?" Louis asked.

"One killed the Otts," Pete said. "We saw him from the cherry trees."

"And the other one killed that mob guy Porky," Gary added, "the one who helped Ronny serve his papers. He shot him right in front of us."

"You've got them here, here in this cave?" Louis asked.

"Oh, shit no," Pete said, "their sittin' in the cave jail. The Badger dug it by himself, and we kicked their asses off the ledge, and the Badger grabbed them and pulled them inside the cave. We give them food and water and check on them sometimes, make sure they ain't dead. Whose deal is it?"

"Can they escape?" Johnny asked.

"Fuck no," Pete said, "if they try, they'll fall down the steep incline onto the rocks below. Don't worry. They're scared shitless."

Louis chuckled and shook his head, "This is unbelievable. You got the two killers right here. Tied up in the cave jail. Unbelievable."

"When the Badger comes back," Mickey said, "we can show you the two mob guys."

"Johnny, Louis," Gary asked. "You want to stay the night here with us?"

"We came out here tonight boys for a reason," Louis said. "The cops will be coming soon to drive you off the tunnel. They know where you are. You best be leaving now, don't you think?"

"Shit no," Pete said, "Let them come. I don't think they'll find us in here and if they do, we have two tunnels we can take and escape into the woods or out to the dam."

"No shit," Johnny said, "that's something else."

"But boys," Louis said, "if you got the two killers in a cave here, why don't you surrender to the police and turn over the killers. It's perfect. It's a perfect way to end this."

"No, it's not," Pete said, "what about the Badger? What will the police do to him? We can't do anything until the Badger comes back and approves what we're doing. That simple."

Louis shook his head. "But boys," he said, "the Badger is a paid killer, what you do in the end can't depend on him. You need to separate yourselves from the Badger the sooner, the better."

"Look at all he's done for us," Gary said. "We might not be alive if it wasn't for him. He caught the two killers, the cops couldn't catch them, but the Badger did. We're not going to run out on him cause you say so. Fuck that."

All Louis could think about was, *we got trouble here.*

"Fellows," Louis said, "I've got to get back. It looks like you have everything under control. I'd love to get in that card game with you someday. Johnny, you coming with me?"

"Hell no," Johnny responded, "can I get in the card game, boys?"

"Sure," Gary answered, "you got money?"

"Oh, no," Johnny replied, "no, I don't.

"Well shit then," Gary said, "this ain't no bank."

"Oh, Johnny said, "okay. It's really cool in there, though."

"Hey Johnny," Pete said, "he's just bustin' them. None of us have any money; we're using little stones."

Gary got up, "Ha, ha, ha, I got that one on you, Johnny," he said, as he playfully drilled his fist into Johnny's side, sort of Gary's trademark when he gets caught busting somebody's balls.

"Look," Johnny said, "I'll play one or two hands, and then I got to get home. Nobody knows I'm gone."

"Okay, Johnny," Pete said, "but don't let the Polack peek at your cards, he cheats every time."

"Gary, can you take me down to the tracks, I've got to get going," Louis said.

"Sure, Louis, come on," Gary answered.

"Why don't you let me deal first," Pete suggested, "then you can leave your hand here, and we'll watch it."

Gary got up, turned, and looked back at us. We all had the famous Hill shit-eatin' grins on our faces. It dawned on him that we looked at his cards when he left to bring Johnny and Louis up.

"Hey, fuck you, guys."

With that, Gary went out the cave entrance to take Louis down, with his friends laughing their asses off.

CHAPTER 51

"Goddamn Hill Kids"

Friday, 8:30 p.m.
Edge of the Woods

Detective Frost pulled in behind Tommy Lochran's car parked at the edge of the woods just off Flat Rock Road. He cut the engine and sat thinking about what he'll do next. Frost had Loch's sandwich, shotgun shells, ankle holster, and .38. He opened the door and got out, went around to open the trunk to get the weapons. He put the sandwich on the hood and crouched down to put the guns and shells inside the right, front tire. He got back up.

It didn't feel right, leaving Lochran by himself in the woods with the mobsters nearby. If anything happened, Frost could never forgive himself. He leaned against Loch's car. *Goddamn him,* Frost thought, *I don't like this.* He looked at his watch. It was late. Frost wasn't going to go home and to bed. Not with his partner in the woods. He went back to his trunk and opened it. He grabbed the other shotgun and opened a box of shells and dumped them in the trunk. He loaded it and put three-four rounds in each of his pants pocket. He closed the trunk.

It was dark, but Frost — like Loch — knew the woods. They played war games there as kids. They camped out there; built forts. It's like riding a bike, Frost reasoned, it never leaves you. Placing the shotgun on his shoulder, he started for the woods and stopped. He went back and felt under the car for the other shotgun. Grabbed the sandwich on the hood and stuffed it into his jacket pocket. He reopened the

RON COSTELLO

trunk, loaded the other shotgun and put more shells into his pockets. He grabbed the ankle holster and gun, kneeled, and strapped it on. He closed the trunk and headed for the woods.

As he approached the edge of the woods, he stopped. He cut through a clump of dense fir trees. A deer bolted out to his right. It scared the shit out of him. *What the hell am I afraid of,* he thought, *I'm carrying two short-barrel shotguns.* He got in a crouch and looked around. He knew where the tunnel was in proximity to the woods. He knew the location of the old logging road. He got back up and cut to his left. He walked slowly, deliberately, and tried to use the small amount of moonlight to his advantage. He stopped by a small creek.

He started up a slight hill and worked his way around some honeysuckle bushes and tried to avoid the vicious stickers, but at night it was nearly impossible. He walked around fallen trees and thickets. At night, in the woods, it's difficult to recognize anything. He figured he'd move as far as he could into the center of the woods and stay there. Maybe in the morning he'd hear or see Loch.

The footing wasn't sound. His shoes were clogged with mud, and his shoelaces were useless. He looked for animal paths he could use to make better time. Animals moved off around him — didn't see them, just heard them. He knew there wasn't anything in the woods that could hurt or attack him, except maybe a stray dog.

He stepped on and crunched down on lots of tree branches and leaves. Being late summer, he was sure the woods were full of ticks and spiders. He was getting tired and started looking for higher ground. He figured he'd been walking for about two hours. That would bring him where he wanted to be, about to the center of the thickest part of the woods.

He meandered up a small incline and stopped. He found a dry spot where he could bed down in front of a large tree. It would protect his back. He stretched his tired legs and leaned back against the tree. He lay the shotguns across his tired legs. Frost felt better, spending the night in the woods near his partner instead of home in bed. As he lay back against the tree, he closed his eyes.

Frost didn't know how long he was out when he heard it. He opened his eyes and stared out at the darkness. *Hearing things is all,* he thought. But it sounded real enough that he reached down and clicked the safeties off on both shotguns. The leaves trashed again accompanied by twigs and sticks snapping. *Oh, yea,* he thought, *there's somebody behind me. Let them come around me; don't make any sudden moves.* Just like turkey hunting near the Pennsylvania Grand Canyon, calling in a tom and knowing the right time to move and shoot.

Then a husky whisper cut through the night air like a barn owl screech, "Frosty, is that you?"

Frost knew the voice but couldn't place it. He knew he heard it before. He turned a little and tried to look out from behind the tree, still ever careful.

"Frosty, it's me, Georgie."

Frost shook his head. "Georgie, what the hell are you doing out here. Get over there in the moonlight so I can see you before I shoot your scrawny ass."

Georgie moved quickly, but complained, "Jesus Christ, a little touchy, aren't you? You should be more grateful considering the information I have for you."

As Georgie moved into the moonlight, Frost, too tired to get up, said, "What information? What are you talking about?"

I was trailing those mob guys. Three of them; they didn't know shit about moving in the woods. Then they came upon your partner."

"Loch?" Frost said as he got up on his knees.

"Yeah," Georgie responded, "he fell and hurt his ankle. Probably broke it. The Mob pricks got the jump on him. But then this crazy shit came along. He was dressed in white, scary as all shit. He got the jump on the mob guys and took control of the situation. But not all three mob guys were there; one stayed back."

"I hope this ends well, Georgie."

"The mob guy who stayed back snuck up on them and fired three shots at the crazy guy dressed in white. I think he missed, but one might have grazed him. Then, Jesus Christ, the crazy guy in white, throws an ax and splits the mob guy's head in half, just like in some monster movie. It was some shit. The only thing missing was Alfred Hitchcock coming out from behind a tree saying, "Good evening.""

"What about Loch, what happened to Loch?"

"Yeah, well, the one mob guy wanted to shoot Loch. But I think Loch talked him out of it."

"Is Loch still alive?"

"Yeah, last I knew, and I haven't heard any shootin'. So, I'd say the chances are good."

"What do you mean you think; didn't you see everything?"

"Yeah, but I couldn't hear them talking. I was a way's back up in an old rotted out tree stand. I'm lucky the mother didn't break up and crash to the ground, or they would have killed me, too."

"Okay, enough of that, what happed to officer Lochran?"

"After Lochran talked them out of killing him, they made a crutch out of a tree limb. I could tell he was in a lot of pain. Then they started moving around. I trailed them until it got dark and they set down for the night. I think Loch was leading them around in circles. Then later I heard you coming."

"How close are we to them right now?" Frost asked.

"Not real close, maybe a half-mile."

"And you heard me coming?"

"Shit yeah," Georgie said, "you were heading right toward them. So, I figured I better cut behind you and warn you."

"Thanks, Georgie. You can go home now. This isn't for you."

"Well, if you don't mind me saying, you move through the woods like a tank. You need me to stay with you and get you close to them. They got some mean-ass firepower."

"Like what? What do they have?"

"To start with, a Tommy gun. The other one has a 16-gauge pump with double ought buck, a real beauty. They got handguns up their asses. No, Frosty, if you want to stay alive and get your partner back, you need me."

Frost leaned back against the tree and thought about it. He looked at the stars through the trees. It was a beautiful night. Georgie was a pain in the ass, but he knew guns, and he knew the woods. Frost figured he could use Georgie's woods' smarts.

"Okay, sit over there. Let me think."

As Georgie moved to a spot to sit," he said, "You gonna give me one of those feather dusters you have, you got two of them."

"No way, Georgie, you can forget that. You're going gun less."

"All right, but if I get shot dead, my Aunt El will sue."

Frost smiled and settled in against the tree. "We'll get up before sunrise. Oh, and Georgie, stop calling me Frosty."

"No problem, Frosty," Georgie replied.

Frost leaned his head back against the tree, smiled, and thought, *"Goddamn Hill kids."*

～

Friday, 11 p.m.
Bottom of the Hill

Just before midnight, Louis Regina hustled down the tracks a mile or so and found the path that took him up past Johnny's house. Once in his car on Leedom Avenue, he went looking for a phone booth. He remembered seeing one past Baffa's bar at the bottom of the hill, so he drove down Jefferson Street and down to the bottom of the hill and pulled into an Esso station. He got out of his car, stepped into the phone booth, and made a collect call to the home of the Newark mob boss, Vito Graziano.

"Sorry to call so late, sir," Louis said.

"I'm sure you have a good reason, Louis," Mr. Graziano said, "is it good or bad?"

"Not sure sir," Louis replied, "I just came from visiting the boys, and there are some things you should know about."

"What is it, Louis?"

"When I got there, they were in a cave the Badger dug, and it had a couple of escape tunnels-built in."

"Not surprising, go on."

"The Badger wasn't there. The boys said he had left late in the morning because he thought he heard something in the woods. He hadn't come back."

"Well, he could be tracking some unfortunate soul, and maybe he's burying him."

"There's more, sir."

"Go on."

"The Badger built a cave jail near the boy's cave on the side of the tunnel, where he put in two of Angelo Morello's hitmen, Crazy Phil, who the boys say killed the Otts, and the Hunchback, who they saw shoot Porky Bananas in the woods."

There was silence on the other end.

"Sir?"

"Are you sure about this, Louis?"

"I didn't see inside the cave jail, but the boys had no reason to lie to me."

"This is not good, Louis. Not good at all. If the Badger turns on us, we could be in trouble, is that what you're thinking?"

"It is exactly, sir."

"Okay fine. You know what you have to do, Louis, right?'

"Yes, I do, sir."

"Okay, so let's break off communication between us. You handle it from here. If you get in trouble, we can get you to Italy, and you'll have the best attorneys in the country. Come see me when it's over."

"Yes, sir."

And Vito Graziano hung up.

CHAPTER 52

"We'll Kick their Asses"

The Final Day – August 13, 1964
Saturday, 4 a.m.
The Woods

"Georgie, you awake?" detective Frost asked. "Georgie, wake up." Frost moved his leg around and kicked Georgie's foot. It was still dark.

"Whoa, who's there?" Georgie exclaimed, "I'm tired; leave me alone."

Frost kicked his foot again. "Georgie, wake up. It's time to go."

Georgie sat up. "Huh? What time is it?"

"Little after four," Frost said. "We better get moving."

"Ah, shit," Georgie said, "I'll take mine easy over and no cream or sugar."

Frost grunted. "If we get Loch back, I'll treat you to that, no problem. Can you get us close to them?"

"Yeah, but what's that gonna do? They outgun us. All they have to do is open up with that Tommy and you and me are having eggs and coffee in heaven."

"What if we separate them?" Frost asked.

"How are you gonna do that? Hire Moses?"

"Jesus, Georgie, I didn't think you knew about Moses, you're a biblical scholar for sure."

"Wait a minute, Frosty, you might have something there. Didn't Moses part something?"

"Yeah, the water so the Israelites could get by."

"Shit, Frosty, we can do the same thing. Only instead of parting the water, we part the mafia."

"I'm listening," detective Frost said.

"What if I get on one side of them and you get on the other, maybe 40 yards or so on each side. We raise a little hell, you know, not much, just enough to get their attention. Then maybe one of them will come out on my side and one on your side. Just like Moses but the mafia instead of water."

"I like it," Frost said, "but it won't work."

"Why not?" Georgie asked. "If they come after us both you can take them."

"What happens if they put a gun to Lochran's head and force us to surrender?" Frost asked. "They'll shoot Loch and us. I can't take that chance."

"So, what do you want to do then?" Georgie asked.

"I should have sent you there last night," Frost said, "that was my mistake."

"Send me where?" Georgie asked.

"Sneak back out of the woods to Mary Waters Ford Road and head to the incinerator. The man who runs the claw there, George Ferraco, starts early, sometimes before sunrise. Have him call the police and report an officer down in the woods between Mary Waters Ford and the tunnel. Tell George to tell the police you'll wait for them at the top of Mary Waters Ford Road at the logging road. You got this?"

"All right," Georgie said, "but I think we can take them ourselves. You know, you and me. We'll kick their asses."

"Georgie," Frost said, "they've got too much firepower. You're unarmed, and I can't match what they have. We'll end up getting Loch killed as well as ourselves. Now go and be quiet."

"What are you going to do?" Georgie asked.

"I'm going to sneak closer. I'm going to trail them, get as close as I can."

"Oh," Georgie replied, "I don't think that's a good idea, Frosty, I heard you coming a mile away. They will, too. If you want to save your partner, let's go together. A lot of old guys think they can be kids again. Well, let me tell you, you can't."

"Georgie," Frost said, "I'm not going to tell you again. Head for the incinerator, now.

～

Saturday, 4:30 a.m.
Leedom Avenue
The Hill

Louis Regina stayed at a motel on City Line Avenue, and after chugging down some coffee, he made his way back to the Hill. He parked on Leedom again, but this time turned his car around to escape fast. He went to the trunk and took out the Beast, a seven-pound double barrel 10-gauge short barrel shotgun.

It was in a sling. The sling held 15 rounds. He looped it over his head and pushed it around to the middle of his back. He also carried a .45 pistol in a chest holster with five magazines stuffed into his pockets. He locked his car and found the path he and Johnny used the previous evening and started down the tracks.

He walked deliberately, keeping his mind on the ties before him, trying not to miss one and twist his ankle. Just like Johnny showed him. "If you're thinkin' about stuff," Johnny told him, "and not concentrating, you'll turn an ankle sure as shit."

Regina has cleaned up messes before, and he's a good cleaner. As consigliere and attorney, his role in the Graziano family was an advisor to the boss, Vito Graziano. But there were times when the boss and the family needed additional help. Like when the black mafia tried to muscle their way into Newark. Just starting to sprout in Harlem in the early sixties, the black mafia got into heroin and was taking business away from the Italian families in New York. The blacks were nowhere near as powerful as New York's five families. Thinking a move to another city might be smart, the Harlem black mob went to Newark — close enough to run business in Harlem, yet away from the heat of the five families. Vito Graziano underestimated the black mob, and after several failed attempts to drive them out, told his consigliere, Louis Regina, "You know what you have to do, Louis, right?"

Regina set up several meetings with the heads of the Newark black mafia. He did what he does best; he lured them to sleep. Once they got somewhat comfortable with Louis, they invited him to address all the heads of the Harlem black mafia in Newark.

After all, he was Vito Graziano's consigliere, attorney and spokesman, and they trusted him. They made a big mistake. He went to the meeting with two 10-gauge shotguns under his raincoat and when he left the restaurant, not only was the black mafia movement into Newark finished, but it was twenty years later before they were able to rebound. Louis got them all.

There were other examples where Louis lured his enemies to sleep — got their trust and confidence, then, when the opportunity presented itself, struck like a hungry rat. As Louis carefully walked on and over the railroad ties, knowing it was in his hands to defend not only his underworld family but several other families as well. This was bigger than four kids in cherry trees. Louis knew that as did Vito Graziano. And both knew what he had to do.

Louis also knew as he approached the tunnel in darkness if he did his job right, his prey would welcome him, just like the heads of the Harlem mafia. When Louis got to the tunnel, he noticed the rope missing. Carrying the Beast and the ammo, Louis couldn't climb up without it. He made some half-ass attempts but gave up. He tried shouting up to the boys, but they didn't answer. He knew he didn't have much time. He decided he'd wait a little and try calling them again. Either that or possibly in daylight he could climb up.

~

Saturday, 5 a.m.
The Woods

It didn't take Georgie long to get to Mary Waters Ford Road, as the morning got brighter. He left the woods and walked out onto the street and headed down the hill. Then he stopped. He looked back. Standing in the middle of the road, he started thinking. *He's going to get them both killed,* he thought, meaning Frosty. A voice inside him kept saying, *don't do it, Georgie, go back. Go back and save them. By the time the cops get here, it will be too late. Go back, go back, go back.*

Georgie stood in the street looking into the woods. He turned around and headed back up the hill, found the logging trail, and went back into the woods. But he stopped again. *Am I doing the right thing? Go man, go,* he told himself. *Go and save them.* He turned and looked toward the road. *Go, man, go, it's the only way you can save them.* Georgie listened to his inner voice. He turned and quietly followed the logging road into the deep woods.

~

Saturday, 5:30 a.m.
The Woods

Detective Lochran didn't get much sleep. The pain in his ankle was intense. During the night he had to pee, but of course, couldn't get up. So, he turned onto his side, opened his zipper, and let it go. Finished, he pushed himself away from the wetness a foot or two.

He lay there, watching the woods get brighter. He thought he heard something. At dawn, deer are active and so are many of the rodent family: squirrels, chipmunks, mice, even porcupines; as well as the reptiles, namely, snakes. As a deer hunter, sitting in a tree stand or against a tall pine, gun across his thighs, he learned to recognize the woods' noises, so he didn't mistake a ground squirrel for a buck tip-toeing around him.

He heard it again. Still, on his side, he got up on his right elbow and peered into the semidarkness. Just that little movement sent pain streaking down his right leg and into his ankle. Leaves crunched, and a twig broke. *Oh, yea, someone's out there,* Loch thought. He looked over at the two mobsters who were beginning to stir. Another branch snapped; leaves shuffled. Sneakers looked up.

He heard it, too. Sneakers lifted his Tommy gun and reached over and hit Whispers on the shoulder. "Someone's here," he said softly to Whispers. Whispers got up on his knees and held the pump shotgun out in front of him. Sneakers pointed to where he heard the noise. Lochran watched the two mobsters. He shuffled his feet a little, trying to make noise. Sneakers glared at Lochran and ran his finger across his throat. Leaves rustled again.

"Okay" Sneakers whispered to Whispers, "I'm going out this way," he said, motioning with his head, "you go over and put your shotgun to his head. If shootin' starts and you hear me yell, kill him. Blow his brains out." Whispers nodded. "I'll try to go around him out there, and then come up behind." Whispers nodded again. "Okay, let's go. Slowly and quietly as we can."

Sneakers got up and eased into the darkness. Although brighter, pockets of the thick woods were still dark. Whispers crawled over to Lochran and grabbed his shirt behind his neck and tried to pull him up. "Get up," he whispered to the detective. Lochran managed to get up in a sitting position, and Whispers put the barrel of the shotgun to the side of his head. "Make one sound or move, and I'll scatter your brains."

Tommy Sneakers worked his way behind Frost. He couldn't see him, only hear him. One thing Georgie said that was right about Frost, his glory days of playing in the woods were over. Frost moved like a clumsy ox. Sneakers figured Frost was on the other side of a thicket of briars and rhododendron. He lifted the Tommy and squeezed the trigger, firing a burst of 10 rounds into the air. Enough to let Frost know what he faced. The thundering sound echoed through the woods. To Frost, the shots were close and terrifying. It shook him to the core.

"The next slugs go right at you," Sneakers said. "There's nothing between us but a bunch of weeds. When my friend hears it, he'll blow the other copper's brains out. It's your move."

"You've got five seconds to decide."

"Okay," Frost answered, "I'm laying my guns down now."

"Stand up so I can see you," Sneakers demanded.

CHAPTER 53

"Are You Going to Shoot Us?"

Saturday, 5:30 a.m.
Top of the Tunnel

G ary got his zipper caught. He had to pee, so he left the cave to a clump of weeds and sumacs maybe 20 yards away. Struggling to pull it up and return to the cave, he heard the burst of machine gunfire.

He froze. *Holy shit*, he thought. He looked into the woods, but it was still dark. Hearing or seeing nothing, he went back to the cave and woke the other boys.

"Hey, wake up, I heard machine gun fire."

"You were dreaming, go back to sleep. It's too early to get up."

"No, I mean it. I was taking a piss, and I heard machine gun fire."

"Did you hear any bombs," Mickey asked. Ronny laughed.

"How about missiles," Pete asked. "Any missiles coming our way? We're in a damn bomb shelter." Ronny laughed again.

"That's right, we're in a bomb shelter," Ronny offered, "so let them come. It's probably Russia."

"All right, I'm done with you assholes. I'm going in the woods to see what it was," Gary exclaimed, knowing that that would get them up.

Mickey sat up. "Whoa, wait, you can't do that," he said.

Ronny and Pete sat up, too. "How far away was it?" Ronny asked.

"I don't know, but it sounded pretty loud," Gary said.

Pete wasn't convinced. "You sure you're not bullshitting again?" Pete asked. "This isn't another of those Wolfman bullshit stories, is it?"

Gary loved the Lon Chaney Wolfman movie. He often explained unexplainable stuff that it was Wolfman. He swore that Wolfman was alive and he'd seen him. Pete laughed and said, "That's it, isn't it, now you're going to swear it was Wolfman."

"Hey, fuck you Bruno," Gary said, which is what Gary said when he actually did get mad. Pete knew how to react.

"Okay, take it easy."

Being cooped up for so long, the boys were getting short-tempered and uneasy. Gary was generally an easy-going guy but piss him off and lookout. They could tell when Gary was done fooling around. But he had such a big heart; ten minutes later he would get Pete in a 'friendly' neck lock and you knew he wasn't mad anymore.

Now they took Gary seriously about the gunfire.

"Louis told us not to leave the cave and when the police come, to use the tunnels to escape," Mickey said, "I think we should stay right here."

"But the Badger is out there somewhere, and he may need our help," Pete said.

"I don't know," Ronny added, "the Badger can take care of himself. I don't think he needs our help."

"Then why didn't he come back, yet?" Gary asked. "He said he'd be back by sunset last night. I got a feeling he's in trouble."

Pete then threw Gary a peace bond. "Your instincts are good, Pecker," he said, "I vote we look for him while we still have the cover of darkness."

"Jughead," Pete said, "what about you?"

"I say we look too," Mickey added, "but how about we do this. Two of us go ahead, and two keep a distance behind following. We stay within eyesight. That way, we move through the woods carefully, prepared to run back to the tunnel and into the cave."

"I like that," Gary said. "If the two in front get shot, the two following behind can make it back. Good thinking, Merk."

"I think we should do it," Ronny said. "We owe it to the Badger. He'd come looking for us."

"All right," Pete added, nodding, "let's go. Who's out front?"

"I'll do it," Gary said.

"Me too," Pete said. "Let's go."

~

Saturday, 9 a.m.
The Woods

By 6 a.m., Tommy Sneakers and Jimmy Whispers had hit the trifecta. They got rid of Little Joey, thanks to the Badger. They had both detectives and, better recognition of the woods. Not that they were anything close to being Boy Scouts, but after spending the night there and getting the two detectives, they had more confidence. Little did they realize they were about to take the whole enchilada.

With both detectives on their knees and their hands clasped behind them, Sneakers heard a noise. Then voices. Sneakers motioned for Whispers to cover the two detectives with his 16-gauge pump, while he investigated the commotion. He took his Tommy gun. Quietly as possible, Sneakers snuck around a small steam and into a patch of goldenrods. He was able to move through the goldenrods like a mouse on the kitchen table. What Sneakers found blew him away. He parted the goldenrods to see better and saw four boys on their knees around the body of Little Joey. The boys were upset. From the goldenrods, Sneakers could see the ax still embedded in Little Joey's head. It looked gruesome.

"Shit, you can see inside his head, his brains and everything."

"Bet the Badger did this."

"No, ten people are walking around in these woods with axes, ass-wipe, of course, the Badger did it."

"Bite me, Polack, somebody else could have done it."

"Think he's a mob guy?"

"Yep. Want to get his wallet?

"I don't know, stripping a drunk guy is one thing, stripping somebody with an ax pounded into their brains is another."

"Well, he's not going to wake up."

"Duh, you think, dumb ass."

"Hey, blow me, jerk off."

"Let's not disturb him, who cares who he is."

"Fine, let's get out of here."

"Where?"

"Back to the tunnel. Let's go."

"What about the Badger?"

"Look at this ass-wipe. The Badger can take care of himself."

"I'm not leaving until we find the Badger."

"All right, but let's move out of here, he's startin' to stink."

"You'd stink too your brains were all over the ground."

As Sneakers watched, he noticed the boy with the dark rim glasses, the Italian looking kid, wiping his eyes. Even the hardened killer Sneakers felt, if only for a few seconds, for the boys. For a brief time, Sneakers thought of his own two kids, a tad older than these boys, but close enough. Here, in the palm of his hand, he had what eluded the mob all summer. With one squeeze of the Thompson's trigger, Sneakers and Jimmy Whispers finished their job. Knock off the two detectives and head for the Golden Nugget in Vegas. But unexpectedly, killing the boys wasn't as crucial to Tommy Sneakers, anymore. They reminded him too much of his own children. Dressed like them, talked like them, and, at least in Sneakers' mind, were them.

But he had a job to do, so he had to elude his personal feelings and take control. "Unless you want to join him on the ground," Sneakers said, in a normal speaking tone, like he was telling his boys to turn off the television and start their homework, "you had better back away from the body. Stay on your knees with your hands clasped behind you."

"Who are you?" one of the kids said.

Sneakers moved closer to the boys. "I told you I heard a machine gun this morning," Gary said, "look at that shit he's holding."

"That's right," Sneakers said, "I can kill all four of you within a few seconds with one simple squeeze on the trigger. One little burst and you don't rat on nobody, and I'm a hero. Now do exactly as I say. Back away from the body."

"Did you kill him?"

"I did not," Sneakers replied, "but I think I know who did."

"Why'd he get killed?"

"He was a hot dog, bragging all the time," Sneakers said. "My partner and I couldn't stand him."

"Your partner? Is your partner here now?"

"I'll introduce you to him in a minute. I want you to stand up, one at a time, and clasp your hands behind your back."

"Are you going shoot us?"

"Not now," Sneakers replied, "but I will. Now, walk single file-like through these wildflowers and across that small creek. If anyone tries to run, I'll mow down all of you. Now move it."

The boys did as Sneakers said. They weren't about to be slaughtered by the "machine gun." Just a little past the creek, they walked into a small clearing where they saw the detectives Frost and Lochran and the partner holding a gun on them. Detective Lochran was lying on his side but sat up when he saw the boys. Frost was already in a sitting position. Neither detective said a word.

"Okay, stop there," Sneakers said, "now get down on your knees, keep your hands behind your back.

"My arms are getting tired," Ronny said, and just after he did, Whispers walked over and kicked him.

"Shut up," he said.

"Whispers," Sneakers hollered, "knock that shit off."

Lochran and Frost exchanged glances like they saw a sign from Sneakers. A sign of which they could take advantage. Whispers went over to Sneakers side and said into his ear, "Let's kill them all now."

"We don't have Crazy Phil and Hunch," Sneakers said.

"Fuck them," Whispers barked, "we didn't come here for them. We got the boys and both detectives. By the time they find them dead, we'll be in Vegas gettin' laid."

Sneakers looked uncomfortable. He fiddled with the Tommy, twisted his neck around and said, "Let's figure this out, first." Lochran and Frost locked eyes.

"Figure what our." Whispers said. "You're not turning soft on me, are you Sneakers? Tommy fuckin' Sneakers?"

"Fuck no, we just need to be careful here. No tellin' who's in these woods, know what I'm sayin?'"

"We got to kill these assholes and get out of here," Whispers said, "don't matter who's in the woods. If you don't want to, then I will."

"They're just kids, for cryin' out loud," Sneakers said. "We never whacked kids before, Whispers."

"Okay," Whispers said, "I get it, you got kids just like them. No problem, Sneakers. Give me the Tommy, and you take the shotgun and take a little walk. I'll take care of business, here."

"Hold it," Sneakers said. "Just back off. I need to think. Back the fuck off."

CHAPTER 54

"My Kind of Soccer You Can"

Saturday, 9:30 a.m.
Belmont Hills

With Lorraine Frost sitting across from her in her living room, Delores Lochran placed a call to Captain Tolan of the Lower Merion police force. The women had not heard from their husbands — strange because they always keep in close touch even on duty. Delores's husband Tommy left for the woods Thursday afternoon. Lorraine's husband, Butch Frost, left early Friday morning before dawn. The women were worried.

"Delores," Captain Tolan said, picking up his desk phone, "what'd Loch do, take a vacation day?"

"No Captain," Delores responded, "we had lunch Thursday at home and Lock said he was going to check on some things in the woods off Mary Waters Ford Road. I haven't heard from him since. Lorraine said Butch went to check on Loch in the woods and she hasn't heard from him, either."

"Wait," the Captain said, "are you sure about this? They didn't call or anything?"

"Nothing, Captain," Delores said, "we've heard nothing, and we're quite worried. Both Lock and Butch always stay in touch with us. It's just not like them."

"Okay, don't worry," the Captain said, "I'm sure there's an answer. I'll send reinforcements to the Hill and to the top of Mary Waters

Ford Road. I'm off to the Hill, too. Sit tight, and don't worry." He hung up.

~

Saturday, 10 a.m.
Belmont Hills Fire Company

Billy, Johnny, and Richie couldn't believe how many kids showed up. The three boys covered the Hill Friday afternoon and Friday night, asking kids to meet at the firehouse. It wasn't difficult to figure out why so many kids came. People on the Hill have been talking about the boys and the Otts' murders for the past two months. Everybody had a theory, and the Manayunk bookies were even taking bets on how long the kids could hide out without getting shot. At the firehouse, all kinds of kids showed up, different ages, different sizes, but all from the Hill.

"Jesus, Billy," Richie Pompizzi said, "I bet there are over a hundred kids here. Something, huh?"

"Richie," Johnny exclaimed, "I bet 200."

"Bill," Richie asked, "where's Georgie?"

"I don't know," Bill said, "we went to his house twice yesterday and his aunt didn't know, either. Okay, let's get this thing started."

"Hey Johnny," a girl in the crowd yelled, "if I do this walk thing, will you teach me to play soccer?"

Johnny Ciarlello beamed and shouted, "Sure."

Another girl in the crowd hollered, "Will you teach me to play soccer in the woods?"

Johnny frowned and hollered back, "Sorry, you can't play soccer in the woods."

To which the girl responded, "My kind of soccer you can."

The crowd of kids erupted in laughter. Johnny smiled and shook his head. "He's cute," another girl in the crowd added.

Billy got up on a small cement platform where he was elevated just above the kids. "All right," he hollered, "let's get this thing started. We're going to walk out to the Flat Rock Tunnel. Johnny Ciarlello will lead us down Highland to Leedom and through a path to the tracks. If you don't want to go, you should leave now."

No one moved.

"Can trains run us over on the tracks," yelled Cheryl Geiger."

"Not unless you stand in the middle of the tracks," Johnny Ciarlello yelled. The kids laughed.

"Frankie might be dumb enough to do that," someone yelled. The kids erupted in laughter.

"Hey Richie," Denise DiCicco hollered, "can you teach us to play soccer after this is over?"

"Sure," Richie replied.

"Okay," Billy said, let's stay in the street, if cars come, they can wait until we pass through. Let's get started."

"Hey Billy," Skip yelled, "what are we going to do when we get out to the tunnel?"

"We're goin' to kick ass," Billy yelled. The kids cheered.

So, they started from the firehouse out to Ashland and down to Highland. The official count was over 300 by the time they started down the Highland hill. But they encountered a problem. Two police cars sat end to end across Jefferson Street blocked their way. As the kids marched down Highland, an officer holding a bullhorn stepped forward.

"Okay," he said, "you can stop right there. Where do you think you're going?"

When the kids got to within shouting distance, Billy stopped them. He yelled, "You're not going to stop us. We're doing what you should have done weeks ago. We're going out to the tunnel."

"You can't do that," the policeman announced, "it's under police surveillance."

"You can't stop us," Billy shouted, "you can't shoot us all."

With that, the kids started walking. Captain Tolan, standing next to the officer with the bullhorn, said, "Let them through, but you go out ahead of them, and I'll follow behind. Let's move the cars first."

The two police cars were moved out of the way as the kids descended Highland Avenue. An officer joined their ranks at the front.

"What are you doing?" Billy asked him.

"I'm going with you son," the officer said, "don't try to stop me."

Billy smiled, and the kids continued down Highland to Leedom Avenue. Johnny led them past his house for the path to the tracks, and they made their way to the tunnel."

Captain Tolan, before he left his car, picked up the dashboard hand-held. "Captain Tolan, here," he said, "I need backup in Belmont Hills."

Roger that Captain, go-ahead

"I need three patrol cars at the top of Mary Waters Ford Road. There's an old logging road at the top, have them find it and stake it out. Don't let anyone in or out. And two patrol cars on Leedom Avenue out front of the Ciarlello home. Contact the state police barracks for back up and reinforcements. Await further instructions. Copy?

Roger that Captain, the officers are on their way.

With that, the Captain had to jog back to rejoin the kids.

~

Saturday, 10:30 a.m.
The Woods

Without a rope, it took Louis Regina several hours to climb up the side of the tunnel. He was near the cave halfway up when he looked out and saw the crowd of kids on the tracks; he figured a mile or so away. "What the…Oh, shit, now what?"

Louis parted the vines and brush and peered into the boy's cave. It was empty. He climbed the rest of the way to the top. He found no one up there, either. He pulled the Beast out of the sling and loaded it. He checked his .45 and made sure it had a full clip. Then he started into the woods. He had no idea where he was going, but only that he had to find the four snotnose kid witnesses; before the cops do. The mob of kids on the tracks forced Louis into the woods.

Meanwhile, four Lower Merion police cars and three state police cars pulled up alongside the entrance to the logging road on the top of Mary Waters Ford. Six officers loaded with revolvers and each holding a shotgun waited for further instructions. At the same time, two FBI agents, accompanied by an FBI sniper boarded a Navy helicopter at the Willow Grove Air Station and headed for the Hill.

"How much time you need to think?" Jimmy Whispers asked his partner Tommy Sneakers. "It's getting late. All we have to do is kill them and find our car."

"How old are you, boy?" Tommy Sneakers asked Mickey.

"Fifteen, we're all 15, sir."

"What's the difference how old they are," Whispers said. "We've been sent here to whack them, and we got them right here so let's whack the mother fuckers. What's wrong with you, Tommy?"

"Because he's a decent human being that doesn't want to shoot kids," detective Lochran said, "the question is what's wrong with you?"

"Shut the fuck up, copper," Whispers said. And Whispers fired a shot into Lochran's leg.

"Ow, shit, you son of a bitch," Lochran yelled and grabbed his thigh. Detective Frost moved over to Lochran. He removed his jacket and shirt to make a tourniquet for his partner.

"See," Whispers yelled, "see how fuckin' easy it is? Now you shoot the other motherfucker."

When the Badger, who had been watching the mobsters from a distance heard the shot, he quickly moved closer. Georgie Scavello also heard it and closed in on the two mobsters from another direction. Further away, Louis Regina heard it as well and began moving — as quickly as he could — toward the shot. Out on Mary Waters Ford Road, an officer picked up his dashboard handheld and contacted the Captain. When the Captain's radio crackled, he pulled it out of his back pocket. "Yea, Captain here."

"Captain," officer Robinson said. "We just heard a gunshot in the woods."

"All right, Robinson," the Captain replied. "spread out and move into the woods. Work your way toward the shot. Do it now."

"Yes, sir."

Captain Tolan jogged through the crowd of kids to the front and stopped them. "That's it," he yelled, "this as far as you go. You must stop here."

"What are you talking about?" Billy yelled as the group of kids slowed their advance. "We're going to the tunnel."

"No, you're not, you're stopping right here. There has been gunfire near the tunnel, and I am not allowing you or anyone else near the scene. If you don't stop, we're going to start making arrests. Stop now!"

The kids stopped.

"How long do we have to wait?" Johnny yelled.

"You don't move until I give the word. Anyone that does is breaking the law and will be arrested."

"Go on," Whispers screamed at Sneakers, "shoot the other one; what are you waiting for?"

Sneakers lifted the Tommy gun and pointed it at Frost. Lochran was holding his leg and moaning. "Don't do it, you son of a bitch," Frost yelled, "don't do it."

Pete looked down and saw the handle of a gun peeking out of the leaves. It was maybe two feet away. *Holy shit*, he thought, *is it loaded*? He looked at Mickey and Ronny, but they had their eyes focused on Sneakers. Gary was behind him. Pete looked back down at the gun. If he leaned on his side and put his hand down, it would go right over the gun. Pete shifted his weight like he was trying to find a comfortable position and extended his arm. He leaned down, and his right hand went over the gun. Nobody noticed. They were all watching Sneakers.

Suddenly, the Badger appeared out of a patch of ferns and yelled, "Death now!" The Badger was carrying a long-handled ax. All eyes shifted to him. "Holy shit," Gary stammered.

Pete wrapped his fingers around the gun handle, lifted it, and flipped it to Ronny — as he did, he yelled, "Ronny." Ronny caught it, but it surprised him, and he didn't know what to do with it.

The Badger lifted the long handle ax over his head, and as he started the downswing, yelled, "Kill you."

"Ronny," detective Frost yelled, "throw it here."

CHAPTER 55

Gunfight in the Woods

Saturday, 10:40 a.m.
500 feet above the ground

The Bell Hydro-Skimmer, a 22-ton, 62-foot-long Navy helicopter left the Willow Grove Air Station and headed for the Hill. Inside were the two FBI agents from the Bureau's division of organized crime, Lou Watts and Ben Hacket. Plus, an FBI sharp-shooter. Within 20 minutes the chopper was over the Hill and at a low altitude headed toward the Flat Rock Tunnel. Watts instructed the pilot to swing around over the tunnel, cut its speed, and hover over the woods. The chopper was just above the treetops.

Captain Tolan pulled his Motorola from his back pocket. "Captain Tolan, here," he said.

"Captain, Ben Hacket of the FBI, we're directly over the woods west of the tunnel. Can you give me an update?"

"I saw you swing around in front of the tunnel, and I see you now. You're right on target. We heard a gunshot about 10 minutes ago, agent." "Haven't heard anything since then. Two of my detectives are in those woods as captives and as far as we know, the killer from Italy. We've located a rental car on an old logging road under phony names. Most likely the Philly mob, so at least one other mobster is in there. I've instructed a dozen offers both local and state police to spread out and move from Mary Waters Ford toward the gunshot."

"Okay, Captain, we'll see what we can find. The woods are pretty thick; I don't know how much we'll see."

"Don't kill any of my men, agent."

"Roger that, Captain."

The helicopter slowly circled the woods. The sharpshooter sat on the left side, strapped in at an open doorway.

In the woods, Louis Regina was close enough to have heard the Badger yell, followed by a burst of machine-gun fire and what sounded like six or seven shots from a handgun. Down on the tracks, the Captain and the large crowd of Hill kids heard the gunfire, too.

"Holy hell," a kid shouted, "sounds like war."

The Captain got back on the radio. "Agent, did you hear the shooting?"

"Roger that, Captain, sounds like just below us and off to the right."

"Robertson," the Captain screeched, "did you hear the gunfire?" Officer Robinson, in a line arm's length apart with 11 other officers with shotguns and gas, cautiously moved through the woods.

"Certainly did, Captain. Not far in front of us."

"Whoa, did you hear that shit," one of the Hill kids shouted.

It was a boom, boom, followed by five or six pop, pops.

"Agent, hear that?" the Captain asked, "sounded like a shotgun and small arms fire."

"Roger that, Captain, right below us."

"Captain," officer Robinson said, "more gunfire in front of us, maybe a thousand feet. Should we stand down?"

"Hell no," the Captain shouted, "proceed with caution."

"We see 'em, Captain" agent Watts radioed, "looks like a hell of a mess down there. We're positioning for a shot."

Then more pops, seven or eight, followed by another round from the shotgun. The Hill kids on the tracks acted like they were at the Narberth fireworks. "Oooh, ahh."

"We see at least two men down," Watts relayed by radio, as the chopper hovered over the scene. "Better get some ambulances out here, Captain, and a medical airlift. We've used half our fuel, got about fifteen-twenty minutes left."

"Roger that, Agent."

~

Saturday, 10:30 a.m.
The woods

Picture this in slow motion, Ronny's toss of the handgun to agent Frost fell short of its mark. The Badger hadn't survived this long as a killer without the survival instincts of a snake. Even as he held the ax over his head, the Badger's sense of perception caught the movement of the Tommy Gun and the 16-gauge pump, both of which swung toward him. He brought the ax down and dove backward — in a somersault — behind the giant oak tree from which he appeared. Seeing the gun Ronny flipped fall short, Frost on his knees, dove toward the gun, grabbed it and rolled over. Ronny, Mickey, Pete, and Gary, seeing the gunfight unfold, scampered on their hands and knees like chipmunks for cover behind any large tree they could find.

Tommy Sneakers turned with the Thompson and from his hip shot off a burst of fire toward the Badger; missed but shredded five feet of bark off the tree.

As he rolled over onto his stomach, Frost opened fire and hit Sneakers with four well-placed shots, one that ripped into his left ear and exited through his right. Sneakers was dead before he hit the ground.

Whispers turned and pointed the pump shotgun — not at Frost, who he didn't have a clear shot at — but at Lochran who was on his back, semiconscious. Just as Whispers squeezed the trigger, a short handle ax ripped into the back of his head and split it open, scattering blood over the detectives and kid witnesses. With the ax blade buried deep in his skull, Whispers dropped to his knees, pumped two shots harmlessly into the woods and fell on his face. On his way down, he whispered something, but of course, nobody heard it.

The Badger, who dove and somersaulted away, ducked behind a large maple tree. He reached around behind him for another ax. Louis Regina stepped out from the trees holding the Beast in front of him and fired once at the Badger. He missed. Louis turned and decided to take out Frost, who was facing the other direction and was an easy target. Frost was a goner, but he managed to crawl away and out of the direct line of fire. Louis, not positioned for a good shot, moved around a tree stalking Frost.

Just above the treetops, the Navy chopper moved into position. The agents could see Louis pursuing detective Frost. From the helicopter, a voice via bullhorn demanded that Louis drop his weapon.

Louis momentarily stopped and looked up at the helicopter hovering on top of him, just above the trees.

Louis fired two rounds in the direction of the kid witnesses, but they were well hidden behind trees, and the buckshot ripped through the woods. He had two shots left, so he figured to get Frost first, and then reload and get the kid witnesses. As he maneuvered to kill Frost, the voice in the helicopter again demanded that he drop his weapon. Twenty feet from Frost, Louis appeared to have a great shot to kill the detective. He raised the Beast to shoot.

Frost was in trouble. The sharpshooter had difficulty getting a clear shot on Louis. Out of nowhere, Georgie came out through the trees in a dead run toward Louis. Just as Louis squeezed the trigger, Georgie body-slammed hard into him from the side and knocked him down. He never got the shot off. Louis tried to get up and shoot Georgie, but two shots rang out from above the trees. The first tore through the back of Louis's shoulder and spun him around. The second shot hit him in the chest. Blood gushed out of Louis's mouth and for a second or two, he tried to lift the Beast. He couldn't, and he fell backward and lay motionless.

The Badger, as he watched the gunfight unfold, sensed the line of police just beyond the trees. He turned and ran back toward the tunnel. Nobody ever saw him again. The cops arrived and ordered the boys, including Georgie and detective Frost to lie on their stomachs, hands behind their backs. They were handcuffed until the police could sort things out. The Navy helicopter turned and sped off toward the Willow Grove Air Station.

The gunfight was over.

Lying handcuffed a few feet from Georgie, detective Frost turned his head toward him and said, "Goddamn, Georgie, I owe you those eggs, easy over and coffee, no cream or sugar."

"Frosty, can I get scrapple, too?"

Epilogue

The Badger used the tunnels he dug from the cave to exit the woods. He stripped off his white killing suit and put to use what he learned from the boys; he escaped back to the Hill through the dump. From there he made his way to Manayunk and caught a train to Center City. After hiding out in South Philadelphia for a month, he returned to Italy with a forged passport and identification.

Detective Tommy Lochran got airlifted out of the woods to Lankenau Hospital, where his right leg was amputated. He became the first case in the United States where an amputee received a prosthetic leg during surgery. A year later he returned to duty as supervisor of the police education program. Officer Lochran retired in 1970. He and his wife Delores continued to live in Belmont Hills until their deaths.

Detective Butch Frost remained a detective until he retired in 1976. He and his wife Lorraine moved to Sarasota, Florida. Detective Frost died in 2008. Both detectives received police accommodation medals for their work in protecting the kid witnesses.

The kid witnesses, Petey, Gary, Mickey, and Ronny, testified in court as witnesses to two murders. 'Phil' Crazy 'Phil' Ruggiero and 'Harry' The 'Hunchback' Battaglia received life sentences: Crazy Phil for killing Mr. and Mrs. Otts, and The Hunchback for the murder of Porky Bananas.

The four boys didn't go near the woods for the rest of the summer and swore they would never camp out again. They entered Harriton

High School in September and discovered they had way better girls to chase. "Sweeter AND smarter," as Gary said. They had great baseball careers at the school and also played three more seasons of American Legion baseball on the Hill.

The Belmont Hills Fire Company held a party at the firehouse for all the kids who followed Johnny, Billy, and Richie down Leedom and out the tracks. They were awarded for bravery and given credit for driving Louis Regina off the top of the tunnel and into the woods. But more than that, they were celebrated for what all kids from the Hill do — ever since the West Manayunk name was dropped — they stuck together to help their own.

Two weeks after the gunfight in the woods, Detective Frost took Georgie out for breakfast, where he got his eggs, over medium, coffee, no cream or sugar, and scrapple. Some fifty years later, Georgie became a gun expert.

The author lives in South Philadelphia with his wife Denise and their three cats.

Past Book

See the Author's last book, *Darkness They Could Not See*. It's historical fiction about Christopher Columbus's first voyage. The unusual book is written in the first person, present tense, with three voices: The cabin boy, the Bloodwoman, and the Admiral. Here are three excerpts from the book.

October 12, 1492
Off the coast of Guanahania
Daybreak
The Cabin Boy

No one utters a word; hardly a sound is made. We watch and wait. Fish break the water — a quick slushing sound magnified by the eerie silence — and feed on hundreds of insects that hop and jump on the water's surface. Gulls and other birds roost on our poles and collapsed sails.

Darkness slowly gives way to the sun on the horizon — its yellow streaks breaking across the dark placid water.

As the mist lifts and the tip of the sun grows, a form appears in the distance. It's land. The ships are closer than first thought. As more of the sun takes over — as if it were changing watch with the night — dark silhouettes loom on the shore. And they move.

People.

The crew is silent, focused, as the rising rays of sunrise illuminate the silhouettes. I put my hands above my eyes to shield the sun and

379

see that there are not just a few silhouettes onshore, but what appears to be hundreds.

Suddenly, a seaman hollers, "Them people is naked!"

Pandemonium erupts on the ship. The seamen go crazy. Far from home for nearly three months, then seeing naked women — many beautiful naked women of all ages — is more than they can handle.

"Get the boats ready!" a seaman screams, "I'm going ashore. Don't anybody get in my way."

They rush toward the ship's boat, pushing and shoving and yelling at each other. Several begin fighting, falling to the deck, swinging their fists, kicking. They've turned into a street mob, each one trying to be the first to get to the ship's boat.

QUIET, the Admiral shouts. QUIET, NO ONE MOVE.

Q-U-I-E-T. HAVE YOU LOST YOUR MINDS?

"But Admiral, there's naked women on that shore, waving to us to join them, we're ready to go so what are we waiting for..."

"Yea, yea, let's go, get them boats ready...

"I SAID Q-U-I-E-T."

October 12, 1492
Landfall
Off the coast of Guanahania
The Admiral

I said four days and four days it is. How did I know? I'll give credit to the birds. It was the birds that told me. They land on top of our sails and say, Cristóbal Colón, you are so close. Release the parrot and make a deal with the men. The birds were right.

As the mist lifts from the quiet water of the inlet, the ship's boat moves slowly toward shore. I kneel as we move through the beautiful turquoise-colored water. It is so clear, and those in the boat with me shift their eyes from shore to the water. It's difficult not to look down at the water, where fish are so abundant.

It seems like thousands of brightly colored fish surround the boat. There appear to be beds of a white, hard substance easily seen through the clear water. A green sea turtle swirls the water around just off the right side of the boat, and it startles the men.

Those in the ship's boat with me are hand-picked: Martin Alonso Pinzón, captain of the Pinta; Martin's brother, Vincente Yáñez Pinsón, captain of the Niña; Rodrigo de Escobedo, secretary of the fleet. Plus, Rodrigo Sánchez of Segovia, comptroller of the fleet; and Luis de Torres, the ship's interpreter, who knows Hebrew and Arabic.

I have asked Mr. Sánchez to record my words when I claim all of the land for the sovereigns of Spain.

Hundreds of people line the shore; most are naked. Sánchez remarks to me that the people appear to have no weapons.

"What do we call them, Admiral? Mr. Sánchez asks.

"We are in the West Indies, Mr. Sánchez," I reply, "we call them Indians, of course." As the ship's boat moves closer to shore, I see that the Indians look happy, as if they are glad to see us. Feeding fish break the water surface, and snakes — nearly as plentiful as the fish — zig and zag across the water in front of the boat.

"Holy hell," Martin Alonso Pinźon says, as he turns and looks at me, "did you see the size of that fish that just went under the boat?" I nod. His brother, seated behind him, says, "I've seen two or three big fish. This place is loaded with them."

October 28, 1492
Sixteen days after landfall
The Bloodwoman

"Wait, we can delay them," Colibri says, "to give Dancing Dog more time. If we delay them, they won't know because they are stupid. All they want are the trinkets from the streams.

"How?" I ask. "How will you delay them?"

"Some of us," Colibri says, "can befriend the clothed men. Then we can try to lead them astray, to give them false hope."

"I will gladly do that," Yari says.

"Me, too," says Guama. "We can do that, they are stupid and believe whatever we tell them. We can delay them for weeks."

Maybe," Cacique Guacanagaric says, "you can invent a story to scare these clothed men away. Maybe then they will not bother us here on Ayiti."

"Story?" Tiburon asks, "I don't understand, cacique."

"I get it," I imply; "yes, you could make up a story. That's a great idea Cacique Guacanagaric."

"Tell them," the Cacique said," that on Bohío there are people who have one eye and have a face of a dog."

The Taínos burst into laughter. The cacique has to settle them down.

"Let me finish, please," the cacique asks, still chuckling himself. "You say they believe everything, Guama, is that right?"

"Yes, Cacique Guacanagaric," Guama answers. "If I told them the gold trinkets were in the belly of the grouper, these clothed men would be fishing all day long and at night, too."

The people erupt in laughter again.

"But the grouper doesn't bite at night," Thing of Death says.

"It doesn't matter, Thing," Guama replies, "if we tell them they do, they will fish and fish."

The cacique waits for the laughter to subside. "Tell them there are people on Bohíto who will eat them," he says.

More laughter.

Cacique Guancanagaric lets them laugh. It is good to hear the laughter; it makes our hearts light, especially with the clothed gods on the way. They have been under much stress. They don't know about the Caribs. I do not want to add that on.

"Okay," the cacique says, "all laughter aside. This is our plan. Guama and Colibri will assist the clothed men and lead them astray, gaining time. You will tell them there are one-eyed people on Bohio with dogfaces and an appetite for human flesh. I will instruct our people to light many fires on the night they arrive, and Guama and Colibri will tell them these are fires to cook the clothed men for a meal. After that, if they still insist on coming to our land, we will avoid them. We will have no contact with them, especially the Taíno women. Whatever plan Dancing Dog has with his disciples, we will help to carry it out. Bloodwoman will work with Dancing Dog and keep us all informed and ready. Are there questions?"

There are no questions.

"Do what you have to do, Guama and Colibri and others, do what you can to delay them, but be careful."

"Don't worry, cacique," Tiburon says, "we will delay them for sure.

"All right," Grandmother Spider adds, "let's kick some ass."

Made in the USA
Middletown, DE
04 January 2020